CRITICS SALUTE <u>RAMSES</u>

"A PLOT AS SINUOUS AS THE RIVER NILE, WITH CHARACTERS LYING LIKE CROCODILES IN THE SHALLOWS. . . . THIS BOOK MAKES ANCIENT EGYPT AS RELEVANT AND 3-D AS TODAY'S NEWS."
　—J. Suzanne Frank, author of *Reflections in the Nile*

"Officially, Christian Jacq was born in Paris in 1947. In fact, his real birth took place in the time of the pharaohs, along the banks of the Nile, where the river carries eternal messages. . . . Who could ever tell that Christian Jacq, Ramses' official scribe, was not writing from memory?"
　—*Magazine Littéraire*

"With hundreds of thousands of readers, millions of copies in print, Christian Jacq's success has become unheard of in the world of books. This man is the pharaoh of publishing!"
　—*Figaro Magazine*

"In 1235 B.C., Ramses II might have said: 'My life is as amazing as fiction!' It seems Christian Jacq heard him. . . . Christian Jacq draws a pleasure from writing that is contagious. His penmanship turns history into a great show, high-quality entertainment."
　—*VSD*

"It's *Dallas* or *Dynasty* in Egypt, with a hero (Ramses), beautiful women, plenty of villains, new developments every two pages, brothers fighting for power, magic, enchantments, and historical glamour."
　—*Libération*

"He's a pyramid-surfer. The pharaoh of publishing. His saga about Ramses II is a bookselling phenomenon!"
　—*Le Parisien*

"Moves at a breakneck pace. . . . A lot of fun."
　—*KLIATT*

RAMSES

VOLUME V

UNDER THE WESTERN ACACIA

CHRISTIAN JACQ

Translated by Mary Feeney

WARNER BOOKS

A Time Warner Company

Originally published in French by Editions Robert Laffont, S.A. Paris, France.

Warner Books Edition
Copyright © 1996 by Editions Robert Laffont (Volume 5)
All rights reserved.

Warner Books, Inc., 1271 Avenue of the Americas, New York, NY 10020

Visit our Web site at
http://warnerbooks.com

 A Time Warner Company

Printed in the United States of America

First U.S. Printing: March 1999
10 9 8 7 6 5 4 3 2 1

Library of Congress Cataloging-in-Publication Data

Jacq, Christian.
    [Sous l'acacia d'Occident. English]
    Under the western acacia / Christian Jacq.
       p. cm. — (Ramses ; v. 5)
    ISBN 0-446-67360-9
    I. Ramses II, King of Egypt—Fiction. I. Title. II. Series:
Jacq, Christian. Ramsès. English ; v. 5.
PQ2670.A2438S6813   1999
843'.914—dc21   98-31258
                                       CIP

Book design and composition by L&G McRee
Cover design and illustration by Marc Burkhardt

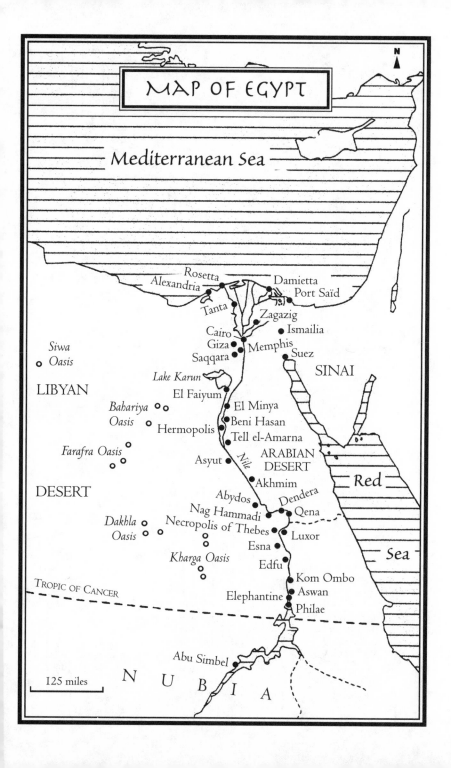

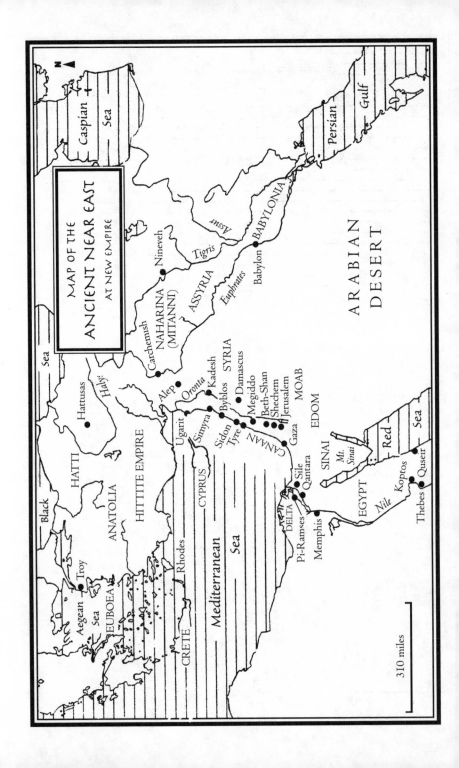

ONE

The setting sun bathed the temples of Pi-Ramses in heavenly gold. Dubbed "the Turquoise City" after the colored tiles on its buildings, the capital Ramses the Great had built in the Nile Delta was the picture of wealth, power, and beauty.

Life was good in Pi-Ramses, but the Sardinian giant Serramanna took no pleasure in the balmy evening or the pink-streaked sky. Decked out in his horned helmet, sword at his side, whiskers curled, the former pirate who had become Ramses' personal bodyguard rode grimly toward the villa where the Hittite prince Uri-Teshoop had spent the last several years under house arrest.

Uri-Teshoop, the deposed son of the late Emperor Muwattali, Ramses' sworn enemy. Uri-Teshoop, who had usurped the throne from his ailing father, only to be outmaneuvered by Hattusili, the emperor's brother. Uri-Teshoop had been spirited out of Hatti by Ahsha, the head of Egyptian diplomacy, who was Ramses' boyhood friend.

Serramanna smiled. The fearless Anatolian warrior, a runaway! The crowning irony was that Ramses, the man Uri-Teshoop hated most in the world, was the one who had granted him political asylum in exchange for information about the Hittite troops and their state of readiness.

During Year Twenty-one of Ramses' reign, to the surprise of both peoples, Egypt and Hatti had signed a peace treaty, pledging mutual assistance in case of outside attack. Uri-Teshoop feared the worst. Would he not make a prime scapegoat, the perfect token for Ramses to offer Hattusili to seal their pact? Yet the Pharaoh, respecting the principle of asylum, had refused to extradite his guest.

By now, Uri-Teshoop no longer counted. And Serramanna thoroughly disliked the mission that Ramses had sent him on tonight.

The Hittite's villa was set in a palm grove on the northern edge of town. At least he'd had a comfortable life in this land of the pharaohs that he had dreamed of destroying.

Serramanna admired Ramses and would serve him faithfully to the end. However reluctantly, he would carry out the king's terrible order.

The entrance to the villa was flanked by two of Serramanna's handpicked guards, armed with clubs and daggers.

"Nothing to report?"

"Nothing, Chief. The Hittite is sleeping it off in the garden, down by the pool."

The hulking Sard went through the gate and lumbered down the path to the pool. Three other guards kept a permanent watch on the former commander-in-chief of the Hittite army, who spent his time eating, drinking, swimming, and dozing.

Swallows swooped high in the sky. A hoopoe grazed Serramanna's shoulder. Jaws tense, fists clenched, eyes glowering, he prepared to do his duty. For the first time, he was sorry that he worked for Ramses.

Like an animal sensing danger, Uri-Teshoop awoke before the giant's heavy tread sounded on the path.

Tall and muscular, Uri-Teshoop had long, flowing locks;

fleecy red hair covered his bare chest. Not even the Anatolian winter daunted him, and he had lost none of his strength.

Lying on the flagstone rim of the pool, eyes half-closed, he watched as Ramses the Great's bodyguard drew nearer.

So tonight was the night.

Ever since the signing of the outrageous peace treaty between Egypt and Hatti, Uri-Teshoop had felt his time running out. A hundred times he had thought of escaping, but Serramanna's men had never given him a chance. He'd escaped extradition only to be bled like a pig, slaughtered by a brute as ruthless as himself.

"Get up," ordered Serramanna.

Uri-Teshoop was not accustomed to being ordered around. Slowly, as if savoring his final act, he rose to face the man sent to slit his throat.

The Sard's expression was one of barely contained fury.

"Go ahead, butcher," spat the Hittite. "Do what your master told you. I won't even give you the pleasure of fighting me."

Serramanna's fingers gripped the pommel of his short sword.

"Clear out."

Uri-Teshoop could hardly believe his ears.

"What do you mean?"

"You're free."

"Free? To do what?"

"To leave this place and go where you please. Pharaoh is applying the law. There's no longer any reason to hold you here."

"Is this some kind of joke?"

"No, it's a sign of peace. But if you make the mistake of staying in Egypt and cause the least trouble here, I'll arrest you. You won't be a political exile anymore, just a common-law criminal. Give me the slightest cause to run you through with my sword, and believe me, I will."

"But tonight you're not allowed to touch me. Am I right?" Uri-Teshoop taunted.

"Get out!"

A reed mat, a kilt, a pair of sandals, a slab of bread, a bunch of onions, and two faience amulets to swap for food: that was all Uri-Teshoop was given upon his release. The Hittite prince had now been wandering the streets of Pi-Ramses for several hours like a sleepwalker. His new-found freedom made his head spin; he could hardly think straight.

There was no finer city than Pi-Ramses, ran the popular song:

> Long live the town of Pi-Ramses,
> Where the hoopoe and nightingale sing
> In the shade of acacia and sycamore,
> Where the poor man lives like a king.
> Long live the boats and the fishes,
> Long live the breeze from the sea.
> Long live the Turquoise City,
> The most wonderful place to be.

Uri-Teshoop fell under the spell of the capital built in a fertile region on a loop of the Nile framed by two broad canals. There were rich grasslands, orchards where prized apples grew, vast olive groves that yielded rivers of oil, vineyards producing a soft, fruity wine, flower-decked cottages . . . Pi-Ramses was far different from rugged Hattusa, the capital of the Hittite empire, a fortified city high in the central Anatolian plateau.

A painful thought wrenched Uri-Teshoop from his torpor. He might never become Emperor of Hatti, but he would get revenge on the Pharaoh who had freed him, the fool. Eliminating Ramses, considered a god since the victory at Kadesh (where he had defeated a coalition that should have crushed him) would plunge Egypt—perhaps even the entire Near East—into chaos. Fate had treated Uri-Teshoop cruelly; his only consolation was that his destructive urges had survived intact.

Milling around him was a colorful crowd of Egyptians, Nubians, Syrians, Libyans, Greeks, and others who had come to admire the capital that the Hittites had hoped to raze—before they caved in to Ramses.

Destroying Ramses . . . how could a fallen warrior possibly pull it off?

"Your Highness," murmured a voice behind him.

Uri-Teshoop wheeled around.

"Your Highness, do you remember me?"

Uri-Teshoop looked down at a compact man with lively dark eyes. A linen headband held his thick hair in place; he sported a trim goatee. This obsequious character wore a brightly striped robe that reached to his ankles.

"Raia . . . is it really you?"

The Syrian merchant bowed.

"But you were our spy. What are you doing back in Pi-Ramses?"

"It's peacetime, Your Highness. A new era has begun. There's been an amnesty. I was a rich trader with a good reputation in Egypt; I've simply started back in business.

No one tried to stop me, and I've rebuilt my upper-class clientele."

Raia had been near the top of a Hittite spy ring that operated for years, attempting to destabilize Ramses' regime. When Serramanna broke up the network, the Syrian had managed to escape and then return to his adopted homeland after a stay in Hattusa.

"Well, good for you, Raia."

"Good for us."

"What do you mean by that?"

"Do you believe that this is a chance meeting?"

Uri-Teshoop studied Raia more attentively.

"You mean you trailed me?"

"I heard conflicting rumors about what might happen to you. For more than a month, my men have kept up a constant watch on your villa. I gave you time to get your feet on the ground, and now . . . well, now here I am. May I offer you a cool beer?"

Uri-Teshoop wavered. It had been an eventful night. Yet his instincts told him that the Syrian merchant could help him move forward with his plans.

In the tavern, their discussion was lively. Raia encouraged Uri-Teshoop's gradual metamorphosis from released prisoner into ruthless warrior, ready for any conquest. The Syrian merchant had not been mistaken: despite years of exile, the former commander-in-chief of the Hittite army was as bloodthirsty as ever.

"I'm not a big talker, Raia. Tell me what you want from me."

The merchant spoke confidentially. "I have only one question, Your Highness. Do you want revenge on Ramses?"

"He humiliated me. Peace with Egypt was no doing of mine! But overcoming this Pharaoh seems impossible."

Raia nodded.

"That depends, Your Highness, that depends . . ."

"Do you doubt my courage?"

"With all due respect, courage won't be enough."

"Why would you, a merchant, want to throw yourself into such risky business?"

Raia smiled a twisted smile. "Because my hate is as ardent as your own."

TWO

Wearing a golden collar and the pharaoh's traditional simple white kilt, Ramses the Great was celebrating the rites of dawn at his Eternal Temple, the Ramesseum, on the West Bank of Thebes. Gently he roused the divine power hidden within the *naos*, or inner sanctum, thanks to which energy would circulate between heaven and earth, Egypt would be at one with the cosmos, and the human tendency toward destruction would be curbed.

At the age of fifty-five, Ramses was tall and athletic, his large head crowned with a mane of red-gold hair. He had a broad forehead, arched eyebrows, and piercing eyes; his curving nose was long and thin, his ears round and delicately rimmed. He radiated magnetism, strength, and natural authority. In his presence, the sturdiest of characters lost their composure. A god clearly lived within this Pharaoh who had covered the country with monuments and flattened every enemy.

Thirty-three years on the throne . . . Ramses alone knew the true weight of the ordeals that he had endured. First came the death of his father, Seti, leaving him rudderless at the very moment the Hittites began to wage war on Egypt. Without the help of Amon, his heavenly father, Ramses, deserted by his own troops, would never have triumphed at Kadesh. There had been years of happiness and peace, certainly, but then his mother, Tuya, the model of rectitude, had joined her illustrious husband in the country of light where the souls of the just dwelt for all eternity. Fate's next blow was even crueler, inflicting a loss from which the king would never recover. His Great Royal Wife, Nefertari, had died in his arms at Abu Simbel in Nubia, where Ramses had built twin temples to glorify the royal couple's indestructible unity.

Pharaoh had lost the three beings he loved most in the world, the three people who had made him who he was and whose love was limitless. Still, he must continue to reign, to embody Egypt with the same faith and the same enthusiasm.

Four other faithful companions had also left him: his pair of war horses, so valiant on the field of battle; Fighter, the pet lion that had more than once saved his life; and Watcher, the yellow dog, now a royal mummy. Another Watcher had taken his place, then a third, who was just a pup.

Gone, too, was the Greek poet Homer, who had ended his days beneath the lemon tree in his beloved Egyptian garden. Ramses nostalgically recalled his conversations with the author of the *Iliad* and the *Odyssey*, who had come to admire the civilization of the pharaohs.

After Nefertari's death, Ramses had been tempted to step down and transfer power to his eldest son, Kha. But his circle of friends had opposed the idea, reminding the monarch that his life was no longer his own and that a pharaoh must serve until he died. No matter what he suffered as a man, he must fulfill his duty to the end. The law of Ma'at required it, and Ramses, like his predecessors, would bow to this principle of justice and harmony.

It was here, in his Temple of Millions of Years, which emitted the magic flux that protected his reign, that Ramses drew strength. Although an important ceremony awaited him, he lingered in the halls of the Ramesseum. It comprised a vast enclosure with two great courtyards where pillars depicted the king as Osiris, a huge hall with forty-eight columns, and a sanctuary where the divine presence resided. Access to the temple was through massive monumental gates, or pylons, inscribed with texts saying that they rose to the heavens. On the south side of the forecourt stood the palace, and around the holy site were an extensive library, storerooms, a treasury containing precious metals, the scribes' offices, and the priests' quarters. The temple complex hummed with activity night and day, for the service of the gods knew no rest.

Ramses spent a few too-brief moments in the part of the shrine dedicated to his wife, Nefertari, and his mother, Tuya. He contemplated the reliefs showing the queen's union with the scent of the god Amon-Ra, at once secret and luminous, and then the scenes where she nursed the Pharaoh, guaranteeing him eternal youth.

They must be growing restless in the palace, he realized. The king tore himself away from his memories, not stopping to look at the colossal statue carved from a single block of pink granite and entitled *Ramses, the Light of Kings,* nor the acacia tree planted in Year Two of his reign. He headed straight for the audience chamber with its sixteen columns, where the foreign diplomats had gathered.

With her saucy green eyes, pert nose, and rounded chin, Iset the Fair was vivacious and charming. Even though she was past fifty, the years never seemed to touch her; she was as graceful and winning as ever.

"Has the king left the temple yet?" she asked her chambermaid, a note of concern in her voice.

"Not yet, Your Majesty."

"The ambassadors will be furious!"

"Don't you worry. An audience with Ramses is such a privilege that no one minds waiting."

To be with Ramses . . . yes, it was the greatest of privileges! Iset recalled their first summer of love, when he was a brash young prince, not yet destined for power. How happy they had been in their reed hut at the edge of a wheat field, secretly discovering pleasure in each other! Then the sublime Nefertari appeared on the scene, unaware that she had all the qualities required of a Great Royal Wife. Ramses had chosen well in Nefertari; yet it was Iset the Fair who had given him two sons, Kha and Merenptah. For a short while she had felt some resentment toward Ramses, until she realized that she was quite unprepared for a queen's overwhelming responsibilities. Her lone ambition was to share the existence of the man she loved, to however great or small an extent he allowed.

Neither Nefertari nor Ramses had shunted her aside. As "secondary wife," according to protocol, Iset had been blessed to stay close to the king, living in his shadow. Some claimed she was wasting her life, but Iset only laughed. To her, even being a servant to Ramses would be better than marrying some stupid, pretentious diplomat.

Nefertari's death had been profoundly distressing. The queen was no rival, but a friend for whom Iset felt the greatest admiration and respect. Realizing that no words could lessen the monarch's heartbreak, she remained on the sidelines, silent and discreet.

And then something inconceivable occurred.

At the end of the mourning period, after Ramses himself had sealed the door to Nefertari's tomb, the king asked Iset the Fair to assume the position of Great Royal Wife. No King of Egypt could reign alone, for Pharaoh united the masculine and feminine principles, joined in harmony.

Iset the Fair had never expected to become Queen of Egypt; any comparison to Nefertari terrified her. Yet Ramses' will was law. Iset assented, despite her anxiety. She became "the Sweet of Love, She Who Sees Horus and Set at One in Pharaoh, Lady of the Two Lands of Upper and Lower Egypt, She Whose Voice Gives joy." These traditional titles were of no importance. The true miracle was sharing Ramses' existence, his hopes and sorrows. Iset was the wife of the greatest king the world had ever known, and his faith in her was enough to make her happy.

"His Majesty is asking for you," said the chambermaid.

In her vulture headdress festooned with two tall plumes, her long white robe and floating red sash, her golden necklace and bracelets, the Great Royal Wife made her way to the audience chamber. Her noble upbringing served her well in official ceremonies. She knew the gathered dignitaries would be watching her like a hawk, just as they watched Pharaoh.

Iset the Fair stopped a few steps from Ramses.

He was her first and only love, yet he never ceased to impress her. He towered over her; she would never take the full measure of his thought. Yet the magic of passion had bridged the yawning gap between them.

"Are you ready?" he asked.

The Queen of Egypt bowed her head.

When the royal pair appeared, the room fell silent. Ramses and Iset the Fair took their place on the throne.

The Pharaoh's boyhood friend and secretary of state, elegant, debonair Ahsha, stepped forward. His refined appearance—impeccable robe, trim mustache, intelligent, sparkling eyes—and somewhat haughty manner made it hard to believe that he had worked as a daring undercover agent in Hittite territory. With his love of women and the finer things in life, Ahsha might have looked on the world with jaded eyes, yet he burned with a mission that nothing and no one could quench: working for the greater glory of Ramses, the one man for whom he felt a boundless, if unspoken, admiration.

"Your Majesty," declared Ahssa, "the south submits to you and brings you its riches, requesting the breath of life from you. The north implores the miracle of your presence. The east offers all its land; the west kneels humbly, its chiefs approach with their heads bowed."

The Hittite ambassador broke away from the crowd of diplomats and kowtowed to the royal couple.

"Pharaoh is the guiding light," he declared, "the fire that gives life or destroys it. May his *ka* live forever, may the weather favor him, may the inundation be provident. It is he who channels divine energy, he in whom heaven and earth are joined. For Ramses has quelled insurrections, and all the world is at peace."

Presents followed the round of speeches. From deepest Nubia to the northern protectorates of Canaan and Syria, the empire paid tribute to its master, Ramses the Great.

The palace was asleep; a single light shone in the king's office.

"What's going on here, Ahsha?" asked Ramses.

"The Two Lands are thriving, every province is prospering, the granaries are full to bursting, you're the life of your people, you—"

"No more official speeches. Why was the Hittite ambassador so fulsome in his praise?"

"Diplomatic language."

"No, I sense something more. Don't you agree?"

Ahsha ran a manicured index finger through his scented mustache.

"I admit that I'm troubled."

"Could Hattusili have second thoughts about our treaty?"

"No, he wouldn't couch it in those terms."

"Tell me what you really think."

"Believe me, I'm puzzled."

"With the Hittites, leaving questions unanswered could be a fatal mistake."

"Am I to understand that you want me to find out the truth?"

"We've had too many peaceful years; lately you've lost your edge."

THREE

Short, slight, and thin despite the enormous quantities of food he consumed at all hours of the day and night, Ahmeni, like Ahsha, was a boyhood friend of Ramses. A scribe to the core, a tireless worker, he reigned over a limited staff of twenty specialized aides who prepared briefs for the Pharaoh on essential issues. Ahmeni displayed remarkable efficiency, and despite the envious souls who heaped unfounded criticism on him, Ramses held him in the highest confidence.

Despite his bad back, Ahmeni always insisted on lugging piles of confidential documents on wooden tablets or papyrus. His face was so drained of color that he often seemed on the verge of fainting. Yet he wore out his assistants, required very little sleep, and wielded reed pens and brushes for hours on end to compose reports for Ramses' eyes only.

Since Pharaoh had decided to spend several months in Thebes, Ahmeni had gone along with several members of his staff. Officially "sandal-bearer to the king," the scribe cared nothing for titles and honors. Following Ramses' example, his sole obsession was the country's prosperity. So he allowed himself no respite, for fear of committing a fatal error.

Ahmeni was shoveling down some barley porridge and farmer's cheese when Ramses entered his document-filled office.

"Finished your lunch?"

"No matter, Your Majesty. The fact that you're here doesn't augur well."

"Your last few reports seemed rather positive."

"*Seemed?* Why seemed? You aren't implying that I'm missing something, are you?"

With age, Ahmeni had grown defensive and snappish.

"I'm not suggesting any such thing," Ramses said serenely. "I'm only trying to understand."

"Understand what?"

"Isn't there one area that concerns you somewhat?"

Ahmeni thought out loud: "The irrigation system is running smoothly; so are the dikes. The provincial governors are obeying directives, with no undue tendency to act on their own. Agriculture is thriving, the people have enough to eat and adequate lodging. Religious feasts are observed as planned, the companies of builders, quarrymen, stonecutters, sculptors, and painters are at work throughout the country. No, I see no problem."

Ramses should have been reassured, for Ahmeni had no equal when it came to spotting flaws in Egypt's administrative and economic system. Yet the king still looked thoughtful.

"Is there something Your Majesty hasn't told me?"

"You know that I can't keep anything from you."

"Then what is this all about?"

"The Hittite ambassador was much too flattering about Egypt."

"Bah! All the Hittites know how to do is make war and tell lies."

"I sense a storm brewing right inside Egypt, a storm with deadly fallout."

Ahmeni took the monarch's premonition seriously. Like his father, Seti, Ramses had strong ties to the terrifying thunder god Set, who also defended the bark of the sun against attacking monsters.

"Right inside Egypt?" repeated the scribe, unnerved. What did this omen mean?

"If Nefertari were still in the land of the living, she could see into the future for us."

Ahmeni rolled up a scroll and straightened his brushes—everyday gestures to dispel the waves of regret that now washed over him as well as Ramses. Nefertari had been the soul of beauty, intelligence, and grace, the peaceful smile of an accomplished civilization. She had almost made him forget his work—unlike Iset the Fair, who was no favorite of the Pharaoh's private secretary. Ramses had no doubt been right to elevate her rank, although in Ahmeni's opinion the role of queen was beyond her. The one real compensation was that she loved Ramses.

"Does Your Majesty have anything specific in mind?"

"I'm afraid not."

"We'll have to be twice as vigilant, then."

"I don't like waiting for trouble."

"I know, I know," grumbled Ahmeni. "Here I thought I might finally take a day off, but I see that will have to wait."

Predominantly white, with touches of red on the top and green on the sides, several feet long, flat-headed and thick-tailed, the horned viper slithered sideways toward the foot of the palm tree where a couple lay entwined. After a day beneath the sand, the reptile had come out to hunt at night-fall. In the hot season its bite was instantly fatal.

Neither the man nor the woman, in their passionate embrace, seemed aware of the danger. Feline, limber, and laughing, the lovely Nubian obliged her lover, a swarthy, solid-looking man of fifty, to call on all the resources of his virility. Now tender, now demanding, the Egyptian stood no chance against the Nubian beauty, making love to her with the eagerness of a first encounter. In the balmy night, their shared pleasure was as torrid as the summer sun.

The viper was within striking distance.

The man gently wrestled the woman onto her back and kissed her breasts. She was ready for him. Eyes locked, they consumed each other hungrily.

Lotus reached out a quick, sure hand to grasp the horned viper by the neck. The reptile hissed and bit into empty air.

"Nice catch," commented Setau, without breaking his rhythm. "We'll get some fine venom without even having to hunt."

Suddenly Lotus seemed to lose interest.

"I have a bad feeling."

"Because of the viper?"

"Ramses is in danger."

Setau always took such pronouncements seriously. He might be a snake charmer, a boyhood friend of the Pharaoh's, and Ramses' man in the province of Kush—but his wife was a sorceress. Together they had caught an incalculable number of reptiles, each one more dangerous than the next, extracting the venom for medicinal purposes.

Fiercely independent, Setau and Lotus had nonetheless accompanied Ramses on his military expeditions in both the north and the south, caring for the sick and wounded.

In peacetime they had been in charge of a vast research laboratory until Pharaoh asked for their help in Nubia, much to their delight. The spineless viceroy to whom they reported would have tried to interfere with their initiatives, yet he feared this couple whose official residence was guarded by cobras.

"What sort of danger?" Setau asked with a frown.

"I don't know."

"Do you see a face?"

"No," replied Lotus. "It was just a sick feeling. For one split second, I sensed a threat to Ramses."

Still gripping the viper firmly, she stood up.

"You've got to do something."

"What can I do here in Nubia?"

"Let's leave for the capital."

"Once we're gone, the viceroy will undo all our good work."

"I'm sorry, but if Ramses needs our help, we ought to be by his side."

Burly Setau took orders from no man, but he had long ago learned never to contradict his soft-spoken wife.

The high priest of Karnak, Nebu, had lived to a great age. As the sage Ptah-hotep wrote in his famous *Maxims,* advancing years meant perpetual fatigue, recurring weakness, and a tendency to doze even during the day. Eyesight and hearing diminished, the heart slowed, speech failed, bones ached, the sense of taste disappeared as nasal congestion increased, and standing and sitting grew equally painful.

Despite these ailments, old Nebu continued to fulfill his mission from Ramses: to tend the temple of Karnak and its vast estates, preserving the riches of the great god Amon. The high priest delegated the daily running of the complex to Bakhen, the Second Prophet, who oversaw eighty thousand construction workers, craftsmen, field hands, fruit growers, vintners, and other employees.

When Ramses first named him high priest, Nebu had no illusions. The young monarch wanted to bring the state-within-a-state under his control. He demanded loyalty. Yet Nebu was no mere figurehead; he had fought to keep other temples from plundering Karnak's wealth and power. Since Pharaoh took care to maintain harmony in the country as a whole, Nebu had considered his tenure blessed.

The old man, who was kept informed by Bakhen, rarely left his modest three-room dwelling near Karnak's sacred lake. In the evening he liked to water the iris beds on either side of his front door. When he found he could no longer care for them, he would ask the king to release him from his duties.

Nebu was astounded to see a stranger pulling weeds in his flower bed. "No one but me touches those irises!" he said testily.

"Not even the Pharaoh of Egypt?"

Ramses stood up and turned to face him.

"Your Majesty, I beg your—"

"You're right to take personal care of this treasure, Nebu. You've done well by Egypt and Karnak. Planting, helping things grow, keeping them alive, so fragile and beautiful . . . is there any nobler calling? After Nefertari died, I considered leaving my cares behind and becoming a gardener."

"Unthinkable, Your Majesty."

"I thought you'd be more understanding."

"An old man like me can retire with a clear conscience, but you . . ."

Ramses contemplated the rising moon.

"A storm is brewing, Nebu. I need reliable, competent men to deal with the forces that may be unleashed. I'm not letting you retire yet, no matter how old and frail you claim to be. Keep running Karnak with a firm hand."

FOUR

The ambassador from Hatti, a wiry little man around sixty, entered the State Department lobby. According to custom, he laid a bouquet of chrysanthemums and lilies on the stone altar and bowed to the looming statue of a baboon. This was the animal form of Thoth, the patron of scribes, god of language and knowledge.

Then the ambassador addressed a lance-wielding officer.

"The secretary is expecting me," he said crisply.

"I'll announce your visit."

Attired in a fringed robe of red and blue, his dark hair shining with aromatic oil, a short beard framing his jaw, the ambassador paced.

A smiling Ahsha came out to greet him.

"I haven't kept you waiting too long, have I? Let's go into the garden, dear friend, where it will be quieter."

Palm and jojoba trees pleasantly shaded a blue lotus pool. On a pedestal table, a servant placed alabaster goblets full of cool beer along with a basket of figs, then withdrew discreetly.

"Rest assured," said Ahsha, "we're quite alone."

The Hittite ambassador hesitated to sit down on a folding wooden chair with a comfortable-looking green linen seat pad.

"What are you so afraid of?"

"You, Ahsha."

The Egyptian diplomat's smile never left his face.

"I've been a spy in your country, I grant you, but that's all in the past. Today I'm an official with a reputation to uphold and no desire at all for wild adventures."

"Why should I believe you?"

"Because, like you, I have only one goal in mind: strengthening the peace between our two peoples."

"Has Pharaoh replied to Emperor Hattusili's latest letter?"

"Of course. Ramses sent excellent news of Queen Iset and his horses, repeating how pleased he is to note that the peace treaty is in full force, forever uniting Egypt and Hatti."

The ambassador's face closed.

"From our point of view, that's quite insufficient."

"What were you hoping for?"

"Emperor Hattusili has been shocked by the tone of Pharaoh's last few letters. They made him feel that Ramses considers him as a subject, not an equal."

The diplomat's own tone was almost aggressive.

"Would you say that his discontent has reached alarming proportions?" inquired Ahsha.

"I'm afraid so."

"How could such a slight misunderstanding affect our alliance?"

"The Hittites are proud. Anyone wounding their pride attracts retribution."

"Aren't we blowing a minor incident out of proportion?"

"From our point of view, it's a major incident."

"I'm afraid I see . . . But couldn't we seek a negotiable solution?"

"Our position isn't negotiable."

Ahsha had been afraid this was coming. At Kadesh, Hattusili had been commander of the coalition that Ramses defeated. Now the emperor was seeking any possible means to reassert his dominance.

"Does this mean you'd consider . . ."

"Breaking the treaty? It does," the Hittite ambassador said flatly.

Ahsha decided to use his secret weapon.

"Would this help to smooth things over?"

He handed the Hittite a letter Ramses had written. Intrigued, the ambassador read it aloud:

> *May this letter find you in the best of health, dear brother Hattusili, and your wife, family, horses, and provinces as well. I have just examined your complaints: you believe that I treat you as one of my subjects, and that grieves me. Be certain that I hold you in all the consideration due your rank, for you alone are emperor of the Hittites. I assure you that I regard you as my brother.*

The envoy was obviously astonished.

"Did Ramses write this?"

"It's in his own hand."

"Is the Pharaoh of Egypt acknowledging his error?"

"Ramses wants peace. And I have an important announcement: an International Center will soon open in Pi-Ramses, permanently staffed and at the disposal of the diplomatic corps. The Egyptian capital will host a permanent dialogue with its allies and vassals."

"Remarkable," conceded the Hittite.

"Our hope is that this initiative will pacify your country."

"I'm afraid it won't."

Now Ahsha began to worry in earnest. "Am I to conclude that nothing will allay the emperor's dissatisfaction?"

"I may as well tell you straight out that Hattusili also wishes to keep the peace. Except that he's proposing one condition . . ."

The Hittite ambassador spelled out the emperor's true intentions. The smile quickly faded from Ahsha's face.

As they did every morning, celebrants said prayers for Seti's *ka*—his spiritual essence—at his magnificent temple of Gurnah on the West Bank at Thebes. The priest in charge of funerary offerings was about to set a tray of grapes, figs, and juniper wood on the altar when one of his subordinates whispered a few words in his ear.

"Pharaoh, here? But no one told me!"

Turning around, the priest spied the monarch's tall silhouette in a white linen robe. Ramses' power and magnetism set him apart from the other celebrants.

Pharaoh took the tray and entered the chapel where his father's soul lived on. It was here at Gurnah that Seti had proclaimed Ramses as his successor, having guided his younger son lovingly yet firmly toward that point ever since adolescence. The twin crowns of Egypt, "Great of Magic," had been carefully fitted to the prince's head. He was the Son of Light, and now his destiny was entwined with Egypt's.

Succeeding Seti had seemed impossible. Yet Ramses' true freedom had lain in having no choice, living the law, and satisfying the gods in order to benefit humankind.

Today, Seti, Tuya, and Nefertari roamed the byways of eternity, sailing in their celestial barks. On earth, their tombs and temples immortalized their name. It was toward their *ka* that humans would turn when they felt the need to pierce the mysteries of the afterlife.

When the service was over, Ramses headed for the temple gardens, which were dominated by a sycamore full of herons' nests.

The sad, sweet sound of an oboe enchanted him. A quiet tune, grave yet lilting, as if saying that hope could bring an end to pain.

Seated on a low wall, framed in foliage, a woman sat playing. Her hair was black and shiny, her features as chiseled as those of a goddess, Meritamon, aged thirty-three, was at the height of her beauty.

Ramses felt a pang, for she was the image of her mother, Nefertari. A gifted musician, Meritamon had known since girlhood that she was suited to the religious life, playing tunes for the gods in some secluded temple. Such a cloistered existence had been Nefertari's dream—an impossible dream once Ramses' love had led her to become his Great Royal Wife. Meritamon could easily have claimed a prominent rank among the temple musicians at Karnak, yet she preferred to remain at Gurnah, close to Seti's soul.

The final notes filtered toward the sun. The lovely musician set her instrument down on the wall and opened her blue-green eyes.

"Father! Have you been here long?"

Ramses took his daughter in a long embrace.

"I've missed you, Meritamon."

"Pharaoh is the spouse of Egypt; all her people are his children. With more than a hundred royal children, I'm flattered that you still remember me."

He stepped back and admired her.

"You know that the title of royal son or daughter is an honorary one. And you're the only child of Nefertari, the love of my life."

"Now you're married to Iset the Fair."

"Do you mind?"

"No, you made the right decision. Iset is devoted to you."

"Would you consider returning to Pi-Ramses?"

"No, Father. I don't care for the outside world. What could be more useful than conducting services each day? I commune with my mother; I'm living her dream, and I'm convinced that my happiness feeds her eternal spirit."

"She left you her beauty and her character. Have I no chance at all of luring you back?"

"None at all," she said, smiling.

He gently took her hands. "Are you sure?"

Her smile was so much like Nefertari's. "Could you be giving me an order?"

"You're the only person that Pharaoh would never dare order around."

"I wouldn't try to resist you, Father. It's just that I'm of more use in the temple than at court. Nurturing my mother's spirit, my grandparents' spirit, seems like the most important task I can perform. Without ties to our ancestors, what kind of world would we build?"

"Keep playing your heavenly music, Meritamon. Egypt will need it."

The young woman's heart skipped a beat.

"What danger do you fear?"

"An approaching storm."

"Surely you can control it."

"Play, Meritamon, for Egypt and for Pharaoh, too. Spread harmony, enchant the gods, make them smile down on our Twin Kingdoms. A storm is brewing, and it will be terrifying."

FIVE

Serramanna slammed his fist into the guardroom wall, sending a slab of plaster flying.

"What do you mean, he's gone?"

"Disappeared, Chief," confirmed the soldier in charge of tailing the Hittite prince Uri-Teshoop.

The hulking Sardinian grabbed him by the shoulders, and though the guard was a sturdy fellow, he felt his bones crack.

"Is this some kind of joke?"

"No, Chief, I swear it isn't!"

"You let him slip right through your fingers?"

"He got lost in the crowd."

"Why didn't you search the neighborhood?"

"Uri-Teshoop is a free man, Chief! We have no authorization to launch a search for him. The vizier would never sanction it."

Serramanna snorted like an angry bull and let go of the soldier. The bumbling idiot was right.

"What should I do next, Chief?"

"We'll put a double guard on Pharaoh. The slightest infraction of discipline and I'll bash your skulls!"

It was not a threat that the members of Ramses' bodyguard took lightly. In a fit of rage, the old pirate might just do it.

To work off his fury, Serramanna sank a series of daggers into the heart of a wooden target. Uri-Teshoop's disappearance did not augur well. The bitter and vengeful Hittite would use his newfound liberty as a weapon against the Lord of Egypt. All that remained to be seen was when and how.

A large contingent of diplomats was on hand as Ramses inaugurated his new International Center. With his customary brio, Ahsha gave a fine speech studded with the words "peace," "understanding," and "economic cooperation." As was fitting, a lavish banquet topped off a ceremony heralding Pi-Ramses' advent as the capital of the Near East and welcoming all its neighbors.

From his father, Ramses had inherited the ability to read people's innermost secrets. Despite Ahsha's practiced composure, the king could tell that his friend was worried, increasingly anxious about the approaching storm.

The moment they could break away from the receiving line, the two men talked.

"Brilliant performance, Ahsha."

"All in a day's work, Your Majesty. I must say I applaud your new initiative."

"What was the Hittite ambassador's reaction to my letter?"

"Oh, excellent."

"But Hattusili is demanding more, isn't he?"

"That may be the case."

"Stop playing the diplomat, Ahsha. I want the truth."

"All right, then. Unless you accept Hattusili's conditions, there will be war."

"I won't cave in to his threats."

"Please listen, Ramses. You and I have worked too hard for peace to see it disintegrate in an instant."

"Tell me his demands."

"You know that Hattusili and his wife, Puduhepa, have a daughter, by all accounts a lovely and highly intelligent young woman."

"So?"

"Hattusili wants to strengthen his ties with Egypt. He thinks a marriage would be the best way."

"Am I to understand . . ."

"You understood from the beginning. To seal our pact, Hattusili demands not only that you marry his daughter, but also that you make her your Great Royal Wife."

"That title belongs to Iset the Fair."

"What does that matter to a Hittite? A wife must obey her husband. If he repudiates her, all she can do is fade into the background."

"This is Egypt, Ahsha, not some barbaric country. Are

you suggesting that I cast Iset aside to marry a Hittite princess, the daughter of my worst enemy?"

"Today he's your best ally," corrected the secretary of state.

"The very idea is absurd and revolting!"

"At first glance, yes. But on second thought, it's not without interest."

"I won't inflict such humiliation on Iset."

"You're no ordinary husband. The grandeur of Egypt must come before your personal feelings."

"You've had too many women, Ahsha. I think you've become a cynic."

"The concept of fidelity is alien to me, I admit, but I'm offering my opinion as your friend and servant."

"It's no use asking my sons Kha and Merenptah if they'd agree. I know what they'd say."

"Who could reproach them for honoring their mother, Iset the Fair, Ramses' Great Royal Wife? Peace or war . . . this is the choice before you."

"Let's dine with Ahmeni. I want to consult with him."

"You can consult with Setau, too. He's just off the boat from Nubia."

"That's the first good news you've given me!"

Setau the snake charmer and champion of Nubia; Ahsha the shrewd statesman; Ahmeni the disciplined and devoted scribe . . . Only Moses was missing. So many years earlier they had made up Ramses' band of boyhood friends, attending the royal academy in Memphis, sharing the pleasures of friendship and debating the nature of true power.

Tonight Ramses' chef had outdone himself: a leek and zucchini timbale; lamb grilled with thyme and a side dish of puréed figs; marinated kidneys, goat cheese, and honey cake with carob sauce. In honor of this reunion, Ramses had called for a special red wine from Year Three of Seti's reign, sending Setau into near ecstasy.

"All praise to Seti!" exclaimed the cobra tamer, dressed in his indestructible antelope-skin tunic, its countless pockets saturated with anti-venom remedies. "Any reign that produced such a marvel was truly blessed by the gods."

"I see that you still haven't learned how to dress," said Ahsha, shaking his head.

"Evidently not," Ahmeni chimed in.

"No one asked for your opinion, scribe. Just keep shoveling in the food. How do you manage to stay so thin?"

"I work hard for king and country."

"Are you implying there's something wrong with my initiatives in Nubia?"

"If that were the case, I would have written you up long ago."

"When you two are finished bickering," interrupted Ahsha, "perhaps we could discuss more serious matters."

"Moses is the only one missing," mused Ramses. "Where is he, Ahsha?"

"Still battling his way through the desert. He'll never reach his Promised Land."

"Moses is on the wrong path, but I'm sure he'll achieve his goal."

"I miss him too," confessed Ahmeni. "But how can we forget that our Hebrew friend is a traitor?"

"This is no time for nostalgia," Setau broke in. "For me, a friend who takes such a drastic step is no longer a friend."

"Wouldn't you take him back if he made amends?" asked Ramses.

"As far as I'm concerned, he's burned his bridges. Forgiveness is for weaklings."

"It's a good thing Ramses didn't put you in charge of diplomacy," Ahsha said dryly.

"With snakes there are no halfway measures. Venom either cures you or kills you."

"I thought we'd changed the subject," said Ahmeni.

"What brings me here is Lotus," explained Setau. "Her psychic gifts said that Ramses is in danger. Or am I mistaken?"

The Pharaoh offered no denial. Setau turned toward Ahmeni.

"Instead of gobbling cake, tell us what you've found out!"

"Why . . . nothing! Everything is in order as far as I can see."

"And you, Ahsha?"

The diplomat rinsed his fingers in a bowl of lemon-scented water.

"Hattusili has made an unexpected demand: he wants Ramses to marry his daughter."

"Where's the problem?" asked Setau, amused. "This type of diplomatic marriage has worked well in the past, and a Hittite princess would just be one more secondary wife."

"In the present case, the situation is more complex."

"Is the bride-to-be hideous?"

"No. The Hittite emperor wants his daughter to be Great Royal Wife."

At that, Setau lost his temper.

"That means our old enemy is requiring Ramses to renounce Iset!"

"To put it bluntly, yes," said Ahsha.

"I hate the Hittites," confessed Setau, draining another goblet of wine. "Iset the Fair isn't Nefertari, of course, but she still deserves respect."

"For once," Ahmeni said hoarsely, "I agree with you."

"You should both reconsider," declared Ahsha. "Peace is at stake here."

"We can't let the Hittites dictate to us!" protested Setau.

"They're no longer our enemies," the secretary of state reminded them.

"You're wrong! Hattusili and his ilk will never stop trying to take over Egypt."

"You're the one who's off base. The Hittite emperor wants peace; he's only redefining his conditions. We at least ought to think it over."

"I prefer to trust my instincts."

"I *have* thought it over," affirmed Ahmeni. "I can't say I care for Iset the Fair, but she is Queen of Egypt, the Great Royal Wife that Ramses chose after Nefertari's passing. No one, even the Emperor of Hatti, has the right to insult her."

"Completely unreasonable!" Ahsha insisted. "Do you want to send thousands of Egyptians to their deaths, cause bloodshed in our northern protectorates, and put the whole country in jeopardy?"

Ahmeni and Setau looked questioningly at Ramses.

"I'll make my decision alone," said the Pharaoh.

SIX

The convoy leader dithered over his route.

Should he head south along the coast, passing through Beirut and crossing Canaan on the way to Sileh, or would it be better to take the road along the Anti-Lebanon range and Mount Hermon, leaving Damascus to the east?

Phoenicia had its charms: there were oak and cedar forests, shady walnut groves, fig trees with their delicious fruit, and villages that made pleasant rest stops.

But Pi-Ramses urgently needed his cargo—olibanum, the painstakingly harvested white frankincense from the Arabian peninsula.

The Egyptians called it *sonter,* "that which makes divine," and mixed it with reddish myrrh, which was no less precious. The rare substances played a crucial role in worship. Temples filled with their heady scent, which rose to the heavens and delighted the gods. Embalmers and physicians also made use of them.

The Arabian frankincense tree was short, with dark green leaves. In August and September it bloomed with golden, purple-hearted flowers, while droplets of white resin beaded beneath the bark. A trained worker could scrape the bark to obtain three harvests per year, reciting the time-honored magic words: *"Be good to me, white frankincense tree, and Pharaoh will make you grow."*

The convoy was also transporting Asian copper, tin, and glass, but these items, while sought-after and easily traded, were far less valuable than olibanum. Once the delivery was made, the merchant would rest at his comfortable home in the Delta.

With his receding hairline and expanding waistline, he enjoyed a good time, yet took his work seriously. He personally checked his chariots and donkeys daily. As for his employees, they were well fed and well treated, but were quickly dismissed if they dared to complain.

The merchant decided to take his convoy down the high road. It was harder but shorter than the coastal route. There would be plenty of shade and the animals would stay cooler.

The donkeys were moving at a steady pace, the twenty drivers were humming, the wind was at their back.

"Boss . . ."

"What is it?"

"I think we're being followed."

The merchant shrugged. "I know, I know. You used to be a mercenary. Well, we're at peace now, and the route is well patrolled."

"All right, but we're still being followed. I can tell."

"We're not the only convoy on the road!"

"If they're vagabonds, I won't give up my food without a fight."

"Stop worrying and tend to your donkeys."

The convoy came to a sudden halt. Furious, the merchant worked his way to the head, where he found a pile of brush blocking their path.

"Clear it away!"

The moment the lead drivers set to work, a volley of arrows mowed them down. Their frantic counterparts tried to run, but met the same fate. The former mercenary brandished a dagger, scrambled up the rocky slope, and hurled himself at the archers. A long-haired strongman intercepted him, bashing in his skull with a hatchet.

The whole incident lasted only a few minutes. Only the merchant himself was left alive. Trembling, unable to move, he watched the hatchet-wielding killer come forward, his broad chest covered with a reddish fleece.

"Let me live . . . I'll make a rich man of you!"

Uri-Teshoop burst out laughing and sank his sword in the poor wretch's belly. The Hittite detested merchants.

His henchmen, all Phoenicians, recovered their arrows from the fallen bodies. The donkeys took orders from their new masters.

The Syrian Raia feared Uri-Teshoop's violent nature, but he had found no better figure to rally opposition to the peace treaty. Certain factions still hoped to overthrow Ramses by any possible means. Raia was growing rich again, yet he was convinced that one day the Hittites would attack Egypt. Uri-Teshoop, the former commander-in-chief, would regroup his forces and urge them on to battle. As the man behind the general's climb back to the top, Raia would be in a privileged position.

When the Hittite appeared in his warehouse, Raia recoiled imperceptibly. He had the feeling that this cruel warrior, at once hot-tempered and coldhearted, might slit his throat for the simple pleasure of killing.

"Back so soon, Your Highness!"

"Aren't you happy to see me, Raia?"

"Of course I am! But your task was not a simple one, and—"

"I made it simple."

The Syrian shivered beneath his goatee. He had asked Uri-Teshoop to make contact with the Phoenicians and buy up the latest shipment of olibanum coming out of Arabia. It might require hard bargaining, but Raia had supplied Uri-Teshoop with enough tin to persuade any merchant. The Syrian had also thrown in a contraband bar of silver, rare vases, and some bolts of fine fabric.

"And how did you simplify it?" Raia asked hesitantly.

"Merchants like to talk; I'm a man of action."

"So you had no trouble persuading the convoy leader to sell you the olibanum."

Uri-Teshoop's smile was a carnivore's.

"No trouble at all."

"Yet the merchant in question drives a hard bargain."

"He didn't bargain with my sword."

"You couldn't have . . ."

"I hired some mercenaries and we slaughtered every last man in the convoy, down to the leader."

"But why?"

"I told you. I don't like to talk, and I got the goods. Isn't that what matters?"

"The incident won't go unnoticed. If there's an investigation . . ."

"We threw the bodies down a ravine."

Raia wondered if he shouldn't stop living a double life. But it was too late to turn back now. If he showed the least hesitation, Uri-Teshoop would eliminate him.

"And now?" asked the prince.

"We need to destroy the cargo," Raia told him.

"But isn't the olibanum worth a fortune?"

"Yes, but any prospective buyer would turn us in. All white frankincense is earmarked for the temples."

"I need weapons, horses, and soldiers."

"Don't even think about selling it!"

"I won't. You're going to sell it for me, in tiny lots, to traders leaving for Greece and Cyprus. And we'll start forming a network of resisters who want an end to this damned peace agreement."

There was a grain of sense in Uri-Teshoop's plan. Through his Phoenician contacts, Raia could liquidate the olibanum fairly safely. Fundamentally hostile to Egypt, Phoenicia would harbor Hittite political dissenters.

"I need a respectable front," the prince continued. "Serramanna will never stop hounding me unless I look like I've settled down."

Raia considered this. "So what you need is a rich and well-connected wife. A love-starved widow, in other words."

"Do you have one in mind?"

Raia scratched his goatee. "My clientele is extensive . . . I have an idea or two. Next week I'll throw a banquet and introduce you."

"When is the next shipment of olibanum due to leave the Arabian peninsula?"

"I don't know yet, but we have time. My informers will keep us posted. But won't another strike bring the Egyptian army down on us?"

"There will be no sign of violence, and the Egyptian authorities will be mystified. We'll corner the whole year's harvest. But what makes you so sure that a shortage of frankincense will have such a drastic effect on Ramses?"

"Religious observations are the backbone of Egypt's culture. Any change in the ancient rituals threatens to throw the country out of balance. When the priests notice the shortage of olibanum and myrrh, they'll turn against Ramses. He'll be forced to admit his oversight. His neglect of the gods will anger both the clergy and the people. If we can spread a few false rumors, thereby adding to the confusion and cutting further into his base of support, there will be protests in the major cities."

Uri-Teshoop imagined Egypt overrun by a pillaging army. He pictured Ramses' crowns trampled by Hittite soldiers, saw the terror in his eyes.

The hatred on the prince's face began to frighten the Syrian merchant. For a few seconds, Uri-Teshoop entered the realm of darkness, losing contact with the world of men.

"I want to strike fast and hard, Raia."

"We must proceed cautiously, Your Highness. Ramses is a formidable adversary. Undue haste will only result in failure."

"I've heard about his magical protection. But that has surely weakened with age, and he no longer has Nefertari to help him."

"Our spy ring included Ramses' brother and Meba, the undersecretary of state," Raia reminded him. "Even though they're gone, I still have valuable contacts in the upper reaches of government. Officials can be talkative; one of them told me that diplomatic relations between Hatti and Egypt are about to deteriorate."

"Why didn't you tell me this sooner? And what's behind it?"

"That's still a secret, but I'll find out before long."

"Our luck is beginning to change, Raia! And I'm no less formidable than Ramses."

SEVEN

Iset the Fair's handmaiden soaped the queen's back thoroughly, then poured warm, scented water over her slender body. The substance she used was rich in saponin, extracted from the bark and pith of the precious and bountiful desert date tree. The Queen of Egypt relaxed, letting the manicurist and hairdresser work on her. A manservant brought her a cup of cool milk.

In Pi-Ramses, Iset the Fair felt more at ease than in Thebes, where Nefertari's tomb stood in the Valley of the Queens on the West Bank and the Ramesseum included a chapel where Ramses often led the prayers for his late wife's soul. Here, in the cosmopolitan capital Pharaoh had created, life was hectic, with less time to think about the past or the world to come.

Iset contemplated herself in a polished bronze mirror, a disk with its handle representing a long-limbed naked woman, her head crowned with a papyrus tuft.

Yes, she was still beautiful. Her skin was as soft as finely woven cloth, her face was as fresh as ever, love shone in her eyes. Yet her beauty would never equal Nefertari's, and she was grateful that Ramses had the honesty never to pretend he would one day forget his first Great Royal Wife. Was Iset jealous? Not at all. In fact, she missed Nefertari. Royalty had never been what Iset wanted. The honor of bearing Ramses' two sons was enough to make her happy.

Two sons, so different from each other! Kha, the elder, was now thirty-seven, a distinguished cleric who spent the majority of his time in temple libraries. His brother, Merenptah, at twenty-seven was as athletic and commanding as his father. One of them might well be called upon to reign; yet the Pharaoh could also choose one of his many royal sons, most of whom were brilliant administrators, as his successor.

Iset cared nothing for power or the future. She was savoring each second of this new miracle that life had offered her. Living at Ramses' side, officiating with him at ceremonies, watching him reign over the Two Lands . . . Was there any existence more marvelous?

The hairdresser braided the queen's hair, perfumed it with myrrh, then adjusted a short wig, topping it with a diadem of pearls and carnelian.

"Forgive me for being overly familiar . . . but Your Majesty looks stunning!"

Iset smiled. She must stay beautiful for Ramses, to make him forget, for as long as possible, that her youth had disappeared.

The moment she stood up, he appeared. No man could compare to him, none possessed his intelligence, force of character, or sheer presence. The gods had given him every gift, which he in turn showered upon his country.

"Ramses! I'm not even dressed yet."

"We need to discuss a serious matter."

Iset the Fair had been dreading this test. Nefertari had had a flair for governing; she had none. Helping to steer the ship of state terrified her.

"You decide," she said meekly.

"It concerns you directly, Iset."

"Me? But I swear that I haven't meddled in anything official, and—"

"Your own position is in question, and peace is at stake."

"Explain what you mean, I beg of you!"

"Hattusili is demanding that I marry his daughter."

"A diplomatic marriage . . . Why not?"

"That's not all he asks. He wants her to become my Great Royal Wife."

Iset the Fair stood motionless for a few seconds. Then her eyes filled with tears. It was the end of the miracle. She must step aside and let a pretty young Hittite princess take her place as the symbol of the entente between Egypt and Hatti. With peace hanging in the balance, Iset the Fair weighed less than a feather.

"The decision is yours to make," declared Ramses. "Will you agree to step down and live in retirement?"

The queen smiled wanly. "This Hittite princess must be very young . . ."

"Her age is of little importance."

"You've made me a happy woman, Ramses. Your will is Egypt's will."

"So you'll give in?"

"It would be criminal to stand in the way of peace."

"Well, *I'm* not giving in! The Emperor of Hatti is not about to dictate to the Pharaoh of Egypt. We're not barbarians who treat their women as inferiors. What Lord of the Two Lands has ever dared repudiate his Great Royal Wife, who is one in being with Pharaoh? No Anatolian warlord will make Ramses violate the law of our ancestors."

Ramses took Iset the Fair's hands tenderly in his own.

"You spoke with Egypt's interests in mind, as a true queen. Now I'll have to act."

Filtering through one of the three tall barred windows that lit Ramses' spacious office, light from the setting sun gilded the statue of Seti. Brought to life by the sculptor's magic, kept alive by the ritual "opening of the mouth and the eyes" at the time of his funeral, the monarch continued to transmit a message of rectitude that only his son could apprehend, as the peace of evening clothed itself in godly splendor.

White walls, a broad table where a map of the Near East was spread out, a straight-backed armchair for the Pharaoh, straw side chairs for his visitors, a library of books on the protection of the royal soul, and a cupboard for papyri: in these stark surroundings Ramses the Great pondered the decisions affecting his country's future.

The monarch had consulted the sages of the House of Life in Heliopolis; the high priests heading the major religious centers; Ahmeni; the vizier; and his cabinet. Then he closeted himself in his office and spoke soul to soul with his father. Not so long ago he could have talked to Nefertari and Tuya. Iset the Fair, however, knew her own limits and made no attempt to help. Solitude weighed on him; soon he would have to test his two sons to find out whether either of them might be suited to continue the work under way since the days of the first Pharaoh.

Egypt was both strong and fragile. Strong because the law of Ma'at—the guiding principle of justice and harmony—would outlast human pettiness; fragile because the world was changing, giving wider berth to tyranny, greed, and selfishness. The pharaohs would no doubt be the last to champion Ma'at, knowing that without the goddess's help the world would become a mere combat zone where barbarians clashed with ever more destructive weapons, aiming to amass more privileges and destroy all ties to the divine.

Thus Pharaoh's task was to replace violence, injustice, hatred, and lies with the harmony of Ma'at, a task he performed in concert with invisible powers. And the Emperor of Hatti's new demand was in conflict with Ma'at.

A guard ushered in Ahsha, wearing an exceptionally well tailored linen robe and long-sleeved shirt.

"I couldn't work in a room this stark," he remarked.

"My father liked things plain, and so do I."

"Being Pharaoh doesn't leave much room for enjoyment. Anyone who envies you must not have a clue. Has Your Majesty reached a decision?"

"My consultations are finished."

"Have my arguments swayed you?"

"No, Ahsha."

"Just as I feared."

The secretary of state gazed at the map of the region.

"Hattusili's ultimatum is an insult. Acquiescing would be a denial of our entire heritage."

Ahsha touched his index finger to the Hittite empire.

"A refusal equals a declaration of war, Your Majesty."

"Are you condemning my decision?"

"It's the decision of Ramses the Great, Pharaoh of Egypt. Your father would have done no differently."

"Was this some kind of test?"

"No. I was only doing my duty as a diplomat, suing for peace. Would I be Ramses' friend if I didn't challenge him?"

A smile flickered on the king's lips.

"When will Your Majesty mobilize the troops?"

"My secretary of state is quite the pessimist."

"Your official reply will provoke Hattusili's fury; he'll be waiting to pounce."

"You lack confidence in your abilities, Ahsha."

"I'm a realist."

"If anyone can still save the peace treaty, it's you."

"In other words, Pharaoh is ordering me to leave for Hattusa, explain our position to the Hittite emperor, and make him reverse his decision."

"You read my mind."

"It will never work."

"Ahsha . . . you've done the impossible before, haven't you?"

"I was younger then, Your Majesty."

"Why let this ridiculous marriage become the main issue? In this situation, we need to take the lead."

The diplomat frowned. He thought he knew Ramses well, yet once more the Pharaoh had managed to surprise him.

"We reached a mutual assistance agreement with our great friend Hattusili," the king continued. "You'll explain that I fear a Libyan attack on our western flank. Since the peace treaty was signed, however, our weaponry has aged and we're experiencing a shortage of iron. You'll therefore request that the Hittite emperor replenish our supply. Thanks to his help, and in keeping with our conventions, we'll be able to defend ourselves against the Libyan aggressor."

Speechless, Ahsha crossed his arms. "Is that really my mission?"

"I forgot one thing: I need the iron delivered as fast as he can get it here."

EIGHT

Kha, the son of Ramses and Iset the Fair, had steered clear of the military and the government. While the secular arena held no interest for him, he felt a true passion for classical literature and Old Kingdom monuments. With a stern, angular face, shaved head, dark blue eyes, thin frame, and stiff gait from his arthritic joints, Kha looked like the born scholar he was. After distinguishing himself in the struggle with Moses, whose magic tricks had produced the famous plagues on Egypt, Kha remained in firm command of the temple of Ptah in Memphis. He had long since delegated his temporal duties, concentrating his energies on the hidden forces that dwelt in air and rock, in water and wood.

The House of Life in Heliopolis preserved the "Souls of Light," the sacred archives dating back to the golden age when the pharaohs built the pyramids and the sages established the liturgy—a blessed era, when men were able to plumb the secrets of life and death. Not content with exploring the mysteries of the universe, these sages had transcribed them in hieroglyphs, thus transmitting their vision to future generations.

Recognized by all as the greatest expert on the country's traditions, Kha had been chosen to organize the first of

Ramses' jubilees, called sed-feasts, marking the thirtieth year of his reign. Such an extended period of wielding power was supposed to exhaust a pharaoh's strength. A festival of regeneration was therefore in order, an assembly of the community of gods and goddesses to renew Pharaoh's energy. Of course, many demons had attempted to thwart Ramses' sed-feast, but in vain.

Kha did much more than merely decipher old scribbles. He was obsessed with projects so ambitious that they would require the Pharaoh's backing. Before submitting his dreams for his father's approval, he must first bring them more in line with reality. That was why dawn found him pacing the quarry of the Red Mountain near Heliopolis, seeking out blocks of quartzite. According to legend, on this site the gods had massacred men who had rebelled against the light; the stone would be forever tinged with their blood.

While he had not been trained as a stonemason or sculptor, Kha instinctively communed with the mineral world. He felt the latent energy coursing through the veins of stone.

"What are you looking for, my son?"

Emerging in the daybreak that conquered the shadows, laying claim to its desert empire, Ramses contemplated Kha.

The king's elder son stopped breathing. Kha knew full well that Nefertari had sacrificed her life to save him from an evil sorcerer's black magic, and he sometimes wondered whether Ramses might secretly resent him for it.

"You're wrong, Kha. In no way do I blame you."

"You've been reading my mind!"

"Didn't you want to see me?"

"I thought you were in Thebes, and here you are at the Red Mountain."

"A grave danger is threatening Egypt. I have to deal with it. Meditating in this holy place is indispensable."

"Aren't we at peace with the Hittites?"

"The peace may prove to be no more than a truce."

"You'll steer clear of war or win if one comes along. No matter what happens, you'll be able to keep Egypt safe from harm."

"Don't you want to help me?"

"I'm useless when it comes to politics. And you'll reign for years to come, if you respect the ancestral rites. In fact, that need was what I wanted to discuss with you."

"What are you proposing?"

"You must undertake immediate preparations for your next sed-feast."

"So soon after the first one?"

"I've concluded from my research that it must be celebrated at three-year intervals."

"Do whatever is necessary."

"You could give me no greater joy, Father. No divinity will be absent from your next sed-feast. Joy will spread throughout the Two Lands; the goddess Mut will stud the heavens with malachite and turquoise."

"You must have another project in mind as well, Kha. What temple will get these blocks of quartzite you're prospecting here?"

"For several years I've been studying our illustrious past. Among the earliest rites was the cult of a bull called Apis, whose speed represented the king's ability to break through the barriers of space. We would do well to continue honoring this extraordinary animal, giving him a tomb in keeping with his importance. And it's not the only old monument that needs restoration. Even certain pyramids have been damaged by time or defaced by the Hyksos invaders. Will you grant me the manpower to complete the work?"

"Choose the master builder and stoneworkers yourself."

Kha's stern face lit up.

"This place is strange," remarked Ramses. "The rebels' blood has soaked into the stone. Here, the eternal combat between the forces of light and darkness has left deep traces. The Red Mountain is a place of power where one had best tread carefully. You haven't come here by chance, Kha. What treasure are you seeking?"

The king's elder son sat down on a dun-colored boulder.

"The Book of Thoth. The book containing the secret of the hieroglyphs. It's somewhere in the necropolis of Saqqara. I mean to find it, even if the quest takes years."

At fifty-four, Dame Tanit was a comely Phoenician whose ample curves attracted admiring glances from much younger men. Her late husband had been a rich trader, a friend of the Syrian merchant Raia's, and had left her a considerable fortune that she now spent lavishly, throwing banquet after banquet in her plush Pi-Ramses villa.

The shapely Phoenician little mourned the mate she had found vulgar and boring. After a few weeks of feigned sadness, she had found consolation in the arms of a magnificent Nubian with outstanding attributes, yet she soon tired of him. Like all her previous lovers, he had trouble keeping up with her, manly as he was. And a woman as hungry for pleasure as Tanit could never forgive this deplorable lack of endurance.

Tanit could have returned to Phoenicia, but she had grown fond of Egypt. Thanks to Ramses' authority and influence, the land of the pharaohs was heaven on earth. Nowhere else was a woman so free to live as she saw fit.

As evening fell, Dame Tanit's guests arrived—wealthy Egyptian business associates, high government officials fascinated by her charm, fellow countrymen who had designs on her fortune, not to mention the new faces she loved to discover. What could be more exciting than a man's frankly appreciative gaze? Tanit knew how to lead men on and when to back away, constantly keeping them off balance. No matter what happened, she was always in control of the situation. Anyone who tried to play the dominant male had no chance at all with her.

As usual, the food would be luscious (particularly the rabbit braised in beer, served with eggplant caviar) and the wines exceptional. Thanks to her palace connections, Tanit had even acquired a few jars of red Pi-Ramses wine dating from Year Twenty-one of Ramses' reign, when the peace treaty with the Hittites was signed. And as usual, the Phoenician would size up the best-looking men, with her sure eye for future conquests.

"How have you been, my dear lady?"

"Raia! So glad to see you again. I'm doing wonderfully, thank you."

"If I weren't afraid you'd accuse me of flattery, I'd tell you that you're lovelier than ever."

"The climate agrees with me. And then the pain of losing my husband is just beginning to fade."

"Fortunately, that's the law of nature. A woman like you isn't meant to be alone."

"Men are liars and brutes," she said teasingly. "I should stay away from them."

"You're wise to use caution, but I'm convinced that fate will grant you another chance at happiness."

"And how is business, Raia?"

"Demanding as ever. Making luxury foodstuffs requires highly skilled workers who demand top wages. The imported vases that are so popular with my select Egyptian clientele keep me on the road a great deal. Serious craftsmen don't sell their wares cheaply. As my reputation rests on quality, I have to keep reinvesting in my business; that's why I'll never be rich."

"You're a lucky man. You seem to have landed on your feet."

"I was falsely accused of being a Hittite sympathizer. It's true that I had dealings with Hatti, but they were never political. The advent of peace set me back in good standing. Renewed ties with our foreign trading partners are even encouraged now. I'd say that peace is Ramses' greatest accomplishment. Don't you agree?"

"Pharaoh is so attractive. Too bad he's out of my league."

The peace treaty, the mutual assistance agreement signed by Ramses and Hattusili, the Hittite empire's loss of its conquering spirit, Egypt triumphant . . . Raia could no longer bear to think of the cowardice and defections that had led to this wretched state of affairs. All his adult life he had fought to see the Anatolian army's supremacy extend throughout the Near East. He wasn't about to give up now.

"May I introduce a friend to you?" he asked Tanit, who was instantly intrigued.

"Who is it?"

"A Hittite prince who's new to Pi-Ramses. He's heard a lot about you, but the social life in Egypt intimidates him. I practically had to drag him here tonight."

"Point him out to me."

"He's standing over there, near the oleanders."

A lamp atop a pillar illuminated Uri-Teshoop, standing apart from the clusters of animated guests. The flickering light revealed a hard face, long thick hair, a strong torso covered with reddish fleece, and the sturdy muscular build of a warrior.

Tanit was too moved to speak. She had never before seen a male animal exuding such intense sensuality. The banquet ceased to exist. A single thought possessed her: getting this stallion into bed.

NINE

R amses was invited to observe his younger son, Merenptah, training with Serramanna. Outfitted in a hinged breastplate, a helmet with flaring horns and a bronze disk on top, plus a round shield, the Sard was slamming his sword into the prince's rectangular shield, forcing the younger man to give ground. Pharaoh had asked his guard captain not to go easy on his son; if Merenptah wanted to prove his valor in combat, he could find no stauncher opponent.

At twenty-seven, the prince, whose name meant "Beloved of the God Ptah," was a fine-looking athlete, brave, alert, and blessed with excellent reflexes. Although the Sardinian giant was past fifty, he had lost none of his strength or fighting prowess. Simply resisting him was an exploit.

Merenptah retreated, attacked again, parried blows, worked his way to one side, then the other. Little by little, he was wearing Serramanna down.

Abruptly, the giant stopped dead, throwing his long sword with its triangular blade to the ground, along with his shield.

"Enough skirmishing. We'll fight hand to hand now."

Merenptah hesitated for a moment, then followed suit. Ramses was reliving his initial unarmed confrontation with the Sardinian pirate on the shore of the Mediterranean.

The king's son was unprepared when Serramanna rushed headlong at him. Military school had never taught Merenptah to fight like a wild beast. Flat on his back on the dusty barracks floor, he felt the old pirate's crushing weight on his chest.

"Class dismissed," declared Ramses.

The two men got up. Merenptah was furious.

"He tricked me!"

"That's what the enemy always does, my son."

"I want to keep fighting."

"No need. I saw what I wanted to see. Now that you've been given this valuable lesson, I'm naming you as commander of the Egyptian army."

Serramanna nodded his approval.

"Within a month," Ramses continued, "I want you to submit a complete and detailed report on the state of our troops and their armament."

As Merenptah caught his breath, Ramses rode off in the chariot that he still drove himself. To whom should he entrust the fate of Egypt: the scholarly Kha or the fiery

Merenptah? If their strengths were united in one single person, the choice would have been easy. And Nefertari was no longer there to advise him. As for his royal sons, all of them were talented, yet none had as strong a personality as Iset the Fair's two sons. And Meritamon, Nefertari's daughter, had chosen the cloistered life in a distant temple.

Ramses must not ignore the advice Ahmeni had given him that very morning: "Your Majesty must draw on the rites of regeneration to remain on the throne until your energy is totally exhausted. For Pharaoh, there has never been any other possible path, nor will there ever be one."

Raia left his warehouse, walked through the streets of craftsmen's shops nearby, passed in front of the palace, and headed for the broad avenue leading to Pi-Ramses' main temples. Lined with shade trees, this street was the image of Ramses' capital city, both majestic and livable.

The merchant passed the temple of Amon on his left and the temple of Ra on his right. At what he hoped was a leisurely pace, he continued toward the temple of Ptah, which he skirted, for anchored in the outer wall were tablets engraved with ears and eyes. Ptah, it was said, heard every secret and saw the most hidden intentions.

"Superstition," scoffed Raia, though he felt uneasy; he rounded the corner where a niche held a statuette of the goddess Ma'at, allowing the people to contemplate the central mystery of pharaonic civilization, the immutable law, conceived beyond the bounds of time and space.

Raia arrived at the craftsmen's entrance to the temple complex; the guard recognized him. They exchanged a few meaningless remarks about the weather; the merchant complained about how stingy some of his customers could be. Then he was admitted to the area reserved for goldsmiths. As an expert on precious vases, Raia knew a good number of the workmen, and made sure to ask after one man's family, another's health.

"I know you want to pry our secrets out of us," muttered an old metal worker who was stacking ingots on a cart.

"I've given up on that," confessed Raia. "Watching you work is enough to make me happy."

"You haven't come here for pleasure, though."

"I wouldn't mind getting hold of one or two nice pieces."

"To sell them for three times as much!"

"That's business, my friend."

The old craftsman turned his back on Raia. The Syrian was used to such rebuffs. Discreet, almost invisible, he observed the apprentices carting ingots to journeymen, who weighed the metal under supervision by specially trained scribes. The gold was then deposited in a sealed vase and fired; a blowtorch fanned the flames. The blowers often kept their cheeks puffed out so as not to lose the rhythm. Other workers poured the molten metal into receptacles in a variety of shapes, handing them over to the goldsmiths. These master technicians worked at a forge, their stone hammers fashioning necklaces, bracelets, vases, statues, and ornamental doors for temples. Trade secrets passed from master to disciple though long years of training.

"Magnificent," said Raia to a goldsmith who had just finished a pectoral.

"It's for the statue of a god," explained the craftsman.

The merchant lowered his voice. "Can we talk?"

"It's noisy enough in here. No one will hear us."

"Your two sons both want to marry, I hear."

"Could be."

"I'd like to help them set up housekeeping."

"What do I have to do?"

"Just get me some information."

"Don't count on me to sell you our trade secrets."

"I'm asking nothing of the sort!"

"Then what do you want to know?"

"Since I've been so successful, I'd like to see my countrymen feel more settled in Egypt. Haven't you hired a Syrian or two to work here?"

"Yes, there's one in the shop."

"Is he satisfied with his lot?"

"More or less."

"If you agree to give me his name, I'll speak to him."

"Is that all you want, Raia?"

"I'm getting older, I have no children, and I'm a man of means. I'd like to find someone I can sponsor."

"Egypt has taught you to be less selfish . . . that's a good sign. It will be in your favor when your soul is judged. Your Syrian is over there with the blowers. The big one with the ears that stick out."

"I hope that your sons enjoy my wedding gifts."

Raia waited until the afternoon break to approach his fellow Syrian. His two previous attempts, with a carpenter and a mason quite content with their situation, had met with total failure. This was exactly the opposite.

The Syrian blower, a onetime prisoner of war taken near Kadesh, refused to admit Hittite defeat and hoped the hostilities would soon resume. Bitter, resentful, and itching for revenge, he was exactly the type of man Uri-Teshoop and Raia needed. Even better, the metal worker had friends who shared his views.

Raia had no trouble convincing the younger man to work

for him and join a resistance group with the express mission of attacking Egypt's vital interests.

Uri-Teshoop bit his new lover on the neck and rammed himself into her. Tanit sighed with satisfaction. At last she was experiencing raw passion.

"Again," she begged.

The Hittite took unbridled pleasure in the comely Phoenician's womanly body. In the fortresses of his home country, he had learned to give the opposite sex what they deserved.

Momentarily, Tanit felt a pang of fright. For the first time, she was no longer in control of the situation. She had never encountered a man so rough, so wonderfully inexhaustible. Despite the warning signal, she knew she would never find another like him, able to fulfill her wildest fantasies.

Deep in the night, she finally begged him to stop.

"Already?"

"You're a monster!"

"No, I'm a man. I guess you've only had boys before me."

She clung to his damp, hairy chest. "You're wonderful. I wish dawn would never come."

"What does it matter?"

"But you'll have to leave! We'll meet again tomorrow night."

"I'm staying."

"Do you know what that means, in Egypt?"

"When a man and a woman live together publicly, it's considered a marriage. So now we're married, you and I."

She drew away in shock.

"I do want to see you again, but . . ."

Uri-Teshoop shoved her onto her back and straddled her.

"You're going to obey me, woman. I'm the son of the last Emperor of Hatti and the legitimate heir to the throne. You're nothing but a Phoenician harlot who'll give me pleasure and satisfy all my needs. I don't suppose you have any idea what an honor it is, me taking you as my wife?"

Tanit tried to protest, but Uri-Teshoop once again entered her forcefully; once again her head whirled.

"If you betray me," the Hittite prince said hoarsely, "you're dead."

TEN

From a rush basket, Setau pulled a triangular loaf of bread, a bowl of oat gruel, dried fish, a braised pigeon, a roast quail, two kidneys simmered in wine, a steak on a bed of fried onions, figs, and a pot of herbed cheese. He carefully placed the dishes one by one on Ahmeni's desk, forcing him to set aside the scrolls he was consulting.

"What is all this?"

"Are you blind? A decent meal, that's what it is. It may even fill you up for an hour or two."

"I didn't need—"

"You certainly do need it. Your brain doesn't work on an empty stomach."

Anger flared in the scribe's pale eyes. "Are you insulting me?"

"It's the only way to get your attention."

"You're not going to start in again on—"

"Of course I am. I want more funds for Nubia and I can't take the time to fill out fifty requests like the other provincial administrators do."

"You should go to your immediate superior, the Viceroy of Nubia."

"He's an imbecile and a do-nothing. All he cares about is keeping his job. He has no interest in the province, and Ramses wants me to put it back on the map. To cover it with temples and chapels, to increase the amount of arable land, I need men and equipment."

"There are also certain procedures you need to follow."

"You and your rules! They take all the fun out of life. Forget the rules, Ahmeni!"

"I'm not an independent agent, Setau. The vizier Pazair and the king himself will demand an accounting."

"Give me what I'm asking for and we'll find the funds for it later."

"In other words, you're making me responsible for your future mistakes."

Setau appeared surprised. "Well, naturally! You scribes know how to make things sound right."

The braised pigeon was delectable; Ahmeni obviously enjoyed it.

"Lotus cooked this, didn't she?"

"My wife is a woman of many talents."

"This borders on bribery, you know."

"Are you going to accommodate me?"

"If Ramses weren't so fond of Nubia . . ."

"Thanks to me, within a few years it will be richer than an Egyptian province!"

Ahmeni attacked the roasted quail.

"Now that we've taken care of business," said Setau, "I can confess that I'm rather worried."

"Why is that?"

"Last night I was making love to Lotus when she sat straight up and said she sensed a monster lurking. She wasn't talking about the two cobras standing watch at the foot of our bed or even the Hittite threat that Ramses could easily dispel a second time, if he had to."

"Did you find out what monster it was, then?"

"There's no doubt in my mind: it's Uri-Teshoop, the Hittite beast."

"We can't pin anything on him."

"Have you put Serramanna on alert?"

"Of course."

"What does he think?"

"He hates Uri-Teshoop, like you do, and believes that setting him free was a big mistake. But as you say, the Hittite's done nothing wrong so far. I think that exile has stolen his thunder. What have we to fear from a fallen prince?"

Serramanna opened his eyes at dawn's first light. On his left a young Nubian woman slumbered. On his right was a slightly younger Libyan. This morning the Sardinian giant couldn't even remember their names.

"Rise and shine, ladies!"

He administered a slap to his bedmates' delicate backsides. As usual, he underestimated his strength, and the girls' shrieks gave him a headache.

"Get dressed and go home," he ordered.

Serramanna dove into the pool that took up most of his garden and swam for some twenty minutes. He knew no better cure for the aftereffects of wine and wantonness.

Feeling better, he was about to polish off a loaf of fresh bread with some onions, bacon, and dried beef when his manservant announced that one of his men had arrived to see him.

"A new development, Chief. We've located Uri-Teshoop."

"Dead, I hope?"

"No, alive and kicking . . . and married."

"Who's the lucky woman?"

"A Phoenician widow, Dame Tanit."

"One of the richest women in Pi-Ramses! You must be mistaken."

"Go see for yourself, Chief."

"I'm on my way."

Still gnawing on a huge chunk of beef, Serramanna jumped on his horse.

The doorman at Dame Tanit's villa should have asked the giant Sard for a search warrant, but Serramanna's angry glare changed his mind. He called the gardener and asked him to take the head of Ramses' personal bodyguard in to see the lady of the house.

Clad in a flimsy linen gown that did little to conceal her

voluptuous charms, Tanit was breakfasting on a shady terrace. Beside her was Uri-Teshoop, who wore nothing but his fleece of reddish hair.

"The illustrious Serramanna!" exclaimed the Hittite, visibly pleased by the Sard's arrival. "Shall we invite him to share our meal, my dear?"

The hulking Sard came to a halt before the mistress of the house, who clung to Uri-Teshoop.

"Do you know who this man is, Dame Tanit?" inquired Serramanna.

"I do."

"Then tell me."

"Uri-Teshoop is a Hittite prince, son of the late Emperor Muwattali."

"He was also the commander-in-chief of the Hittite army and Egypt's worst enemy."

"That was all long ago," Uri-Teshoop interrupted mockingly. "Before Ramses and my uncle signed their treaty. Now Pharaoh has set me free, and everyone's happy. Don't you agree, Serramanna?"

The Sard noted bite marks on the comely Phoenician's neck. "This Hittite has spent the night under your roof and seems determined to move in with you. Are you aware of what that implies, Dame Tanit?"

"Of course I am."

"He's forcing you to marry him, isn't he, under threat of violence?"

"Answer him, sweetheart," ordered Uri-Teshoop. "Tell him that you're a free woman, that you make your own decisions like any of your Egyptian sisters."

Tanit was emphatic: "I love Uri-Teshoop and take him as my husband! There's no law against it."

"Think carefully, Dame Tanit. If you admit that this

individual has assaulted you, I'll arrest him on the spot and you'll be out of danger. I'll make sure he's charged, and he won't get off lightly. Mistreating a woman is a serious offense."

"Get out of my house!"

"I'm surprised," Uri-Teshoop said coolly. "I thought that you'd come as a friend, and here you're acting like a policeman. Do you happen to have a warrant, Serramanna?"

"Take care, Dame Tanit. You're heading for trouble."

"My wife and I could file a grievance," added the Hittite. "But I'll let it go this time. Off with you, Serramanna. Newlyweds need privacy, you know."

Uri-Teshoop planted a passionate kiss on the comely Phoenician. Oblivious of the Sard, she stroked her new husband without the least restraint.

The shelves and cupboards in Ahmeni's office threatened to cave in under the weight of official documents. The king's private secretary had never had so many pressing matters to deal with at once; since he checked every detail personally, he had been sleeping only two hours a night, and over his staff's protests he had canceled leave time for the entire next quarter. Only a sizable bonus had prevented a mutiny.

Ahmeni was implementing Setau's plans for Nubia, countering the do-nothing viceroy's objections. He advised Pazair, the vizier, who mistrusted his staff economists. He met with Ramses daily after carefully preparing the data the sovereign requested. And then there was the rest, all the rest, since Egypt must remain a great nation, a unique land he would continue to serve without a thought for his own welfare.

Still, when Serramanna burst into his office, the pale and hollow-faced scribe wondered how much more his frail shoulders could handle.

"What now?"

"Uri-Teshoop has gone and married a rich Phoenician widow named Tanit."

"He's done well. She's well endowed in every sense of the word, I hear."

"It's a catastrophe, Ahmeni!"

"Why do you think so? Marriage may tame our warrior prince at last."

"I won't be able to shadow him anymore. If he spots my men, he'll go to the authorities. He's a free man now; officially, I have no cause to keep him under surveillance. But I'm sure he has something up his sleeve."

"Did you talk with this Tanit?"

"He hit her and threatened her, I'm sure of it. But she seems to be in love with him."

"Love? I'd forgotten there were people with time to think about that. Don't worry, Serramanna. Uri-Teshoop has finally made a conquest, but this one will retire him from the battlefield for good."

ELEVEN

Hattusa, the capital of the Hittite empire, was the same as ever. Built on the central Anatolian plateau, exposed to blazing summers and frigid winters, the fortified city was composed of a lower town (notable for the temple of the Storm God and Sun Goddess) and an upper town. Atop the upper town, a forbidding citadel stood watch over five miles of ramparts bristling with towers and battlements.

Ahsha was not unmoved at the sight of the city, which cast the empire's military might in stone. This was the place where he had nearly lost his life during a particularly dangerous espionage mission prior to the battle of Kadesh.

The Egyptian secretary of state's convoy had trekked through arid steppes and negotiated inhospitable passes to reach the capital, surrounded by peaks that presented a daunting obstacle to potential attackers. Hattusa loomed like an impregnable fortress terraced up rocky slopes, an incredible feat of engineering. A far cry from Egypt with its warm, open, welcoming cities!

Five fortified gates controlled access to the capital—two in the lower town's walls, three in the upper town. The Hittite escort that had been accompanying the Egyptian delegation for the last few days of their journey now led them to the uppermost point of entry, the Sphinx Gate.

Before passing through it, Ahsha celebrated the Hittite ritual of breaking three loaves of bread, pouring wine on the stone, and saying the time-honored words: *"May this rock be eternal."* All around he noticed containers full of oil and honey, intended to keep demons at bay. Emperor Hattusili, he saw, had not interfered with tradition.

This time Ahsha had found the journey fatiguing, whereas in his younger days he was always on the move and had loved taking risks and courting danger. The older he got, the less he liked leaving Egypt. This trip was depriving him of the chance to do what he loved best: watching Ramses govern. Upholding the law of Ma'at, Pharaoh knew that *"listening is the best of all,"* to quote the sage Ptah-hotep, Nefertari's favorite author. Ramses would let his cabinet members speak at length, remaining attentive to each intonation, each nuance of body language. Then, with the lightning quickness of the crocodile Sobek surging through deep water to bring the sun back to life, the Pharaoh would make his decisions. He would utter a simple phrase, luminous, obvious, and definitive. He steered the rudder with a peerless touch, for he alone was the ship of state and its pilot. The gods who had chosen him had made no mistake, and men were right to obey them.

Two officers in helmet, breastplate, and boots guided Ahsha into Emperor Hattusili's audience chamber. The palace sat on an imposing summit with three tall peaks. Its high towers and battlements were under constant watch by specially trained troops. The lord of the land was safe from any outside attack. That was why past usurpers had usually preferred poison over a futile attempt on the palace.

Hattusili would have been forced to use poison on Uri-Teshoop, were it not for Ahsha's exceptionally deft manipulation, which convinced the heir apparent to flee the country. Seeking refuge in Egypt, Uri-Teshoop had supplied Ramses with useful information on the Hittite army.

A lone entrance led into the "Great Fortress," as the awestruck inhabitants called the citadel. When the heavy bronze door swung shut behind him, Ahsha felt he was being taken prisoner. The message he was delivering to Hattusili did not leave him inclined to be optimistic.

He was reassured to note that the emperor did not keep him waiting. Ahsha was shown into a freezing hall with thick pillars and walls hung with heavy tapestries.

Short and slight, his hair held in place with a headband, a silver collar around his neck and a copper band at his left elbow, Hattusili was dressed in his habitual long red and black robe. A superficial observer might have concluded that he was rather insignificant, even harmless. That would fail to take into account his stubborn character and gift for strategy. After all, this onetime high priest of the Sun Goddess had finally outmaneuvered Uri-Teshoop in their long power struggle. His wife, the lovely priestess Puduhepa, whose intellect commanded the respect of military men and merchants alike, had seconded him. Ahsha bowed to the imperial pair, seated on their squat and massive thrones.

"May all the gods of Egypt and Hatti smile upon Your Imperial Highnesses, and may your reign be durable as the heavens."

"We've known one another long enough to dispense with formalities, Ahsha. Come sit beside us. How is my brother Ramses?"

"Extremely well, Your Highness. May I say that the empress's beauty illuminates the palace?"

Puduhepa smiled. "Flattery is still part of the diplomat's

arsenal, I see."

"We're at peace now; I no longer need to flatter you. My declaration is no doubt improper, but it's sincere."

The empress blushed.

"If you're still the ladies' man you used to be," concluded the emperor, "I'd better be on my guard."

"I'm afraid I haven't changed. It's not in my nature to be faithful."

"Yet you saved Ramses from the pitfalls that Hatti set in his path, and dismantled our network of spies in Egypt."

"Let's not overstate the case, Your Highness. I carried out Pharaoh's plan, and luck was with me."

"But why dwell on the past? Our task is to build the future."

"Ramses agrees completely: his top priority is strengthening the peace agreement with Hatti. The happiness of both our peoples depends on it."

"We're glad to hear it," murmured Puduhepa.

"Allow me to stress that Pharaoh's intentions are peaceful," continued Ahsha. "As he sees it, the era of conflicts is over, and we must never allow our past differences to rekindle."

Hattusili grew somber.

"Is there something behind your insistence?"

"Not at all, Your Highness. Your brother Ramses merely wishes to acquaint you with his innermost thoughts."

"You're to thank him for showing such trust in me and tell him that we're in perfect accord."

"To the joy of our two countries and their allies. Nevertheless . . ."

The head of Egyptian diplomacy laid his chin on his clasped hands, at chest level, in a meditative pose.

"What is it, Ahsha?"

"Egypt is a rich country, Your Highness. It can never

stop attracting envy."

"Is there some new threat?" questioned the empress.

"Unrest in Libya. Again."

"Can't Pharaoh deal with it easily?"

"Ramses would like to act quickly and use effective weaponry."

Hattusili's inquisitive gaze fixed on Ahsha.

"Surely Egypt's arsenal is adequate?"

"Pharaoh would like his brother the Emperor of Hatti to ship us large quantities of iron that we can use to manufacture new arms and crush the Libyan initiative."

A long silence followed the diplomat's request. Then Hattusili rose, nervously pacing the audience chamber.

"My brother Ramses is demanding a fortune from me! I have no iron; if I did, I'd keep it for my own army. Is Pharaoh seeking to bankrupt me and ruin Hatti, when Egypt is such a wealthy nation? My reserves are empty, and it's no time for mining iron."

Ahsha remained impassive.

"I understand."

"Let my brother Ramses dispatch the Libyans with the weapons he has on hand. Later, if he still needs iron, I'll send a reasonable quantity. Be sure to tell him that this request surprises and shocks me."

"I'll let him know, Your Highness."

Hattusili returned to his throne.

"Now let's get down to basics: when will my daughter be leaving Hatti to become Ramses' Great Royal Wife?"

"Well . . . the date hasn't been set."

"You've come all the way here to tell us there's no decision?"

"Such an important proposal demands due consideration, and—"

"Enough diplomacy," interrupted the empress. "Does Ramses agree to repudiate Iset the Fair and make our daughter Queen of Egypt, or doesn't he?"

"It's a delicate situation, Your Highness. Egyptian justice does not condone such a repudiation."

"Is a woman going to dictate the law?" Hattusili asked curtly. "Who cares what this Iset wants? Ramses only married her to replace Nefertari, a true queen who was instrumental in bringing about the peace. The new consort doesn't count. To seal our pact for good, Ramses must marry a Hittite princess."

"Perhaps your daughter could become a secondary wife and—"

"She'll be Great Royal Wife, or else . . ."

Hattusili's voice trailed off, as if he himself were frightened by the words he meant to say.

"Why does Ramses insist on rejecting our proposal?" the empress asked in a more conciliatory tone.

"Because, as I've told you, a pharaoh doesn't repudiate a Great Royal Wife. It's not in keeping with Ma'at."

"Is that position irreversible?"

"I'm afraid so, Your Highness."

"Is Ramses aware of the consequences?"

"Ramses has only one concern: acting with rectitude."

Hattusili rose.

"This audience has ended. Give my brother the Pharaoh this message from me: either he must set a date for his marriage to my daughter in the very near future, or it will mean war."

TWELVE

Ahmeni had a bad back, but never found the time for a massage. As if he weren't already overburdened with work, now he was supposed to lend Kha a hand with the preparations for Ramses' sed-feast, his second jubilee. Arguing that his health was excellent, the king wanted to postpone it; but his elder son invoked the authority of traditional texts.

Ahmeni appreciated Kha's high standards and enjoyed discussing literature with him. Yet his daily cares were so overwhelming that the Pharaoh's private secretary and sandal-bearer was rarely able to indulge his taste for fine prose.

After a council meeting during which the king implemented a vast reforestation project in the south and lectured the official in charge of the dikes because repairs were behind schedule, Ahmeni and Ramses were strolling in the palace gardens.

"Has Your Majesty had news of Ahsha?"

"He arrived safe and sound in Hattusa."

"It won't be easy to make Hattusili back down."

"Ahsha's had trickier assignments."

"This time he doesn't have much room to maneuver."

"Now tell me, Ahmeni, what you couldn't bring up in front of the cabinet."

"First there's Moses. Then an incident we need to check on."

"Moses?"

"In a tight corner with his Hebrews. Everyone is afraid of them; they have to fight tooth and nail to survive. If we intervened, the Hebrew problem could be resolved in short order. But we're dealing with Moses, our boyhood friend, and I know you'll let destiny take its course."

"Since you know the answer, why ask me the question?"

"The desert patrol is still on alert. If the Hebrews wanted to come back to Egypt, would you let them?"

"When they come back, neither Moses nor I will be living. Let's move on to the incident that troubles you."

"We won't be getting the expected shipment of olibanum."

"Why not, Ahmeni?"

"I've had a long report from the Phoenician middleman who deals with the producers. A hailstorm hit the trees, and before that they suffered some kind of blight. There'll be no harvest this year."

"Has that ever happened before?"

"I've consulted the archives, so I can tell you that it's not unprecedented. Fortunately, it's a rare phenomenon."

"Do we have enough reserves?"

"No restrictions will be placed on the temples. I've ordered our Phoenician suppliers to bid early on the next harvest so that we can replenish our stock."

Raia was jubilant. Ordinarily abstemious, he'd celebrated by knocking back two quick goblets of strong beer. He felt a bit lightheaded, but then he would have even without the drink. His small victories were finally adding up to something major.

The contact with his fellow Syrian expatriates had exceeded all his expectations. Raia had sparked a renewal of interest and activity among the downtrodden, the bitter, the envious. The Hittites, disappointed with Hattusili's policies, jumped on the bandwagon. The emperor was soft; he'd never try to conquer Egypt. When all the factions met secretly with Uri-Teshoop at one of Raia's warehouses, there was widespread enthusiasm. A leader of the prince's stature would one day soon bring power within their reach.

And Raia had plenty of other good news for Uri-Teshoop—as soon as the prince was through ogling the three naked Nubian dancing girls that he and Dame Tanit had hired to entertain their guests. The new expatriate couple was by now the toast of Pi-Ramses.

Tanit was experiencing both heaven and hell on earth. It was bliss having a real man, always ready to satisfy her at any hour of the day or night, whose hot, hard love made her wild with pleasure. Yet it was hell, too, because he was so rough and unpredictable; she never knew when he might strike out at her. Tanit, who had always lived as she pleased, had become a willing yet troubled slave to Uri-Teshoop.

The hundred-odd guests had eyes only for the three dancing girls. Their round, firm breasts hardly jiggled. Their long slim legs tantalized even the most blasé of the spectators. But these delightful entertainers were untouchable. Once their number was finished, they would disappear without a word to anyone. Their fans would have to wait for their next appearance at some equally lavish banquet.

Uri-Teshoop left his bride deep in discussion with two businessmen so mesmerized by the performance that they would have signed any contract. The Hittite prince grabbed a bunch of grapes and settled into a pile of cushions near a column decorated with painted grapevines. Behind it sat Raia. Without looking at each other, the two men could talk in low voices as the band was playing.

"What's so urgent, Raia?"

"I talked with an old courtier who gets a discount on my best vases. He tells me the palace is in an uproar over a rumor that's circulating. I've been trying to confirm it for the past two days. The situation does sound serious."

"Does it affect us?"

"They say that to seal the pact between Egypt and Hatti, the emperor is demanding that Ramses marry his daughter."

"Another diplomatic marriage . . . What would that change?"

"You don't understand. Hattusili insists that she become the Great Royal Wife!"

"A Hittite princess on the throne of Egypt?"

"Exactly."

"Unthinkable!"

"They say Ramses has refused to give in to Hattusili's ultimatum. He won't repudiate Iset the Fair."

"In other words . . ."

"Yes, Highness—a hope of war!"

"That upsets all our plans."

"Too soon to say; in my opinion, it's preferable not to make any changes until we have solid information. Ahsha is supposed to be in Hattusa negotiating with the emperor. I still have a lot of friends up there, so we'll soon find out what's happening. And that's not all . . . I have an interesting person I'd like you to meet."

"Where is this person?"

"Hiding in the garden. We could—"

"Bring him to my bedchamber and wait for me there. Go through the vineyard and enter the house through the laundry. As soon as the banquet is over, I'll catch up with you."

When the last guest had departed, Tanit draped herself around Uri-Teshoop. She burned with a fire that only her lover could quench. Almost tenderly, he led her toward their bedchamber, a love nest full of expensive furniture, floral arrangements, and clouds of scent. Before she was through the door, the comely Phoenician whipped her dress off.

Uri-Teshoop shoved her inside the room.

Tanit thought this was some new game, but she froze at the sight of Raia, the Syrian merchant, accompanied by a strange man with a square face, wavy hair, and black eyes that flashed with cruelty and madness.

"Who is this?" she stammered.

"They're friends," replied Uri-Teshoop.

Terrorized, Dame Tanit clutched at a linen sheet and covered her ample curves. Raia, momentarily speechless, could not understand why the Hittite was letting her in on the meeting. The man with the cruel eyes sat still.

"I want Tanit to hear all that goes on here," declared Uri-Teshoop. "She should become our accomplice and ally. From now on, her fortune will serve our cause. One wrong move, and she'll be eliminated. Are we all in agreement?"

The stranger nodded; Raia followed suit.

"You see, darling, you have no chance of escaping the three of us or those we command. Have I made myself understood?"

"Oh, yes. Yes!"

"Then we can count on your unconditional support?"

"You have my word, Uri-Teshoop!"

"You won't be sorry."

His right hand lightly brushed her breasts. This simple gesture quelled Tanit's rising panic.

The Hittite turned to face Raia.

"Introduce your guest to me."

Reassured, the Syrian merchant spoke slowly. "We've had a stroke of luck. You may recall that a Libyan sorcerer named Ofir ran our former spy ring. Despite his exceptional talent and the damage he did to the royal family, he was arrested and executed, a terrible loss for our side. But someone has decided to take up the torch and avenge Ofir: his brother, Malfi."

Uri-Teshoop looked the Libyan over from head to foot.

"A worthwhile plan . . . but how will he execute it?"

"Malfi heads the best-armed tribe in Libya. Combating Egypt is his sole mission in life."

"Will he obey me without question?"

"He'll place himself under your orders, on the condition that you destroy Ramses and his empire."

"It's a deal. You'll serve as the intermediary between our Libyan ally and me. His men should start training and prepare to march at a moment's notice."

"Malfi will be ready, Your Highness. Libya has been waiting so long to pay Pharaoh back in blood for all his insults!"

"He can go home. He'll be hearing from me."

The Libyan vanished without having said a word.

THIRTEEN

Although it was long past sunrise, the royal palace at Pi-Ramses was in a profound silence. The servants went about their work as usual, but without a sound. Everyone, from cooks to chambermaids, moved like a shadow.

Ramses' ill temper had the entire palace staff terror-stricken. The oldest members, who had known the monarch since he was a boy, had never seen him in such a state. Set's power tore through him like a thunderstorm that left its victims dazed.

Ramses had a toothache.

For the first time in his fifty-five years, his body would not obey him. The palace dentists and their ineffective treatment made him so furious that he banished them from his sight. With the exception of Ahmeni, no one knew that another source was also feeding the Pharaoh's anger: Hattusili was detaining Ahsha in the Hittite capital, allegedly to pursue negotiations, more likely to hold him hostage.

The court's hopes rested on a single individual: the chief physician of the realm. Unless a new treatment worked, the king's mood was liable to worsen.

Despite the pain, Ramses worked on, with the only person who could handle him in such a state: Ahmeni, himself an old grouch who detested the mincing airs of the courtiers. Working together, they had no need to be agree-able. As far as his secretary was concerned, it was business as usual.

"Hattusili is baiting us," Pharaoh said flatly.

"Perhaps he's looking for a way out," suggested Ahmeni. "Rejecting his daughter is an intolerable insult, but the Emperor of Hatti is the one who'll opt to reopen the hos-tilities."

"I know the old fox will try to pin it on me!"

"Ahsha is playing him with finesse. I'll bet that Hattusili doesn't know which way to turn."

"You're wrong! He's plotting his next move against me."

"As soon as we hear from Ahsha, we'll know what's what. His code will tell us whether he's had free dealings or been held prisoner."

"If he weren't being held against his will, we would have had word by now."

There was a tentative knock at the door.

"I don't want to see anyone," decreed the king.

"It could be the chief physician," countered Ahmeni, rising to answer.

In the doorway, the grand chamberlain quaked with fear at the thought of disturbing the monarch.

"The chief physician has arrived," he murmured. "Will Your Majesty permit a consultation?"

The grand chamberlain stepped aside, and in came a young woman as lovely as dawn in springtime, a blossoming lotus, a shimmering wave on the Nile. Her hair was on the light side, her face pure and finely drawn. Her eyes were the shade of a summer sky, her gaze clear and direct. She wore a lapis lazuli necklace around her slender neck, and strands of carnelian at her wrists and ankles. Her linen dress hinted at her high, firm breasts, slim, shapely hips, and long, tapering legs. Her name was Neferet, meaning "beautiful, perfect, accomplished." What other name would do? Even Ahmeni, who had no time for women (he considered them flighty creatures, unable to sit for hours deciphering hiero-glyphs), was forced to admit that the young doctor's beauty was almost on a plane with Nefertari's.

"You've taken your time," grumbled Ramses.

"My apologies, Your Majesty. I was out of town per-forming surgery on a little girl. We may have saved her life."

"The doctors on your palace staff have no idea what they're doing!"

"Medicine is an art as well as a science. Perhaps they simply don't have my touch."

"It's a good thing Dr. Pariamaku finally retired. Some of his patients may have a chance to recover."

"I can tell you're in pain."

"I have no time for pain, Neferet! Cure me as fast as you can."

Ahmeni rolled up the scroll he'd just been showing to Ramses, said goodbye to Neferet, and retreated into his office. He'd never been able to bear cries of pain or the sight of blood.

Neferet took her illustrious patient to a quiet spot where she could examine him. Before attaining the sought-after rank of physician, she had studied and practiced a number of specialties, from dentistry to surgery, including ophthal-mology along the way.

"A competent dentist should treat you, Your Majesty."

"It will be you and no one else."

"I can suggest a highly skilled specialist . . ."

"I want you, and I want you now. Your job is on the line."

"Come with me, please, Your Majesty."

The palace treatment center was airy and sunlit; on the white walls were paintings of medicinal plants.

The king was settled in a comfortable armchair, his head bent back, neck resting on a pillow.

"For local anesthesia," explained Neferet, "I'll use one of Setau's pharmaceuticals. You won't feel a thing."

"What's the nature of the problem?"

"A cavity with infectious complications, resulting in an abscess that I'm about to drain. Pulling the tooth won't be necessary. I'll make a filling with a mixture of resin and mineral substances. For the other sore tooth, I'll grind a specific remedy to 'stuff the ache,' as we say in our medical jargon. The main ingredients are medicinal ocher, honey, quartzite powder, gashed sycamore fruit, bean paste, cumin, bitter apple, acacia gum, and sap."

"How did you come up with that?"

"I consult old treatises written by the sages, Your Majesty, then check the formulation with my favorite instrument."

Between her thumb and index finger, Neferet showed him a strand of linen from which a small granite pendant was suspended. When held over the correct ingredient, the stone began to spin.

"You practice divining, like my father," commented Ramses.

"And yourself, Majesty. I've heard how you found water in the desert. Now, in addition to the procedure you'll be undergoing today, you'll have to care for your gums by chewing a paste made of bryony, juniper, absinthe, sycamore nutlets, and medicinal ocher. For pain, I'm pre-

scribing an extract of willow; it's a most effective analgesic."

"What other bad news do you have for me?"

"Your pulse and your eye examination show that you're
endowed with exceptional energy, allowing you to fight off
most illness, but as the years go by your joints will continue
to bother you . . . and you'll have to live with it."

"I hope to die before I'm crippled with arthritis!"

"You're Egypt's peace and happiness, Your Majesty; the
people hope to see you reach a ripe old age. Sages live to a
hundred and ten, so they say; that's how old Ptah-hotep was
when he wrote his *Maxims*."

Ramses smiled.

"Watching you and listening to you eases my pain."

"The anesthesia is taking hold, Your Majesty."

"How are my health policies working, Neferet?"

"I'll compose my annual report for you soon. Overall,
the situation is satisfactory, but public and private health
measures need constant upgrading. They're all that keeps
Egypt safe from epidemics. Your director of the Double
House of Gold and Silver must not skimp on purchasing
the rare and expensive ingredients used in medicinal com-
pounds. I've just learned that we won't be receiving the usual
shipment of olibanum, which I can't do without."

"You needn't worry; we have plenty in reserve."

"The anesthetic has taken effect by now. Ready, Your
Majesty?" she asked, approaching him.

Facing thousands of bloodthirsty Hittites at Kadesh,
Ramses had never flinched. But he closed his eyes when he
saw the dentist's instruments zeroing in on his mouth.

Serramanna was having trouble keeping up with Ramses' chariot. Since Neferet had applied her remarkably effective treatment, the monarch was twice as energetic as ever. Only Ahmeni, as frail as he was, could match the Pharaoh's capacity for work.

A coded message from Ahsha had reassured Ramses on his account. The secretary of state had not been taken prisoner, but was staying in Hattusa to pursue negotiations for an indeterminate period. As Ahmeni had supposed, the Hittite emperor was reluctant to initiate a conflict with an uncertain outcome.

As the floodwaters subsided from lower Egypt, the late-summer weather was balmy. The king's chariot drove along a canal serving local villages. No one, not even Ahmeni, knew the nature of Ramses' highly personal and urgent mission.

The death of the king's older brother, Shaanar, and his accomplices had made it somewhat easier to provide security for Ramses. Yet having Uri-Teshoop at large worried Serramanna, the more so since the monarch's fearlessness was undiminished with age.

Ramses pulled up beneath a lush tree at the edge of the canal.

"Come see, Serramanna! According to the records at the House of Life, this is the oldest willow tree in Egypt. An extract from its bark soothed my toothache. That's why I've come to give thanks. And I'll do better: with my own hands, I'll plant willow shoots in Pi-Ramses, and order that the same be done throughout the country. The gods and nature have given us so much; let's take care to multiply their treasures."

"No other land," mused the former pirate, "could have produced a king like this one."

FOURTEEN

A frigid wind blew across the high Anatolian plateau; in Hattusa, winter came close on the heels of autumn. Ahsha had no complaints about Hattusili's hospitality, however. The food was decent, if nothing fancy, and the two Hittite girls sent to entertain him performed with zeal and conviction.

But he missed Egypt. Egypt and Ramses. Ahsha wished he could grow old in the shadow of the monarch whom he had served his whole life and on whose account he had agreed, with concealed enthusiasm, to confront the worst dangers. As a youth at the royal academy in Memphis, Ahsha had sought true power. Only Ramses had it—not Moses, as he had once briefly believed. Moses fought for a truth that had been revealed to him, while Ramses built upon the truth of a civilization and a people, day after day, offering his every act up to Ma'at, to the invisible, to the principle of life. Like his predecessors, Ramses knew that stasis meant death. He was like a musician who could play several instruments, constantly creating new melodies with the same timeless notes. Ramses took his power from the gods; he wielded it not as a club, but rather a striving for rectitude. Adherence to the law of Ma'at meant that no pharaoh of Egypt would become a tyrant. His function was not to subjugate men, but to liberate them from themselves. To watch Ramses reign was to contemplate a stoneworker sculpting the face of a divinity.

Wearing a red and black woolen robe like the one his late brother had favored, Hattusili entered the Egyptian diplomat's private suite.

"Are you satisfied with your welcome, Ahsha?"

"It's more than adequate, thank you, Your Highness."

"The cold snap isn't affecting you, I hope?"

"I'd be lying if I said it didn't. The weather is so mild on the banks of the Nile at this time of year."

"Every country has its advantages. Don't you like Hatti anymore?"

"The older I get, Your Highness, the more of a home-body I become."

"Then I have good news for you. I've made up my mind. You can leave for Egypt by tomorrow morning. But I also have bad news: I'm standing firm on my position, and my demands are the same. My daughter must become Ramses' Great Royal Wife."

"What if Pharaoh continues to refuse?"

Hattusili turned his back on the Egyptian. "Yesterday I convened my generals and told them to prepare our troops for combat. Since my brother the Pharaoh has asked me for iron, I've had a special present made for him."

The emperor turned back to face Ahsha, pulling an iron dagger from an inner pocket and handing it over.

"A marvel, isn't it? Light and easy to handle, yet able to cut through the toughest shield. I showed the dagger to my generals and promised to retrieve it myself from the corpse of my brother Ramses if he rejects my proposal."

The sun sank behind the temple of Set, the strangest building in Pi-Ramses. The home of this angry deity, the "Instigator of Confusion," had been built on the site of the former Hyksos capital, razed when the first kings of the Eighteenth Dynasty had expelled the hated Asiatic invaders. Ramses had transformed the ill-fated place into a pole of positive energy, for he had confronted Set the Destroyer and appropriated his power.

It was here, in this forbidden domain where only Set's son dared to tread, that Pharaoh would draw the strength necessary to wage the forthcoming combat.

When Ramses emerged from the temple, his younger son, Merenptah, approached him.

"My task is completed, Father."

"You've worked fast."

"I've inspected every barracks from Pi-Ramses to Memphis."

"You give credit to reports from the commanding officers?"

"Well . . ."

"Speak your mind."

"None, Your Majesty."

"Why is that, Merenptah?"

"I've observed them. They've gotten soft. The commanders are so sure that your peace will hold that they've neglected training. Our army has rested on its laurels so long that it's gone to sleep."

"What's the state of our arsenal?"

"The quantity of arms is adequate, but the quality isn't what it should be. The foundries have slowed production over the past several years, and a good number of the chariots need an overhaul."

"See to it."

"I may bruise a few egos in the process."

"When the fate of Egypt is at stake, that hardly matters. Act like a true commander-in-chief, retire any officers who've grown lax, name reliable men to responsible positions, and furnish our army with the weapons it needs. Don't come back to see me until you've fulfilled your mission."

Merenptah bowed to Pharaoh and left for headquarters.

It was not the way a father ought to speak to his son; but Ramses was the Lord of the Two Lands and Merenptah his potential successor.

Iset the Fair was losing sleep, even though she felt truly blessed.

Every day she was able to see Ramses, exchange confidences with him, take part in religious ceremonies and official appearances at his side . . . and her two sons, Kha and Merenptah, both had brilliant careers.

Yet Iset the Fair felt sadder and sadder, more and more alone, as if this surfeit of happiness had sapped her vitality. The cause of her sleepless nights was clear: where Nefertari had built a bridge to peace, she, Iset, was becoming a symbol of conflict. Just as Helen had been the origin of the terrible Trojan War, she, Iset, would be seen as the cause of a new confrontation between Egypt and Hatti.

Under Merenptah's guidance, Pi-Ramses was in the grip of rearmament fever. Intensive training and arms production had begun in earnest.

The queen's hairdresser was worried.

"When can I do your makeup, Your Majesty?"

"Is the king up?"

"Oh, for ages."

"Will we be lunching together?"

"He sent word to your majordomo that he'll be in meet-ings all day with the vizier and the fortress commanders from Canaan."

"Then send for my sedan chair and bearers."

"Your Majesty! Your hair isn't done, I haven't put on your wig or painted your eyes, I—"

"Be quick about it."

Iset the Fair was an easy burden for the twelve sturdy bearers who took her from the palace to Ahmeni's office. And since the Great Royal Wife had asked them to hurry, they looked forward to a healthy tip and an extra hour's rest.

The queen made her way through the busy staff room. The twenty scribes working for Ahmeni dealt with a con-siderable number of issues and had no time for idle chatter. They had to pore over documents, write briefs for the king's private secretary, sort, file, and struggle to keep up with the workload.

Iset walked through a broad room full of columns; some of the scribes didn't even spare her a glance. When she entered Ahmeni's office, he was chewing a slice of bread smeared with goose fat and composing a critique to the head of the royal granaries.

Ramses' sandal-bearer rose in astonishment.

"Your Majesty . . ."

"Sit down, Ahmeni. I need to talk to you."

The queen closed the wooden door to the office and

drew the latch. The scribe felt ill at ease; much as he'd admired Nefertari, he'd always clashed with Iset the Fair. It was also unusual to see her looking less than presentable, with dull eyes, a drawn face, and no hint of makeup.

"I can't do without your help, Ahmeni."

"I don't see how I can help, Your Majesty . . ."

"Stop playing games with me. I know full well that the court would be relieved if Pharaoh repudiates me."

"Your Majesty!"

"That's how it is, and nothing I do will change it. You know what's going on in this country: what do the people think?"

"It's rather delicate . . ."

"I want to know the truth."

"You're the Great Royal Wife, and public opinion should be of no consequence."

"The truth, Ahmeni."

The scribe lowered his eyes, as if concentrating on the scroll he held.

"You have to understand the people, Your Majesty. They're used to peace now."

"The people loved Nefertari. They haven't much use for me. That's the truth you're afraid to tell me."

"I can't deny it, Your Majesty."

"Speak to Ramses. Tell him I understand how serious the situation is and that I'm ready to step down in order to avoid a conflict."

"Ramses has made his decision."

"Reason with him, Ahmeni, I beg of you."

The king's private secretary was convinced of Iset the Fair's sincerity. For the first time, he saw her as worthy of being the Queen of Egypt.

FIFTEEN

"Why are you delaying your departure?" Emperor Hattusili inquired of Ahsha.

"Because I still hope to change your mind."

Frigid gusts blew over his capital's ramparts; the lord and master of Hatti, cap on head, was tightly bundled in his red and black woolen robe. The Egyptian wore an ample cape, but still felt the biting cold.

"Impossible, Ahsha."

"Do you want to start a pointless war over a woman? Troy served as an example. Why get caught up in a killing frenzy? Queens are supposed to give life, not death."

"Your arguments are excellent, but so Egyptian! Hatti would never forgive me for losing face. If I back down to Ramses I'll lose my hold on the throne."

"No one is challenging you."

"If I do anything that causes humiliation to the Hittite army, I won't live long. We're a warrior people, Ahsha; bear in mind that my replacement would be far worse than I am."

"Ramses wants to make sure your reign will last, Your Highness."

"Can I believe you?"

"I swear on what I hold dearest: Ramses' life."

The two men walked a short way down the wall walk

surrounding the capital, bristling with watchtowers. The military presence was always felt in Hattusa.

"Aren't you tired of waging war, Your Highness?"

"Soldiers bore me. But without them there would be no more Hatti."

"Egypt has no taste for combat. We prefer the art of love and building temples. Let's leave the battle of Kadesh in the past."

"Ahsha, don't force me to say that I wish I'd been born an Egyptian!"

"Any new conflict between Egypt and Hatti would be a disaster. It would weaken our two countries and play into Assyria's hands. Why not allow a diplomatic marriage between your daughter and Ramses, and leave Iset the Fair in place as Great Royal Wife?"

"I can't back down now, Ahsha."

Ramses the Great's secretary of state looked out over the lower town, in the heart of which stood the temple of the Storm God and the Sun Goddess.

"Men are perverse and dangerous animals," he mused. "Eventually they'll spoil the earth and wipe out their own kind. Once the downward spiral begins, there's no stopping it. Why are men so bent on their own destruction?"

"Because humans have grown farther and farther apart from the gods," replied Hattusili. "When the final link has been severed, there will be nothing left but fanatics manipulated by tyrants; the people will be like ants."

"It's curious, Your Highness . . . You force me to admit that I've spent my life fighting for Ma'at, the harmonious balance between heaven and earth. In the end, it's all that matters."

"And isn't that what made you Ramses' friend?"

The wind blew harder, accentuating the cold.

"We'd better go back inside, Ahsha."

"It seems such a waste, Your Highness."

"I quite agree, but you and I can do nothing about it. Let's hope that the gods of Hatti and Egypt will witness our good faith and perform a miracle."

A teeming crowd milled along the river landing at Pi-Ramses. Earlier in the day several boats from Memphis, Thebes, and other cities to the south had been unloaded, and the local market's customary bustle had reached unprecedented proportions. The merchants with the choicest locations, including a number of women vendors, were sure to make a killing.

Hand in hand, Uri-Teshoop and Tanit strolled through the marketplace, looking at fabric, sandals, chests of precious wood, and other luxury goods. All of Pi-Ramses was out shopping, and the comely Phoenician smiled through clenched teeth at her many acquaintances, who were attracted by the Hittite prince's manly charms.

Uri-Teshoop noted with satisfaction that Serramanna's henchmen were no longer tailing him. Harassing an honest citizen was an offense; the prince would be within his rights to file a grievance.

"Can I buy a few things?" Tanit asked plaintively.

"See here, darling, you're free to do as you please."

His bride shopped compulsively to calm her nerves, stopping at stand after stand and eventually reaching Raia's. The Syrian merchant was featuring pewter drinking cups, slender alabaster vases, and colored perfume vials that elegant ladies were snapping up. As Tanit bargained with one of Raia's assistants, the Syrian approached Uri-Teshoop.

"Excellent news from Hattusa: Ahsha's negotiations are at a standstill. The emperor refuses to withdraw his demands."

"Have the talks broken down for good?"

"Ahsha is on his way back to Egypt. Hattusili's reply to Ramses is an iron dagger that he's promising to retrieve from the Pharaoh's body when the Hittites defeat him in battle."

Uri-Teshoop paused, finally saying, "I want you to deliver my wife's purchases in person. Come by tonight."

Setau, still in his prime, was more amazed by the day.

How did Lotus, his lovely Nubian wife, manage to stay so young? She used no unguents or pomades; it must be her witchcraft that preserved the charms her husband found so hard to resist. With her, love was a delightful game, with inexhaustible variations.

Setau nuzzled Lotus's breasts.

Suddenly she grew tense.

"Did you hear a noise?"

"Your heart, I think it's beating faster . . ."

Then she relaxed as Setau made it impossible for her to concentrate on anything other than their mutual and mounting pleasure.

The unexpected visitor froze. When she slipped into the laboratory, she had hoped to find it empty. But when Setau and Lotus were staying in Pi-Ramses, they liked to remain close to their containers of venom from the royal cobra, black cobra, puff adder, and horned viper. They were currently conducting important research in conjunction with the chief physician of the realm. Banquets and the social whirl bored them; between endless hours of empty conversation and the study of substances that could induce death or possibly save lives, it was no contest.

Sighs and heavy breathing reassured the visitor. Setau and Lotus were fully occupied. All she needed to do was watch her step and get her hands on a flask of venom without making the slightest sound. Which one should she choose? A useless question; one poison would be as effective as the next. In their unrefined, undiluted state, the effect would be deadly.

One step, then another, and a third . . . The bare feet glided over the floor tiles. Just a few more steps and the interloper would reach the heart of this forbidden domain.

Suddenly, a form reared up.

Terrified, the intruder stopped in her tracks. In the dim light, she identified a royal cobra swaying from side to side. Her fear was so intense that she couldn't utter a sound. Her instinct told her to back away, extremely slowly, moving almost imperceptibly.

It felt as if her flight took hours. When she was out of sight, the guardian cobra went back to sleep.

Ahmeni counted the scrolls again: forty-two, one per province. The results would vary according to the number of canals and bodies of water. Thanks to the huge lake developed by the pharaohs of the Middle Kingdom, the Faiyum region, already rich in various species of trees, had a head start. In keeping with Ramses' orders, willow trees would be planted all over Egypt. Temple laboratories would extract the analgesic substance from the bark, making it more readily available to doctors.

The additional assignment had been the last straw for Ahmeni. He took his frustration out on his subordinates, but never questioned Pharaoh's directives. The only good thing was that the king's official sandal-bearer wasn't required to make preparations for war on top of everything else! Merenptah was handling that job very well, never coming to cry on Ahmeni's shoulder.

Loaded down with papyrus scrolls, the scribe intercepted Ramses on his way to perform the evening rites in the temple of Amon.

"Could Your Majesty spare me a minute?"

"Only if it's an urgent matter."

"All right, I won't insist . . ."

"You wouldn't stop me on the spur of the moment, Ahmeni. What's on your mind?"

"Iset the Fair came to consult me."

"Is she taking a new interest in affairs of state?"

"She doesn't want to be the cause of a conflict with Hatti. I must confess that her sincerity moved me."

"If Iset's charm is working on you at last, the kingdom must be in peril."

"It's serious, Your Majesty. The Great Royal Wife dreads becoming the cause of another Hittite war."

"I stand by my decision, Ahmeni. If we give in to the Hittites now, our earlier struggles will have been for nothing. Repudiating a Great Royal Wife would mean opening to the door to barbarism. Iset the Fair bears no responsibility for this impasse. The only culprit is Hattusili."

SIXTEEN

An icy rain fell on Hattusa; the Egyptian delegation was about to depart. Elegant and regal in her fringed red dress, indifferent to the cold, the empress came to bid Ahsha farewell.

"The emperor has taken to his bed," she revealed.

"Nothing serious, I hope?"

"A slight fever; it shouldn't last."

"Tell him I hope that he'll get well soon, Your Highness."

"I'm terribly sorry that the negotiations broke down," admitted Puduhepa.

"So am I, Your Highness."

"Will Ramses agree in time?"

"Let's not fool ourselves."

"I've never seen you so pessimistic, Ahsha."

"There are only two things we can hope for: a miracle and, well, you. Couldn't you soften your husband's stand?"

"Until now I haven't been able to . . . but I'll keep trying."

"Your Highness, I wanted to say— No, it's not important."

"Go ahead."

"It's nothing, really."

How could Ahsha confess to the Empress of Hatti that

of all the women he'd ever met, she was the only one he would have wanted as a wife? Telling her would be an unforgivable lapse in taste.

Ahsha studied Puduhepa intently, as if trying to engrave the memory of an unattainable face on his mind. Then he bowed.

"Don't leave sad, Ahsha. I'll do all I can to avoid the worst."

"So will I, Your Highness."

When the convoy began to move, Ahsha did not look back.

Setau felt wonderful. He crept from the bedchamber without waking Lotus, whose naked, inviting body never failed to stir him. He hesitated a moment, then made his way to the laboratory. The horned viper venom they'd gathered the previous night would have to be processed before the day was out. His work as administrator of a Nubian province did not mean that the old snake charmer had forgotten the tricks of his trade.

A servant girl carrying a tray froze in her tracks at the sight of him. This gruff-looking man, she knew, must be the magician who handled poisonous snakes without fear of being bitten.

"I'm hungry, child. Go find me some dried fish, milk, and fresh bread."

Trembling, the servant girl obeyed. Setau went out into the garden and lay in the grass to soak up the smell of the earth. He ate hungrily; then, humming off-key, he headed back to the laboratory.

But he couldn't find his working uniform anywhere. It was an antelope-skin tunic saturated with antidotes for snakebite. These products must be used with care, for the cure could prove worse than the bite itself. In his tunic, Setau was a walking medicine chest, able to cure any number of illnesses.

When he and Lotus began to make love, he'd let the tunic fall on a low seat. No, that couldn't be right . . . it was in another room. Setau inspected the antechamber, a small hall with columns, the shower room, the privies.

He searched in vain.

There was one last place: the bedroom. Yes, of course. That must be where he'd left his precious tunic.

Lotus was waking up; Setau caressed her tenderly.

"Tell me, darling . . . where have you put my tunic?"

"I never touch it."

Setau nervously combed the bedchamber, without success.

"It's disappeared," he concluded.

Serramanna hoped that this time Ramses would take him along to fight the Hittites. For years now, the former pirate had wanted to slit the throats of the Anatolian foe and tally the amputated hands of the dead. When the king had waged the famous battle of Kadesh, the giant Sard had been ordered to remain behind in Pi-Ramses and watch over the royal family. Since that time, he had trained enough men to provide adequate security in his absence. His only dream was marching off to war.

The Sard was somewhat surprised to have Setau burst into the barracks where he was training. The two men had not always been on the best of terms, yet they had come to a grudging agreement based on their mutual loyalty to Ramses.

The old pirate stopped hitting the wooden dummy he had been shattering with his bare fists.

"A problem, Setau?"

"My most precious possession has been stolen: my antelope-skin tunic."

"Any suspects?"

"A jealous doctor, no doubt. And he won't even know how to use it!"

"Can you be more specific?"

"I wish I could."

"Someone must be playing a trick on you because you're making such a reputation for yourself in Nubia. They're not very fond of you at court."

"We have to search the palace, the noblemen's villas, the tradesmen's workshops, the—"

"Calm down, Setau! I'll put two men on the case, but with the army newly mobilized, finding your tunic can't be a top priority."

"Do you know how many people that tunic has saved?"

"I've heard about it, but wouldn't it be better just to get hold of another one?"

"Easy for you to say. I was used to that one."

"Please, Setau! Stop making such a fuss and come have a drink with me. Afterwards we'll go see the best tanner in town. That's the best I can do to save your skin!"

"This isn't a joke, Serramanna. Help me find out who took it."

Ramses read the latest report from Merenptah. It was clear and concise. His younger son was proving to be unusually lucid. When Ahsha returned from Hatti, the Pharaoh would attempt his final negotiations with Hattusili. But the emperor was no fool, and like the King of Egypt he would use the interim to prepare his army for combat.

The elite Egyptian troops were in better shape than Ramses might have supposed. It would be easy to hire experienced mercenaries and step up the pace of training for the new recruits. As for rearmament, extra shifts at the foundries meant that it would soon be complete. The officers that Merenptah had appointed with Ramses' endorsement would form battalions able to overpower any Hittite force.

When Ramses took his place at the head of his army and led them north, the certainty of triumph would inspire his regiments.

It was a mistake for Hattusili to break the peace. Egypt would not only fight its hardest to survive, it would also take its enemies by surprise. This time Ramses would storm the fortress of Kadesh.

Yet the king was in the grip of an anxiety he rarely felt, as if uncertain how to proceed. Without Nefertari to light the way for him, the monarch must consult with one of the gods.

Ramses ordered Serramanna to prepare him a fast boat for Hermopolis in middle Egypt. Just as the sovereign set foot on the gangway, Iset the Fair arrived to plead with him.

"May I come with you?"

"No, I need to be alone."

"Have you had news of Ahsha?"

"He'll be back soon."

"You know my feelings, Your Majesty. Give an order and I'll obey it. Egypt's happiness is more important than mine."

"I'm grateful to you, Iset; but there can be no happiness if Egypt condones injustice."

At the edge of the desert, near the necropolis where the high priests of the god Thoth were buried, grew an immense dum palm, much taller than its counterparts. Here, according to legend, Thoth appeared to his faithful, providing that they had kept themselves free from idle chatter. For those who knew how to keep their tongue, the god of language and patron of scribes was like a cool spring, yet this spring remained inaccessible to anyone who talked too much. Therefore the king stopped to meditate for a day and a night at the foot of the dum palm, to calm the churning waters of his thoughts.

At dawn, a loud cry greeted the returning sun.

Less than ten paces from Ramses stood a colossal ape, a dog-faced baboon with powerful jaws. The Pharaoh met his gaze.

"Open the way for me, Thoth, you who know the mysteries of heaven and earth. You revealed the law to gods and men, you put its power into words. Help me find the right path, the path that is best for Egypt."

The huge baboon reared up on its hind legs. Taller than Ramses, it lifted its hands toward the sun in a sign of adoration. The king did the same, with his unique ability to stare at the sun without fear of being blinded.

The voice of Thoth sprang forth from the heavens, the dum palm, and the mouth of the baboon. Pharaoh heard and took it to heart.

SEVENTEEN

Rain had been falling for several days, and fog interfered with the Egyptian convoy's progress. Ahsha admired the way the donkeys kept a steady pace despite the heavy loads and nasty weather. Egypt considered these animals to be one of the god Set's incarnations, representing inexhaustible strength. Without donkeys, there could be no prosperity.

The secretary of state was eager to exit northern Syria, traverse Phoenicia, and enter the Egyptian protectorates. Usually he enjoyed traveling, but this time it was sheer drudgery. The scenery bored him, the mountains made him uneasy, the rivers were awash with foreboding.

The military attaché in charge of the convoy was a veteran of Kadesh, a member of the auxiliary force that had come to Ramses' aid as he battled the Hittites single-handed. The man knew Ahsha well and held him in high regard. The diplomat's exploits as a secret agent and his knowledge of the terrain commanded respect. The secretary of state was also reputed to be a pleasant companion and a brilliant conversationalist, yet from the outset he'd been glum and silent.

At a rest stop by a sheepfold where men and beasts warmed themselves, the officer sat down beside Ahsha.

"Feeling ill, sir?"

"Just tired."

"You're bringing back bad news, aren't you?"

"It could be better, but as long as Ramses is on the throne the situation will never be desperate."

"I know about the Hittites. They're bloodthirsty brutes at heart. A few years' rest has only made them more eager to fight."

"This time the problem is somewhat different: a woman. No ordinary woman, it's true; we're talking about the Great Royal Wife. Ramses is right; we must make no concessions where the fundamental values of our civilization are concerned."

"That doesn't sound very diplomatic!"

"I'm approaching retirement. I promised myself I'd resign when traveling got old for me. That time has come."

"The king will never let you go."

"I'm as determined as he is and I'll negotiate to win. Finding someone to succeed me will be easier than he imagines. Not all the royal sons are merely courtiers; a few of them are top-notch civil servants. In my profession, when curiosity fades, it's time to quit. Politics no longer interests me. My only desire is to sit in the shade of the palm trees and watch the Nile flow by."

"Couldn't it be a passing fatigue?" asked the officer.

"I'm just not interested in deal-making anymore. My decision is final."

"This is my final mission, too. Then peace at last!"

"Where do you live?" inquired the diplomat.

"In a small town near Karnak. My mother is very old. I'll be glad to help make her last years happy."

"Are you married?"

"Never had time."

"Neither did I," said Ahsha wistfully.

"You're young yet."

"I'd rather wait until old age extinguishes my passion for women. Until then, I'll bear my weakness as bravely as I can. Let's hope that the gods will overlook it when it's time for my soul to be judged."

The old soldier lit a fire with flint and dry wood.

"We have some fine dried meat and pretty fair wine."

"A cup of wine will do for me."

"Are you losing your appetite, sir?"

"For some things. Perhaps that's the first sign of wisdom?"

The rain had finally let up.

"We could go a bit farther today," suggested Ahsha.

"The men and animals have had a rough time of it," objected his companion. "Once they're rested, we'll pick up the pace."

"I'll go get some sleep myself," said Ahsha, knowing that rest would elude him.

The convoy next crossed a green oak forest atop a steep, boulder-strewn crevasse. The winding trail was so narrow that they were forced to march single file. Clouds trooped across the restless sky.

A strange feeling haunted Ahsha, a feeling he was unable to name. He tried to banish it by dreaming about the banks of the Nile, the shady garden at the Pi-Ramses villa where he would while away his days, the dogs, cats, and monkeys that he'd finally have time to look after . . . but to no avail.

His right hand rested on the iron dagger Hattusili had given him as a double-edged gift to Ramses. If he hoped to make Ramses nervous, Hattusili was seriously misjudging the Pharaoh! Threat would have no effect on him. Ahsha felt like tossing the weapon into the river below, but he knew the dagger was only a symbol of the problem.

At one time, Ahsha had been in favor of trying to eliminate regional differences; now he thought exactly the opposite. Uniformity would only create monsters, faceless states in the grip of profit seekers pretending to advance the cause of humanity, the better to stifle initiative and maintain control.

Only Ramses was capable of keeping humanity on the straight and narrow, steering clear of stupidity and indolence and leading men toward the divine. If the world never produced a second Ramses, it would veer into a nightmare of chaos and fratricidal conflict.

How comforting Ahsha found it to leave the final decisions to Ramses! Pharaoh took his guidance from the great beyond. At one with God in the inner sanctum of the temple, he was also alone with his people, whom he must serve without a care for his personal glory. For several millennia, pharaonic rule had overcome all obstacles and faced all crises precisely because it was not of this world.

Once his days as roving ambassador were over, Ahsha would gather the ancient texts on the pharaoh's twin nature, celestial and earthly, and present the collection to Ramses. They'd discuss it on balmy evenings beneath an arbor or sitting by a pond thick with lotus blossoms.

Ahsha had been lucky in life, very lucky. To be Ramses' friend, to help him foil plots and repel the Hittites . . . what could have been more exalting? A hundred times Ahsha had been on the brink of despair, considering human baseness, treachery, and mediocrity; yet a hundred times Ramses had pulled him back, making the sun shine brightly once again.

A dead tree.

A tall tree, with a broad trunk and exposed roots, still appearing indestructible.

Ahsha smiled. This dead tree, was it not a source of life? Here birds took refuge, insects fed. It fully symbolized the mysterious interrelationship of all living things. What were the pharaohs, after all, if not immense trees, touching the heavens, offering food and protection to a whole people? Ramses would never die, for during his lifetime his kingship had taken him through the gates of the invisible world. A knowledge of the supernatural was what gave a king his earthly bearings.

Ahsha had spent little time in the temples. However, he had been close to Ramses, and by osmosis had been initiated into certain secrets that each pharaoh knew and kept. Perhaps Ramses' secretary of state was already outgrowing his retirement, before it had even begun. Wouldn't it be more exciting to leave the everyday world behind and live a cloistered life, to embark on the spiritual life as a new adventure?

The path grew steeper. Ahsha's horse panted. One more pass and they would begin the descent toward Canaan, then start on the road to Egypt's northeastern border. For a long time Ahsha had refused to believe he could ever be happy with a simple existence in the land where he was born, far from the hue and cry of public life. The morning they left Hattusa, snow had come early to the mountains of Anatolia, and he had spotted his first gray hair in the mirror—a clear signal that the old age he had dreaded was closing in.

Ahsha alone was aware of the toll he was paying for too

many voyages, too many risks, too much danger. Neferet, the chief physician of the realm, would know how to soothe his pain and slow the aging process, but unlike Ramses, Ahsha could not use magical rites to renew his energy. The diplomat had worn himself out. His life span was nearing its end.

Suddenly came the terrifying scream of a mortally wounded man. Ahsha reined in his horse and turned around. From behind him rose other cries. Below there was fighting, and arrows whizzed from the treetops.

From both sides of the path sprang Libyans and Syrians armed with short swords and lances.

Half of the Egyptian contingent was exterminated within a few minutes. The survivors managed to kill a few of their attackers, but were sorely outnumbered.

"Run!" the officer in charge yelled to Ahsha. "Gallop straight ahead!"

Ahsha didn't hesitate. Brandishing the iron dagger, he fell on a Libyan archer, easily identified by the twin plumes stuck in his black and green headband. With one broad stroke, the Egyptian slit his throat.

"Watch out, watch . . ."

The veteran officer's warning trailed off in a rattle. A heavy sword had just crushed his skull. Wielding the sword was a long-haired demon with reddish fleece on his chest.

In the same instant, an arrow hit Ahsha in the back. Unable to breathe, he slumped on the damp ground. All the fight had gone out of him.

The red-haired demon approached the wounded man.

"Uri-Teshoop . . ."

"Yes, Ahsha, I've finally paid you back. Those diplomatic tricks of yours were my downfall. And now that you're out of the way, it will be Ramses' turn! Ramses will think the coward Hattusili is the one responsible for this slaughter. What do you think of my plan?"

"That . . . the coward . . . it's you."

Uri-Teshoop grabbed the iron dagger and sank it in Ahsha's heaving chest. Already the pillaging had begun. He'd have to take control or the Libyans would end up killing each other.

Ahsha knew that he didn't have the strength to write Uri-Teshoop's name with his blood. With his index finger, drawing on the last shred of his dying energy, he traced a single hieroglyph on his tunic, above his heart, then let his head drop.

Ramses would know what that lone hieroglyph meant.

EIGHTEEN

The palace was dead silent. Just back from Hermopolis, Ramses knew immediately that something serious had happened. The courtiers were conspicuously absent, government officials were lying low in their offices.

"Go find Ahmeni," the king ordered Serramanna, "and meet me out on the terrace."

From the highest point in the palace, Ramses contemplated the capital that Moses had helped him build. The white houses trimmed in turquoise slumbered beneath the palm trees. People strolled and chatted in the gardens by cooling ponds. Flagstaffs flew banners above the monumental gates, affirming the presence of the divine.

The god Thoth had asked the monarch to preserve the peace, no matter what sacrifices it demanded. In the labyrinth of ambitions, it was his responsibility to find a way around massacres and misery. By broadening the king's heart, the god of knowledge had given him a new will. Ramses, the son of Ra, the divine light, was also the son of Thoth, who represented the sun at night.

Ahmeni was paler than usual. His eyes were infinitely sad.

"You, at least, will dare to tell me the truth!"

"Ahsha is dead, Your Majesty."

Ramses was stone-faced.

"In what circumstances?"

"His convoy was attacked on the way into Canaan. A shepherd discovered the corpses and alerted the local police. When they arrived on the scene, one of them recognized Ahsha."

"Has his body been positively identified?"

"Yes, Your Majesty."

"Where is it now?"

"At a fort, along with the remains of the other members of his delegation."

"No survivors?"

"None."

"Any witnesses?"

"No witnesses."

"Let's send Serramanna to the scene of the attack. He should search for clues and bring back the remains. Ahsha and his companions will rest in Egyptian soil."

The giant Sard and a small group of mercenaries had gone through several horses on the way to the fort and back. As soon as he returned to Pi-Ramses, Serramanna had left Ahsha's remains with an embalmer to wash, perfume, and prepare the body before it was presented to the Pharaoh.

Ramses had taken his friend in his arms and laid him on a bed in one of the palace bedchambers.

Ahsha's face was serene. Wrapped in a white shroud, he seemed to be asleep.

Above him stood Ramses, flanked by Ahmeni and Setau.

"Who killed him?" asked Setau, his eyes red-rimmed.

"We're going to find out," promised the king. "I'm waiting for Serramanna to report."

"Ahsha's House of Eternity is ready," reported Ahmeni. "Men have judged him worthy, and the gods will bring him back to life."

"My son Kha will conduct the funeral rites and say the ancient prayers for resurrection. Ahsha's work here below will continue in the next world; his love of country will protect him from the dangers of the underworld."

"I'll kill his murderer with my own hands," announced Setau. "I won't rest until I do."

Serramanna was shown into the room.

"What have you found out?"

"Ahsha took an arrow near the right shoulder blade, but the wound wasn't fatal. Here's what killed him."

The former pirate handed the dagger to Ramses.

"Iron!" exclaimed Ahmeni. "A sinister gift from the Emperor of Hatti! The message is clear: he's assassinated the Egyptian ambassador, a close friend of Pharaoh's!"

Serramanna had never seen Ahmeni so furious.

"We know who the murderer is, then," concluded Setau. "Let Hattusili try and hide in his citadel! I'll find a way to get in and toss his corpse back over the ramparts."

"Perhaps we shouldn't be too hasty," ventured the Sard.

"Don't tell me you think I can't do it!"

"I'm sure you could do as you say, Setau. It's the identity of the murderer I wonder about."

"The iron dagger is a Hittite piece, isn't it?"

"Of course it is, but I found another clue at the scene as well."

Serramanna produced a broken plume. "It's the Libyans' war regalia."

"Libyans fighting with Hittites? It's impossible."

"When the forces of evil decide to unite," asserted Ahmeni, "nothing is impossible. It's all quite clear: Hattusili wants a showdown. Like his predecessors, he dreams only of destroying Egypt, and he'd sign on with demons from hell to do it!"

"There's another point to consider," commented Serramanna. "Ahsha's delegation was a small one. There must have been forty or fifty of the attackers. A band of looters that laid a trap for them, not a regular army."

"That's only your interpretation," objected Ahmeni.

"No, it's a fact. When you look at the terrain, the width of the path, and the prints the riders left, there's no room for doubt. I'm sure there wasn't a single Hittite chariot in the vicinity."

"What does that change?" asked Setau. "Hattusili ordered his shock troops to execute Ahsha with a special gift for Ramses, this iron dagger! Since Pharaoh refuses to wed his daughter, the Emperor of Hatti counters by having one of his close friends assassinated. Even though Ahsha was a diplomat, a negotiator. Nothing can change a nation's mind-set; the Hittites will always be inarticulate barbarians."

"Your Majesty," Ahmeni said gravely, "I abhor violence and detest war. But leaving this crime unpunished would be an intolerable affront to justice. As long as Hatti remains unchecked, Egypt will be in mortal danger. Ahsha gave his life to make us see it."

Without betraying the least emotion, Ramses listened to it all.

"What else, Serramanna?"

"Nothing, Your Majesty."

"Did Ahsha write anything on the ground, perhaps?"

"He wouldn't have had time. The blow from the dagger was forceful and death would have followed quickly."

"What about his baggage?"

"Stolen."

"His clothing?"

"The embalmer removed it all."

"Bring me what he was wearing."

"But . . . it must be destroyed by now."

"Bring it here, and fast."

The king gave Serramanna the fright of his life. Why would he be so interested in a blood-spattered tunic and cloak?

The Sard left the palace at a run, leapt on the back of his horse, and galloped to the embalmers' settlement outside of town. The senior embalmer had prepared Ahsha's corpse for the final earthly encounter between Pharaoh and his friend.

"Ahsha's clothing," demanded the Sard.

"I don't have it anymore," replied the undertaker.

"What did you do with it?"

"Well . . . the usual. Gave it to the neighborhood washerman."

"Where does he live?"

"Last house on the curve that runs along the canal."

The hulking Sard flew off again, forcing his steed to jump walls, riding through gardens, hurtling down alleyways as pedestrians scattered. He reached the curve at full gallop.

At the last house, he pulled on the reins to stop his sweating horse, jumped off, and pounded on the shutters.

"Where's the washerman?"

A woman appeared in the window.

"Down at the canal. He's working."

Leaving his horse behind, Serramanna ran down to the canal, used only for doing laundry. A man was just beginning to soap Ahsha's tunic when Serramanna grabbed him by the hair.

On the cloak there were traces of blood. On the tunic, too, but with a visible difference: Ahsha's unsteady finger had drawn something there.

"It's a hieroglyph," Ramses announced. "What do you make of it, Ahmeni?"

"Two outstretched arms, open palms held downward . . . a negative meaning."

"The sign for 'no.' I read it the same as you."

"The beginning of a name or a word . . . What did Ahsha mean?"

Setau, Ahmeni, and Serramanna were perplexed. Ramses reflected.

"Ahsha knew he had only a few seconds before he died, time to write only one hieroglyph. He also knew the conclusion we'd reach, that only Hattusili could be behind this abominable act, forcing me to declare war immediately. So Ahsha left this last word to prevent a tragedy. 'No.' No, the real culprit is not Hattusili."

NINETEEN

Ahsha's funeral was a stately occasion. Dressed in a panther skin, Kha performed the ritual opening of the eyes, ears, and mouth above the gilded acacia-wood coffin containing the distinguished diplomat's mummy. Then Ramses sealed the door to his eternal dwelling.

When silence fell once again upon the tomb site, the king remained alone in the mortuary chapel opening toward the outside. He would be first to fill the role of priest to his late friend's *ka* by placing a lotus blossom, some irises, a loaf of fresh bread, and a cup of wine on the altar. Henceforth, a priest in the employ of the palace would bring offerings each day, maintaining Ahsha's eternal memory.

Moses was gone in pursuit of his dream; Ahsha was in

the next world. The circle of boyhood friends was growing tighter. At times, Ramses began to regret that he had reigned so long, with so many dark passages. Like Seti, Tuya, and Nefertari before him, Ahsha was irreplaceable. He had kept to himself, passing through life with feline grace. He and Ramses had no need to talk at length; each instinctively grasped the other's most secret meaning.

Nefertari and Ahsha had built the peace agreement. Without their determination and courage, Hatti would never have agreed to a halt in the old hostilities. Fortunately, Ahsha's killer had no idea how strong the understanding between true friends could be. As he lay dying, Ahsha had summoned his final spark of energy to contradict a lie.

It was a moment when any man would be justified in drowning his sorrows in wine or easing his pain by reminiscing with loved ones. Any man except Pharaoh.

To see Ramses the Great one-on-one, even when you were both his younger son and commander-in-chief of his army, was enough to take your breath away. Merenptah tried to stay cool, knowing that his father would judge him, like the god Thoth weighing souls in the Judgment Hall of the Dead.

"Father, I wanted to say—"

"Don't bother, Merenptah. Ahsha was my old friend, not yours. Condolences won't lessen my grief. All that matters is that his *ka* will last, beyond the fact of physical death. Now tell me, is my army ready for combat?"

"Yes, Your Majesty."

"From this point on, there's no room for carelessness.

The world is about to undergo a great change, Merenptah. We must be ready to defend ourselves at any time. You should be constantly on your guard."

"Am I to understand that you're declaring war?"

"Ahsha helped us spot a trick that might have made us the party breaking the peace treaty. Still, the situation is delicate. To save his honor, Hattusili will be forced to invade Canaan and launch a broad offensive against the Delta."

Merenptah was astonished.

"Are we going to let him?"

"He'll think we're disorganized and unable to react. We'll attack once he gets lost in the maze of branches of the Nile, dividing his troops. On our terrain, the Hittites won't be able to maneuver."

Merenptah seemed on edge.

"What do you think of this plan, my son?"

"It's . . . bold."

"You mean dangerous?"

"You're Pharaoh and I must obey you."

"Be honest, Merenptah."

"I'm confident, Your Majesty. I trust in you, as all of Egypt does."

"Be ready then."

Serramanna trusted his pirate's instincts. He could not believe that Ahsha's death had happened during an organized raid by Emperor Hattusili's shock troops. And this same instinct told him that there was a beast to track, someone capable of murder if it might weaken Ramses and deprive him of his friend's precious, even indispensable support.

Which was why the Sard was lurking near Dame Tanit's villa, waiting for Uri-Teshoop to emerge.

The Hittite left the house early in the afternoon, riding off on a black horse with white spots, checking first to see if he was followed.

Serramanna approached the doorman.

"I want to see Dame Tanit."

The lady of the house received the Sard in a handsome salon with two columns, lit by four tall windows that let in both air and light. The comely Phoenician looked thinner.

"Is this an official visit, Serramanna?"

"A social call, for the time being. The rest will depend on your answers, Dame Tanit."

"So it's an interrogation."

"No, a simple interview with an upstanding citizen who's fallen into bad company."

"I don't understand."

"Of course you know what I'm getting at. A serious event has just occurred: Ahsha, the secretary of state, was murdered on his way home from Hatti."

"Murdered . . ." Tanit blanched. To get rid of Serramanna all she needed to do was call for help, and the four Libyans hiding in her villa would instantly dispose of the Sard. But eliminating Ramses' security chief would cause an investigation, and Tanit would be caught in the wheels of justice. No, she must keep her head.

"I'd like a detailed account of your husband's whereabouts for the past two months."

"Uri-Teshoop has spent most of his time here in this house. We're still very much in love. When he does go out, it's to visit a tavern or walk in town. We've been so happy together!"

"When did he leave Pi-Ramses and when did he come back?"

"Since he's been with me, he hasn't left the capital. He enjoys it here. He's gradually forgetting his past. Thanks to our marriage, he's become one of Pharaoh's subjects, just as you and I are."

"Uri-Teshoop is a criminal," Serramanna said firmly. "He's threatened and terrorized you. If you tell me the truth, I'll put you under my protection, and the justice system will take care of him."

For a second, Tanit was tempted to run into the garden. Serramanna would follow her, she'd warn him about the Libyans, and she could be her own woman again . . . But that would be the last she'd ever see of Uri-Teshoop, and she wasn't ready to give him up. While he was away, she'd fallen ill. She'd never had such a lover; she needed him like a drug.

"Even if you drag me into court, Serramanna, I won't say anything different."

"Uri-Teshoop will destroy you, Dame Tanit."

She smiled, thinking of the feverish lovemaking that had ended only minutes before the Sard's arrival.

"If you've finished making your unfounded accusations, you may go."

"I'd like to save you, Dame Tanit."

"I'm not in danger."

"If you change your mind, get in touch."

She teasingly ran a soft hand over the Sard's enormous forearm.

"You're a good-looking man . . . Too bad I've already met my match."

Decked out in a golden collar with a lapis lazuli scarab, turquoise bracelets at her wrists and ankles, tall feathers in her queenly headdress, and wearing a tucked dress of royal linen and rose-colored cape, the Great Royal Wife Iset the Fair slowly rode through Pi-Ramses in her chariot. The driver had chosen two steady horses outfitted with a brightly colored caparison and sporting blue, red, and yellow ostrich plumes.

The spectacle was magnificent. News of the queen's passage spread quickly, and soon a crowd gathered to admire her. Children scattered lotus petals in front of the horses as cheers rose. Seeing the Great Royal Wife so close would bring good luck. Rumors of war were forgotten in the groundswell of approval for Ramses' decision. He must never repudiate Iset the Fair, no matter what the repercussions.

Raised in an aristocratic milieu, Iset the Fair savored this contact with her people, where social classes and cultures mixed. All the inhabitants of Pi-Ramses cheered in support of her. Despite the chariot driver's reluctance, the queen demanded to visit the humblest neighborhoods, where she was given a warm welcome. How good it felt to be loved!

Back at the palace, Iset the Fair collapsed on her bed as if intoxicated. There was nothing more moving than being the repository of the people's trust, their hope of a rosy future. Emerging from her cocoon, Iset the Fair had discovered the country of which she was queen.

That evening, at a dinner for the provincial governors, Ramses had announced that conflict was imminent. Everyone noted that Iset the Fair was radiant. Though unable to equal Nefertari, she was growing into her title and inspired respect from veteran courtiers. For all and sundry she had a word of reassurance. Egypt had nothing to fear from Hatti; all would be well, thanks to Ramses. The governors were touched by the queen's conviction.

When Ramses and Iset were alone on the terrace overlooking the city, he held her tenderly to him.

"You did beautifully tonight, Iset."

"Are you proud of me at last?"

"I chose you as Great Royal Wife and was right to do so."

"Have negotiations with Hatti broken down for good?"

"We're ready for battle."

Iset the Fair laid her head on Ramses' shoulder.

"No matter what happens, you'll be the winner."

TWENTY

Kha was obviously distressed.

"War . . . but why?"

"To save Egypt and permit you to find Thoth's book of knowledge," answered Ramses.

"Is it really impossible to mend relations with Hatti?"

"Their troops are closing in on our northern protectorates. It's time to deploy our contingent; I'm going with Merenptah and leaving you in charge while I'm gone."

"Father! I can't replace you, even temporarily."

"You're wrong, Kha. With Ahmeni's help, you'll be able to do as I ask."

"What if I make mistakes?"

"Concentrate on the people's happiness and you'll know what to do."

Ramses climbed into his chariot, which he would drive himself at the head of the regiments he planned to post at strategic points in the Delta and along the northeastern frontier. Behind him would come Merenptah and the generals with the four main battalions.

Just as the king prepared to give the departure signal, a rider burst into the barracks courtyard.

Serramanna jumped off his horse and ran up to Ramses' chariot.

"Your Majesty, I must speak to you!"

Pharaoh had ordered his security chief to watch over the palace. He knew it was a disappointment to the Sard, who for years had longed to see action with the Hittites; but who else would take better care of Kha and Iset the Fair?

"I won't reconsider, Serramanna. You're staying in Pi-Ramses."

"It's not about me, Your Majesty. Come, I beg you."

The Sard looked stricken.

"What's happened?"

"Come, Your Majesty, come with me . . ."

Ramses asked Merenptah to let the generals know their departure would be delayed.

Pharaoh's chariot followed Serramanna's horse as they sped toward the palace.

The chambermaid, the lady-in-waiting, and the servant girls were huddled in the hallways, weeping.

Serramanna stopped at the doorway to Iset the Fair's bedchamber. The Sard's face was a mixture of misery and confusion.

Ramses went in.

A heady smell of lilies filled the room, bright with the noonday sun. Iset the Fair, clothed in a white ceremonial robe and a turquoise tiara, lay on her bed, arms at her side and eyes wide open.

On the sycamore night table was an antelope-skin tunic—Setau's old standby, stolen from his workshop.

"Iset . . ."

Iset the Fair, Ramses' first lover, the mother of Kha and Merenptah, the Great Royal Wife for whom he was fully prepared to do battle . . . Iset the Fair was looking into the next world.

"The queen chose death to keep us out of war," explained Serramanna. "She poisoned herself with the venom from Setau's tunic so that she'd no longer stand in the way of peace."

"You're not making sense, Serramanna!"

Ahmeni spoke up. "The queen left a message. I read it and asked Serramanna to come and find you."

In keeping with tradition, Ramses did not close the dead woman's eyes. She must confront the afterlife with a frank gaze and an open face.

Entombed in the Valley of the Queens, Iset the Fair was given a more modest resting place than Nefertari's. Ramses himself performed the rites of resurrection over her mummy. The queen's *ka* would be kept alive by the constant prayers of special mortuary priests and priestesses.

On the Great Royal Wife's sarcophagus the Pharaoh had placed a branch of the sycamore tree he had planted in the garden of Iset's Memphis mansion when they were seventeen. This token of their youth would keep Iset's soul blooming.

At the end of the ceremony, Ahmeni and Setau requested an audience with Ramses. Without replying, the king climbed a nearby slope. Setau scrambled after him, and despite the toll on his frail constitution, Ahmeni did likewise.

The sand, the rocky incline, Ramses' rapid pace that set his lungs on fire . . . Ahmeni muttered all the way up the path. Still, he made it to the top, where the king gazed out on the Valley of the Queens and the eternal dwellings of Nefertari and Iset the Fair.

Setau kept silent, the better to appreciate the magnificent sight. Ahmeni sat on a boulder and wiped his forehead with the back of his hand.

He dared interrupt the king's meditation.

"Your Majesty, there are urgent decisions to be made."

"Nothing is more urgent than contemplating this land beloved of the gods. The gods spoke; their voice became the sky, mountains, water, and earth. In Set's red land we have dug our tombs, with their chamber of resurrection bathed in the primordial ocean that surrounds the world. Through our rites we preserve the energy of the first morning, and our country is born again each day. All else is meaningless."

"To live again, our country has to survive! If Pharaoh

neglects the world of men, the gods will retreat into their invisible realm."

Setau expected that Ahmeni's sharp tone would earn him a blistering rebuke from Ramses. But the king contented himself with studying the marked contrast between desert and cultivated land, between the everyday and the eternal.

"What's the latest pitfall you're imagining, Ahmeni?"

"I wrote to Hattusili, the Emperor of Hatti, to announce the news of Iset the Fair's passing. While the country is in mourning, engaging in war would be out of the question."

"No one could have saved Iset," added Setau. "She took too much of too many different substances, and the combination was deadly. I burned that wretched tunic, Ramses."

"I don't hold you responsible, Setau. Iset thought she was acting in Egypt's best interest."

Ahmeni stood up. "She was right, Your Majesty."

Stung, the monarch wheeled around. "How dare you say such a thing, Ahmeni?"

"Much as I fear your wrath, I have to state my opinion: Iset left this world to preserve the peace."

"What do you think, Setau?"

Like Ahmeni, Setau felt the power of Ramses' blazing eyes. Yet the least he could offer was his honesty.

"If you refused to understand Iset the Fair's message, Ramses, she'd die a second death. Make sure that her sacrifice wasn't in vain."

"And what should I do about it, according to you?"

"Marry the Hittite princess," Ahmeni declared gravely.

"Nothing stands in the way of it any longer," added Setau.

Ramses clenched his fists. "Are your hearts hard as granite? Iset has barely been laid in her tomb and you're telling me to remarry?"

"You're not just any widower mourning his loss," Setau said bluntly. "You're the Pharaoh of Egypt, whose duty it is to preserve the peace and save his people. The people care nothing for your personal feelings; they only demand that you govern them wisely."

"A Pharaoh and a Hittite Great Royal Wife . . . wouldn't that be a travesty?"

"Quite the contrary," Ahmeni chimed in. "What else could bring our two countries closer together? If you consent to this marriage, the specter of war will recede for the foreseeable future. Imagine how your father, Seti, and your mother, Tuya, will celebrate up among the stars! Not to mention Ahsha, who gave his life to build a lasting peace."

"You're starting to sound like a politician, Ahmeni."

"I'm only a scribe in failing health, not especially bright, but honored to be sandal-bearer to the Lord of the Two Lands. I have no wish to see those sandals splattered with blood again."

"The law of Ma'at requires you to reign in conjunction with a Great Royal Wife," Setau pointed out. "You really can't lose if you marry this foreigner."

"I hate the woman already!"

"Your life isn't your own, Ramses. Egypt demands this sacrifice of you."

"And so do you, my friends."

Ahmeni and Setau nodded in unison.

"Leave me alone now. I need to think."

Ramses spent the night on the cliffs. After nourishing himself with the rising sun, he lingered in the Valley of the

Queens, then rejoined his escort. Without a word, Ramses climbed into his chariot and drove at full speed to the Ramesseum, his Eternal Temple. He celebrated the rites of dawn and prayed in Nefertari's chapel. Then the Pharaoh retired to his palace, where he proceeded with long ablutions, drank some milk, ate some figs and fresh bread.

His face refreshed as if he had slept for several hours, the monarch pushed open the door to Ahmeni's office. The scribe was frowning over his correspondence.

"Take a new sheet of top-quality papyrus and write to my brother the Emperor of Hatti."

"And what might be the content of this letter?"

"Announce that I've decided to make his daughter my Great Royal Wife."

TWENTY-ONE

Uri-Teshoop drank a third cup of strong oasis wine. Fortified with spices and resin, this was a substance embalmers used to preserve the viscera; physicians also prized its antiseptic properties.

"You drink too much," observed Raia.

"You don't know how to enjoy what Egypt has to offer. This wine is a treat! Did anyone follow you?"

"Put your mind at ease."

The Syrian merchant had waited until the middle of the night before slipping into the comely Phoenician's villa. He had detected nothing suspicious.

"Why this unexpected visit?"

"Important news, Highness, very important."

"The war has started?"

"No, Highness, no. There will be no war between Egypt and Hatti."

Uri-Teshoop threw down his cup and grabbed the Syrian by the collar of his tunic.

"What are you talking about? My setup was perfect!"

"Iset the Fair is dead and Ramses is preparing to marry Emperor Hattusili's daughter."

Uri-Teshoop released his partner in crime.

"A Hittite queen of Egypt . . . Unthinkable! You must be mistaken, Raia!"

"No, Highness. The news is official. You murdered Ahsha for nothing."

"Getting rid of that miserable spy was crucial. Our hands are no longer tied. None of Ramses' other advisers is as smart as Ahsha."

"We've lost, Highness. It's peacetime again, a peace no effort of ours can break."

"Imbecile! Do you know the woman who's going to become Pharaoh's Great Royal Wife? A Hittite, Raia, a real Hittite princess, proud, shrewd, indomitable!"

"She's the daughter of your enemy Hattusili."

"She's my cousin. But a Hittite first and foremost! She'll never submit to an Egyptian, Pharaoh or not. This is our chance."

Raia sighed. The wine was going to the warrior prince's head. Bereft of any hope, he was imagining things.

"Perhaps you ought to leave Egypt," the Syrian suggested to Uri-Teshoop.

"Suppose that this Hittite princess were on our side, Raia. We'd have an ally in the very heart of the palace!"

"You're dreaming, Highness."

"No, this is a sign that destiny is sending us, a sign I'll turn to my advantage!"

"You'll be sorely disappointed."

Uri-Teshoop drained a fourth glass of wine.

"We've omitted one detail, Raia, but there's still time to act. You'll use the Libyans."

A curtain rustled, and the Syrian merchant pointed his finger toward the suspect location.

Like a cat, Uri-Teshoop sprang toward the curtain, pulled it roughly aside, and hauled out a trembling Tanit.

"Were you listening?"

"No, no, I was coming to find you . . ."

"We have no secrets from you, darling, since you can't betray us."

"You have my word!"

"Go to bed. I'll be there in a minute."

Tanit's longing gaze promised a lively bedtime. In a few crisp phrases, Uri-Teshoop gave his orders to Raia.

The main Pi-Ramses foundry was still busy turning out swords, lances, and shields. So long as the Pharaoh's marriage to the Hittite princess had not been celebrated, preparations for war would continue as before.

Weapons seized from the Hittites were sent to a workshop near the foundry, where Egyptian craftsmen studied them closely. One of the metal workers, a highly inventive young man, took an interest in the iron dagger the palace had just sent over.

The quality of the metal, the width of the blade, the ease of handling—everything about it was remarkable.

Copying this piece would not be easy. It would take several tries. His mouth almost watering, the craftsman weighed the dagger in his hand.

"Someone to see you," announced an orderly.

The visitor was a blunt-featured mercenary.

"What do you want?"

"The palace wants the iron dagger back."

"Do you have a written order?"

"Of course."

"Let's see it."

From a leather pouch that hung from his belt, the mercenary produced a wooden tablet and showed it to the metal worker.

"But these aren't hieroglyphs!"

With a wicked uppercut, Raia's Libyan hireling knocked the craftsman cold. Then he retrieved the tablet and the fallen dagger and ran from the workshop.

At the end of a lengthy interrogation, Serramanna was convinced that the metal worker was not in league with the thief who had taken the dagger. It must be just some soldier of fortune with an eye for profit, like so many others in the Egyptian army.

"A ruffian working for Uri-Teshoop," the Sard told Ahmeni.

The scribe kept on writing.

"Do you have proof of that?"

"My gut instinct is enough for me."

"Is this even worth pursuing? Uri-Teshoop has money now, or at least his wife does; why would he try to steal Hattusili's dagger?"

"Because he's thought of some new way to harm Ramses."

"Any conflict with the Hittites is impossible at this point. The essential thing is your inquest into Ahsha's murder. Any progress there?"

"Not yet."

"Ramses is demanding to know the assassin's identity."

"The murder and the theft of the dagger . . . it's all tied up together. If anything happens to me, go after Uri-Teshoop."

"What's going to happen to you?"

"If I'm to get anywhere with this investigation, I'll have to infiltrate Libyan circles. And if they figure out what I'm doing, they'll try to get rid of me."

"You're the captain of the royal bodyguard! No one will dare take you on."

"They didn't stop at killing Pharaoh's secretary of state, who was also his boyhood friend."

"Couldn't you try something less dangerous?"

"I'm afraid not, Ahmeni."

In the heart of the Libyan desert, far from any oasis, Malfi's tent was a makeshift fort, guarded by trustworthy lieutenants. The tribal chief was drinking milk and eating dates; he never touched wine or beer, considering them the devil's potions because they jumbled his thoughts.

Malfi's personal bodyguard was composed of natives from his village who would have remained poor peasants without his help. Eating their fill, properly clothed, armed with lances, swords, bows, and slings, and popular with the ladies, they practically worshiped Malfi. To them he was a powerful desert spirit, swift as a panther, with razor-sharp fingers, and eyes in the back of his head.

"My Lord, there's a fight!" his water bearer reported.

Malfi stood up, unalarmed. He had a square face with a broad forehead half hidden beneath a white turban. He slowly emerged from his tent.

The training camp was home to fifty-odd men, who were practicing with mock weapons and bare fists in the afternoon sun. Malfi enjoyed the extreme conditions that the desert heat and sand offered; only men possessing the true warrior spirit would survive here.

And this test of their skill was crucial in view of the task awaiting the fledgling Libyan army: overcoming Ramses' forces. Malfi constantly pondered the generations of Libyan chieftains humiliated by the pharaohs. The hostilities had lasted for centuries, punctuated by the defeats the Egyptians inflicted on the brave but disorganized desert tribes.

Ofir, Malfi's older brother, had used a weapon that he hoped would be decisive: black magic, in the service of the pro-Hittite spy ring he also directed. He had paid for his failure with his life, and Malfi had sworn revenge. Little by little he was forming a federation of Libyan tribes, whose uncontested master he was bound to become.

His meeting with the Hittite prince Uri-Teshoop was a boon. With an ally of that standing, a Libyan victory was no mere pipe dream. Malfi would soon avenge long centuries' worth of shame and rage.

A heavyset soldier, unusually aggressive, seemed to have forgotten he was in a training exercise and was pummeling two opponents, despite the fact they were taller and armed with lances. When Malfi approached him, the soldier began to show off, grinding his foot into one of his victim's heads.

Malfi drew a dagger from beneath his tunic and sank it into the back of the heavyset soldier's neck.

The fighting broke up. All heads turned toward Malfi.

"Continue your training and keep control of yourselves," he ordered. "Remember that the enemy can come from nowhere."

TWENTY-TWO

The great audience chamber at the Pi-Ramses palace was truly stunning. Even courtiers who had already climbed the monumental staircase—decorated with figures of vanquished enemies won over to the will of Pharaoh and the law of Ma'at—found it a deeply moving experience. The main door was wreathed with Ramses' coronation names, blue on a white background, enclosed in cartouches whose oval shape symbolized the cosmic circuit over which the Lord of the Two Lands reigned.

Plenary audiences, convening the entire court, were not a

frequent occurrence. Only events with a direct impact on Egypt's future led Ramses to address the elite assembly.

The atmosphere was tense. Rumor had it that the Hittite emperor was holding his ground. Ramses' initial rejection of the proposal to marry Hattusili's daughter had surely been taken as an insult. The Pharaoh's eventual acceptance had probably failed to cancel the affront.

The floor of the great hall was tiled with lacquered terra-cotta, featuring scenes of pools, flowering gardens, ducks swimming in a blue-green pond, and fish darting through white lotus blossoms. Priests, scribes, cabinet members, provincial governors, givers of offerings, keepers of secrets, and court fixtures were present, admiring the extravaganza of pale green, yellow-gold, and off-white on the walls with their scenes of flitting hoopoes, hummingbirds, titmice, nightingales, and kingfishers. Higher up, the eye delighted in a floral frieze of interwoven poppies, lotuses, daisies, and cornflowers.

A hush fell when Ramses ascended the stairs leading to his golden throne. The highest step was decorated with a lion closing its mouth around a lurking enemy from the underworld, representing the disorder that constantly threatened to disrupt Ma'at's harmony.

Pharaoh wore a double headdress, the white of upper Egypt entwined with the red of lower Egypt. The twin crown was imbued with magic, like the uraeus on his forehead, the image of a female cobra spitting fire to dispel the forces of darkness. In his right hand the king held the scepter called "Magic," resembling a shepherd's crook. For just as the shepherd watches over his flock and returns strays to the fold, Pharaoh must unite the scattered field of energies. For a few seconds the monarch's eyes lingered on a sublime painting, the face of a young woman meditating in front of massed hollyhocks. This was a portrait of Nefertari, whose beauty illuminated the reign of Ramses the Great even from beyond the grave.

But Pharaoh had no time for nostalgia. The ship of state moved forward; the rudder must be manned.

"I have called you together so that you may transmit some essential facts to the whole country. Wild rumors have been circulating in the capital, and I intend to reestablish the truth, which you will broadcast."

Ahmeni was seated in the last row, with other scribes, as if he occupied some lesser post. This way he would be more in tune with the audience's reactions. Serramanna, on the other hand, had chosen the front row. At the slightest sign of unrest, he would pounce. As for Setau, he occupied his place in the hierarchy, to the left of the Viceroy of Nubia, among the most visible dignitaries, many of whom stole repeated glances at Lotus, clothed in a pink dress with straps that left her breasts uncovered.

The governor from the province of the Prince, in lower Egypt, came forward and bowed to the monarch.

"May I have the floor, Your Majesty?"

"Yes, speak."

"Is it true that the secretary of state, Ahsha, is actually a prisoner in Hattusa, and the peace treaty with the Hittites has been broken?"

"My friend Ahsha was murdered on his way back to Pi-Ramses. He has found eternal rest on Egyptian soil. The investigation into his death continues; the guilty parties will be identified and punished. The peace with Hatti is in large part Ahsha's work, and we will make it his monument. Our nonaggression pact is still in force and shall remain so for some time to come."

"Your Majesty . . . may we ask who the next Great Royal Wife will be?"

"The daughter of Hattusili, Emperor of Hatti."

A buzz ran through the crowd. Finally a battalion commander requested the floor.

"Your Majesty, isn't that too great a concession?"

"As long as Iset the Fair was queen, I rejected Hattusili's proposal. Today, this marriage is the only means of consolidating the peace that the people of Egypt desire."

"Will we have to tolerate the presence of a Hittite army on our soil?"

"No, General, only a Hittite princess."

"Forgive my impudence, Your Majesty, but a Hittite on the throne of the Two Lands . . . won't it be a slap in the face to those who fought in the Anatolian campaigns? Thanks to your son Merenptah, our troops are combat ready and well equipped. What have we to fear from a conflict with the Hittites? Rather than backing down to their blatant demands, we ought to confront them."

The officer's outspokenness seemed likely to cost him his post.

"Your remarks are not devoid of intelligence," appraised Ramses, "but your outlook is biased. If Egypt were to launch an attack, we would be breaking the peace treaty and betraying our word. Is that any proper way for a pharaoh to behave?"

The general backed away and blended into the crowd of courtiers who were in general agreement with the monarch.

The supervisor of canals requested the floor.

"What if the Emperor of Hatti reverses his decision and refuses to send his daughter to Egypt? Wouldn't you judge that attitude intolerable, Your Majesty?"

Dressed in his ceremonial leopard skin, the high priest of Memphis, Prince Kha, stepped forward.

"Will Pharaoh permit me to answer?"

Ramses nodded.

"From my point of view," declared the king's elder son, "politics and diplomacy are not an adequate basis for making a vital decision. Keeping our word and respecting the law of Ma'at are of prime importance, but we must also heed our ancestral legacy of magic. In Year Thirty of his reign, Ramses the Great celebrated his initial sed-feast; henceforth our sovereign must frequently replenish the invisible forces he needs in order to govern. That is why the most urgent task he faces in the thirty-third year of his reign is planning his second sed-feast. Then the horizon will clear and the answers to our questions will come unbidden."

"It's a complicated and costly undertaking," protested the director of the House of Gold and Silver. "Wouldn't it be better to postpone this for a while?"

"Impossible," retorted Kha. "Our study of the texts and the astrologers' calculations lead to the same conclusion: Ramses' second jubilee must be held without fail before two months are out. We must coordinate our efforts to ensure the attendance of all the gods and goddesses, and focus our thoughts on safeguarding Pharaoh."

The commander-in-chief of the fortresses strung along the northeastern border felt he must put in a word. A career soldier, a man of experience, he had the ear of many influential figures.

"With all due respect for the high priest's position, what happens in the event of a Hittite attack? When Hattusili learns that Egypt is planning this jubilee without regard to his daughter's wedding, he may take it as an insult and strike out at us. While Pharaoh is busy celebrating the sed-feast, who will be giving orders?"

"Religious ceremonies are the very thing that will protect

us," Kha asserted in his fine, deep voice, "as they have done since time immemorial."

"So says a priest well versed in the temples' secrets. A military man sees things somewhat differently. Hattusili is reluctant to attack us because he fears Ramses, the victor of Kadesh. He knows what supernatural feats our Pharaoh can perform. If the king isn't at the head of his troops, the Emperor of Hatti will be more likely to try a preemptive strike."

"Egypt's best protection is in the realm of magic," Kha reiterated. "Our foes, Hittite or otherwise, are merely the instruments of the forces of darkness. No human army can stop those forces. Remember that Amon was the one who gave strength to Ramses' sword arm at the battle of Kadesh."

The argument hit home. No other officer voiced an objection.

"I'd like to attend the sed-feast," said Merenptah, "but shouldn't I be at the border in Pharaoh's stead?"

"With two of the royal sons, you'll keep watch over our frontier while the jubilee proceeds."

Ramses' decree reassured the assembly, but the ranking celebrant priest, visibly irritated, made his way to the front of the audience. He had a shaved head, a long, thin face, and a rather ascetic figure.

"If Your Majesty will allow me, I have a few questions to ask of the high priest."

The king made no objection. Kha had been dreading this ordeal, but had hoped it would at least take place in an unofficial setting.

"At what site does the high priest of Memphis plan to celebrate this second sed-feast?"

"In the Pi-Ramses temple constructed for the purpose."

"Does the king possess the testament of the gods?"

"He does."

"Who will preside over the ceremonies?"

"Seti's immortal soul."

"Whence comes the light that provides Pharaoh with celestial energy?"

"That light is born of itself and reborn continuously in Pharaoh's heart."

The priest gave up quizzing Kha, realizing that the prince was flawlessly prepared. With a grave expression, the dignitary turned back to face Ramses.

"Despite the high priest's qualifications, Your Majesty, I deem it impossible to celebrate this sed-feast."

"Why?" asked Kha in amazement.

"Because the Great Royal Wife plays an essential role in it. Yet Pharaoh is a widower and has not yet taken this Hittite princess as his wife. However, no foreigner has ever had access to the mysteries of regeneration."

Ramses rose.

"What makes you think that Pharaoh is unaware of this difficulty?"

TWENTY-THREE

Techonk had been a tanner since he was a child. The son of a Libyan arrested by the Egyptian police for sheep rustling and sentenced to several years' hard labor, he had not followed his father home to preach armed revolt against Pharaoh. At Bubastis, then Pi-Ramses, Techonk had found work and gradually made a name for himself in his trade.

Approaching fifty, he began to feel pangs of remorse. He was fat and happy, but only because he'd sold out, ignoring Egypt's humiliating treatment of his native land. As a prosperous craftsman with a staff of thirty, he willingly opened his door to needy Libyans. Over time, he became a one-man aid society for his fellow expatriates. Some of them quickly found their place in Egyptian society. Others kept a chip on their shoulder and never adjusted. But now something new was in the air, a movement that frightened Techonk, who was no longer so convinced that the Two Lands should perish. Still, suppose Libya finally did have its day, and a Libyan sat on the throne of Egypt? Only first they'd have to get rid of Ramses . . .

To quiet his mind, Techonk returned to his work. He checked a fresh shipment of hides from goats, sheep, antelopes, and other desert animals. After the skins were dried, salted, and smoked, a team of specially trained workers would coat them with dirt and soften them with urine, droppings, and dung. It was the foulest-smelling procedure performed in the workshop, which underwent regular public health inspections.

A fast-acting curing process using oil and alum was followed by true curing with a product rich in tannic acid, derived from Nile acacia pods. If necessary, the hides underwent a second soaking in oil, then were pounded and stretched to soften them. Techonk was successful because he refused to settle for a simple tanning with animal fat. What was more, he had a special talent for draping and cutting the finished product. That was why his clientele was large and varied. Techonk's workshop produced bags, dog collars and leashes, ropes, sandals, cases and scabbards for daggers and swords, helmets, quivers, shields, and even writing stands.

Using a knife with a semicircular blade, Techonk was cutting a strap from a top-grade antelope skin when a whiskery giant barged into his establishment.

Serramanna, the head of Ramses' security detail . . . The blade raced along the leather, slid off track, and sliced through the craftsman's middle finger. Techonk cried out in pain as the blood spurted. Ordering an assistant to clean the hide, he washed his wound and prepared to daub it with honey.

The hulking Sardinian stood motionless, watching the scene. Techonk bowed to him.

"Excuse me for keeping you waiting . . . a foolish accident."

"Strange . . . I heard that you had a sure hand with the knife."

Techonk was trembling with fear. As the descendant of Libyan warriors, he should have been able to stare down any opponent. But Serramanna was an old pirate, a Sard, and colossal.

"Is there something I can do for you?"

"I need a wristband in your best leather. Wielding my hatchet, I've begun to feel a slight weakness lately."

"I can offer you a choice of several different models."

"I'm sure that you keep the best ones in your back room."

"No, I—"

"I told you I'm sure, Techonk. Let's go."

"Yes, I remember now."

Techonk was sweating like a pig. What had Serramanna found out? Nothing, he could know nothing. The Libyan must get hold of himself, not show signs of some completely unfounded fear. Egypt was a law-abiding country; the Sard would never dare use violence without legal repercussions.

The tanner led Serramanna into the cubbyhole where he kept the masterpieces he never intended to sell. Among them was a splendid red leather wristband.

"Are you trying to bribe me, Techonk?"

"Of course not!"

"A piece like this is fit for a king."

"You flatter me."

"You're a fine craftsman, Techonk. You've done well, with a large clientele, a promising future . . . What a shame!"

The Libyan blanched.

"I don't understand . . ."

"With everything going so well, why throw it all away?"

"Throw it away?" he echoed dumbly.

Serramanna ran his hand over a magnificent brown leather shield, suitable for a commanding general.

"I'm sorry to tell you, Techonk, but you may be in for some serious trouble."

"But why?"

"Do you recognize this piece?" asked the bodyguard, producing a leather tube serving as a scroll case. "It came from your workshop, didn't it?"

"Yes, but—"

"Yes or no?"

"All right, I admit it's my work."

"Who ordered it?"

"A priest at the main temple."

The Sard smiled. "You're an honest man, Techonk. I knew it."

"I have nothing to hide, sir!"

"Yet you made one serious mistake."

"What?"

"Using this case to deliver a subversive message."

The Libyan was short of breath. His tongue felt thick and his temples throbbed.

"It's . . . it's . . ." he choked.

"It got switched around somehow," Serramanna explained. "The priest was quite surprised to find it contained a document calling for all Libyans in Egypt to unite in an armed revolt against Ramses."

"No, no . . . it's impossible!"

"You admitted that this scroll case comes from your shop, Techonk. And you're the one who sent out the message."

"No, sir, I swear I wasn't!"

"I admire your work, Techonk. You should never have gotten mixed up in a plot that's too deep for you. At your age and in your situation, it's hard to fathom. What got into you?"

"Sir, I—"

"Don't make any false statements, or you'll suffer the

consequences in the next world. You've gone astray, Techonk, but I can believe you were manipulated. We all lose our bearings from time to time."

"It's all a misunderstanding, I—"

"Don't waste your breath, Techonk. My men have been monitoring you for the past several months. We know that your workshop shelters Libyan rebels."

"Not rebels, sir! Only men in trouble, who need a helping hand. Isn't that natural?"

"Don't downplay your role. Without you, no under-ground network could form."

"I'm an honest tradesman, I—"

"Let's get down to brass tacks, friend. I have evidence that can hang you, or at least get you life without parole. I only need to show this scroll to the vizier and he'll write out a warrant for your arrest. You'll have a well-publicized trial and a punishment to fit the crime."

"But I'm innocent!"

"That's what you say. But with hard evidence, the judges won't hesitate. You're trapped, Techonk . . . unless I decide to help you."

"What will make you decide?" gulped the tanner.

Serramanna stroked the leather shield.

"No matter what his position, every man has unfulfilled desires. I'm no exception. I earn a good living, my lodgings are more than adequate, I have all the women I want . . . but I'd like a nest egg, something for my old age. So you see, I could say nothing and suppress this evidence . . . but for a price, Techonk."

"How high?"

"Don't forget that I have to keep the priest in question quiet. A fair percentage of your profits would satisfy me."

"If we reach an agreement, will you leave me in peace?"

"I still have to do my job, friend."

"What do you want?"

"The name of the Libyans responsible for killing Ahsha."

"Sir, I have no idea!"

"Even if that's the truth, you can find out for me. Be my special investigator, Techonk, and you won't regret it."

"What if I can't get results?"

"That would be unfortunate . . . but I'm sure you'll find a way. In my official capacity, I'm here to place an order for a hundred shields and scabbards. When you come to the palace, ask for me."

Serramanna exited, leaving a bewildered Techonk behind. Ahmeni had convinced the Sard to pose as a man on the make, ready to betray his king for gold. If Techonk fell for the act, he'd be less afraid to talk and would lead Serramanna in the right direction.

TWENTY-FOUR

In this thirty-third year of the reign of Ramses the Great, the Theban winter, sometimes fraught with icy winds, turned out to be mild. A wide, cloudless blue sky. A peaceful Nile, its banks lush green from the summer floods.

Donkeys laden with forage trotting from one village to the next. Cows with milk-swollen udders driven to pasture by cowherds and dogs. Girls playing with dolls on the doorsteps of whitewashed houses while boys ran after a rag ball . . . Egypt moved to its eternal rhythm, as if nothing, ever, was bound to change.

Ramses savored this simple moment frozen in time. How right his ancestors had been to choose the West Bank for building their Temples of Millions of Years, to dig their houses of eternity, where each morning their astral bodies were born anew with the rising sun! Here the border between this world and the other side blurred, and human life was absorbed into mystery.

After celebrating the rites of dawn at the temple of Gurnah, where Seti's *ka* was preserved, Ramses prayed in the chapel. His father's soul was expressed in each hieroglyph carved into the walls. Deep in the silence, he sensed his father's voice, the voice of a pharaoh reborn as a star. As the Pharaoh made his way though the great courtyard, bathed in soft light, a procession of priestesses emerged from the hall of columns, singing and playing their instruments. The moment Meritamon spotted her father she broke away from the group, went to meet him, and bowed, crossing her arms over her chest.

She looked more like Nefertari every day. Clear as a spring morning, her beauty seemed to have fed on the temple's wisdom. Ramses took his daughter's arm and the two of them walked slowly down the avenue of sphinxes, lined with acacia and tamarisk trees.

"Do you keep abreast of events in the outside world?"

"No, Father; I know you're defending Ma'at, combating the forces of darkness and chaos. Isn't that all that matters? Rumors from the secular world never cross the temple walls, and rightly so."

"It's the life your mother would have chosen, if fate hadn't dictated otherwise."

"Weren't you the master of her fate?"

"Pharaoh's duty is to act in the world, although his innermost thoughts may remain with the temple. Today I must preserve the peace, Meritamon. To that end I plan to marry the daughter of Emperor Hattusili."

"Will she become Great Royal Wife?"

"She will, but I need to celebrate my second sed-feast before the wedding. Which leads me to a decision I cannot make without your consent."

"I have no desire to play a role in the government, as you well know."

"The sed-feast cannot take place without the active participation of a native-born Great Royal Wife. Would you consider acting as a stand-in?"

"Meaning I'd have to leave Thebes, go to Pi-Ramses, and what then?"

"Although you'd officially be Queen of Egypt, you could return here to the life you've chosen."

"I won't be called to a public life in the future?"

"I'll only ask for your help with my jubilees, which Kha plans to schedule every three or four years until the end of my lifetime. You're free to accept or refuse, Meritamon."

"Why me?"

"Because years of meditation have given you the spiritual and magical capacity to fulfill a demanding religious role."

Meritamon stood still, gazing back at the temple of Gurnah.

"You ask too much of me, Father, but you are Pharaoh."

Setau grumbled. Far from his beloved Nubia, a fabulous hunting ground for snakes, he felt exiled. Still, he had plenty to do. Lotus's nightly excursions into the countryside yielded fine specimens, and the venom he extracted from them by day had been the basis for many improved remedies, breathing new life into the royal laboratories. Also, acting on Ahmeni's advice, he was making good use of this stay in Pi-Ramses to hone his management skills. As he matured, Setau had been forced to admit that his enthusiasm was not enough to convince high officials to grant him the resources he needed for his little corner of Nubia. Without becoming a practiced courtier, he had grown more adept at presenting his requests, and the results were pleasing.

Leaving the office of the head of the merchant marine, who had agreed to earmark three new cargo ships for him, Setau encountered Kha, whose face looked less serene than usual.

"Problems?"

"Organizing this sed-feast requires almost constant attention . . . and I've just had some upsetting news. The inspector of temple supplies for the Delta, who should be able to supply me with most of the sandals, linen, and alabaster cups that we'll need, has almost nothing on hand. That throws off all my calculations."

"Has he offered you any explanation?"

"He's away on business; his wife is the one who wrote me."

"He doesn't take his job very seriously! I'm only a junior official, but I'd never act that way. Let's go ask Ahmeni about this."

Munching on a goose drumstick, absentmindedly dipping it in red wine sauce, Ahmeni perused the reports the inspector in question had sent from his headquarters north of Memphis.

Ramses' private secretary quickly reached a conclusion, and it was unequivocal.

"Something doesn't click. Kha was well within his rights to request extra supplies for the sed-feast, and according to my records the inspector should have no problem supplying his needs. I don't like the look of it . . . not at all."

"Could there be some mistake in the inspector's calculations?"

"Perhaps, but I checked them against my own books, and I know there's no mistake there."

"This may have an impact on the celebrations," confessed the high priest. "To welcome the gods and goddesses we need the finest temple linen available, the best sandals, the—"

"I'll call for an audit at once," announced Ahmeni.

"Just what a scribe would propose," railed Setau. "An audit will be long and complicated, and Kha has no time for that. Let's try something less official. Name me as your deputy and I'll clear this up in no time."

Ahmeni frowned. "We'd be stretching the law . . . And what if it's dangerous?"

"I have some reliable helpers. Let's not waste time talking. Write me my orders, Ahmeni."

Deep in the warehouse district north of Memphis, Dame Cheris was directing operations with the skill of a seasoned general. Small, dark, attractive, and strong-willed, she directed the mule drivers arriving with laden convoys, divided tasks among the packers, checked invoices, and waved her big stick in the face of anyone who dared cross her.

A woman of character, the kind that appealed to Setau.

With his disheveled hair, several days' growth of beard, and new antelope-skin tunic that was somehow even shabbier than the old one, Setau quickly caught her eye.

"No loitering here," she warned him.

"I'd like to speak with you."

"No time to talk. I have work to do."

"Your work is exactly what I was hoping we could discuss."

Dame Cheris flashed him a malicious grin. "Could it be that you don't like to see a woman running things?"

"No, I simply wonder whether you're credentialed to act in an official capacity."

Her dark eyes registered astonishment. A vagabond would never express himself in those terms.

"Who are you?"

"A deputy auditor named by the central government."

"Pardon me, but I had no idea, the way you're dressed . . ."

"My superiors disapprove, but they humor me because I get results."

"Speaking of credentials, would you mind showing me your written orders?"

"Here you are."

The papyrus bore all the necessary seals, including the vizier's stamp of approval.

Dame Cheris read and reread the text which gave this deputy auditor the right to examine the warehouses as he saw fit.

"In fact, my orders were to present this document to your husband."

"He's out of town."

"Shouldn't he be overseeing the operations?"

"His mother is very old, and she needed him."

"So you're filling in, I take it."

"I know the job and I do it well."

"A serious problem has arisen, Dame Cheris. You seem unable to supply the palace with the items required for the king's upcoming sed-feast."

"Well . . . the order was unexpected . . . and it's true that we're experiencing shortages."

"And how do you explain that?"

"I don't know all the details, but apparently there's been a large transfer of goods to a secondary site."

"What site is that?"

"I wasn't told."

"Who authorized the transfer?"

"I wouldn't know, but as soon as my husband is back he can answer all these questions to your satisfaction, I'm quite certain."

"Tomorrow morning I'll start examining your books and inspecting the warehouses."

"Tomorrow I'd planned a cleaning detail and—"

"Remember, Dame Cheris, I'm on a special mission. My superiors want a report as soon as possible. You're to give me free access to your books."

"You won't know where to begin!"

"I'll manage. See you tomorrow, Dame Cheris."

TWENTY-FIVE

Dame Cheris had no time to lose. Once again, her imbecile of a husband had overreacted to an official requisition. When he showed her a copy of his reply, she'd flown into a violent rage. Too late to intercept the courier . . . Cheris had promptly packed her husband off to a village south of Thebes, hoping the incident would blow over and the palace would fall back on other resources.

Unfortunately, the government reaction had been quite different. His bizarre appearance notwithstanding, this deputy auditor seemed determined and resolute. Cheris had momentarily considered trying to buy him off, but that was too risky. She'd have to activate her emergency plan.

At closing time she had four packers stay behind with her. Her losses would be major, but this was the only way to escape detection. Still, it would be hard to sacrifice the goods they'd so patiently misappropriated.

"We'll meet just past midnight," Cheris ordered her four strong men. "Go inside the building to the left of the main warehouse."

"It's always locked," objected one of the packers.

"I'll unlock it for you. You'll transfer the contents to the main warehouse—fast as you can, and without a sound."

"It's outside regular hours, Mistress."

"That's why I'm offering an extra week's pay for this one night of work. And a bonus besides, if you do a good job."

Broad smiles spread over the four men's faces.

"After tonight, you'll forget about what you did here. Do we understand each other?"

The threat in Cheris's sharp voice was barely veiled.

"Understood, Mistress."

The warehouse district was deserted. At regular intervals, policemen patrolled the area with guard dogs.

The four packers hid inside a large building where sledges used to haul heavy goods were stored. After a meal of beer and fresh bread, they slept in shifts.

When the night was darkest, Dame Cheris's imperious whisper sounded.

"Come on."

She had pulled the wooden bolts and broken the dried-mud seals barring entry to the building where her husband supposedly stored copper for use in temple workshops. Without asking questions, the packers removed a hundred jars of top-quality wine, four hundred fifty lengths of finest linen, six hundred pairs of leather sandals, a number of disassembled chariots, thirteen small chunks of iron ore, three hundred rolls of wool, and a hundred alabaster cups.

Just as the packers were loading the last of the contraband, Setau popped out of a dark corner where he had been watching the drama unfold.

"Nice try, Dame Cheris," he said coolly. "You've put back everything that you and your husband stole from the government. Nice try, but it's too late."

The small dark woman kept her head. "What are you demanding in exchange for your silence?"

"The names of your fences. We want to know who's redistributing temple goods."

"It's not important."

"Talk, Dame Cheris."

"You won't take a cut?"

"It's not my style."

"Too bad you're all alone, and I have four helpers."

"Don't worry, I've brought a partner."

Lotus was suddenly framed in the warehouse doorway. Bare-breasted, a brief papyrus kilt covering her slim hips, she held a reed basket with a leather lid.

Dame Cheris felt like laughing. "Some help she'll be!" she said acidly.

"Call off your henchmen," Setau said calmly.

"Seize these two," Dame Cheris curtly told the burly packers.

Lotus set the basket down and opened it. Out slithered four highly excited puff adders, easily identified by the three blue and green bands on their necks. Their exhalation produced a terrifying hiss.

Scrambling over the bolts of cloth, the four packers made a hasty getaway.

The vipers surrounded Dame Cheris, who was looking green herself.

"You'd better talk," advised Setau. "The venom from these snakes is highly toxic. It might not kill you, but the internal damage would be irreversible."

"I'll tell you everything," promised the small brunette.

"Whose idea was it to misappropriate temple property?"

"My . . . my husband's."

"Is that the whole truth?"

"All right. My husband's and mine."

"How long has this been going on?"

"A little over two years. If this new sed-feast hadn't come up with all its special demands, no one would ever have noticed."

"You must have had to pay off the temple scribes."

"Nothing that complicated. My husband kept two sets of books, we sold the goods in lots of varying sizes, according to how things came in. The shipment I was just preparing was quite a large one."

"Who's your buyer?"

"A merchant captain."

"His name?"

"I'm not sure."

"Describe him, then."

"Tall, bearded, brown eyes, a scar on his left forearm."

"Is he the one who pays you?"

"Yes, with gemstones and a little gold."

"When were you due to make the transfer?"

"The day after tomorrow."

"Well then," concluded Setau with a grin, "we'll have the pleasure of making his acquaintance."

The barge made its landing after an uneventful day on the river. It was hauling huge terra-cotta jars that kept drinking water fresh for an entire year, thanks to a trade secret known only to middle Egypt's potters. But on this barge the jars were empty, for the captain would be using them to stash the contraband he received from Dame Cheris.

The captain had made his career in the merchant marine,

and his fellow officers considered him highly professional. No serious accident to mar his record, no mutinous crews, a reputation for on-time deliveries . . . But he kept a string of mistresses, and his expenses had grown much faster than his income. After some hesitation, he had agreed to move stolen goods. His share of the traffic allowed him to live on the grand scale he craved.

Dame Cheris was as well organized as he was. As usual, the cargo would be ready and waiting, the transfer from warehouse to barge would be swift and smooth. No one would take any notice, especially since the crates and baskets were labeled as foodstuffs.

Before the goods were loaded, however, he would be subjected to stiff negotiations. He was squeezed between Cheris's escalating demands and his client's attempts to pay less each time. The discussions could take hours, but eventually they would come to terms.

The captain headed for Cheris's official residence. According to their agreement, she waved to him from her balcony, the all-clear signal.

The captain strode through the courtyard and entered a salon with two blue-painted columns and padded benches along the walls.

Dame Cheris's light footsteps sounded on the stairs. Following her was a gorgeous Nubian woman.

"But . . . who's this with you?"

"Don't turn around, Captain," said Setau's husky voice. "There's a cobra at your back."

"It's true," confirmed Dame Cheris.

"Who the hell are you?" asked the captain.

"The Pharaoh's deputy. My mission is to put a stop to your illegal dealings. But I also need to find out who your boss is."

The old sailor felt trapped in a nightmare. His world was crashing down around him.

"Tell me who's in charge," insisted Setau.

The captain knew what consequences were facing him. He'd bring the ringleader down as well.

"I only met him once."

"Did you know his name?"

"Yes . . . He's called Ahmeni."

Dumbfounded, Setau took a few steps and halted in front of the captain.

"Describe him!"

Finally the captain got a good look at his inquisitor. He'd bet this deputy was the only snake around! Convinced that the reptile was an invention, he turned and bolted.

The snake uncoiled and bit him in the neck. The pain and shock sent the captain tumbling to the ground in a heap.

Her way now clear, Dame Cheris ran into the courtyard.

"No!" yelled Lotus as the second cobra, a female, struck the pretty little woman in the back as she ran through her doorway. Breathless, her heart in a vise, Dame Cheris crawled a short distance, clawing the ground, then went still. The reptile went slinking back to its mate.

"There's no way to save them," said Lotus regretfully.

"They robbed their country," Setau reminded her. "And they'll be judged harshly in the afterworld."

Setau sat down, head in his hands. "But Ahmeni mixed up in this business? I can't believe it."

TWENTY-SIX

Emperor Hattusili's latest letter was a masterpiece of diplomacy. Ramses had read it carefully a good ten times and still couldn't tell what Hattusili was saying. Did he want war or peace? Would he still have his daughter marry Ramses, or was he cloaked in outraged dignity?

"What do you make of this, Ahmeni?"

The king's official sandal-bearer and private secretary looked thinner than ever, despite the quantities of food he consumed throughout the day. After an in-depth consultation, Neferet the chief physician had given Ahmeni a clean bill of health but advised him to reduce his workload.

"We need Ahsha here. He would have known what to make of this convoluted prose."

"But what do you think?"

"Although I'm usually inclined to be pessimistic, I have the feeling that Hattusili is giving you an opening. Your sed-feast begins tomorrow; magic will give you the final answer."

"I'll be glad to spend some time with the assembled gods and goddesses."

"Kha has done a magnificent job," appraised Ahmeni. "Everything will be in place. Have you heard how Setau caught the thieves that were skimming temple goods? The recovered items are already in Pi-Ramses."

"And the culprits?"

"They met an accidental death. The case will be submitted to the vizier's tribunal, with a probable sentence of obliteration of the guilty parties' names."

"I'm retiring now until dawn."

"May your *ka* be with you, Majesty, so that your light may shine upon Egypt."

At summer's end, the night was clear and warm. Like most of his compatriots, Ramses had decided to sleep beneath the stars, on the terraced roof of the palace. Lying on a simple reed mat, he contemplated the sky, where the souls of pharaohs who had passed into light now sparkled. The axis of the universe passed through the pole star; the immortals clustered around it, beyond time and space. Since the era of the pyramids, the wisdom of the sages had been written in the sky.

At the age of fifty-five, after thirty-three years on the throne of Egypt, Ramses halted the flow of hours to ponder his actions. Until now he had never stopped moving forward, overcoming all obstacles, refusing to concede that anything was impossible. Although his energy was undiminished, he no longer faced the world like a ram with his horns down, barreling full speed ahead. Reigning over Egypt did not mean imposing one man's will, but rather infusing the law of Ma'at with new life, with Pharaoh as her first servant. The young Ramses had hoped to forge ahead with an entire society in tow, changing hearts and minds, delivering Egypt forever from pettiness and baseness. As he grew more experienced, the dream had faded. Humans would always be what they were, enmeshed in falsehood and evil; no doctrine, no religion, no government could change their nature. Only the practice of justice and the continual application of the law of Ma'at kept chaos at bay.

All that his father, Seti, had taught him, Ramses had endeavored to uphold. His desire to be a great pharaoh, to set his seal on the destiny of the Two Lands, no longer counted. Having lived the most fortunate of lives, having climbed to the pinnacle of power, he had only one remaining ambition: to serve.

Setau was drunk, yet kept on swilling strong oasis wine. He stumbled angrily around the bedchamber.

"Don't go to sleep, Lotus! This is no time to rest. We need to think and decide."

"You've been saying the same thing for hours now."

"Yes, and you ought to listen. You and I know the truth. We know that Ahmeni is a sellout, totally corrupt. I hate the little scribe, I'd like to see him boil in the cauldrons of the destroyers of souls . . . But he's my friend, he's Ramses' friend. As long as you and I keep quiet, he won't stand trial for his crimes."

"Do you think Dame Cheris's operation could have some connection to a plot against Ramses?"

"We need to think and decide . . . If I go see the king . . . no, I can't. It's the eve of his sed-feast. I can't spoil his jubilee. If I go see the vizier . . . he'll arrest Ahmeni! And you're no help!"

"Get some sleep. You'll think better if you're rested."

"We don't just need to think, we need to decide! How

can we decide if we're asleep? Oh, Ahmeni . . . what have you done, Ahmeni?"

"The right question at last," Lotus said dryly.

Stiff as a statue, despite his trembling hands, Setau stared at his lovely wife.

"What do you mean by that?"

"Before you give up sleep for good, ask yourself what Ahmeni has actually done."

"It couldn't be clearer, since the barge captain gave us his name. Someone's been skimming temple goods in the Delta, and that someone is Ahmeni. My friend Ahmeni."

Serramanna was sleeping alone. At the end of an exhausting day, putting the various elements of his sed-feast security detail in place around the main temple, he had sunk into bed without a thought for the delectable body of his latest mistress, a Syrian girl who was supple as a reed.

Shouts wrenched him from a deep sleep.

The hulking Sard shook and stretched like an animal, then ran into the hall, where his steward was tussling with a visibly tipsy Setau.

"We have to investigate, right away!"

Serramanna pulled the steward aside, grabbed Setau by the collar of his tunic, dragged him into the bedchamber, and poured a jug of cool water over his head.

"What the . . ."

"It's only water. Must be a while since you've tried any."

Setau plopped onto the bed. "I need you," he told the Sard.

"Don't tell me your godforsaken snakes claimed another victim."

"No, we have to investigate."

"Investigate what?"

"Ahmeni's finances," Setau finally blurted out.

"Excuse me?"

"Ahmeni has a hidden fortune."

"What have you been drinking, Setau? It's worse than snake venom."

"Ahmeni has been dealing in stolen goods. And it may even be worse! Suppose his activities threaten Ramses?"

"Explain what you mean, man."

Disjointedly, but omitting no vital detail, Setau related how he and Lotus had uncovered Dame Cheris's skimming operation.

"And you believe a bandit like that barge captain?" Serramanna said at length. "Under pressure, he might have picked a name at random."

"He seemed honest," objected Setau.

Serramanna was stunned. "Ahmeni . . . the last one I'd ever suspect of betraying king and country."

"You mean you would have suspected me first?"

"Don't tell me I've hurt your feelings! It's Ahmeni's integrity we're questioning."

"We need to investigate."

"Investigate! That's easy for you to say. During the sed-feast there are heightened security demands. And Ahmeni has a finger in everything. If he *has* done anything dishonest, and figures out that we know, he'll cover his tracks. Did you think we could accuse him without solid proof?"

Setau buried his head in his hands. "Lotus and I were witnesses. The barge captain gave only one name."

It made Serramanna's stomach turn to think that Ahmeni, the most faithful of faithful servants, might be just another corrupt official. If so, there was no hope for human nature. The worst part was the possibility that Ahmeni could be involved in a plot against Ramses. Were his hidden riches arming the Pharaoh's opponents?

"Maybe I'm drunk," admitted Setau, "but I've told you everything. Now three of us know about it."

"I wish I didn't."

"What will we do, Serramanna?"

"Ahmeni has rooms in the palace, but he almost always sleeps in his office. We'll have to lure him out and conduct a careful search. If he's hoarding gold or gemstones, we'll find them. We'll put a tail on him and note the identity of all his callers. He must be in contact with the other members of his network. Let's hope that none of my men slip up. If the vizier's police get wind of this, I'll be in serious trouble."

"We have to think of Ramses, Serramanna."

"Who else would I be thinking of, Setau?"

TWENTY-SEVEN

All of Egypt prayed for Ramses that morning. After such a long reign, how well would he absorb the formidable energy that emanated from the gathering of gods and goddesses? If his physical body were no longer in a state to serve as a receptacle for the *ka*, or spiritual essence, it could be broken like an over-fragile container. The fire of Ramses' reign would meld with the celestial fire, while his mummy returned to the earth. On the other hand, if the king's regeneration was successful, new blood would circulate in the country's veins.

At the Temple of Regeneration in Pi-Ramses, Kha had assembled the statues of the divinities arriving from both the northern and southern provinces. For the duration of the feast Pharaoh would lodge among them, isolated from the outside world.

Dressing at dawn, Ramses thought about Ahmeni. How endless these days must seem to his longtime secretary! All during the sed-feast he was kept from consulting with the king, and any number of matters he considered urgent would have to be tabled. According to Ahmeni, Egypt was never run well enough and no official took his role as seriously as he should.

Crowned with the traditional twin headdress, wearing a tucked linen robe, gilded kilt, and golden sandals, Ramses appeared in the palace doorway.

Two royal sons bowed low to the monarch. Wearing sectioned wigs with side panels and long shirts with billowing sleeves, they carried poles topped with carvings of a ram, one of the incarnations of Amon, the hidden god.

Slowly the two standard-bearers preceded Pharaoh to the towering granite portal of the Temple of Regeneration. In front of it stood obelisks and colossal statues symbolizing the royal *ka*, like their counterparts at Abu Simbel. The original plans for Pi-Ramses, conceived in Year Two of Ramses' reign, had left room for this temple, as if the king sensed he would remain on the throne for more than thirty years.

Two priests in jackal masks greeted the monarch. One of

these procession leaders opened the way to the south, the other to the north. They guided Ramses through the hall of tall columns, toward the vestry, where the king stripped and donned a short, shroudlike linen tunic. In his left hand he held his shepherd's crook; in his right hand was the three-pronged scepter, representing Pharaoh's three births, in the underworld, on earth, and in the heavens.

Ramses had already undergone many a physical test, from facing down a wild bull to single-handedly battling thousands of frenzied Hittites at Kadesh; yet the sed-feast was a more intense kind of combat, where invisible forces came into play. The self must die, returning to the uncreated matter from which it had issued. Ramses must be reborn in the love of the gods and goddesses. He must succeed himself. This act of alchemy would forge an inalterable bond between his symbolic person and his people, between his people and the divine powers assembled within him.

The two priests in jackal masks again guided the sovereign to a large open-air courtyard, like Pharaoh Djoser's at Saqqara. This was the work of Kha, such an admirer of ancient architecture that he had commissioned the replica within Ramses' Temple of Regeneration.

She was walking toward him.

Meritamon, the only daughter of Nefertari, now became Nefertari herself, reborn to give Ramses rebirth. A long white robe, understated gold collar, headdress with two tall plumes symbolizing Life and the law. She was dazzling, the Great Royal Wife. She took her place behind him, where at every stage of the ritual she would protect him with the magic of litany and song.

Kha lit the flame that illuminated the divine statues, the chapels in which they stood, and the royal throne upon which Ramses would sit if he emerged victorious. The high priest would be assisted by the great council of upper and lower Egypt, whose members included Setau, Ahmeni, the high priest of Karnak, the chief physician of the realm Neferet, and a number of royal sons and daughters. Setau, sobered up, was no longer obsessed with investigating Ahmeni. All that mattered was the ritual that must be perfectly staged to renew Ramses' vital powers.

The great dignitaries of upper and lower Egypt prostrated themselves before Pharaoh. Then Setau and Ahmeni, in their role as the king's "sole companions," washed his feet. Thus purified, his feet would take him through space, water, earth, or fire. The water jug used in the ritual was in the shape of the hieroglyph *sema*, depicting the cardiopulmonary juncture and signifying "unity." This sanctified water made Pharaoh a coherent being, the unifier of his people.

Kha had organized everything so well that the days and nights of the festival flew by like a single hour.

Forced to walk slowly in his form-fitting tunic, Ramses activated the offerings of food that lay on the chapel altars. His gaze and the holy words "Pharaoh gives this" released the foods' spiritual gifts. The queen, in her symbolic role as celestial cow, was supposed to feed the king on milk from the stars, ridding his body of weakness and disease.

Ramses worshiped each divine power, preserving the multiplicity of creative impulses flowing into him. Thus he drew precisely on the inalterable unity concealed within each statue, at the same time giving them magical life.

For three days it was one procession, litany, and offering

after another in the great courtyard. Short stairways led to the radiating chapels that sheltered the gods and goddesses, defining the sacred space and diffusing their energy. By turns lively or contemplative, the music of tambourines, harps, lutes, and horns accompanied the various parts of the ritual set out in the scroll that the celebrant priest unrolled.

Assimilating divine energy, exchanging dialogue with the bull Apis and the crocodile Sobek, wielding a harpoon to keep the hippopotamus at bay, Pharaoh forged links between the great beyond and the people of Egypt. The king's actions rendered the visible invisible, building a harmonious relationship between man and nature.

A platform had been raised in an outlying courtyard; here sat three adjoining thrones. To reach them Ramses had to go up several steps. When he sat on the throne of upper Egypt, he wore the white crown; for lower Egypt, the crown was red. And one aspect or another of the royal person, a duality in motion, enacted each phase of the ritual. It was an apparent contradiction in terms, resolved in the oneness of Pharaoh. Thus the Two Lands were one, yet remained distinct. Seated alternately on the two thrones, Ramses became either Horus, with his piercing gaze, or the almighty Set, with a third identity of his own that reconciled the two warring brothers.

On the next-to-last day of the festival, the king shed his white tunic to don the traditional kilt worn by pharaohs since the days of the pyramids. A bull's tail hung from the waistband. The time had come to ascertain that the reigning pharaoh had correctly assimilated the divine energy and could now take possession of the earth and sky.

After acting out the drama of the two warring brothers, Horus and Set, Pharaoh was prepared to receive anew the

Testament of the Gods, making him the rightful heir of Egypt. When Ramses' fingers closed around the small leather swallowtail case containing the invaluable document, everyone's heart skipped a beat. Would a human hand, even that of the Lord of the Two Lands, be strong enough to take hold of a supernatural object?

Firmly gripping the Testament of the Gods, Ramses next laid his hand on a rudder, representing his ability to steer the ship of state in the right direction. Then he strode boldly across the great courtyard, equating it with Egypt as a whole, the image of earth and sky. The king completed the ritual circuit eight times in all—four each as lord of upper and lower Egypt. Pharaoh's footsteps transfigured the Two Lands' provinces, affirming the reign of the gods and the presence of the celestial hierarchy. Through him, all past pharaohs were restored to life, and Egypt was rededicated to the divine.

"I have gone the course," proclaimed Ramses. "I have held the Testament of the Gods in my hand. I have traversed the earth and touched its four corners. I have covered it according to my heart. I have gone the course, crossing the ocean of origins. I have touched the four sides of heaven. I have gone as far as light and have offered the fertile earth to her queen, the law of Life."

This final day of the sed-feast was a time of celebration in towns and villages. The word was out that Ramses had triumphed; his reign would be full of new energy. Yet the feasting could not begin until the rejuvenated monarch displayed the Testament of the Gods to his people.

At dawn, the Pharaoh mounted a sedan chair borne by his highest officials. Hard as it was on Ahmeni's back, he insisted on taking part. Ramses was carried to the four points of the compass, and at each he drew his bow and shot an arrow to proclaim Pharaoh's continuing reign to the entire universe.

Then he mounted a throne, the underside of which was decorated with a dozen lion's heads, and addressed the directions of space, announcing that the law of Ma'at would reduce the forces of evil to silence.

Crowned anew, Ramses paid homage to his ancestors. Those who had gone before, opening the doors to the invisible, were the base on which the monarchy rested. Even Setau, who prided himself on being strong, could not hold back his tears. Never had Ramses been so great, never had Pharaoh so thoroughly embodied the light of Egypt.

The king left the great courtyard where time had been abolished. He crossed the hall of columns and climbed the stairs leading to the top of the monumental gateway. Appearing between the pylon's two tall towers, like the sun at its height, he showed the Testament of the Gods to his people.

A ringing cry rose from the crowd. By acclamation, Ramses was recognized as fit to govern; his words would be life, his deeds would join earth to heaven. The Nile would be life-giving, reaching into the valleys, depositing fertile silt on the fields, providing clean water and abundant fish. The gods' blessing made glad the hearts of all the king's subjects. Thanks to him, food would be plentiful as grains of sand on the banks of the Nile. And so it was said of Ramses the Great that he shaped the country's prosperity like dough in his own hands.

TWENTY-EIGHT

Two months and a day.
A stormy day, after two months of discreet and painstaking investigation. Serramanna had not skimped on manpower: he had used his best operatives, experienced mercenaries, to tail Ahmeni and search his rooms without attracting attention. The Sard had warned them that if they were caught, they were on their own; if they implicated him, he'd strangle them with his own hands. Bonuses were also promised, in the form of additional leave days and special rations.

Keeping Ahmeni away from his office for any length of time proved difficult. A last-minute inspection tour of the Faiyum gave Serramanna the break he needed, but the search yielded nothing. The scribe's nearly unoccupied rooms, the storage chests and shelves in his office, even his library, concealed nothing suspicious. Ahmeni continued to work night and day, eat copiously, and sleep little. As for his callers, they were all upper-level government officials, summoned as needed to go over their accounts and prime their enthusiasm for public service.

Listening to the Sard's negative results, Setau wondered if he might have been dreaming; yet both he and Lotus had clearly heard the barge captain name Ahmeni. It was impossible to erase the blot on his memory.

Serramanna was ready to call off the investigation. His men were on edge and likely to commit some blunder before long.

But on that stormy day the old pirate's worst fears were confirmed. Just after noon, when Ahmeni was alone in his office, the king's sandal-bearer had a highly unusual visitor: a rough-looking character with one good eye and a bushy beard.

Serramanna's operative trailed him to the Pi-Ramses harbor and had no trouble identifying the man as a barge captain.

"Are you sure?" Setau asked Serramanna.

"The fellow sailed south with a shipment of jars. The conclusion is obvious."

Ahmeni was fronting a gang of thieves. Ahmeni, who knew his way around the government better than anyone, was using that knowledge for his personal profit. And that might not be the worst of it . . .

"Ahmeni took his time," noted the Sard, "but he finally had to make contact with one of his men."

"I still don't want to believe it."

"Sorry, Setau. Now I'll have to tell Ramses what I've found out."

"Forget your grievances," Emperor Hattusili wrote to the Pharaoh of Egypt. *"Stay your sword arm; permit us to breathe. In truth, you are the son of the god Set! He promised you the land of the*

Hittites, and they will bring you all that you desire in tribute. Are they not at your feet?"

Ramses showed the tablet to Ahmeni.

"Read it yourself . . . a surprising change of tone!"

"The peace faction must have won out, with Puduhepa leading the way. Your Majesty, all you need do now is write an official proposal for a Hittite princess to become Queen of Egypt."

"Compose a flattering letter and I'll set my seal on it. Ahsha didn't die in vain; this diplomatic coup will be his crowning achievement."

"I'll run to my office and write you the letter."

"No, Ahmeni, do it here. Sit on my chair and use what's left of the daylight."

"Me, sit in Pharaoh's chair? Never!"

"Afraid?"

"Of course I am! Lightning has struck men for presuming less."

"Let's go up on the roof terrace."

"But the letter . . ."

"It can wait."

The view was spellbinding. Ramses' capital, magnificent and tranquil, was settling down for the night.

"The peace we so desire is right before our eyes, don't you think, Ahmeni? We should savor it like a rare fruit, enjoying each precious moment. Yet men only seem to want to upset the balance, as if harmony were more than they can stand. Why, Ahmeni?"

"I don't know, Your Majesty," he said in a faltering voice.

"Haven't you ever asked yourself the question?"

"I've never had time. And I have Pharaoh to answer my questions."

"Serramanna spoke to me," revealed Ramses.

"What about?"

"A visitor to your office."

Ahmeni seemed unperturbed. "Who would that be?"

"Can't you tell me?"

The scribe reflected for a few seconds. "He must mean the barge captain who showed up unannounced and forced his way into my office. Certainly not the sort of person I usually see! He rambled on about dock workers and late shipments . . . I had to call a guard to get rid of him."

"Was that the first time you'd seen him?"

"Yes, and the last! But why all these questions?"

Ramses' gaze became as penetrating as Set, the storm god's. His eyes blazed, piercing the dusk.

"Have you ever lied to me, Ahmeni?"

"Never, Your Majesty. And I never will. I swear it on the life of Pharaoh!"

For a few endless seconds, Ahmeni stopped breathing. He knew that Ramses was judging him and was about to hand down his verdict.

"I trust you, Ahmeni."

"Why have they been watching me?"

"You were accused of skimming goods from the temple warehouses so that you could amass a private fortune."

"What would I want with a fortune?"

"We have work to do. Peace seems to be within our reach, but we still should convene a war council without delay."

Setau threw his arms around Ahmeni while Serramanna mumbled excuses.

"What a relief, if Pharaoh pronounced you innocent!"

"But you two thought I was guilty?" asked the scribe, wide-eyed, as Ramses stood quietly observing the scene.

"I admit I believed the worst," said Setau. "But I was only thinking of Ramses' safety."

"In that case," judged Ahmeni, "you did right. And if you ever have cause to doubt me again, do the same. Safeguarding Pharaoh is our most pressing duty."

"Someone tried to discredit Ahmeni in His Majesty's eyes," Serramanna pointed out. "Someone whose tidy little operation Setau broke up."

"I want to hear all about it," Ahmeni said resolutely.

Setau and Serramanna filled him in on the episode.

"The real head of this fencing operation used my name," concluded the scribe. "He lied to that barge captain who got on the wrong side of Setau's snake. Someone planned to cast doubt on my integrity and my work. All it took was sending another barge captain to my office, and you were convinced of my guilt. With me out of the way, the administration would be in a state of flux."

Ramses suddenly came to life. "Slinging mud at my closest advisers is an insult to my country's government. Someone is trying to undermine Egypt just as we've reached a turning point with Hatti. It's not a simple case of thievery, even on a large scale. It's a deeper corruption that has to be stopped at once."

"Let's find that sailor who came to see me," Ahmeni suggested.

"I'll get right on it," said Serramanna. "The fellow will lead us straight to the ringleader."

"I'll do whatever I can to help Serramanna," proposed Setau. "I think I owe it to Ahmeni."

"Just watch your step," cautioned Ramses. "I want the real head of the operation."

"What if it turns out to be Uri-Teshoop?" proposed the Sard. "If you ask me, he's out for revenge."

"It can't be," objected Ahmeni. "He wouldn't have the inside knowledge of how goods are distributed to the temples."

Could it be that Uri-Teshoop was trying to prevent Ramses' marrying Hattusili's daughter? It was one way to get back at the uncle who'd thrust him from power . . . The king considered the merits of his bodyguard's theory.

"It could be someone who's in league with Uri-Teshoop," insisted Serramanna.

"Enough discussion," Ramses said bluntly. "Let's stop wasting time and get to the bottom of this. Ahmeni, I'm assigning you new offices in the palace annex."

"But why?"

"Because you're officially under investigation for corruption. We want our ringleader to believe that everything went as planned."

TWENTY-NINE

A strong, icy wind buffeted the ramparts of Hattusa, the fortified capital city of the Hittite empire. On the high Anatolian plateau, fall had abruptly turned to winter.

Torrential rains left the roads muddy and interrupted trade. Emperor Hattusili, feeling the cold, huddled by the fire sipping mulled wine.

The letter he'd just received from Ramses had made him very glad. Never again would Hatti and Egypt be at war. Although a show of force was sometimes necessary, Hattusili preferred diplomacy. Hatti was an aging empire, suffering battle fatigue. Since Hattusili had reached an agreement with Ramses, the people had become accustomed to peace.

Finally, Puduhepa was back. The empress had spent several hours in the Storm God's temple, consulting the oracles. Majestic and striking, the high priestess was respected as a leader, even among the generals.

"What news?" inquired Hattusili nervously.

"Nothing good. The storms will only get worse, with the temperature dropping."

"Well, I have some wonderful news for you!" The emperor waved the papyrus from Pi-Ramses.

"Has Ramses given his final consent?"

"His daughter took the symbolic role of Great Royal Wife to help him through the regeneration rituals. Now that the jubilee is over, our dear brother the Pharaoh of Egypt has agreed to marry our daughter. A Hittite as Lady of the Two Lands . . . I never thought I'd see the day."

Puduhepa smiled. "It's only because you backed down to Ramses."

"On your advice, my dear . . . your sage advice. Words are of no importance; achieving our ultimate goal is all that matters."

"Unfortunately, the weather is against us."

"It's bound to improve."

"The omens are dubious."

"If we delay sending our daughter, Ramses will think it's a trick."

"What are we to do, Hattusili?"

"Tell him the truth and request his help. Egyptian magic is second to none; we can use it to tame the elements and send our daughter on her way. Why don't we sit down now and write to our dear brother?"

His face stern and angular as ever, head shaved, and gait sometimes stiff from aching joints, Kha roamed the immense necropolis of Saqqara, where he felt more at ease than in the land of the living. As the high priest of Ptah, Ramses' elder son rarely left the ancient city of Memphis. Yet the pyramids fascinated him, and he spent long hours contemplating the three stone giants on the Giza plateau—the pyramids built by Khufu, Khephren, and Menkauré. When the sun reached its zenith, their white limestone flanks reflected the light, illuminating the funerary temples, the gardens, and the desert. The pyramids represented the primordial stone emerging from the original ocean at the dawn of time; they were also petrified rays of sunshine containing changeless energy. And Kha had plumbed one of their truths: each pyramid was a letter in the great book of wisdom that he was seeking in the country's archives.

Yet something was troubling the high priest of Memphis. Near the Pharaoh Djoser's great architectural complex, dominated by the step pyramid, stood the pyramid of Wenis, badly in need of restoration. Dating from the end of the Fifth Dynasty and already more than a thousand years old, the venerable monument had suffered serious wounds. Several ornamental blocks must soon be replaced.

Here, in Saqqara, High Priest Kha communed with the souls of the ancestors. Lingering in the chapels of their eternal dwellings, he deciphered the columns of hieroglyphs that dealt with the afterlife and the happy destiny of those who possessed a "just voice," having lived a life according to the law of Ma'at. In the act of reading these inscriptions, Kha restored life to the tombs' occupants, who remained present on a silent plane.

The high priest of Ptah was walking the perimeter of Wenis's pyramid when he spied his father coming toward him. It struck him that Ramses resembled one of those luminous spirits that appeared to clairvoyants at certain hours of the day.

"What are your plans here, Kha?"

"In the short term, stepping up restoration on the Old Kingdom pyramids most in need of repair."

"Have you found the Book of Thoth?"

"Only hints of it . . . but I won't give up. There are so many treasures in Saqqara that I'll need a long life to study them."

"You're only thirty-eight; they say the sage Ptah-hotep waited until the age of a hundred and ten before writing his Maxims!"

"In this holy place, Father, eternity has fed on human time and transformed it into living stone. These chapels, these hieroglyphs, these entities that venerate the secret of life . . . is this not the best our civilization has to offer?"

"Do your thoughts ever turn to affairs of state, my son?"

"Why should they, when you're here to reign?"

"The years are passing, Kha, and one day I too will go to the land that loves silence."

"Your Majesty's *ka* has just been regenerated, and I plan to do even better for your next sed-feast three years hence."

"You know nothing about the government, the economy, the army . . ."

"I have no taste for such subjects. The strict observance of ritual is the true foundation of our society, don't you agree? Our people's happiness depends on it, and with each passing day I intend to devote myself more fully to my religious duties. Do you think I'm heading in the wrong direction?"

Ramses raised his eyes to the top of Wenis's pyramid.

"Seeking the highest, the most vital, is always the right direction. But Pharaoh must also descend into the underworld and confront the monster that tries to dry up the Nile and destroy the bark of light. Without Pharaoh waging this daily battle, what rites would we have left to celebrate?"

Kha stroked the ancient stone, as if it nourished his thoughts.

"How best, then, can I serve Pharaoh?"

"The Emperor of Hatti wishes to send his daughter to Egypt as my bride. In their part of the world, the weather has made it impossible for the delegation to leave. Hattusili requests that our magicians incite the gods to improve conditions. What you can do is find me the text that will let us do precisely that."

The barge captain, Rarek, had found a hideout where no one would ever track him. Following his performance at the palace, spouting gibberish at some pale-faced scribe, Rarek had taken up residence in Pi-Ramses' Asian quarter. It was what the man who hired him had advised. Somewhat inconvenient, but still, the job paid well, better than three months' sailing on the Nile. Rarek had reported back to his boss, who seemed more than satisfied. Everything had gone as planned, it seemed. The only drawback was that now the boss wanted Rarek to shave. He was proud of his manly beard, and tried to protest, but since his personal safety was at stake, he relented. Clean-shaven and under another name, he soon would sail south once more and remain out of sight.

Rarek spent his days sleeping on the upper floor of a small white house. His landlady roused him when the water bearer came by. She also brought him the onion- and garlic-filled pastries that were his favorite food.

"The barber's out in the square," she announced on this morning.

The sailor yawned. Without his beard he might have trouble attracting women. Fortunately he still had other masculine attributes that were just as convincing.

Rarek looked out the window.

In the little square below, the barber had pounded in four stakes that held an awning to protect his customers from the sun. Beneath the shelter he set two stools, a taller one for himself, a shorter one for his client.

With ten or so men already in line, the wait would be long. Three of them were playing dice, the others dozing against a house front. Rarek decided to take a nap.

His landlady shook him.

"You'd better get down there! You'll be the last."

This time there was no escaping. Bleary-eyed, he went downstairs and out of the little house to take his place on the three-legged stool that groaned beneath his weight.

"What will it be?" asked the barber.

"Take the whole thing off."

"Why would you want to shave such a beautiful beard?"

"None of your business."

"It's your call, friend. How are you paying?"

"With a pair of sandals and a papyrus scroll."

"It's a big job . . ."

"If you don't want it, I'll go somewhere else."

"All right, all right . . ."

The barber moistened Rarek's skin with soapy water and tested the razor's sharpness on his left cheek. Swiftly and suddenly, he held the blade to the sailor's neck.

"If you try to run, if you lie, Rarek, I'll slit your throat."

"Who . . . who are you?"

Setau let the razor slice the skin, dripping blood on the sailor's chest.

"Someone who'll kill you unless you talk."

"Ask me anything!"

"Ever meet a barge captain with brown eyes and a deep scar on his left forearm?"

"Yes . . ."

"Do you know Dame Cheris?"

"I've worked for her."

"Fencing stolen goods?"

"We've done business."

"Who's your boss?"

"His name is Ahmeni."

"You're going to take me to him."

THIRTY

A slight smile lighting his grave face, Kha appeared before Ramses, seated at his desk.

"I spent three days and three nights in the library at the House of Life in Heliopolis, Your Majesty, and I found the book of spells that will stop the bad weather over Hatti. The goddess Sekhmet's messengers have caused disturbances in the atmosphere to keep the sun from piercing the clouds."

"What's the procedure?"

"Reciting litanies nonstop until they have an effect on Sekhmet. Once she calls her emissaries back from the north, the skies will clear. Her priests and priestesses are already at work. The vibration from the chanting and the invisible effect of the rituals should bring a rapid resolution."

Kha withdrew just as Merenptah came running in. The two brothers greeted each other warmly.

The king observed his sons, so different yet so complementary. In his own way, Ramses mused, Kha had acted just like a statesman. He was high-minded enough to govern, while Merenptah had the strength necessary to command. As for their half sister, she would be back in Thebes by now, leading prayers that gave life to the royal statues in Seti's funerary temple as well as the Ramesseum.

The Pharaoh thanked the gods for giving him three exceptional children. In their own way, each of them transmitted the spirit of Egyptian civilization and attached more importance to values than to personal interest. Their mothers, Nefertari and Iset the Fair, could rest in peace.

Merenptah bowed to Pharaoh.

"You called for me, Majesty?"

"Hattusili and Puduhepa's daughter is preparing to leave the Hittite capital for Pi-Ramses. Upon our diplomatic marriage, she will become Great Royal Wife, and this union will set the final seal upon our peace agreement with Hatti. The treaty may not sit well with certain interest groups. Your mission will therefore be providing security for the princess once she leaves Hittite territory and enters our protectorates."

"You can rely on me. How many men will I be able to take?"

"As many as you need."

"An army would be useless, too slow and unwieldy. I'll assemble a force of a hundred veteran soldiers, well armed and familiar with the territory, plus several couriers with the fastest available horses. In case of attack, we'll be well prepared, and I'll send regular dispatches back to Your Majesty. If one of the couriers is late, the nearest fortress will send help at once."

"Your mission is of the highest importance, Merenptah."

"I won't disappoint you, Father."

Since early that morning, a cloudburst had been pounding Hattusa, threatening to flood the lower town.

Panic was rising when Empress Puduhepa addressed the population. Not only were the priests of Hatti praying hard for the Storm God's mercy, she reassured them; magicians from Egypt had also been consulted.

Puduhepa's speech restored calm. A few hours later, the rain stopped. Heavy black clouds hung low in the sky, but to the south it was clearing. The princess might be able to leave after all. The empress went to her daughter's rooms.

At the age of twenty-five, the princess had the savage beauty of Anatolian women, blond and sloe-eyed, with a thin, almost pointed nose and an ivory complexion. She was fairly tall, long-limbed, and carried her head high as befits a princess, yet the overall impression she gave was one of sensuality. Her slightest movements had a feminine quality, both inviting and aloof. There was no well-born man in Hatti who hadn't dreamed of winning her.

"The weather's improving," said Puduhepa.

The princess arranged and scented her long hair, not waiting for a maid.

"Then I should get ready to go."

"Are you nervous?"

"I'm the first Hittite princess to marry a pharaoh, and what a pharaoh! Ramses the Great, the pride of Egypt, the peacemaker . . . In my wildest dreams, I never imagined a more fabulous destiny."

Puduhepa was surprised. "We'll be saying goodbye for good, and you'll never again see your homeland. Won't that be hard for you?"

"I'm a woman and I'm going to marry Ramses, travel the land of the gods, reign in splendor, live in luxury, enjoy a perfect climate, and who knows what else! But marrying Ramses won't be enough for me."

"What do you mean?"

"I want him to love me, too. When he agreed to the marriage, Pharaoh wasn't thinking of a woman, only of diplomacy and peace, as if I were only an article in a treaty. I'll make him change his mind."

"You may be disappointed."

"Am I stupid and ugly?"

"Ramses is no longer a young man. He may not even lay eyes on you."

"I'll make my own destiny; no one else will do it for me. If I can't win Ramses' heart, what use will my exile be?"

"Your marriage will guarantee the future prosperity of two great countries."

"I won't stand for being a servant or a shut-in, only a Great Royal Wife. Ramses will forget I'm a Hittite, I'll reign at his side, and all of Egypt will bow to me."

"I hope it comes true, my darling."

"I'll make it come true, Mother. My will is just as strong as yours."

The sun peeked weakly from behind the clouds. Winter was on its way, with its procession of wind and cold, but the southward route to the Egyptian protectorates would soon be negotiable. Puduhepa wished she could talk more with her daughter, but there was no time. Ramses' future bride was now a stranger in her own citadel.

Raia could not calm down.

A violent dispute had erupted between him and Uri-Teshoop, and the two men had parted without an understanding. The former commander of the Hittite army firmly believed that the arrival of Hattusili's daughter could be turned to Ramses' disadvantage, and therefore no move must be made to stop her. Raia, on the other hand, considered that the diplomatic marriage would stamp out any flicker of warring instinct still left in Hatti.

By giving up the fight, Hattusili was playing into Ramses' hands. The thought made Raia so furious that he felt like pulling out his goatee and ripping his brightly striped tunic to shreds. His hatred of Ramses had become an obsession, and he would willingly run any risk to topple the pharaoh whose colossal statues loomed in front of his country's great temples. It seemed that Ramses' every endeavor met with success. It was too unfair, and it had to stop.

Uri-Teshoop had gone soft, a rich widow's plaything. But he, Raia, had not lost the will to fight. Ramses was only a man; hit often enough and hard enough, he would fall. The first blow was to keep the Hittite princess from ever reaching Pi-Ramses.

Without telling Uri-Teshoop and his Hittite friends, Raia would organize a strike force with Malfi's help. When the Libyan chieftain learned that Ramses' own son, Merenptah, was heading the Egyptian escort troops, his mouth would water. Why, they could eliminate a Hittite princess on her way to marry Ramses and a prince of the blood in one fell swoop!

Not one member of the convoy would be left alive. Pharaoh would believe it was last-ditch resistance from some renegade Hittite army faction. They could scatter some typical weapons at the scene and dress a few dead peasants as Hattusili's soldiers. They would certainly meet with stiff resistance, and there would be Libyan losses, but that would never daunt Malfi. The prospect of a brutal, bloody, and victorious engagement would be too appealing.

Hattusili would lose his daughter, and Ramses his son. The two leaders would seek revenge in their most bitter confrontation ever. Ahsha was no longer there to smooth things over. As for Uri-Teshoop, he'd be forced to fall in line, or else Malfi would deal with him. Raia had no lack of ideas for disrupting Egyptian politics from within. He'd never let Ramses rest.

A knock came at the door of the small stockroom where the Syrian merchant stored his most precious vases. At this late hour, it could only be a customer.

"Who's there?"

"Captain Rarek."

"I don't want to see you here!"

"I've had a close call. I need to tell you what happened."

Raia opened the door a crack.

He only caught a glimpse of the sailor's face before Rarek was pushed from behind, sending both of them tumbling head over heels, while Serramanna and Setau stormed into the stockroom.

The Sardinian giant poked a finger at Raia. "What's this man's name?"

"Ahmeni," replied the captain.

Shackled by handcuffs and a rope around his ankles, Rarek could barely move. Retreating to a dark corner of the stockroom, Raia darted like a snake and climbed the ladder leading to the roof. With a little luck he could shake his pursuers.

Sitting on one corner of a roof, a handsome Nubian woman shot a stern glance at him.

"Stop right there."

Raia whipped a dagger from beneath the sleeve of his tunic.

"Out of the way, or I'll kill you!" As he sprang, arm

raised to strike, a marbled viper bit him in the right heel. The pain was so intense that Raia let go of his weapon, bumped against a ledge, lost his balance, and tumbled over.

When Serramanna found him, he shook his head in frustration. The fall had broken Raia's neck.

THIRTY-ONE

Woozy with satisfaction, amazed by her lover's stamina, Dame Tanit clung to Uri-Teshoop's powerful torso.

"Do it again," she begged hoarsely.

The Hittite prince was ready to oblige, but the sound of footsteps distracted him. He rose and pulled a short fighting sword from its scabbard.

There was a knock at the bedchamber door.

"Who is it?"

"The steward."

"I told you not to disturb us!" Tanit yelled crossly.

"A friend of your husband's is here . . . claims it's an emergency."

The comely Phoenician grabbed Uri-Teshoop's wrist to hold him back, saying, "It may be a trap."

"I can defend myself."

Uri-Teshoop called to a Hittite guard posted in the garden. Proud to serve his former commander, he made his report in a hushed voice, then disappeared.

When her lover returned to the bedchamber, Tanit, still naked, threw her arms around his neck and smothered him with kisses. Sensing his mind was elsewhere, she pulled away and poured him a drink of cool wine.

"What's going on?"

"Our friend Raia is dead."

"An accident?"

"He fell off a roof trying to escape from Serramanna."

The Phoenician blanched. "That awful Sard! Do you think he'll make the connection to you?"

"He may."

"You need to get away from here this minute!"

"Absolutely not. Serramanna is watching me closely; if Raia didn't have time to talk, I'm still beyond his reach. We're well rid of the Syrian, if you ask me. He was beginning to lose his head. Since he put me in contact with the Libyans, he'd outlived his usefulness anyway."

"Do you still need me?" Tanit asked cajolingly.

Uri-Teshoop pawed her luscious breasts. "Be a nice quiet wife and I'll make you happy," he murmured.

When he took her hungrily, she swooned once again with pleasure.

The hunters displayed their animal pelts to Techonk. The Libyan personally chose his raw material; he trusted no one's judgment but his own and maintained strict standards, rejecting three-quarters of what was offered him. That very morning he had dismissed two hunters who tried to sell him second-rate skins.

Suddenly a brightly striped tunic landed at his feet.

"Does this look familiar?"

Pains shot through the tanner's midsection; he rubbed his round belly.

"It's common enough."

"Take a good look at it."

"I tell you, it means nothing special to me."

"Let me refresh your memory, Techonk. This tunic belonged to the Syrian merchant Raia, a dubious character who was up to something. When we cornered him, he jumped off a roof. His past caught up with him, you might say. He was a notorious spy. I'm sure of one thing: the two of you were acquaintances, even partners."

"No, I never—"

"Don't interrupt me, Techonk. I have no proof, but I don't doubt that our late friend Raia was hatching some plot against Ramses, along with you and Uri-Teshoop. Let the Syrian's death serve as a warning. If you or your co-conspirators try to harm the king again, you'll end up like Raia. And what about the commission you owe me?"

"I'll have a leather shield and a pair of my best sandals delivered to your house."

"That's a start . . . Now how about some names?"

"Nothing's going on with the Libyans here in Egypt! We all acknowledge Ramses' authority."

"That's what you should keep on doing. I'll be in touch, Techonk."

Serramanna's horse had barely rounded the corner when the Libyan, clutching his stomach, ran to the privy.

Emperor Hattusili and his wife, Puduhepa, were having a disagreement. Ordinarily the empress acknowledged the wisdom of her husband's views, yet in this instance they were on opposing sides of a heated argument.

"We should let Ramses know that our daughter is on her way," insisted Puduhepa.

"No," retorted the emperor. "This is the perfect opportunity to flush out rebel factions within our army."

"You mean you'd let your daughter's convoy be attacked? You're willing to use your own flesh and blood as bait?"

"She'll be perfectly safe, Puduhepa. In case of aggression, our finest Hittite soldiers will protect her and annihilate the rebels. And we'll accomplish two things at once: eliminating the last vestiges of military opposition to our regime, and sealing the pact with Ramses."

"I refuse to put my daughter at risk."

"My decision is final. She'll leave tomorrow. Only when she's approaching the Egyptian sphere of influence will I notify Ramses that his bride is en route."

How fragile the princess looked, surrounded by Hittite officers and enlisted men with their heavy armor and menacing headgear! Equipped with fresh weapons and healthy young horses, her elite escort troops appeared invincible. Emperor Hattusili realized that his daughter would indeed be exposed to a certain risk, but the opportunity was simply too good to miss. A head of state, he mused, must sometimes put national security above the welfare of his own family.

The sky was clear, the temperature unusually warm for

the season. Beneath their winter cloaks the soldiers were sti-
fling and sweating. February suddenly seemed like summer.
This freak weather couldn't last; in a few hours some rain
was sure to fall and replenish the cisterns.

The princess knelt before her father, who anointed her
with the special oil of betrothal.

"Ramses himself will perform the anointment of marriage," he told his daughter. "Safe journey, future Queen of
Egypt."

The convoy pulled away. Behind the chariot carrying the
princess came another vehicle of the same size, just as com-
fortably outfitted. And on it, seated on a lightweight
wooden throne, sat Empress Puduhepa.

"I'm not letting her go alone," she called as her coach
passed the emperor. "I'll ride along to the border."

Unfriendly mountains, steep passes, unsettling gorges,
thick woods where attackers might lurk . . . Empress
Puduhepa found her own country frightening. The soldiers
guarding them remained on alert, and their number should
be enough to discourage any assailant; still, Hatti had long
been the theater of bloody civil strife. It was quite conceiv-
able that Uri-Teshoop, or one of his ilk, might make an
attempt on the princess, a living symbol of peace with
Egypt.

The young woman remained imperturbable, as if the
ordeal had no effect on her. She haughtily blazed the trail
with a fierce determination to reach her goal.

When the pines rustled, when the rush of a waterfall
sounded like armed men advancing, Puduhepa jumped.

Where were the rebels hiding? What strategy would they use? Strange noises often woke her at night. All day she scanned the woods, bluffs, and riverbanks.

The princess and her mother did not talk. Walled in silence, Puduhepa's daughter refused all contact with her former existence. For her, Hatti was dead, and the future was named Ramses.

Suffering from the heat, thirsty, exhausted, the convoy passed through Kadesh and arrived at the frontier post of Aya in southern Syria. There stood an Egyptian fortress, at the northern limit of Pharaoh's sphere of influence.

Archers were poised in the battlements. The great gates were shut. The garrison was prepared for an attack. The princess got down from her chariot and straddled one of the horses that were part of her dowry. She galloped toward the fort, pulling up at the foot of the ramparts. No Egyptian archer had dared fire.

"I am the daughter of the Emperor of Hatti, and the future Queen of Egypt," she declared. "Ramses the Great is expecting me. Extend me a royal welcome, or Pharaoh's anger will burn you like fire."

The fortress commander stepped forward, protesting, "You've brought an army with you."

"Not an army, only my escort."

"They look like Hittite fighting men to me."

"You're wrong, Commander. I've told you the truth."

"I've received no such orders from the capital."

"Inform Ramses immediately that I've set foot on Egyptian soil."

THIRTY-TWO

Sniffling, red-eyed, and coughing, Ahmeni had a cold. The February nights were freezing, and the pale winter sun didn't manage to warm the air in daytime. Ahmeni had ordered a large quantity of heating wood, yet the delivery had been delayed. In a foul mood, he was preparing to vent his frustrations on his staff when an army courier deposited a dispatch on his desk—a message from the fortress at Aya in southern Syria.

Ahmeni deciphered the coded message, sneezing as he read. At once he threw a woolen mantle over his heavy linen gown, wrapped a scarf around his neck, and ran to Ramses' office, though his lungs seemed to be on fire.

"Your Majesty . . . incredible news! Hattusili's daughter has arrived in Aya. The fortress commander awaits your instructions."

At this late hour the king worked in the light of oil lamps with smudge-proof wicks. Positioned on sycamore stands, they gave off a soft, even light.

"There must be some mistake," assessed Ramses. "Hattusili would have told me his daughter was coming."

"The fortress commander was greeted by a Hittite fighting force that claims to be a bridal party!"

The king paced briefly in his vast office, which was heated with braziers.

"It's a ploy, Ahmeni. Hattusili must have wanted to test his power at home. The convoy could have been attacked by rebel soldiers."

"He'd use his own daughter as bait?"

"Hattusili's mind is at ease now. Have Merenptah leave at once for Syria with his special forces. They'll keep the princess safe on the rest of her journey. Order the fortress commander to open the gates and let Aya welcome the Hittites."

"What if . . ."

"I'll take the risk."

In mutual amazement, the Hittites and Egyptians fraternized, feasted, drank, and ate together like old comrades in arms. Puduhepa, relieved, could turn back toward Hattusa, while her daughter, surrounded by dignitaries and a token Hittite honor guard, would continue south toward Pi-Ramses under Merenptah's protection.

Tomorrow they would separate for good. Her eyes misting over, Puduhepa looked at her beautiful, strong-willed daughter.

"You feel no regret?" she asked.

"I'm too excited."

"It's the last time we'll ever see each other."

"That's how life is. Each person has a destiny . . . and mine is the best of all!"

"I hope you find happiness, my child."

"I'm happy already."

Hurt, Puduhepa refrained from embracing her daughter. The final link had been severed.

"It's completely unheard of," noted the fortress commander, a square-faced, gruff-voiced career soldier. "At this time of year, the mountains should be covered with snow, and we'd have some rain every day. If this heat wave continues, our cisterns will soon run dry."

"We came at a forced march," Merenptah reminded him. "Regrettably, several of my men fell ill. Along the way we found a number of empty wells and dried springs. I'm afraid I'm taking the princess on a rather perilous adventure."

"Completely unheard of," repeated the commander. "Only a god could upset the weather this way."

These were the words Merenptah had been dreading. "I'm afraid you may be right, Commander. Is there a shrine that protects the fortress?"

"Yes, but it can't keep away all the evil spirits surrounding us—not enough to change the weather. We'd have to call on a god with the force to rule the heavens."

"Can you spare us water enough for the return journey?"

"I'm sorry, Your Highness, but no! You'll have to stay here and wait for rain."

"If this unseasonable heat persists, we'll run out of water on the journey, and so will our Hittite companions."

"Still, this is winter. The dry spell can't last."

"As you've said yourself, Commander, it isn't natural. Leaving here is risky, but so is staying."

Deep creases appeared in the officer's forehead.

"But . . . what do you plan to do?"

"Inform the Pharaoh. He'll know what to do."

Kha unrolled three long papyrus scrolls on Ramses' desk, his finds from the archives in Heliopolis.

"The texts are explicit, Your Majesty. A single god controls the climate of Asia: Set, the Destroyer. But no body of magicians is qualified to enter into direct contact with him. You and you alone must convince him to restore the seasons to their proper order. And yet . . ."

"Go ahead, son."

"Yet I can't encourage you to confront him. Set's might is uncontrollable."

"Are you afraid I'm too weak?"

"You are the son of Seti, but changing the weather means dealing with thunder, lightning, and winds. And Set is unpredictable. Egypt can't spare you, Father. Let's send a shipment of holy statues and emergency food supplies to Syria instead."

"Do you believe that Set will let them through?"

Kha hung his head. "No, Your Majesty."

"Then he leaves me no choice. I have to answer the god's challenge, or else Merenptah, the Hittite princess, and everyone with them will die of thirst."

Ramses' elder son had no argument to offer.

"If I don't return from the temple of Set," Pharaoh said to Kha, "be my successor, son, and dedicate your life to Egypt."

The Hittite princess, quartered in the fortress commander's suite, demanded to speak to Merenptah. He considered her an unknown and somewhat dangerous quantity, but showed her all the consideration due a highborn lady.

"Why aren't we leaving for Egypt at once?"

"Because that's impossible, Princess."

"The weather is splendid."

"It's a drought in the middle of the rainy season, and we're short of water."

"You don't mean we're stuck in this horrible fortress!"

"Heaven is against us; some divine will is keeping us here."

"Don't your magicians know what they're doing?"

"I've called on the greatest magician in the land: Ramses himself."

The princess smiled. "You're an intelligent man, Merenptah. I'll recommend you to my husband."

"Let's hope that heaven hears our prayers, Your Highness."

"Oh, it will! I haven't come this far to die of thirst. I know that Pharaoh has heaven and earth in the palm of his hands."

Setau and Ahmeni could do nothing to change Pharaoh's mind. At dinner, Ramses had eaten a thick steak cut from a steer, an animal embodying Set's strength. He drank strong oasis wine, which was also among the god's symbols. Then, after purifying his mouth with salt (which Set exuded, an earthly fire so essential to the preservation of food), the king prayed before the statue of his father, whose very name, Seti, had laid a claim to the storm god's terrifying power.

Without his father's help, Ramses had no chance of coming to terms with Set. The slightest error—a ritual gesture that was less than precise, a moment's inattention—and thunder would strike. There was only one effective weapon against Set's sheer power; that weapon was rectitude, the code instilled in Ramses during his apprenticeship with Seti.

In the middle of the night the king entered the temple of Set, built on the site of Avaris, the hated capital of the earlier Hyksos invaders. A place dedicated to silence and solitude, a place only Pharaoh could enter without fear of immediate annihilation.

Confronting Set meant conquering fear, then regarding the world with eyes of fire, acknowledging its violence and convulsions. It meant becoming the force at the origin of the world, in the heart of the cosmos, where human intelligence never penetrated.

On the altar, Ramses laid a cup of wine and a miniature oryx carved from acacia. Set's fire dwelt within this desert animal, enabling it to withstand extreme heat and survive in a hostile environment.

"The heavens are in your hands," the king told the god. "The earth is at your feet. The world is at your command. Restore the winter rains in the north, take back your parching heat."

Set's statue did not react. The eyes were stony.

"I, Ramses, son of Seti, so address you. No god has the right to reverse the seasons. Even the divine is subject to the law of Ma'at, and you are no exception."

The statue's eyes glowed red. Heat blasted the chapel.

"Do not turn your power against Pharaoh, in whom the

brothers Horus and Set are united. You are within me; your strength is what I use to fight the forces of darkness and banish chaos. Obey me, Set, bring rain to the lands in the north!"

Lightning flashed through the sky and thunder boomed over Pi-Ramses.

A night of combat was beginning.

THIRTY-THREE

The princess confronted Merenptah.

"This waiting is unbearable! Take me to Egypt at once."

"My orders are to deliver you safely. As long as the heat wave continues, it would be unwise to travel."

"Why doesn't Pharaoh do something?"

A drop of water fell on the princess's left shoulder. A second splashed on her right hand. She and Merenptah simultaneously looked up to see dark clouds swirling. A bolt of lightning shot through the sky, followed by a thunderclap. Heavy rain began to fall, lowering the temperature in a matter of minutes.

"There's your answer," said Merenptah.

The Hittite princess threw her head back, opened her mouth, and swallowed the life-giving rain in gulps.

"Let's go. Let's go this minute!" she said.

Ahmeni paced outside the king's bedchamber. Sitting with his arms crossed, scowling, Setau stared straight ahead. Kha read a magical scroll, chanting the spells on it to himself. For at least the tenth time, Serramanna cleaned his short sword with a cloth soaked in linseed oil.

"What time did Pharaoh leave the temple of Set?" the Sard asked again.

"At dawn," sighed Ahmeni.

"Did he speak to anyone?"

"No, he didn't say a single word," Kha declared. "He shut himself up in his room. I called the chief physician and he admitted her."

"She's been in there for over an hour!" grumbled Setau.

"Visible or not, the burns Set inflicts are deadly," the high priest noted. "Neferet knows what she's doing. Let's leave her alone."

"I've been giving him regular doses of my potions to strengthen his heart," Setau reported.

Finally the bedchamber door opened. The four men rushed to surround Neferet.

"Ramses is out of danger," the chief physician of the realm reassured them. "A day of rest, and he can resume his normal activities. But you'd better watch out; we're in for some rain."

The sky darkened over Pi-Ramses.

United like brothers under Merenptah's command, the Egyptians and Hittites made their way through Canaan, took the coastal route along the Sinai peninsula, and arrived in the Delta. At each stop along the way there was feasting. During the trip, several of the soldiers traded their weapons for trumpets, flutes, and tambourines.

The Hittite princess was wide-eyed, drinking in the verdant scenery—palm groves, fertile fields, irrigation ditches, papyrus swamps. What she found here bore no resemblance to the stark Anatolian plateau she had left behind.

When the delegation arrived in Pi-Ramses, the streets were jammed with people. No one could have said how the information spread, but everyone knew that the Emperor of Hatti's daughter would soon make her entry into Ramses the Great's northern capital. The rich mingled with the poor, dignitaries standing elbow to elbow with ditchdiggers. Everyone was feeling expansive.

"Extraordinary," commented Uri-Teshoop, in the front row of spectators along with his wife. "This Pharaoh has done the impossible."

"He convinced the god Set to send rain," beamed Dame Tanit. "There's nothing that Ramses can't do."

"Ramses is his people's air and water," a stonemason added. "His love is the bread we eat and the clothes we wear. He's the father and mother of Egypt!"

"His gaze can plumb minds and search souls," chimed in a priestess from the temple of Hathor.

Uri-Teshoop was undone. How could he fight a pharaoh so endowed with supernatural powers? Ramses commanded the elements; he could even change the weather in Asia. His invisible allies could vanquish any human army. Just as Uri-Teshoop had supposed, nothing could have prevented the safe arrival of the emperor's daughter. Any attack against the convoy would have met with certain failure . . .

The Hittite prince shook himself. No, he would not succumb to Ramses' magic! His goal in life, his only goal, was to bring down this man who had ruined his chance to be emperor and reduced a proud commander to the state of vassal. No matter what his powers were, this Pharaoh was no god, but a human being, with a man's weaknesses and failings. Lulled by his victories and his popularity, Ramses would eventually falter; time would also dull his thinking.

And now he was marrying a Hittite princess, Uri-Teshoop's own cousin! In her veins flowed the blood of an unruly and vengeful nation. Believing that this union would seal the peace might just turn out to be Ramses' greatest mistake.

"There she is!" cried Dame Tanit, whose cry was taken up by thousands of enthusiastic citizens.

In the shelter of her chariot, the princess was putting the finishing touches on her face. She painted her eyelids green with a paste of copper sulfate and drew a black oval around her eyes with a wand dabbed in lead sulfate, silver, and charcoal. She looked in the mirror and was satisfied with her work.

With a hand from Merenptah, the bride-to-be stepped down from the chariot.

Her beauty stunned the crowd. Dressed in a long green gown that set off her ivory complexion, she looked every bit the queen.

Suddenly, every head turned toward the town's main avenue, where the clatter of galloping horses and chariot wheels was heard.

Ramses the Great was coming to meet his future wife.

The two proud young horses were descendants of the pair that, along with the lion Fighter, had been Pharaoh's only allies at Kadesh, when his soldiers abandoned him to fight the Hittites single-handed. Each magnificent steed wore a headdress of blue-tipped red plumes. A caparison of red, blue, and green cotton covered their backs. The reins were attached to the monarch's belt, since he held the scepter of illumination in his right hand.

The gilded chariot advanced at a quick and steady pace. Ramses guided his horses with his voice, never raising it. He wore his blue headdress, recalling the celestial origins of the pharaonic line, and was dressed entirely in gold.

He arrived like the sun, shedding light on his subjects. When the chariot rolled to a halt a short distance from the Hittite princess, the clouds parted and the sun reigned as absolute master in the newly blue sky. Ramses, the Son of Light, was surely responsible for this latest miracle.

The young woman kept her eyes lowered. The king noted that she had opted for simplicity. A discreet silver necklace and bracelets, a simple dress . . . The absence of artifice accented her beautiful figure.

Ramses anointed her forehead with precious oil.

"This is the oil of marriage," declared the Pharaoh. "It makes of you the Great Royal Wife of the Lord of the Two Lands and banishes the forces of evil. On this day you are born to your new position, according to the law of Ma'at. You will take the name Mat-hor-neferu-ra, 'She Who Sees Horus and the Perfection of Divine Light.' Look at me, Mathor, my bride."

Ramses reached his arms out toward the young woman, who very slowly placed her hands in Pharaoh's. She, who had never known a moment's fear, was petrified. The moment she had longed for, the chance to display her countless charms, had finally arrived, and she felt she might faint like some shy little maiden. Ramses radiated such magnetism that she sensed she was touching the flesh of a god, tumbling headlong into another world, a world without landmarks. Winning his love was only a wild dream, she realized, but now there was no turning back, although she wished she could run and go home to Hatti, far, far away from Ramses.

Her hands still held in the king's firm grip, she finally dared to look up at him.

At fifty-six, Ramses was a striking man with unequaled presence. He had a broad forehead, a prominent arch to his thick eyebrows, piercing eyes, strong cheekbones, a long, arched nose, shapely ears, a deep chest—the ideal combination of strength and virile good looks.

Mathor, though newly Egyptian, felt the Hittite in her fall instantly and violently in love.

Ramses invited her into his chariot.

"In this thirty-fourth year of my reign," declared the Pharaoh in a ringing voice, "peace with Hatti will henceforth prevail. Stelae commemorating this marriage will be placed at Karnak, Pi-Ramses, Elephantine, Abu Simbel, and all the temples of Nubia. Feasts will be held in every town and village, with wine provided by the palace. From this day forward, the borders between our two countries will be opened. People and goods will circulate freely within a vast area now free from war and hatred."

A mighty cheer greeted Ramses' declaration.

Caught up in the moment despite himself, Uri-Teshoop joined in.

THIRTY-FOUR

Flaring from the upper edge of the double mast to the planks, the rectangular linen sail swelled with the north wind. The royal flagship sailed fast against the current toward Thebes. In the prow, the captain took frequent soundings in the Nile with the aid of a long pole. He knew the river so well that no mishap would interfere with Ramses and Mathor's journey. Pharaoh had hoisted the sail himself, while his young bride slept on in a cabin festooned with flowers and the cook plucked fowl to be served for dinner. Three helmsmen tended the rudder, which had two magic eyes carved into it showing the right direction. A sailor drew water from the river, dangling by one hand from the guardrail; a ship's boy, agile as a monkey, climbed to the top of the mast to scan the horizon and alert the captain to potential dangers such as herds of hippopotami.

The crew had been treated to an exceptional vintage from the great Pi-Ramses growers, a vintage from Year Twenty-two of Ramses' reign, the memorable date of the peace treaty with the Hittites. This incomparable harvest had been aged in cone-shaped terra-cotta jars, a rosy brown, their straight necks sealed with plugs of clay and straw. They were painted with lotus flowers and a picture of Bes, the master of initiation into the great mysteries, a stocky character with a thick torso and short legs, sticking out his red tongue to denote the almighty Word.

Ramses drank deeply of the fresh air rising from the river, then returned to the cabin amidships, where Mathor was now awake. Perfumed with jasmine, bare-breasted, wearing only a very short skirt, she was as lovely as the morning.

"Pharaoh is all that is wonderful," she said in a soft voice. "A shooting star, a raging wild bull with sharp horns, the crocodile staking out the pond, the falcon seizing its prey, the divine griffin that no one can conquer, the flame that pierces the darkest shadows."

"You have an excellent knowledge of our traditional literature, Mathor."

"It's one of the subjects I've studied, including almost every word written about Pharaoh. Who wouldn't be fascinated by the most powerful man in the world?"

"If you've read all you say, then you must know that Pharaoh detests any form of flattery."

"But I mean it. I'm happier than I ever dreamed. I fantasized about you, Ramses, while my father was fighting you. I was convinced that only the Light of Egypt would give me life. Today I know that I was right."

The young woman clung to Ramses' right leg, stroking it tenderly.

"Am I forbidden to love the Lord of the Two Lands?"

A woman's love . . . it had been the last thing Ramses was looking for. Nefertari had been the love of his life, Iset the Fair his youthful passion. He had considered that part of his life dead and gone until his young bride revived his forgotten desire. Artfully scented, willing yet not provocative, she knew how to be seductive without losing her nobility. Her sheer beauty and sloe-eyed charm moved him deeply.

"You're so young, Mathor."

"I'm a woman, Your Majesty, and also your wife. Isn't it my duty to win your love?"

"Come to the prow and look at Egypt with me. I belong to her first and foremost."

The king wrapped a cape around Mathor's shoulders and led her to the front of the boat. He told her the names of the provinces, towns, and cities, described their riches, detailed the irrigation systems, outlined their customs and festivals.

And here was Thebes.

On the East Bank, Mathor's wondering eyes contemplated the immense temple of Karnak and the shining temple of Luxor, home to the *ka* of all the gods. On the West Bank, with the looming Peak where the goddess of Silence resided, the Hittite princess was struck dumb with admiration for the Ramesseum, the Pharaoh's mortuary Temple of Millions of Years, and the gigantic statue embodying the king's *ka* in stone, identifying him with the divine powers.

Mathor knew that one of Pharaoh's names, "He Who Is Like the Bee," was fully justified, for Egypt was indeed a hive where idleness was out of place. Everyone had a function to fulfill, in accordance with a hierarchy of tasks. The temple itself buzzed with activity: countless workers maintained the temple complex and estates, while inside the shrine priests and priestesses observed religious rites. Even at night, astronomers were busy making observations.

Ramses allowed the new Great Royal Wife no time at all

to adapt. Lodged in the palace at the Ramesseum, she must immediately assume her responsibilities and learn her duties as queen. She realized that obedience was a key element in winning Ramses' love.

The royal chariot drew up to the village of Deir el-Medina, guarded by the police and the army. There followed a convoy carrying food to the craftsmen digging and decorating the tombs in the Valleys of the Kings and Queens. It was the usual fare: loaves of bread, sacks of dried peas and beans, fresh vegetables, excellent fish, slabs of dried, marinated meat. The government also furnished sandals, cloth to make garments, and salves.

Ramses handed Mathor down from the chariot.

"What are we coming here to do?"

"For you, the most important thing."

To the cheers of the workers and their families, the royal pair made their way to the two-story whitewashed house of the local leader, a man in his fifties whose talent as a sculptor had earned him universal admiration.

"How can we thank Your Majesty for his generosity?" the headman asked, bowing deeply.

"I know the worth of your hand and that you and your gang have worked tirelessly. I am your protector and I shall enrich your community so that what you build may last forever."

"Only give us your orders, Majesty, and we will carry them out."

"Come with me, my good man. I will show you where two new work sites are to be dug at once."

When the royal chariot turned onto the track leading to the Valley of the Kings, Mathor cringed. The sight of the sunbaked, seemingly lifeless cliffs filled her with anxiety. Fresh from the comfort and luxury of the palace, the bare rock and forbidding desert came as a shock to her.

At the edge of the Valley of the Kings (where guards stood watch night and day), a group of sixty-odd dignitaries of various ages awaited Ramses. They had shaved heads, chests covered with broad collars, long tucked kilts, and carried staffs with ostrich plumes topping the sycamore handles.

"These are my royal sons," explained Ramses.

They raised their staffs in an honor guard, then followed in the monarch's wake.

Ramses came to a halt not far from the entry to his own tomb.

"Here," he told the headman from Deir el-Medina, "you will dig a huge tomb with columned halls and as many burial chambers as there are royal sons. With help from Osiris, I will protect my children forever."

Next Ramses handed the builder a set of plans he had personally drawn up on papyrus.

"This will be the eternal dwelling of the Great Royal Wife Mathor; you will dig this tomb in the Valley of the Queens, a good distance from Iset the Fair's and far away from Nefertari's."

The young queen turned pale. "My tomb?" she stammered.

"It's our tradition," Ramses told her. "Any person assuming important responsibilities must begin to think of the afterlife. Death is our greatest counselor, for it puts our life in perspective and allows us to focus on what is most important."

"I don't want to think about such depressing things!"

"You're no longer an ordinary woman, Mathor. You can't be a pleasure-loving Hittite princess anymore; you're the Queen of Egypt. Duty is all that counts now, and to understand it you must come to terms with your own death."

"I refuse!"

Ramses' disapproving look made Mathor wish she could eat her words. She fell to her knees.

"Forgive me, Majesty."

"Rise, Mathor. It isn't me you must serve, but Ma'at, the law of the universe that created Egypt and will outlive it. Now let us proceed to meet your fate."

Proud despite her fear, managing to contain her anxiety, Mathor toured the Valley of the Queens, which, though desertlike, seemed less harsh than the Valley of the Kings. It was not closed in by steep cliffs, but open onto the world of the living, which seemed close at hand. The young queen kept her eye on the clear blue sky and recalled the beautiful scenery in Egypt's true valley, the Nile, where she planned to spend countless hours of pleasure.

Ramses thought of Nefertari resting there in the Golden Chamber of a magnificent eternal dwelling. She rose from it constantly, in the form of a phoenix, a ray of light, or a puff of wind traveling to the ends of the earth. Nefertari sailed forever on a splendid bark, upon the heavenly river, in the heart of light.

Mathor remained silent, not daring to interrupt the king's meditation. Despite the gravity of the moment, her husband's presence, his power, stirred her to the depths of her being. No matter what she must do to prove herself, she intended to reach her goal. She would *make* Ramses fall in love with her.

THIRTY-FIVE

Serramanna was running out of patience. The indirect approach, the gentle touch, had gotten him nowhere, so the Sardinian bodyguard had decided to fall back on a more direct method. After fortifying himself with steak and chickpeas, he left on horseback for Techonk's workshop.

This time the Libyan would talk. This time he'd give the name of Ahsha's murderer.

When he dismounted, Serramanna was surprised to find a crowd gathered in front of the tanner's workshop. There were women, children, old people, workers, each talking louder than the next.

"Make way," ordered the Sard. "I'm coming through."

The hulking bodyguard had no need to repeat the order. A hush fell.

Inside the shop, the smell was always overpowering. Serramanna, who had adopted Egyptian standards of cleanliness, almost balked at entering. But the sight of the whole gang of tanners, clustered near a pile of antelope skins, told him that he needed to investigate. He pushed past strands of acacia pods (rich in tannic acid), strode past a yellow-brown tub, and laid a huge hand on the shoulders of two apprentices.

"What's going on here?"

The apprentices stepped aside. Serramanna saw Techonk's dead body, his head submerged in a trough full of dung and urine.

"An accident, a terrible accident," explained the foreman, a stocky Libyan.

"How did it happen?"

"Nobody knows. . .The boss was supposed to be coming in early, and we found him like that when we got here."

"No witnesses?"

"None."

"It doesn't look right. Techonk was an experienced tanner, not the kind to make such a stupid mistake. No, this is murder, and one of you knows something."

"You're wrong," the foreman said weakly.

"I'm going to see for myself," promised Serramanna, glowering. "It's time for an interrogation."

The youngest apprentice darted out of the workshop like an eel and exited at full speed. The good life had not slowed Serramanna's reflexes; he was after the man in a flash.

The young apprentice knew his way around the neighborhood's back alleys, but the Sard's sheer power helped him catch up. The apprentice was trying to scale a wall when Serramanna's iron fist closed around his kilt.

The fugitive lost his grip, screamed, and fell hard on the ground.

"My back . . . I think it's broken!"

"We'll take care of that once you tell me what you know. Talk fast, boy, or I'll break your wrists, too."

The terrified apprentice spoke in gasps. "A Libyan killed the boss . . . a man with black eyes, a square face, and wavy hair . . . called Techonk a traitor . . . the boss argued with him, swore that he'd told you nothing . . . but the man

refused to believe him . . . strangled Techonk and dunked his
head in the dung trough . . . then he turned to us and threatened us. 'Sure as my name is Malfi and I'm the new master
of Libya, if any of you go to the police, I'll get you, too.'
And now that I've told you everything, I'm a dead man!"

"Stop talking nonsense, boy. You won't set foot back
inside the tannery; I'll find you a job with the palace
steward."

"You're not sending me to prison?"

"I like a lad with courage. Up with you now!"

The apprentice hobbled along behind a glowering Serramanna. The Sard had hoped he'd be able to charge Uri-
Teshoop, but someone else was Techonk's murderer.

And what if Uri-Teshoop, the fallen Hittite prince, was in
league with this Malfi, a cold-blooded killer from Libya,
Egypt's hereditary enemy? Yes, the two of them must be plotting together. But how would he ever make Ramses see it?

Setau was washing the copper bowls, the gourds and fil-
ters of various sizes, while Lotus cleaned the laboratory
shelves. Then the snake venom expert took off his antelope-
skin tunic, soaked it in water, and wrung it to extract the medicinal solutions. It would be up to Lotus to turn the tunic
back into a portable pharmacy with potions from the black
cobra, puff adder, horned viper, and their ilk. The lovely
Nubian bent over the brown, viscous liquid. Diluted, it
would make an effective medicine for circulatory problems
and heart disease.

When Ramses walked into the laboratory, Lotus bowed,
but Setau went on with his work.

"You're in a foul temper," observed the king.

"You're right, as usual."

"You disapprove of my marriage with this Hittite princess."

"Right again."

"Why is that?"

"She'll do you no good."

"What makes you so sure?"

"Lotus and I know snakes. To find life within their venom, you have to be an expert. And this Hittite viper is liable to strike in a way that even the reptile expert couldn't predict."

"But you've made me immune to snakebite."

Setau grumbled. In fact, starting in their teens, he had been dosing Ramses with a potion containing tiny amounts of venom, building up to a point where the king could survive any type of bite.

"You put too much faith in your power, Majesty. Lotus thinks you're practically immortal, but I'm convinced the Hittite woman is up to no good."

"They say she's madly in love," Lotus murmured.

"Exactly!" exclaimed her husband. "And when love turns to hate, it's a terrifying weapon. This woman will obviously seek revenge for her country. She's found the perfect battle-field—the royal palace! But of course, Ramses won't listen to me."

The Pharaoh turned to Lotus.

"What's your opinion?"

"Mathor is beautiful, shrewd, ambitious, and . . . Hittite."

"I won't forget it," promised Ramses.

The king was carefully reading the report Ahmeni had submitted. Balder and more pallid than ever, the king's private secretary had summed up Serramanna's incendiary claims in a steady and elegant hand.

"Uri-Teshoop as Ahsha's murderer, and the Libyan Malfi as his accomplice . . . It all fits together, but we have no proof."

"No court would hear the case," Ahmeni agreed.

"Have you ever heard of this Malfi?"

"I looked through the records at the State Department, studied Ahsha's notes, and questioned our Libyan specialists. Malfi, it seems, is a warlord with a grudge against Egypt."

"Is this just a bunch of misfits or a real threat to Egypt?"

Ahmeni thought before replying. "I wish I could say he's harmless, but rumor has it that Malfi has formed a federation of several formerly warring clans."

"Is that rumor or fact?"

"The desert patrol hasn't been able to locate their camp."

"And yet this Malfi has entered Egypt, killed a fellow Libyan in his tannery here in Pi-Ramses, and gotten clean away!"

Ahmeni dreaded Ramses' anger; he rarely let it show, but when it broke loose, it was violent.

"We have no idea what kind of harm he can do."

"If we don't know our enemies, how can we govern the country?"

Ramses rose and walked to his tall office window, where he could stare straight at the sun without damaging his eyes. The sun was his astral protector; each day it gave him the energy to fulfill his office, no matter how difficult the tasks he faced.

"We mustn't overlook Malfi," declared the king.

"The Libyans are in no position to attack us!"

"A handful of demons can sow trouble, Ahmeni. This Libyan lives in the desert, gathering destructive forces that he dreams of using against us. It wouldn't be a war like the one we led against the Hittites, but another kind of confrontation, more indirect, yet no less violent. I sense Malfi's hatred. It's growing, and it's heading my way."

Not so long ago, Nefertari had been at his side, using her psychic gifts to guide his course. Since she had taken her place in the heavens, Ramses had sensed that her spirit lived on in him and continued to inform his decisions.

"Serramanna can conduct an in-depth investigation," Ahmeni proposed.

"Anything else we need to go over, old friend?"

"A scant hundred problems, the same as any other day, all highly urgent."

"I suppose it's no use asking you to get some rest."

"The day there are no more problems to solve is the day I rest."

THIRTY-SIX

With ashes and natron (a mixture of sodium carbonate and bicarbonate), the deftest of the palace masseuses rubbed Mathor's skin to cleanse it of impurities. Then she lathered the young queen with soap made from the bark and cortex of the desert date, a tree rich in saponine, and asked her to lie down on the heated tiles for a rubdown. The specially scented pomade eased muscle tension and perfumed the body.

Mathor was in heaven. Her father may have been Emperor of Hatti, but at home no one had ever tended her with such care and skill. Makeup artists and manicurists plied their trade to perfection, and the new Great Royal Wife felt more beautiful by the day. And she needed to be beautiful if she were to win Ramses' heart. Radiant with love and happiness, the young queen felt irresistible.

"Now for the wrinkle cream," announced the masseuse.

"At my age? You must be mad," Mathor bridled.

"The fight against aging should begin before it's too late."

"But . . ."

"Trust me, Your Majesty. To me, a Queen of Egypt's beauty is an affair of state."

Won over, Mathor let the masseuse apply costly pomade to her face, prepared from honey, red natron, powdered alabaster, fenugreek seed, and ass's milk.

The initial sensation of coolness gave way to a pleasant warmth, banishing old age and ugliness.

Mathor attended banquets and receptions, was entertained in the homes of the rich and noble, and visited the harems where women were taught weaving, music, and poetry. Each day her initiation into the Egyptian art of living brought exciting new discoveries.

Everything was even more beautiful than she'd dreamed.

She barely thought of Hattusa, the sad gray capital of her youth, a living emblem of Hatti's military might. Here in Pi-Ramses there were no high walls, but rather palm trees, ponds, and houses inlaid with colorful tiles that made Ramses' capital the Turquoise City, a garden of earthly delights.

The Hittite princess had dreamed of Egypt, and now Egypt belonged to her! She was its queen, respected by all.

Still, she wondered what power was really hers. She knew that Nefertari had shared the daily work of governing with Ramses and had taken a real part in conducting affairs of state. She had been the force behind the peace agreement with Hatti, even helping to draft the treaty.

Yet while Mathor basked in queenly privilege, she saw so little of Ramses! He did make passionate and tender love to her, but remained distant. She held no dominion over the king. And she had learned nothing about state secrets.

Mathor considered this a temporary stalemate. Eventually she would win Ramses' love; she would dominate him. Intelligence, beauty, and deceit would be her three weapons. The battle would be long and difficult, for Ramses was a worthy opponent; yet the young Hittite did not doubt the outcome for a moment. She had always gotten anything she really wanted. And what she wanted now was to become a queen so renowned that she would replace even the memory of Nefertari.

"Your Majesty," murmured the chambermaid, "I think that Pharaoh is out in the garden."

"Go see, and if he is, come right back and tell me."

Why hadn't Ramses stopped to see her? The king was not in the habit of taking a late-morning break. What unusual event could have made him depart from his schedule?

The chambermaid returned in a tizzy. "It's Pharaoh, all right, Your Majesty."

"And he's alone?"

"He is."

"Give me my lightest and simplest dress."

"Why not the sheer linen with red embroidery and—"

"No, something plain. Just hurry."

"What jewelry shall I bring?"

"None."

"And your wig?"

"No wig, either. Now get going!"

Ramses was sitting cross-legged at the foot of a sycamore tree with a broad crown and shimmering foliage, laden with green and red fruit. The king was dressed in the traditional kilt that Old Kingdom pharaohs had worn when the pyramids were being built. On his wrists were two golden bracelets.

As Mathor watched him, she could see he was talking to someone.

Barefoot, she crept closer. A light wind sent a silken rustle through the sycamore leaves. The young queen was stunned to discover that Ramses was indeed deep in conversation—with his lounging dog, Watcher.

"Your Majesty . . ."

"Come, Mathor."

"How did you know it's me?"

"Your perfume gives you away."

She sat down beside Ramses. Watcher rolled over and sat like a sphinx.

"You were talking to this animal?"

"All animals talk. When they're close to us, like my lion

and this latest member of the Watcher dynasty, they have a lot to say, if we know how to listen."

"But what can he tell you?"

"About faithfulness, trust, and forthrightness. He says where he plans to guide me in the afterlife."

Mathor made a face. "Death . . . Why must you always mention that horror?"

"Only humans commit horrors. Death is a simple physical law, and what lies beyond it may bring fulfillment, if your existence has been just and in keeping with the law of Ma'at."

Mathor drew closer to Ramses and fixed him with her sloe-eyed gaze.

"Aren't you afraid of soiling your dress?"

"I'm not really dressed yet, Your Majesty."

"A plain dress, no jewelry, no wig . . . Why such simplicity?"

"Does Your Majesty object?"

"You have a rank to uphold, Mathor. You can't behave like an ordinary woman."

The Hittite balked. "Have I ever done so? I'm an emperor's daughter, and now the wife of the Pharaoh of Egypt! My existence has always been subject to the demands of protocol and power."

"Protocol, yes; but why do you say power? You had no official function at your father's court."

Mathor felt caught in a trap. "I was too young . . . and Hatti is a military state where women are considered inferior. Here everything is different! The Queen of Egypt has a duty to serve her people, doesn't she?"

The young woman spilled her hair over Ramses' knees.

"Do you feel truly Egyptian, Mathor?"

"I've completely forgotten Hatti, if that's what you mean."

"Have you forsaken your father and mother?"

"Of course not, but they're so far away!"

"It's been a difficult adjustment for you."

"Difficult? This is what I always dreamed of! I don't want to dwell in the past."

"Without an understanding of the past, there's no preparing for the future. You're young, Mathor, still trying to get your bearings. It won't be easy."

"My future is settled: I'm Queen of Egypt!"

"A reigning monarch earns his title day by day. It's never final."

The Hittite was piqued. "I . . . I don't understand."

"You're the living emblem of peace between Egypt and Hatti," declared Ramses. "The route leading up to that peace was strewn with fatalities. Thanks to you, Mathor, joy has replaced great suffering."

"Am I only a symbol, then?"

"It will take you years to penetrate Egypt's secrets. Learn to serve Ma'at, the goddess of truth and justice, and your life will be full of light."

The young woman rose and looked straight at the Lord of the Two Lands.

"I wish to reign as your consort, Ramses."

"You're only a child, Mathor. Forget your whims, uphold your rank, and let time do the rest. Now, if you don't mind, I need to be alone with Watcher. We still have a lot of talking to do."

Mathor bit her lip and ran back to her rooms, determined not to let Ramses see her tears of rage.

THIRTY-SEVEN

In the months that followed her upsetting talk with Ramses, Mathor behaved impeccably. Gorgeously dressed, she dazzled the high society of Thebes with her charm and beauty, playing the queen content to be a figurehead. Heeding the king's advice, she familiarized herself with the court and its customs. She also broadened her knowledge of Egypt's ancient culture and was fascinated by its depth.

Mathor encountered no hostility from Ahmeni, yet could not make inroads with the scribe generally agreed to be the king's closest friend. Setau, his other confidant, had returned to Nubia with Lotus to collect venom from his precious snakes and to apply his ideas for improving the regional government.

The young queen possessed everything yet had nothing. Power seemed so near, yet so far, and bitterness began to invade her heart. Still she strove in vain to win Ramses' love; for the first time, doubts began to assail her. Determined not to let the Pharaoh notice her growing frustration, she threw herself into the social whirl, of which she was the undisputed queen.

One autumn evening, Mathor felt weary. She dismissed her servants, lay down and stared at the ceiling, the better to dream of Ramses, all-powerful and unattainable.

A gust of wind lifted the linen shade covering her window. Or so she thought, until a man burst through it, a long-haired man with an imposing build.

Mathor sat up and crossed her arms over her chest.

"Who are you?"

"A fellow Hittite."

A shaft of moonlight gave the queen a better view of the unexpected visitor's face.

"Uri-Teshoop!"

"Do you remember me, little girl?"

"How dare you break into my bedchamber!"

"It wasn't easy. I've been watching you for hours. With that devil Serramanna always on my tail, I've had to delay approaching you."

"Why would I want to see the man who overthrew Emperor Muwattali and tried to kill my father and mother?"

"All that is in the past. Today we're two Hittites exiled in Egypt."

"Are you forgetting who I am?"

"A bird in a gilded cage, the way I see it."

"I'm Ramses' wife and the queen of this country!"

Uri-Teshoop sat down on the end of the bed.

"Stop dreaming, little girl."

"I'll call the guards."

"Go right ahead."

Uri-Teshoop and Mathor locked eyes. The young woman rose and poured herself a glass of cool water.

"You're nothing but a monster and a brute. Why should I listen to someone with so much blood on his hands?"

"Because we belong to the same tribe, and Egypt will always be the enemy of our people!"

"You're raving. The peace treaty is engraved in stone."

"And you're dreaming if you think Ramses sees you as anything but a pawn in his game. Soon he'll be shutting you up in a harem."

"You're wrong!"

"Has he given you even one shred of power?"

Mathor said nothing.

"In Ramses' eyes, you don't exist as a person. You're part of the price he had to pay for peace. Once he feels sure that your father has called for demobilization, he'll invade Hatti. Ramses is cruel and underhanded. He set a clever trap and Hattusili fell for it. And your own father sacrificed you! Enjoy the high life while it lasts, Mathor. Your youth will be gone much more quickly than you'd ever imagine."

The queen turned her back to Uri-Teshoop.

"Are you quite finished?"

"Think about what I've just told you, and you'll see how much truth there is in it. If you want to see me again, find a way to send me a message without alerting Serramanna."

"What on earth would I want to say to you?"

"You love Hatti as much as I do. And you can't accept either defeat or humiliation."

Mathor waited a long time before turning around again.

A light breeze lifted the linen curtain. Uri-Teshoop had disappeared. Had it all been a nightmare, or was it a call to awaken?

The six men inside the huge vat beneath the vine arbor were singing at the top of their lungs and enthusiastically stomping fermented grapes in time to the music. The wine should be excellent; they were already half drunk on the fumes. Somewhat unsteadily, they clung to the overhanging vines. Outdoing them all was their leader, Serramanna.

"Someone is asking for you," a farmhand shouted.

"Keep going," Serramanna ordered his men. "Don't slow down!"

The man asking for him was an officer in the desert patrol. Weathered, square-jawed, he had his bow, arrows, and short sword at the ready.

"I've come to report, sir," he told Serramanna. "Our men have been combing the Libyan desert for months now, looking for Malfi and his rebel band."

"Have you finally located them?"

"Unfortunately, no. The desert is immense, and we only control the portion closest to Egypt. Venturing farther west would be risky. The Bedouins spy on us and warn Malfi off whenever we get close. He's harder to catch than a shadow."

It was not what Serramanna had wanted to hear. The desert patrol knew what it was doing; of that much he was certain. Their fruitless search proved just how tough an opponent Malfi was proving to be.

"Do we know for sure that Malfi has federated several tribes?"

"I'm not convinced of that," replied the officer. "It may be just another rumor."

"Do you know if he carries an iron dagger?"

"I've never heard it mentioned."

"Keep your men on alert. If anything at all turns up, inform the palace."

"As you wish. But what have we to fear from the Libyans?"

"We're sure that Malfi is up to some kind of mischief. Plus, he's a murder suspect."

Ahmeni never discarded a single document. Over the years, his Pi-Ramses office had turned into an archive of papyrus scrolls and wooden tablets. Three adjoining rooms held inactive files. His staff had repeatedly urged him to eliminate some of the excess, but Ahmeni wanted to keep the maximum amount of information on hand, since requests to other government departments seemed to be filled at a snail's pace.

Ahmeni worked fast. From his point of view, setting aside a problem only tended to make it worse. Most of the time it made more sense to rely on his own solutions than to call in a host of experts who tended to disappear once the going got rough.

He had just eaten a huge dinner of boiled meat that, as usual, would add no weight to his slender frame. He was working by lamplight when Serramanna entered his office.

"Still reading?"

"Yes, somebody has to take care of business."

"You're going to ruin your health, Ahmeni."

"I did that long ago."

"May I sit down?"

"As long as you don't move anything."

The Sard remained standing.

"Nothing new on Malfi," he said regretfully. "He's still on the run in the desert."

"What about Uri-Teshoop?"

"Oh, leading the high life. If I didn't know him like a hunter knows his prey, I'd swear he was a solid citizen with nothing in mind but keeping his rich wife happy."

"It's a possibility. They say that marriage can work wonders."

"They do, do they?"

The Sard's arch tone intrigued Ahmeni.

"What are you getting at?"

"You're an excellent scribe, but time flies, you know, and you're not a young man anymore."

Ahmeni put down his brush and crossed his arms.

"I've met a woman . . . charming, but very shy," continued Serramanna. "Obviously not right for me, but you might like her . . ."

"You're trying to marry me off?"

"I need variety, but you'd make a faithful husband."

Ahmeni saw red. "My life is this office and public affairs! Can you picture a woman in here? She'd sort and clean till I couldn't find a single thing!"

"I only thought—"

"Don't think about me. Just concentrate on finding Ahsha's murderer."

THIRTY-EIGHT

Ramses' Eternal Temple was a large complex on the West Bank at Thebes. According to the Pharaoh's wishes, the pylons seemed to touch the sky, trees shaded freshwater ponds, the doors were of gilded bronze, the floors of silver, and statues vibrating with the life force of the *ka* stood in the great courtyards. Surrounding the temple precinct were a library and storerooms. Within it were chapels to Ramses' father, Seti, his mother, Tuya, and his beloved wife Nefertari.

The Lord of the Two Lands returned frequently to this magical domain where the gods resided. He liked to honor the memory of the loved ones whose presence was always with him. Even so, this visit was special.

Meritamon, Ramses' daughter with Nefertari, was to perform a ceremony immortalizing the reigning Pharaoh.

When he caught sight of her, Ramses was once again struck by her resemblance to her mother. In her form-fitting dress adorned with two rosettes at chest level, Meritamon embodied Sechat, the goddess of writing. Her delicate face, framed by disk-shaped earrings, was fragile and luminous.

The king took her in his arms.

"How are you, my dear daughter?"

"Thanks to you, I'm able to pray in this temple and play music for the gods. I sense my mother's presence at every turn."

"It's at your request that I've come to Thebes. As the sole Queen of Egypt recognized by the temples, what mystery do you wish to unveil?"

Meritamon bowed to the sovereign. "Please step this way, Your Majesty."

In her role as the goddess, wearing the ibis mask of the god Thoth, she led Ramses to a chapel. Under Ramses' gaze, Thoth and Sechat inscribed the king's five coronation names on the leaves of a great tree carved upon the stone wall.

"Your annals are hereby established millions of times," said Meritamon. "They will now last forever."

Ramses was strangely moved. He was only a man upon whom fate had thrust a heavy burden, but the two gods referred him to another reality, as Pharaoh, whose soul passed from king to king through the dynasties.

The concelebrants withdrew, leaving Ramses to contemplate the tree of millions of years on which his eternal name had just been placed.

Meritamon was on her way back to the choir room when a young blond woman, lavishly dressed, barred her way.

"I'm Mathor," she said aggressively. "We've never met, but I have to talk to you."

"You're my father's official wife. We have nothing to say to each other."

"But you're the true Queen of Egypt."

"My role is strictly religious."

"In other words, essential."

"Interpret the facts as you like, Mathor. For me, there's only one Great Royal Wife—Nefertari."

"But she's dead, and I'm alive! Since you won't be queen, why stand in my way?"

Meritamon smiled. "Your imagination is running away with you. I live a cloistered life here and have no interest at all in worldly affairs."

"But you attend state ceremonies as Queen of Egypt!"

"At Pharaoh's request. Do you question his wishes?"

"Speak to him, convince him to give me my rightful place. Your influence will sway him."

"What is it you really want, Mathor?"

"I have the right to reign; my marriage gives it to me."

"Egypt can never be conquered by force, only by love. On this earth, if you flout the law of Ma'at by forgetting your duties, you'll end up sadly disillusioned."

"Your sermons don't interest me, Meritamon; what I need is your help. *I'm* not renouncing the world."

"Then you're braver than I. Good luck, Mathor."

Ramses meditated at length in the huge hypostyle hall in the temple of Karnak, which his father, Seti, had begun and he himself had completed in his role as son and successor. Filtered through the screened stone windows, sunlight fell on one after another of the painted and sculpted scenes that showed Pharaoh making offerings to the gods, winning their consent to reside on earth.

Amon, the great soul of Egypt who gave breath to every nostril, remained mysterious but everywhere in evidence. *He comes on the wind,* revealed one hymn, *but is never seen. The night is filled with his presence. All that is high, all that is low, is the work of his hands.* Attempting to learn about Amon, while realizing that he would always elude human intelligence, was the way to keep away evil and darkness, perceive the future, and organize the country in the image of heaven—according to the holy text called *The Book of Coming Forth by Day.*

The man now approaching Ramses had a square, unprepossessing face that age had done nothing to soften. A former soldier and chief inspector of the royal stables, he had entered the Karnak priesthood and worked his way up through the ranks to become the Second Prophet of Amon. His head was shaved, his linen robe spotless. He came to a halt just beside the monarch.

"My joy at seeing you again is great, O Majesty."

"Thanks to you, Karnak and Luxor are worthy of the gods that dwell here. How is Nebu?"

"The high priest no longer leaves his little house by the

sacred lake; he's old beyond reckoning, yet he continues to rule his domain."

Ramses appreciated Bakhen's loyalty. He was one of those exceptional beings without personal ambition, whose sole concern was right action. The management of Egypt's greatest temple complex and estates was in good hands.

Yet Bakhen seemed less serene than usual.

"Is something wrong?" asked Ramses.

"I've just received a number of complaints from smaller temples in the region of Thebes. They'll soon run out of the olibanum, incense, and myrrh required for their daily religious observances. In the short term, Karnak can supply them, but my own reserves will be depleted within two or three months."

"Won't the temples receive deliveries before the beginning of winter?"

"Of course, Your Majesty, but we can't be sure of the quantities. The recent harvests have been so poor that we may experience shortages of these essential supplies. If offerings can't be made in a satisfactory manner, what will become of the country's harmony?"

As soon as Ramses returned to the capital, Ahmeni appeared at his office with an armload of official documents. Everyone wondered where the frail-looking scribe found the strength to carry such heavy burdens.

"Your Majesty, we must take immediate action! The tax on barges is excessive, and . . ."

Ahmeni fell silent. The serious expression on Ramses' face told him not to bother the king with details.

"How is our supply of olibanum, incense, and myrrh?"

"I can't say off the top of my head, I'll have to check . . . Nothing to be alarmed about, as far as I know."

"How can you be certain?"

"Because I have a system for tracking it. If the reserves dipped below an acceptable level, I'd know."

"Still, it sounds as if there's a potential shortage around Thebes."

"Let's use the overstocks in the Pi-Ramses warehouses and hope that the upcoming harvest will be plentiful."

"Delegate your less important tasks and take care of this problem immediately, Ahmeni."

Ahmeni called a meeting with the head of reserves at the Double White House, the Treasury secretary, and the director of the House of Pine, who checked all shipments of merchandise from foreign countries. The three high officials were all well into their fifties.

"I had to leave an important meeting," complained the Treasury secretary, "so I hope you have some good reason for bringing us here."

"All three of you are responsible for our reserves of olibanum, myrrh, and incense," Ahmeni pointed out. "Since none of you has alerted me to the shortages, I suppose the situation is under control."

"I'm almost out of olibanum," confessed the director from the Double White House, "but that certainly can't be the case with my colleagues here."

"I have only a small supply remaining," the Treasury secretary noted, "but since it hadn't quite reached the official shortage level, I didn't think it wise to alarm my colleagues."

"My situation is exactly the same," said the director of

the House of Pine. "If the shortage had continued over the next few months, I would have reported it."

The three high officials had missed the point of his instructions and had focused instead on the details. And as was too often the case, they had not communicated with one another.

"I want exact figures from each of you."

Ahmeni's calculations were swift. By the next spring there would not be one speck of incense in Egypt; the temples and laboratories would be completely out of myrrh and olibanum.

And throughout the country a feeling of revolt would be born and grow against Ramses' failure to provide.

THIRTY-NINE

Still as lovely as a spring morning, Chief Physician Neferet was putting the final touches on an amalgam filling of pistachio tree resin, honey, copper flakes, and a bit of myrrh, intended for the tooth of her illustrious patient.

"No sign of abscess," she explained to Ramses, "but your gums are fragile and your tendency toward arthritis seems more pronounced. Your Majesty mustn't forget the mouthwash and willow bark tonic that I've prescribed."

"I've planted thousands of willows along the river and

inland lakes. You'll soon have a good supply of your anti-inflammatory remedies."

"Thank you, Majesty. I'm also giving you a paste to chew, composed of bryony, juniper, sycamore pods, and incense. Speaking of incense and myrrh, which are so effective in treating pain, I ought to inform you that we're experiencing shortages."

"I know, Neferet, I know . . ."

"When will new supplies be available for my doctors and surgeons?"

"It won't be long."

Sensing the monarch's unease, Neferet refrained from asking the questions that burned on her lips. The problem must be serious, but she trusted Ramses to lead the country out of this predicament.

Ramses had spent a long time with his father Seti's statue; the sculptor's genius had imbued the face with life. In the stark white-walled office, Seti's presence linked the Pharaoh's thoughts to those of his predecessor. Whenever he had to make decisions involving the kingdom's future, Ramses consulted the soul of his father and teacher, whose rigorous training methods would have broken lesser men.

Seti had been right to test him. Ramses felt that he owed his endurance to the demanding education he had received. As he matured, the fire within him burned no less intensely, but the passion of youth had been transformed into an ardent desire to build up his country and his people as his ancestors had done before him.

When Ramses' eyes came to rest on the large map of the Near East that he often consulted, the Pharaoh thought about Moses, his boyhood friend. He too had burned with a consuming fire, his true guide in the desert as he sought the Promised Land.

On several occasions, against the advice of his military advisors, Ramses had refused to take action against Moses and the Hebrews, believing that they must follow their destiny.

Ramses admitted Ahmeni and Serramanna to his office.

"I've reached several decisions. There's one in particular that ought to please you, Serramanna."

Hearing the king out, the hulking Sard was overjoyed.

Tanit, the shapely Phoenician, never tired of Uri-Teshoop's body. Although the Hittite brutalized her, she gave in to all his demands. Thanks to him, she felt young again. Each day was replete with pleasure. Uri-Teshoop had become her god.

The Hittite kissed her savagely, then rose and stretched like some wild beast, splendidly naked.

"You're a fine filly, Tanit. At times you almost make me forget my country."

Tanit left the bed and joined her lover, crouching to kiss his ankles.

"We're happy, so happy! Let's not think of anything but our love . . ."

"We're leaving tomorrow for your villa in the Faiyum."

"It's so dull there, darling. I'd rather stay here in Pi-Ramses."

"As soon as we arrive, I'll leave again. But you'll act as if we're together in your love nest."

Tanit stood up and pressed her heavy breasts to Uri-Teshoop's chest, embracing him fervently.

"Where are you going? How long will you be gone?"

"You don't need to know. When I get back, if Serramanna questions you, just say that we were never out of each other's sight."

"You can trust me with your secret, darling, I—"

The Hittite slapped her so hard that she cried out in pain.

"You're a female, and a female should keep her nose out of men's business. Do as I say and everything will be fine."

Uri-Teshoop was to rendezvous with Malfi. The two would waylay the convoy bringing olibanum, myrrh, and incense to Egypt. Once they destroyed these precious commodities, Ramses' popularity would plummet and the country would be in a state of turmoil. Conditions would be favorable for a surprise attack by the Libyans. In Hatti, the anti-treaty faction would run Hattusili off the throne and reinstate Uri-Teshoop, the only commander able to conquer Pharaoh's armies.

A frantic servant appeared in the doorway.

"Mistress, it's the police! A giant with a helmet and sword . . ."

"Send him away," ordered Tanit.

"No," countered Uri-Teshoop. "Let's see what our friend Serramanna wants. Tell him we'll be right down."

"I refuse to speak to him. He's so uncouth."

"Settle down, darling. Are you forgetting that we're the most famous pair of lovebirds in Egypt? Throw on a dress that leaves your breasts bare and splash on some perfume."

"Care for some wine, Serramanna?" asked Uri-Teshoop, hugging a languid Tanit to him.

"I'm here on official business."

"How does it concern us?" inquired the Phoenician.

"Ramses gave Uri-Teshoop the right to asylum in difficult times, and the way he's become part of Egyptian society is gratifying to the king. That's why he's granting the two of you a privilege that you can be proud of."

Tanit was astonished. "What do you mean?"

"The queen is leaving on a tour of all the harems in Egypt, where festivities will be arranged in her honor. The Pharaoh is extending an invitation for you to join her on the journey."

"That's . . . that's wonderful!" exclaimed the Phoenician.

"You don't look so happy about it, Uri-Teshoop," remarked the Sard.

"Of course I am . . . such an honor for a foreigner like me . . ."

"Queen Mathor is your cousin, isn't she? And your wife is a Phoenician. As long as people abide by the laws, they're welcome in Egypt. Your conduct has made you an authentic subject of Pharaoh."

"Why were you sent to invite us?"

"Because I'll be providing security for the royal entourage," the Sard replied with a grin. "And I won't let you out of my sight for a second."

They numbered only a hundred, but they were powerfully armed and perfectly trained. Malfi had assembled a strike force that included only his best men, a mixture of experienced fighters and energetic young soldiers.

After final drills, during which a dozen unqualified men

perished, the commando left the secret camp in the heart of the Libyan desert and headed north toward the western fringe of the Delta. Advancing in skiffs or along muddy trails, they crossed it from west to east, then turned toward the Arabian peninsula for their rendezvous with Uri-Teshoop. His men would give them precious information on how to escape detection by Egyptian patrols and lookouts.

The first phase of the conquest would be a triumph. The oppressed Libyans would find new hope, and Malfi would become the hero of a people desperate for revenge. The Nile would turn into a river of blood. Yet first they must strike at Egypt's core values: religious ritual and expression of the law of Ma'at. Without olibanum, without myrrh and incense, the priests would feel abandoned and would accuse Ramses of breaking his pact with heaven.

Malfi's scout retraced his steps.

"We can't go any farther, sir," he reported.

"What kind of nonsense is this?"

"Come see for yourself."

Lying prone on a mound of soft earth, hidden by thorn bushes, Malfi could not believe his eyes.

The Egyptian army occupied a wide band of ground between the sea and the marshlands. Boats full of archers skimmed the waters. Lookouts stood on tall wooden towers. There must be several thousand men, commanded by Merenptah, Ramses' younger son.

"We can't get through," the scout advised. "We'll be spotted and massacred."

Malfi could not lead his men to death; they were his finest, the future spearhead of the Libyan army. Destroying a caravan would have been easy, but skirmishing with a huge force like this would be suicide.

Fuming, the Libyan grabbed a thorny tuft and ground it to bits in his hand.

FORTY

The caravan boss felt dazed. He was a Syrian who had traded all over the Near East, and though he was nearing sixty he had never seen such riches in one place.

His producers were supposed to meet him at the northwestern point of the Arabian peninsula, an arid and desolate region where the temperature was torrid by day and often frigid by night, to say nothing of the danger from snakes and scorpions. The spot was ideal for sheltering a secret cache. For three years now, the Syrian had been stockpiling the treasures he had skimmed from the Egyptian government.

His partners in crime, the Libyan Malfi and the Hittite Uri-Teshoop, believed him when he claimed to have torched what remained of the year's paltry harvest of incense products. Malfi and Uri-Teshoop were warriors, not businessmen; they wouldn't realize that no sensible merchant ever destroys the goods.

With limp black hair framing his moon face, a thick torso set on short legs, the Syrian had been lying and cheating since his teens, not forgetting to buy silence along the way. One of his contacts had been another clever Syrian, Raia, who had recently met a violent death.

The caravan boss had amassed quite a nest egg over the

years. Now it paled in comparison to the incredible prize that had just been deposited in his warehouse.

Standing an average of ten feet high, the incense trees of Arabia had yielded three harvests so abundant that three times as many seasonal workers than usual had to be hired. The dark green leaves and golden flowers with purple centers were not half as beautiful as the superb brown bark. Scraping it released droplets of resin; specialized workers would roll it into tiny balls that released their marvelous scent when burned.

Words failed the cavavan boss when he contemplated the incredible quantity of olibanum. Its whitish, milky, fragrant resin had flowed like honey from the gods. The droplets of white, gray, or yellow had nearly made him weep with joy. He was acquainted with this costly and sought-after product's numerous virtues. It was an antiseptic, an anti-inflammatory, and an analgesic. In ointments, plasters, powders, sometimes in liquid form, Egyptian doctors used it to counteract tumors, ulcers, abscesses, eye and ear infections. Olibanum stopped hemorrhages and helped wounds heal faster; it was even an antidote to poison. Neferet, the famous chief physician of the realm, would pay a fortune for this indispensable substance.

And there was green galbanum resin gum, dark laudanum resin, thick, sticky balsam oil, myrrh . . . He was on the brink of ecstasy. Such a fortune was beyond any merchant's wildest dreams.

The Syrian had taken care to set a decoy for his clients, dispatching a caravan on the route where Uri-Teshoop and Malfi were expecting him. He feared it had been a mistake sending only a modest cargo, for news of the exceptional harvest was already spreading and might reach his foreign partners' ears too quickly.

How could he buy some time? Within two days the Syrian was expecting Greek, Cypriot, and Lebanese traders, who would snap up the contents of his warehouse. Then he planned to head for Crete, where he would spend the rest of his days in comfort. For the next two days he'd just have to pray that Uri-Teshoop and Malfi didn't find him out.

"A Hittite is here to see you," one of his servants announced.

The Syrian's mouth went dry. His eyes stung. The worst had happened. A suspicious Uri-Teshoop was here to check on the rumors. And if he demanded to inspect the warehouse . . . Was there any way to reason with the former commander-in-chief of the Hittite army, or should he run?

Paralyzed with fear, he hesitated. Then he saw that the man coming toward him was not Uri-Teshoop.

"Are you a Hittite?" the caravan boss asked haltingly.

"I am."

"And a friend of—"

"No names, please. Yes, I'm a friend of the general's, the only man capable of saving Hatti from dishonor."

"Good, good . . . May the gods smile upon him! When will he be arriving?"

"You'll have to be patient."

"Nothing has happened to him, I hope?"

"Don't worry, he's merely been detained at official ceremonies in Egypt. He trusts that you'll honor the terms of your contract to the letter."

"He can rest assured that the contract has been executed. Everything went as he wished."

"Good. I'll let the general know."

"Tell him I hope he's satisfied. As soon as I get to Egypt, I'll be in touch."

Once the Hittite was out of sight, the caravan boss

gulped down three shots of strong liquor. He couldn't believe his luck! Uri-Teshoop detained in Egypt . . . Some god of crooked deals must be looking after him.

He would still have to deal with Malfi, a dangerous madman who displayed the occasional flash of lucidity. The sight of blood usually went to the Libyan's head. Slaughtering the decoy caravan would have given him as much pleasure as bedding a woman, and he would have forgotten to examine the cargo closely. But if anything set off an alarm, he'd track the caravan boss like an animal.

The Syrian had many strengths, but physical courage was not among them. The thought of confronting Malfi made him panic.

In the distance, a cloud of dust.

They were expecting no one . . . It could only be the Libyan and his bloodthirsty commando!

The caravan boss collapsed on a mat, cursing his luck. Malfi would enjoy slitting his throat, watching him die a slow death.

The cloud of dust was moving slowly. Horses? No, they'd be going faster. Donkeys? Yes, it was donkeys. Then this must be a caravan! But where had it come from?

Hopeful but unsure, the merchant rose to watch the heavily laden convoy's slow, steady progress. And he recognized the drivers: the men he had sent to their death on the route where Malfi lay in wait!

Could it be a mirage? No, here came the lead driver, a fellow Syrian somewhat older than himself.

"A good trip, friend?"

"Fine, fine."

The caravan boss concealed his stupefaction. "No trouble along the way?"

"Not in the least. But we're all in a hurry to drink, eat, wash, and sleep. Will you take care of the cargo?"

"Of course, of course . . . Go relax."

The caravan was safe and sound, the goods intact. There was only one possible explanation: Malfi and the Libyans had been stopped. Perhaps the warlord had been killed by the desert patrol.

It was all turning out as he'd hoped. The risk and anxiety would all be worth it!

Slightly giddy, the Syrian ran to the warehouse, to which he held the only key.

The wooden bolt was broken.

Livid, he pushed in the door. Between him and his heaps of treasure stood a man with a shaved skull, draped in a panther skin.

"Who . . . who are you?"

"Kha, the high priest of Memphis and Ramses' elder son. I've come for what belongs to Egypt."

The Syrian gripped his dagger.

"Don't do anything rash . . . Pharaoh is watching you."

The thief looked behind him. As far as he could see, the sandy hillocks bristled with Egyptian archers. And there in the sunshine stood Ramses the Great, in his tall blue crown, erect in his chariot.

The caravan boss fell to his knees.

"Pardon . . . I'm not guilty . . . they made me . . ."

"You'll stand trial," announced Kha.

The very idea of court, of the probable sentence, made the Syrian take flight. Raising his dagger, he rushed at an archer who was coming toward him with wooden handcuffs, and sank the knife into the soldier's arm.

Seeing their comrade in mortal danger, three other archers drew their bows. The thief fell, his body bristling with arrows.

Over Ahmeni's objections, Ramses had insisted on

heading the expedition himself. Thanks to information from the desert patrol, as well as the use of his divining rod, the king had located the missing shipments of crucial incense products. He had also detected another irregularity that he wanted to check for himself.

The Pharaoh's chariot took off through the desert, followed by a cohort of military vehicles. Ramses' two horses were so swift that they soon outdistanced his escort.

All the way to the horizon was nothing but sand, rocks, and hillocks.

"What is the king doing out in the middle of nowhere?" a chariot lieutenant asked the archer who rode with him.

"I was at the battle of Kadesh," replied the archer. "Ramses does nothing by chance. It's a divine force that guides him."

The monarch passed by a sand dune and came to a halt.

As far as the eye could see were magnificent trees with gray and yellow bark around a soft white core—an extraordinary plantation of olibanum trees, enough to provide Egypt with precious resin for years to come.

FORTY-ONE

Uri-Teshoop was at the breaking point. The beauty of the gardens, the quality of the food, the charm of the music—nothing could make him forget Serramanna's constant presence and unbearable smile. Tanit, on the other hand, was enjoying her tour of the harems in the company of a dazzling queen. Mathor, who charmed the dourest of administrators, loved being the center of attention.

"Excellent news," Serramanna announced to the Hittite. "Ramses has just performed a new miracle. Pharaoh discovered a huge olibanum plantation in Arabia, and the caravans made their way back to Pi-Ramses safe and sound."

The Hittite clenched his fists. Why hadn't Malfi carried out their plan? If the Libyan had been arrested or killed, Uri-Teshoop would never be able to wreak havoc in Egypt.

Tanit was talking with some local businesswomen at Merur, the harem where Moses had worked long ago. Uri-Teshoop sat apart, on a low stone wall at the edge of an artificial lake.

"Enjoying the view, cousin?"

The former commander-in-chief of the Hittite army raised his eyes to focus on Mathor, now at the height of her beauty.

"I'm too depressed."

"What seems to be the problem?"

"You, Mathor."

"Me? You can't be serious!"

"Haven't you figured out Ramses' strategy yet?"

"Tell me your theory, Uri-Teshoop."

"You're living the final moments of your dream. Ramses has just led a military expedition to the colonies, asserting his hold over the native populations. You'd have to be blind not to see that he's consolidating his bases, getting ready to launch a new assault against Hatti. Before he does that, he'll have to get rid of two stumbling blocks—you and me. I'll be put under house arrest and probably fall victim to some convenient accident. You'll be shut up in one of these harems you so enjoy visiting."

"Harems aren't prisons!"

"You'll be given an honorary position, and that will be the last you'll see of the king. Ramses has his mind set on war, believe me."

"How can you be so sure?"

"I have my network of friends, Mathor. I get solid information, things that would never reach your ears."

The queen looked troubled.

"What are you proposing?"

"The king is a gourmet. He especially enjoys a dish created in his honor, a marinade of garlic, onions, and red oasis wine over beef and filets of Nile perch. A Hittite princess should know how to exploit a weakness for good food."

"You can't be suggesting that I—"

"Don't play innocent! In Hattusa, you learned the uses of poison."

"You're a monster!"

"If you don't get to Ramses first, he'll destroy you."

"That's the last word you'll ever say to me, Uri-Teshoop."

The fallen prince was playing for high stakes. If Mathor was unconvinced, she might well denounce him to Serramanna. But if Uri-Teshoop had successfully planted the seeds of doubt in his cousin's mind, the battle was half won.

Kha was worried.

Yes, the restoration program he had undertaken at Saqqara had already brought remarkable results. Djoser's step pyramid, the pyramid of Wenis that housed the earliest "Pyramid Texts" (secret formulas for resurrecting the royal soul), and the monuments of Pepi I had all been carefully refurbished.

And the high priest of Memphis had not stopped there. He had also asked his teams of builders and stonemasons to patch up the Fifth Dynasty pharaohs' temples and pyramids at Abu Sir, just north of Saqqara. In Memphis, Kha had enlarged the temple of Ptah, adding a chapel to Seti's memory and leaving room for a shrine to the glory of Ramses.

Suddenly overcome with fatigue, Kha went to the spot where the First Dynasty tombs had been dug, at the edge of Saqqara's desert plateau, overlooking palm groves and cultivated fields. Here King Djet had been buried with three hundred sculpted bulls' heads, inlaid with genuine horns that protruded from the walls that surrounded his sepulchre. The visit gave Kha the necessary energy to strengthen the bonds between past and present.

The high priest had not yet discovered the Book of Thoth. At times he felt he would never do so. He attributed his failure to a lack of vigilance and his neglect of the cult of the sacred bull. While he vowed one day to address the problem, he knew he must first see his restoration program to completion.

But would it ever be finished? For the third time since the beginning of the year, Kha told his driver to take him to the pyramid of Mycerinus, where he hoped to leave an inscription once the project was completed.

For the third time, he found the work site empty, except for an old stonecarver munching on bread rubbed with garlic.

"Where is everyone?" asked Kha.

"Gone home."

"The ghost again?"

"Yes, it's back. Several men saw it this time, with its hands full of snakes and threatening to kill anyone who came near. As long as the ghost is hanging around, no one will want to work here, no matter how high the pay."

Kha's worst fears were confirmed: refurbishing the monuments on the Giza plateau would be impossible. The ghost was loosening stones and causing accidents. Everyone knew that it was a tormented soul, returning to earth to cause trouble among the living. Not even Kha's strong magic had been able to stop it.

A chariot approached; it must be Ramses. Kha took heart. He'd requested his father's help. Yet if the king failed, part of the plateau of Giza would have to be declared off limits, and ancient masterpieces would continue to crumble.

"The situation is worsening, Your Majesty. The workers have fled."

"Have you tried the usual incantations?"

"They've had no effect."

Ramses contemplated the pyramid of Mycerinus, with its powerful granite foundations. Each year, the Pharaoh made a pilgrimage to Giza, drawing on the energy its builders had captured in stone—rays of light uniting earth with heaven.

"Do you know where this ghost is lurking?"

"None of the workmen dared follow it."

The king noticed the old stonecarver, still busy eating, and approached him. Startled, the man dropped his piece of bread and fell to his knees, hands outstretched, forehead to the ground.

"Why didn't you run like the others?"

"I . . . I don't know, Your Majesty."

"You know the ghost's hiding place, don't you?"

Lying to the king would mean eternal damnation.

"Take us there."

Trembling, the old man guided the king through the streets of tombs where Mycerinus's followers reposed; in the hereafter, they would continue to serve as his faithful servants. Some of these structures were now more than a thousand years old and needed work, as Kha's trained eye was quick to see.

The stonecarver entered a small open-air courtyard strewn with chunks of limestone. In one corner was a crumbling pile of hewn building blocks.

"It's here, but don't go any farther."

"Who is this ghost?"

"A sculptor whose memory wasn't honored. He's getting revenge by attacking other stoneworkers."

"According to the inscriptions, the man directed a team of builders in Mycerinus's day."

"Let's clear that pile of blocks," ordered Ramses.

"Your Majesty . . ."

"Get to work."

The rim of a rectangular well emerged; Kha threw a pebble down it, and the fall seemed endless.

"Almost fifty feet," concluded the stonecarver when he heard it hit. "Don't venture into that hellhole, Your Majesty."

A knotted rope hung down one wall of the well.

"Someone has to go," Ramses said firmly.

"In that case, I should be the one to take the risk," the workman decided.

"If you meet the ghost," objected Kha, "will you know the right words to neutralize it?"

The old man hung his head.

"As high priest of Ptah," said Ramses' firstborn son, "the task falls to me. Don't keep me from going, Father."

Kha began a descent that he thought would never end. Yet the bottom of the well was not dark: a strange glow emanated from the limestone walls. The high priest finally set foot on uneven ground and proceeded down a narrow corridor ending in a false door. On this was a portrait of the dead man, surrounded by columns of hieroglyphs.

Then Kha understood.

A wide crack ran the full length of the portrait, depriving the beneficiary of the hieroglyphs' formulas for resurrection. Prevented from inhabiting his image, the man's spirit had taken the form of a destructive ghost, furious with the living for neglecting his memory.

When Kha resurfaced, he was exhausted yet radiant. As soon as the underground door was repaired and the dead man's face lovingly sculpted, the curse over the work site would lift.

FORTY-TWO

Uri-Teshoop was back in Pi-Ramses, and still seething. With Serramanna watching his every move for weeks, unable to act and deprived of information, he felt like massacring all of Egypt, beginning with Ramses. What was more, he had to put up with the cloying Tanit, still eager for her daily ration of love.

And here she was, half-naked, in her cloud of fragrance.

"Darling . . . the Hittites!"

"What Hittites?"

"Hundreds of them! Pi-Ramses is full of Hittites!"

"Have you lost your mind, woman?"

"My servants have seen them."

"Hittites attacking the heart of Ramses' kingdom? If it's true, Tanit, that's fabulous news."

Uri-Teshoop pushed his wife away and dressed in a short black and red striped tunic. It felt like the old days. He hopped on a horse, excited, ready for battle.

Hattusili had been overthrown, the faction calling for all-out war had triumphed, the Egyptian defense lines had been broken in a surprise attack, and the fate of the Near East hung in the balance!

On the broad avenue leading from the temple of Ptah to the royal palace, a colorful crowd was celebrating.

There was no soldier in sight, not the slightest sign of combat.

Speechless, Uri-Teshoop spoke to a grinning policeman.

"I heard that Hittites have invaded Pi-Ramses."

"It's true."

"But where are they?"

"At the palace."

"Have they killed Ramses?"

"What are you talking about? These are the first Hittites who've come to visit Egypt. They're paying tribute to our Pharaoh."

Tourists! Dumbfounded, Uri-Teshoop broke through the crowd and headed for the palace gates.

"We were hoping you'd come!" Serramanna boomed heartily. "Want to watch the ceremony?"

The crestfallen prince let the Sard show him to the audience chamber, thick with courtiers.

In the front stood the visitors' delegates, their arms heaped with gifts. When Ramses appeared, conversation ceased. One by one, the Hittites presented the king with lapis lazuli, turquoise, copper, iron, emeralds, amethysts, carnelian, and jade.

The sovereign lingered over some superb turquoise nuggets; they could only have come from the Sinai mines. As a young prince, Ramses had traveled there with Moses. The red and yellow mountain was unforgettable, with its looming boulders and secret ravines.

"These are splendid," he said to the delegate. "Could you have crossed paths with Moses and his Hebrew followers?"

"No, Your Majesty."

"Have you heard about their exodus?"

"Everyone in the region fears them. They're quick to do battle, and Moses still insists they'll find their homeland."

So Ramses' boyhood friend was still pursuing his dream. The monarch took little note of the growing piles of presents, his mind flooding with memories of his estranged companion.

The head of the delegation was the last to bow to Ramses.

"Are we free to come and go in all of Egypt, Your Majesty?"

"Indeed, as our peace agreement stipulates."

"May we honor our gods in your capital?"

"To the west of town is the temple of the Syrian goddess Astarte, our Set's companion. She protects my chariot and horses; I've also asked her to keep the Memphis waterfront safe. The Storm God and Sun Goddess you worship in Hattusa are equally welcome in Pi-Ramses."

As soon as the delegation left the audience chamber, Uri-Teshoop approached one of his fellow Hittites.

"Do you recognize me?"

"No."

"I'm Uri-Teshoop, son of Emperor Muwattali."

"Muwattali is dead now. Hattusili is emperor."

"This visit . . . it's a front, isn't it?"

"What do you mean? We've come to tour Egypt, and other Hittites will follow us. The war is over for good."

For several long minutes, Uri-Teshoop stood stunned in the middle of Pi-Ramses' main avenue.

The head of the Treasury, who was trailing behind Ahmeni, had finally been convinced to appear before Ramses. Up to this point, he had thought it safer to hold his tongue, hoping that scandal could be avoided and reason would win the day. But the arrival of the Hittite visitors, or more exactly the value of their gifts, had occasioned such blatant excess that the high official could no longer keep silent.

Facing Ramses would be too much for him, so the Treasury secretary had gone to Ahmeni. The king's private secretary heard him out, stone-faced, then requested an urgent meeting with the monarch. Now the dignitary was repeating his accusations word for word, as instructed, not omitting the slightest detail.

"You have nothing to add, Ahmeni?"

"Would that really be useful, Your Majesty?"

"Did you know about this irregularity?"

"It slipped by me, I admit, although I did issue warnings."

"Both of you can consider the problem solved."

Relieved, the Treasury secretary avoided the king's stern gaze. He felt lucky not to have been held responsible. As for Ahmeni, he was counting on Ramses to establish the law of Ma'at in the heart of his own palace.

"At last, Your Majesty!" exclaimed Mathor. "I was afraid I'd never see you again. Why wasn't I at your side when you greeted my countrymen? They would have been glad to see how well you treat me."

Superb in her red robe with silver rosettes, Mathor sailed around a ballet of servant girls pursuing their daily tasks—banishing the smallest speck of dust, carrying jewels and gowns for her to wear, tending the hundreds of flowers that scented the queen's wing of the palace.

"Dismiss your staff," ordered Ramses.

The queen froze.

"But . . . I have no reason to."

The man Mathor saw now was no lover, but the Pharaoh of Egypt. The same expression must have been on his face when he counterattacked at Kadesh, rushing single-handed at thousands of Hittite soldiers.

"Out of here, all of you!" cried the queen.

Unaccustomed to such treatment, the servants slowly withdrew, dropping all they carried on the tile floor.

Mathor attempted a smile.

"What's going on, Your Majesty?"

"Do you think you're behaving like a Queen of Egypt?"

"I'm living up to my rank, as you demanded."

"On the contrary, Mathor. Your willful behavior is capricious and unacceptable."

"What have I done wrong?"

"You've been badgering the Treasury secretary to release assets belonging to the temples, and yesterday you signed a decree appropriating the precious metal your fellow countrymen brought as a gift to Egypt."

"I'm the queen. It all belongs to me!" the young woman snapped.

"You're sadly mistaken. The state doesn't run on greed and selfishness, but the law of Ma'at. This land is the property of the gods; they transmit it to Pharaoh, whose duty is to maintain it in good condition, prosperous and happy. Your first concern, Mathor, ought to be right action. When a head of state is no longer a role model, the country is courting decadence and ruin. Your behavior is an insult to Pharaoh's authority and his people's welfare."

Ramses had not raised his voice, but his words cut like a blade.

"I . . . but I didn't think . . ."

"A Queen of Egypt must think before she acts. And you have acted badly, Mathor. I've reversed your unjust decree and taken measures to keep you from doing more harm. Henceforth you are to reside at the harem of Merur and will appear at court only at my request. You will want for nothing, but will make no further requisitions."

"Ramses . . . you can't refuse my love!"

"Egypt is my bride, Mathor. You've never able to understand that."

FORTY-THREE

The Viceroy of Nubia could no longer bear Setau's interfering presence. With valuable help from Lotus, his Nubian sorceress of a wife, Setau had become so involved in the economic development of the southern province that every single tribe was now productive, and not the least conflict between them! The viceroy never would have believed it was possible.

Furthermore, Setau had won respect among the building trades as he dotted the countryside with temples and chapels to the glory of Pharaoh and his patron deities. It was Setau, too, who had made improvements in farming, established tax rolls, and collected revenues!

The viceroy had to face facts: this aging snake charmer, whom he had considered a harmless eccentric, was turning out to be a capable administrator. If Setau continued to get such remarkable results, the viceroy's own position would become untenable. Accused of incompetence and laziness, he would be recalled.

Negotiating with Setau was impossible. Stubborn, refusing to slow his pace, Ramses' old friend would scoff at a compromise. The viceroy hadn't even considered bribing him; Setau and Lotus lived simply, in contact with the natives, and displayed no apparent taste for luxury.

There was only one solution: a fatal accident, carefully arranged so that nothing would seem suspicious. That was why the viceroy had asked a Nubian ex-convict to meet him at Abu Simbel. The man had a long police record and no discernible conscience. Recently released from jail again, he also needed money.

The night was dark. Forming the facade of the great temple, the four colossal seated statues that embodied Ramses' *ka* looked off into the distance, seeing time and space as human eyes could never see them.

The Nubian was waiting. He had a narrow forehead, prominent cheekbones, full lips, and an impressive spear.

"I'm the viceroy."

"I know. I saw you once at the fortress where I was in prison."

"I need your help."

"I hunt for my village now. I'm settling down."

"You're lying. I have evidence that implicates you in a robbery."

Furious, the Nubian sank his spear in the ground.

"What kind of evidence?"

"If you don't cooperate, you'll go back to jail for good. But do as I say and you'll be rich."

"What do you want from me?"

"Someone is standing in my way; you'll help me get rid of him."

"A Nubian?"

"No, an Egyptian."

"The price will be high, then."

"You're in no position to bargain," the viceroy said crisply.

"Who's my mark?"

"Setau."

The Nubian grabbed his spear and waved it at the sky. "He's worth a fortune!"

"You'll be well paid, as long as Setau's death is made to look like an accident."

"Understood."

The viceroy suddenly swayed and plopped down on his behind. The Nubian's whoop of laughter was cut short when the same thing happened to him. The two men tried scrambling to their feet, but again lost their balance.

"The ground is moving," exclaimed the Nubian. "The Earth God is angry!"

The cliff emitted a groan. The statues shook. Paralyzed with fear, the viceroy and his hireling saw one of the colossal heads break loose.

Ramses' face flew toward the criminals and crushed them beneath its weight.

Dame Tanit was desperate. It had been more than a week since Uri-Teshoop last made love to her. He left early every morning, galloped through the countryside all day long, came home exhausted, wolfed down his dinner, and fell asleep without a word to her.

Tanit had only dared question him once, and he'd struck her so hard she'd almost lost consciousness. The comely Phoenician found comfort only with her little tabby cat. She'd lost all interest in her once-thriving business.

A horse's trot . . . Uri-Teshoop was home.

He appeared, a hungry look in his eye. "Come here, sweetheart!"

Tanit ran to her lover's arms. He ripped off her dress and pushed her down on a pile of cushions. "Darling . . . you've come back to me!" she sighed.

Uri-Teshoop's rampant desire overwhelmed her.

"What's been bothering you?" she asked when it was over.

"I thought I'd been abandoned . . . but Malfi is still alive and at work on the Libyan front. One of his men got in touch with me; there's hope again. The battle goes on, Tanit, and Ramses can't be invulnerable."

"Forgive me for saying so, darling, but Malfi frightens me."

"The Hittites have turned into cowards. Only the Libyans can bring them to their senses, and Malfi's the man for the job. We have no other choice than a fight to the death . . . And count on me to win it!"

Tanit slept, sated with pleasure. Sitting on a caned chair in the garden, Uri-Teshoop, his head full of bloodthirsty dreams, gazed at the rising moon and asked for its help.

"I can be of more use than a heavenly body," a feminine voice said behind him.

The fallen prince whirled around.

"Mathor! What are you doing here? It's a risk . . ."

"The queen still has the right to go where she pleases."

"You seem disillusioned . . . Has Ramses repudiated you?"

"No, of course not!"

"Then why have you come here in secret, cousin?"

The beautiful young woman lifted her eyes to the starry skies.

"You were right, Uri-Teshoop. I'm a Hittite and that's what I'll always be. Ramses will never truly accept me as Great Royal Wife. I'll never be the equal of Nefertari."

Mathor couldn't restrain her sobs. Uri-Teshoop tried to comfort her, but she waved him away.

"I'm stupid . . . Why cry over defeat? That's for the weak of heart. A Hittite princess has no right to bemoan her fate."

"You and I were born to conquer."

"Ramses humiliated me," confessed Mathor. "He treated me like a servant. I loved him, I was ready to become a great queen, I did as he bade me, but he wouldn't have me."

"And you want revenge?"

"I'm not sure what I want."

"Wake up, Mathor! Allowing Ramses to shame you would be the coward's way out. You're made of better stuff than that. Just coming here means you've already made your decision."

"Careful, Uri-Teshoop!"

"I won't be careful any longer! Hatti hasn't been humbled yet. There's still time to act. I have powerful allies, Mathor, and we have a common enemy: Ramses."

"Ramses is my husband."

"No, he's a tyrant who's scorned and rejected you. Do what I'm asking, Mathor. You can get your hands on the poison."

Kill her dream . . . Could Mathor throw away the future she'd so desired, destroy the man she'd loved so passionately, the Pharaoh of Egypt?

"Make up your mind," ordered Uri-Teshoop.

The queen vanished into the night.

A smile on his lips, the Hittite warrior went up to the roof terrace, closer to the moon, where he could thank the goddess.

"Who goes there?" he said at the sound of footsteps behind him.

"It's me, darling."

Uri-Teshoop grabbed Tanit by the throat.

"Were you spying on us?"

"No, I—"

"You heard everything, didn't you?"

"Yes, but I'll never tell, I swear it!"

"Of course, sweetheart. You'd never make such a fatal error. Look, Tanit, look!"

From under his tunic flashed an iron dagger. He pointed it at the moon.

"Take a good look at this knife. It's the one that killed Ramses' friend Ahsha. It's the one that I'll use to kill Pharaoh. And you too, if you cross me."

FORTY-FOUR

To celebrate his birthday, Ramses had planned a dinner with his two sons, Kha and Merenptah, as well as his old and faithful friend Ahmeni. The scribe asked the palace chef to surprise the Pharaoh with his favorite dish of beef and fish in special marinade, served with a special vintage dating back to Year Three of Seti's reign.

Fortunately for the future of Egypt, no rivalry existed between Kha and Merenptah. The elder son, a theologian and priest, pursued his quest for knowledge studying ancient texts and the monuments of the past; the younger son was a general, watching over the safety of the realm. No other royal son possessed their maturity, high standards, and statesmanship. When he decided the time had come, Ramses would designate his successor with an easy mind.

Yet no one even considered succeeding Ramses. At sixty, he still drew admiring glances from the palace beauties. What was more, his renown had long since spread beyond Egypt's borders. Storytellers repeated his legend from southern Nubia to the island of Crete. Was he not the world's most powerful sovereign, the Son of Light, the great builder? The gods had never showered so many gifts on a single human.

"Let's drink to the glory of Ramses," proposed Ahmeni.

"No," objected the monarch. "Let's drink to Egypt, our home, the earthly image of heaven."

The four men shared an abiding love for the country they had served all their lives, a land and culture so full of marvels.

"Why isn't Meritamon here?" asked Kha.

"She's playing music for the gods as we speak. That was her wish, and I respect it."

"You didn't invite Mathor," remarked Merenptah.

"She's gone to live at the harem of Merur."

"What?" said Ahmeni in amazement. "I thought I just saw her in the palace kitchens."

"She was supposed to be gone by now. Ahmeni, look into this for me tomorrow. See that she's on her way. Merenptah, have you learned anything more about Libya?"

"Nothing new, Your Majesty. It seems that Malfi is a madman and his dream of conquest is only a delusion."

"The Giza ghost has disappeared," Kha reported. "The stonemasons are back at work."

The palace steward came in and presented the king with a dispatch. Bearing Setau's personal seal, it was labeled "Urgent."

Ramses broke the seal, unrolled the papyrus, read his friend's brief message, and got to his feet.

"I'm leaving for Abu Simbel at once. You can finish without me."

But Kha, Merenptah, and Ahmeni didn't linger; none of them touched the special dinner. The chef briefly considered sharing it with his assistants, but this was the royal meal. Eating it would be improper; it would also be pilfering. Regretfully, the chef dumped the contents of the platter—including the poison that Uri-Teshoop had provided and Mathor had sprinkled into the food.

Once again, Ramses fell under the spell of Nubia. The clear air and sheer blue sky; the enchanting green of palm trees and the thin strip of cultivated land that the Nile carved out of the desert; the flight of pelicans, cranes, flamingos and ibises; the scent of mimosa; the ocher magic of the hills: all put the soul in touch with the hidden forces of nature.

Ramses did not leave the bow of the cutter taking him to Abu Simbel. He had kept his escort to a minimum and had handpicked a tireless crew of elite sailors, familiar with the dangers of navigating the Nile.

Not far from their destination, the monarch took refreshment in his cabin, seated on a folding chair with ivory-encrusted feet in the shape of ducks' heads. Suddenly the boat slowed.

Ramses hailed the captain.

"What's going on?"

"There's a herd of crocodiles on the banks, all of them twenty feet long, at least! And hippos in the water. For the moment, we can't go forward. I'd even advise Your Majesty to disembark. The beasts look nervous. They may attack."

"Steady as she goes, Captain."

"But Your Majesty . . ." he protested weakly.

"Nubia is a land of miracles."

The sailors set to work, their nerves taut.

The hippos stirred in the water. On the riverbank, an enormous crocodile shook its tail, slithered forward with frightening speed, then stopped again.

A huge bull elephant trumpeted, parting the low branches of an acacia tree with his trunk. Ramses had felt his old friend's presence even before he emerged, sending flocks of birds skyward and terrifying the sailors.

Some of the crocodiles took refuge in half-submerged reeds; others charged at the hippos. The struggle was brief but violent; then the Nile grew calm once more.

The big bull trumpeted again, calling to Ramses, who waved back. Many years earlier Seti's son had saved the elephant as a wounded calf. More than once, the great beast had returned the favor.

"Shouldn't we capture that monster and bring it back home?" suggested the captain.

"We should value its freedom as we do our own," replied the king.

Two rocky outcroppings, a backwater with golden sand, a valley between the cliff's twin spurs, acacias scenting the shimmering air, the spellbinding beauty of Nubian sandstone . . . Ramses felt a stab of pain arriving at Abu Simbel's perfect site, for here was the monument to his eternal union with Nefertari.

As the king had feared, Setau's description of the damage was accurate. The temple had definitely suffered an earthquake, with the face and torso of one of the four colossal statues toppled.

Setau and Lotus greeted the monarch.

"Was anyone hurt?" asked Ramses.

"There were two casualties: the Viceroy of Nubia and an ex-convict."

"What were they doing together?"

"I have no idea."

"What happened inside?"

"See for yourself."

Ramses entered the larger sanctuary. In the great hall, damaged pillars had already been propped up.

"Has Nefertari's temple suffered as well?"

"No, Your Majesty."

"The gods have been merciful, Setau."

"We'll set straight to work, and every trace of this disaster will disappear. The statue will be the hardest. I have several plans to submit to you."

"Don't try to repair it."

"You're going to leave the facade in such a state?"

"This earthquake was a message from the Earth God. Since he decided to redo the facade, let's leave it the way he wants."

Pharaoh's decision shocked Setau, but Ramses would not be dissuaded. Only three intact colossi would perpetuate the royal *ka;* the mutilated fourth statue would serve as a reminder of the imperfection inherent in human endeavors. The shattered stone giant would not detract from the majestic whole, but rather would reinforce the power and might of its three companions.

The king, Setau, and Lotus dined at the foot of a palm tree. The snake charmer had not asked the monarch to daub himself with asafetida, a resin from the root of the Persian ferula plant, so evil-smelling that it repelled snakes. Instead, he had given him red berries from a shrub containing an antidote to poison.

"You've increased the quantity of divine offerings," said

Ramses to Setau. "You've filled the granaries to bursting, established peace in this turbulent region, built places of worship all over Nubia, and everywhere championed truth over lies. What would you think of representing Ma'at as the province's chief justice?"

"But that's the viceroy's prerogative!"

"I know that, old friend. And you're the new Viceroy of Nubia, named by decree in this thirty-eighth year of my reign."

Setau searched for a way to refuse, but Ramses allowed him no time to answer.

"You can't turn me down. The earthquake was a sign to you. Your existence is moving into another dimension, Setau. You know how much I love this country; take good care of it for me."

The snake charmer wandered off into the fragrant night. He needed to be alone to digest the fact that he was now one of Ramses' most important administrators.

"May I ask an impertinent question, Your Majesty?" said Lotus.

"It's a special night, isn't it?"

"Why did you wait so long to appoint Setau as viceroy?"

"He was unconsciously learning how to run the province. It's become his vocation; now he's ready to answer the call that gradually came to him. No one has been able to corrupt or slander him, since his will to serve Nubia informs his every action. And he needed time to find it out."

FORTY-FIVE

Alone, Ramses entered the great temple of Abu Simbel to celebrate the rites of dawn. The monarch followed the beam of light that led to the *naos*, or inner sanctum. It fell first on the seated statues of Amon and the royal *ka*, then those of the royal *ka* and Ra. Pharaoh—the gods' earthly representative, not the man—acted in concert with the hidden god Amon and the divine light of Ra, the two great creators forging a complete entity under the name of Amon-Ra.

The fourth statue, of the god Ptah, remained in shadow. As the son of Ptah, Ramses was the builder of his realm and his people. Through Ptah he transmitted the Word that made all things real. The king thought of his son Kha, the god's high priest, who had chosen to plumb this very mystery.

When the monarch emerged from the temple, a soft light bathed the tree-lined esplanade. The Nubian sandstone began to glow, its warm gold like the flesh of the gods. Ramses headed for the temple dedicated to Nefertari, for whom the sun rose.

And this sun, Egypt's nourishing father, would rise until the end of time for the Great Royal Wife who had graced the Two Lands with her beauty and wisdom.

The queen, immortalized by sculptors and painters, made Ramses wish he could pass to the great beyond and be with her once more. He begged her to take him by the hand, to spring from these walls where she lived on, eternally young and beautiful, along with her brother gods and sister goddesses, making the fields turn green and the Nile sparkle. But Nefertari, sailing in the bark of the sun, merely smiled at Ramses. The king's work on earth was not finished. A pharaoh, no matter what his human suffering, belonged to the heavenly powers and to his people. As an imperishable star, Nefertari the sweet and wise would continue to guide Ramses' footsteps in line with the law of Ma'at, until such time as the great goddess finally granted him rest.

The day was waning when Nefertari's magic sent the king back to the outside world, the world where he must not falter.

On the esplanade were hundreds of Nubians in ceremonial dress. Wearing bright red headdresses, golden earrings, full-length white robes, and flowered kilts, the tribal chiefs and their retinue had come bearing gifts—panther skins, gold rings, ivory, ebony, ostrich eggs and plumes, sacks full of precious stones, and fans.

Accompanied by Setau, the designated elder advanced toward Ramses.

"Praise be the Son of Light."

"Praise be the sons of Nubia who have chosen peace," replied Ramses. "May the twin temples of Abu Simbel, so dear to my heart, become the symbol of your union with Egypt."

"Your Majesty, all Nubia already knows that you have named Setau as viceroy."

A heavy silence reigned. If the tribal chiefs disapproved

of the decision, trouble would brew again. But Ramses would stand firm, knowing that his friend was born to run the province and help it prosper.

The tribal elder turned to Setau, who was clad in his well-worn antelope-skin tunic.

"We thank Ramses the Great for choosing this man who knows how to save lives, who has won our hearts by speaking from his own."

Moved to tears, Setau made a deep bow to his sovereign.

And what he saw terrified him: a horned viper slithering beneath the sand, heading straight for the king's foot.

Setau tried to warn Ramses, but the Nubian dignitaries were crowding around him, hoisting him on their shoulders. Their cheering drowned out his frantic shouts.

As the viper reared to strike, a white ibis swooped out of nowhere, then soared away with the snake in its beak.

Those who saw the scene had no doubt: the god Thoth, in the guise of a sacred bird, had saved the monarch's life. And since Thoth had blessed the occasion, Viceroy Setau's administration was sure to be just and wise.

Finally extricating himself from his supporters, Setau spoke to the king.

"To think that viper—"

"What were you afraid of, after the way you've immunized me? Have a little more faith in yourself, old friend."

Twice as bad, if not three times, or ten! Yes, it was much worse than Setau had ever imagined. Since his appointment, he had been overwhelmed with work, hearing a thousand and one petitions, each request more pressing than the last.

In a matter of days, he discovered just how brazen people could be when it came to defending their own interests.

Much as he wanted to fulfill his new mandate from the king, Setau was tempted to resign. Catching dangerous reptiles was easier than resolving conflicts between rival factions.

But the new Viceroy of Nubia had help from two unexpected sources. Lotus, always capable in the field as well as in bed, now proved a competent administrator as well. Her beauty, intact despite the years, also proved a useful distraction during discussions with warring tribal chiefs.

His second ally was even more surprising: Ramses himself. The monarch's presence at Setau's initial discussions with commanders from the Egyptian border fortresses was crucial. The officers, narrow-minded as they were, understood that Setau was no figurehead and had the king's full support. Yet Ramses said not a single word, letting his friend shine.

At the end of the new viceroy's inaugural at the fortress of Buhen, Setau and Ramses walked on the ramparts.

"I've never been good at thank-yous," confessed Setau, "but . . ."

"Nothing could have kept you from this job; I may have helped you end up in it a little faster, that's all."

"You've given me your magic, Ramses, and that's a force nothing could replace."

"Your love for this country has taken over your life, and you've accepted that fact because you're a true warrior, as ardent and uncompromising as Nubia."

"A warrior you've sent to make peace?"

"Peace is the best food of all, isn't it?"

"You'll have to be leaving soon, Ramses."

"You're the viceroy. Your wife is remarkable. The two of you will do wonders for Nubia."

"Will you be back again?"

"I don't know."

"But you love it here as much as I do."

"If I lived here, I'd sit beneath a palm tree along the Nile, facing the desert, and watch the sun while I thought of Nefertari, without a care for affairs of state."

"I'm only now realizing how much is on your shoulders."

"Because you no longer belong to yourself, Setau."

"But you're so much stronger than I am, Majesty. Won't this burden be too much for me to bear?"

"Your snakes taught you how to master fear. Nubia will teach you how to wield power without becoming a slave to it."

Serramanna kept in training with a punching bag, archery, running, and swimming. Yet the extra exercise could not cool his hatred for Uri-Teshoop. The Hittite had kept his head, never committing the slip that the Sard had hoped for, never giving him grounds for an arrest. And his unlikely marriage let him hide behind a cloak of respectability.

As Ramses' bodyguard said his goodbyes to a superb Nubian dancing girl whose playful sensuality had provided some relief, one of his subordinates burst into the room.

"Have you eaten, boy?" Serramanna asked.

"No, sir."

"Nile perch, kidney pie, stuffed pigeons, fresh vegetables . . . how does that sound?"

"Fine, sir."

"I can't hear a thing when I'm hungry. Let's eat, then you'll report to me."

When their meal was finished, Serramanna stretched out on some cushions.

"What brings you here, my lad?"

"I did what you told me, sir, and watched Dame Tanit's house while she was away. A man with wavy hair and a striped outfit came to the gate three times."

"Did you follow him?"

"That wasn't in your orders, sir."

"Can't fault you, then."

"Well, the third time, I just had to see where he was going. I hope you're not mad."

Serramanna rose and clapped his huge hand on the young mercenary's shoulder.

"Good job, my boy! Sometimes it's best to ignore your orders. What did you find out?"

"I know where he lives."

FORTY-SIX

It took Serramanna some time to decide. Should he go ahead and make this suspect talk, or would it be better to consult Ahmeni first? In the past he wouldn't have hesitated, but the former pirate had become an Egyptian; now it seemed to him that respect for the law was the glue that held society together. So the Sard appeared in Ahmeni's office when he knew that the scribe would be alone, working by lamplight.

Poring over wooden tablets, Ahmeni was supping on bean stew, fresh bread, and honey cakes. And still, by some miracle, he stayed thin as a reed.

"When you come to see me so late," he said to Serramanna, "it's not a good sign."

"You're wrong. I have an interesting lead, but I haven't followed up yet."

Ahmeni was surprised.

"Has the god Thoth taken you under his ibis wing, to make you so wise and cautious? You've done right, Serramanna. The vizier doesn't bend the law, as you know."

"The suspect in question is a rich Phoenician, Narish. He called at Tanit's villa several times; lives in a mansion himself."

"It could have been a social call, if they're old acquaintances."

"Narish didn't know that Tanit and Uri-Teshoop were away, touring the harems with the queen. Since they came back, he's only been back once, in the middle of the night."

"Have you been keeping Tanit's house under surveillance without official permission?"

"Of course not, Ahmeni. I learned all this from a neighborhood watchman."

"You're not only playing me for a fool, you're acting like a diplomat! Bravo, Serramanna!"

The scribe suddenly pushed his dish aside. "I've lost my appetite," he announced.

"Have I done something wrong?" the Sard asked anxiously.

"No, you've done everything right. It's the mention of Narish that worries me."

"He's a wealthy man, and no doubt influential, but why would that affect his case?"

"He's more influential than you know. Narish is a trader from the city of Tyre, sent to work with our State Department to arrange the king's upcoming visit to Phoenicia."

The Sard's eyes blazed. "It's a trap! Narish is in contact with Uri-Teshoop!"

"He has business dealings with Dame Tanit; no one can prove that he's in league with the Hittite."

"Let's not be blind, Ahmeni."

"I'm in a difficult position. After several months spent establishing Setau's authority in Nubia, Ramses has turned his attention to the northern protectorates and our trading partners there. He found that our ties to Phoenicia have weakened slightly, and hopes to reinforce them with an official tour. You know the king: the threat of assassination would never deter him from going."

"We have to pursue the investigation and prove that Narish is plotting with Uri-Teshoop!"

"Did you think I'd tell you to wait and see?"

The waters of the Nile reflected the gold of the setting sun. In the homes of rich and humble alike, the evening meal was being prepared. The souls of the dead, after traveling the sun's course and feeding on its energy, drifted back to their eternal dwellings to find rebirth in another form of energy, that of silence.

Yet tonight the guard dogs around the vast necropolis at Saqqara remained on alert, for there were two distinguished visitors on site, Ramses the Great and his son Kha, both unusually animated.

"I'm so happy to welcome you to Saqqara, Your Majesty."

"Have you unearthed the Book of Thoth at last, son?"

"We're in the final phase of restoring the ancient monuments. As for the Book of Thoth, I'm piecing it together page by page; one of those pages is what I want to show you. While you were away in Nubia, the god Ptah kept my builders and stoneworkers busy."

His son's obvious pleasure filled Ramses with happiness. Rarely had he seen Kha so joyous.

The vast domain of Saqqara was dominated by the mother pyramid of Djoser and Imhotep, its steps forming a stairway to heaven. Yet it was not toward this extraordinary monument that Kha led his father. He took an untrodden path that snaked to the northwest of the pyramid.

A chapel with raised columns, their bases bearing plaques to the gods and important state figures, marked the entry to an underground passageway flanked by two priests holding torches.

"As a symbol of power, Pharaoh has always worn a bull's tail in the waistband of his ceremonial kilt," recalled Kha. "That power comes from the bull Apis, allowing the Lord of the Two Lands to overcome all obstacles. It was Apis who bore the mummy of Osiris on his back, reviving the god on his course through the heavens. I vowed to build a shrine to the dynasty of Apis bulls, in keeping with the greatness of their line. The work is now finished."

Preceded by the torch-bearing priests, the monarch and his elder son entered the underground shrine. Over the generations, the god's soul had passed from bull to bull, transmitting his supernatural force without interruption. A series of chapels held their enormous sarcophagi. Mummified like humans, the Apis bulls were buried with treasures from their reigns—jewels, precious vases, even bull-headed *shabti* figurines that would magically come to life and serve them in the next world. The builders had dug impressive galleries linking the various chapels together.

"Every day special celebrants will bring offerings here, so that the great soul of Apis may endow Pharaoh with the strength he needs. I've also built a sanatorium where patients will be housed in whitewashed rooms and undergo sleep cures. Won't your chief physician, Neferet, be pleased?"

"Your work is magnificent, son. It will last through the centuries."

"Here comes Apis now, Your Majesty."

Emerging from the darkness, a colossal black bull slowly advanced toward the Pharaoh. The reigning Apis moved like a beneficent monarch. Ramses remembered the terrifying moment when his father had brought him face to face with a wild bull, long ago on the outskirts of Abydos. So many years had passed since that decisive incident that had sealed his destiny as Son of Light . . .

The bull came nearer, yet Ramses did not move.

"Come to me in peace, brother."

Ramses touched the bull's horn, and its rough tongue licked his hand.

The upper-level State Department officials had greeted Ramses' plans with the highest praise, congratulating the Pharaoh on his remarkable initiative, sure to be welcomed by all the principalities under the joint protection of Egypt and Hatti. No one uttered the slightest criticism or even a suggestion, for weren't Ramses' ideas divinely inspired?

Entering the monarch's office, Ahmeni immediately sensed his old friend's mood.

"Shall I summon Neferet, Your Majesty?"

"I'm suffering from an illness even she can't cure."

"Let me guess; you're fed up with flattery?"

"I've reigned for almost thirty-nine years now. Thirty-nine years of spineless and hypocritical courtiers, officials who sing my praises instead of thinking for themselves, and so-called directors who only follow my directions . . . It's not a pretty picture."

"You're just seeing all this now that you're in your sixties? It's not like you to be so pessimistic, Your Majesty. And you're hurting my feelings. The gods may not have given me your breadth of vision, but I do express my own opinions."

Ramses smiled.

"So you don't think I should leave for Phoenicia?"

"According to Serramanna, there's a plot against you."

"That's always a risk in the northern regions. But as long as my magic protects me, I've nothing to fear."

"Since Your Majesty is unlikely to cancel his plans, I'll tighten security measures as much as possible. Must you really travel to Tyre? Our trade envoy can handle almost any problem."

"Are you underestimating the importance of my mission?"

"So you have a hidden agenda?"

"Your intelligence is a comfort, Ahmeni."

FORTY-SEVEN

Uri-Teshoop rose late and took breakfast in the sunlit garden.

"Where's my wife?" he demanded of the steward.

"Dame Tanit is attending to matters in town."

The Hittite prince was not pleased. Why hadn't Tanit told him of her plans? As soon as she got home, he lashed out at her.

"Where have you been?"

"Now and then I have to look after my business."

"Who did you meet with?"

"Another Phoenician."

"What's his name?"

"Don't tell me you're jealous, darling!"

Uri-Teshoop slapped Tanit hard.

"You . . . you hurt me!"

"His name!"

"Narish. He's a rich merchant who wants to increase the volume of trade with Egypt. He's here in Pi-Ramses to arrange the Pharaoh's upcoming tour of Phoenicia."

Uri-Teshoop kissed his wife on the lips.

"Fascinating, sweetheart. Why didn't you tell me right away? You know it's wrong to make me angry. When will you see this Narish again?"

"We've already come to terms, and I—"

"Come up with some new proposal and pump him about this tour of Phoenicia. You can charm anything out of a man."

Tanit tried to object, but Uri-Teshoop caught her in an embrace. Once again, she was under his spell; there was no resisting her lover's desire.

"All banquets have been canceled," Tanit announced to Uri-Teshoop as he was having his manicure.

"What happened?"

"The Apis bull has just died. During the official mourning period, no feasting is allowed."

"A ridiculous custom!"

"Not to the Egyptians."

Tanit dismissed the manicurist. "The Pharaoh's strength is at stake," she explained to her husband. "Within a few days he has to find another bull to become the new incarnation of Apis."

"Ramses won't have any trouble."

"It's not as easy as it sounds. The bull has to match a specific description."

"And what is that?"

"You'd have to ask a priest involved in Apis worship."

"Get us invited to the funeral."

The last Apis bull had died in its pen at the temple in Memphis. Now its remains lay on a bier in the "pure room," where a wake had been held, with Ramses and Kha in attendance. All night there were prayers for his resurrection. Apis, the magical power of Ptah, the god of builders, must be treated with all the consideration due his rank.

When the mummification process was complete, the bull was placed on a solid wooden sledge and transferred to the royal barge for the journey on the Nile. Then a procession led to the underground burial chamber at Saqqara.

Ramses performed the ceremony opening the animal's mouth, ears, and eyes, bringing it back to life in the Golden Chamber. Neither Uri-Teshoop nor Tanit was allowed to observe these mysterious rites, but they did manage to meet a talkative priest, eager to show off his knowledge.

"To be a candidate for Apis, a bull must have a black hide with white markings, a white blaze on its forehead, a crescent on the chest and another on the flank, plus a tail with both black and white hairs."

"Aren't there plenty of animals that fit the description?"

"No, the gods will make only one."

"What if Pharaoh can't find it?"

"He'd languish, and various ills would beset the country. But Ramses won't fail at his task."

"Of course not," the pair agreed.

Uri-Teshoop and Tanit moved away. "If such an animal does exist," said the Hittite, "let's find it first and kill it off."

Ahmeni's face was drawn and tired. How could he be anything other than tired? Ramses himself had never been able to convince his friend to slow his pace, despite his frail physique.

"All kinds of good news, Your Majesty! For instance—"

"Start with the bad news, Ahmeni."

"Who told you?"

"You've never been good at hiding your feelings."

"All right, then. Emperor Hattusili has just sent you a letter."

"Nothing out of the ordinary; our diplomats correspond regularly."

"He's addressing you, his brother Pharaoh, because Mathor has complained about her situation. The news took Hattusili by surprise; he's demanding an explanation."

Ramses' eyes blazed.

"The woman has probably slandered you to make her father angry and revive the discord between our two peoples," offered the scribe.

"Let's send a suitable reply to my brother the emperor."

"I went over Ahsha's Hittite papers and drafted a letter that ought to smooth things over."

Ahmeni produced a wooden tablet, worn from having been used and scraped clean so many times.

"A fine diplomatic style," said Ramses. "You never cease to amaze me."

"Can I have one of my staff make a final copy?"

"No, Ahmeni."

"But why?"

"Because I'm going to compose the answer myself."

"Forgive me, Your Majesty, but I fear . . ."

"Do you fear the truth? I'll simply explain to Hattusili that his daughter is unsuitable as Great Royal Wife and will spend the rest of her days in comfort at the harem, while Meritamon appears with me at official functions."

Ahmeni blanched.

"Hattusili may be your brother, but he's a proud ruler. A blunt reply may provoke an equally brutal reaction."

"No one should try to gloss over the truth."

"Your Majesty . . ."

"Get back to business, Ahmeni. My letter will go out by tomorrow morning."

Uri-Teshoop had chosen the perfect wife—attractive, sensual, well connected, and rich, very rich. Thanks to Dame Tanit's fortune, the Hittite had been able to hire a considerable number of spotters to locate full-grown black bulls with white markings. Ramses had not even started looking, so Uri-Teshoop hoped this head start would be an advantage.

The story was that the comely Phoenician wanted to start raising cattle and was looking for breeding bulls. First they combed the area around Pi-Ramses, then branched out into the provinces between the capital and Memphis.

"Why is Ramses waiting?" Uri-Teshoop asked Tanit when she returned from a palace meeting with officials from the Double White House, the king's economic advisers.

"He spends most of his time with Kha. The two of them are reformulating the ancient blessing of the Apis bull."

"Have they even found the beast yet?"

"Only Pharaoh can find the right one."

"Then why doesn't he get started?"

"The mourning period isn't over yet."

"If we could deposit the corpse of the new Apis bull in front of the temple, it would be such a blow to Ramses . . ."

"My steward has a message for you."

"Hand it over!"

Uri-Teshoop grabbed a shard of limestone from Tanit's hands. According to one of the scouts, a bull corresponding to the desired description had been spotted in a small village north of Memphis. The owner was demanding an exorbitant price.

"I'm leaving this instant," announced Uri-Teshoop.

FORTY-EIGHT

It was a sleepy summer afternoon in the little village. By the well, beneath a cluster of palm trees, two girls were playing with dolls. Nearby, their mother was repairing wicker baskets.

Uri-Teshoop's horse burst into this peaceful scene, sending the two little girls dashing back to their mother, who was herself terrified by the violent-looking rider with the long, flying hair.

"Woman," he shouted, "tell me where I can find the owner of a strong black bull."

The housewife backed away, clutching her daughters to her.

"Talk, or you'll feel my fists on you."

"On the way out of the village, a farm with a pen . . ."

The horse rode off in the direction to which she pointed. A few minutes of galloping and Uri-Teshoop spotted the pen.

A splendid bull, its black coat sprinkled with white, stood motionless, chewing its cud.

The Hittite jumped down and examined the animal closely. It did indeed bear all the distinctive marks of an Apis bull.

He ran toward the main building where farmworkers were returning from haying.

"Where's your boss?"

"Under the pergola."

Uri-Teshoop was closing in on his goal; he didn't even care about the price.

Lounging on a reed mat, the owner opened his eyes.

"How was the ride?"

"You!"

Serramanna stood up slowly, stretching his immense carcass.

"You're interested in raising cattle, Uri-Teshoop? An excellent idea! It's one of Egypt's strong points!"

"But you're not—"

"The owner of the farm? Oh yes, I am! A nice little place I was able to buy thanks to Ramses' generosity. I plan to retire here. I see you're interested in my prize bull?"

"No, you're mistaken, I—"

"When Ahmeni and I noticed you were nosing around, the king's private secretary had an amusing idea: dyeing my bull's hide with the Apis markings. You don't mind a practical joke, do you?"

The mourning period would soon be over, and the priests were beginning to worry. Why wasn't the king out looking for the new Apis? After visiting the underground shrine to the mummified bulls, then working for days on the First Dynasty resurrection ritual, Ramses let his son, the high priest of Ptah, tell him all about the builder god's ceaseless activity—at work in the heavenly reaches as well as inside beehives or mountains. Ptah's creative Word was revealed in the heart and enacted by the tongue, for every living thought must come to life in a true and fitting form.

A week before the appointed date for the consecration of the new Apis, however, Kha himself could no longer hide his concern.

"Your Majesty, the mourning . . ."

"Yes, son. I know where to find a successor to the late Apis. You needn't worry."

"If the bull is far from here, it will take you some time to reach it."

"Tonight I'll sleep in the burial chamber and ask the gods and Nefertari to guide me."

When night fell, the king remained alone in the underground abode. He knew each of the Apis dynasties by name and appealed to their single linked soul. Lying on a priest's simple cot, Ramses entrusted his soul to sleep—not to the simple repose of body and senses, but to dreams that could take him on an endless flight. As if he had suddenly sprouted a bird's wings, the king left the earth, soared through the heavens, and saw.

He saw all of upper and lower Egypt: the provinces, the towns and villages, the great temples and small shrines, the Nile and her irrigation ditches, the desert and the cultivated fields.

A vigorous north wind pushed the white-sailed ship toward Abydos. In the prow, Ramses tasted the pleasure, one that he always craved, of admiring his country from the water.

Kha had firmly informed the celebrant priests attached to the court that he was leaving with his father to bring the new Apis bull back to Saqqara. Aware of how disastrous it would be if their mission failed, the high priest refused to entertain the possibility.

"We're almost there," he said to the monarch.

"This journey has gone so quickly . . . Such overwhelming beauty seems to do away with time."

The entire clergy of Abydos was assembled to greet the king at the landing; the temple's high priest saluted Kha.

"Has His Majesty come to prepare the mysteries of Osiris?"

"No," replied Kha. "Ramses is convinced that we'll find the new incarnation of Apis here."

"If such were the case, we would have informed His Majesty."

"Then Pharaoh must know something that you don't know."

The high priest of Abydos was confounded. "Haven't you tried to reason with your father?"

"He's Ramses."

Everyone expected the monarch to explore the surrounding countryside, but he made straight for the desert, where the tombs of the First Dynasty pharaohs lay. While their mummies lay at rest in Saqqara, their luminous being endured at Abydos.

Tamarisks shaded the monuments. There, in the foliage, Ramses saw him.

A magnificent black bull raised its head, turning toward the approaching human.

All was exactly as it had been in the Pharaoh's dream that night in the underground chamber.

The beast showed no signs of aggression. He almost seemed to be greeting an old friend after a long separation.

On the bull's forehead was a white blaze, a white crescent on the chest and flanks. The hairs in its tail were both black and white.

"Come, Apis," said Ramses. "I'm taking you to your home."

When the royal ship docked at Memphis, the festivities had already begun. Dignitaries from Pi-Ramses had left the capital to admire the new Apis, whose strength would add years to Pharaoh's reign. But Ahmeni was in no mood to celebrate. He had come bearing bad news.

Cheers rose as the bull and the king, side by side, disembarked and made their way to the temple of Ptah, where the bull-god would live in a huge pen, surrounded by a herd of ravishing cows.

At the gate to the temple grounds an ancient rite was being enacted: a highborn woman of excellent repute stood facing the bull. She lifted her dress to the waist, unveiling her sex, as the crowd roared with laughter. This was the Hathor priestess, welcoming the male that would impregnate her sacred cows and continue the Apis line.

In the front row, Uri-Teshoop squirmed. This bizarre scene, this shameless woman sharing in the crowd's hilarity, this impassive bull, the people that seemingly worshiped Ramses . . . Ramses who seemed so indestructible!

Anyone else would have given up by now. But Uri-Teshoop was a Hittite, a warlord, and Ramses had deprived him of his place as emperor. He could never forgive the Pharaoh for reducing the Hittite nation, once proud conquerors, to a bunch of cringing cowards.

The temple's double gates swung closed. Outside, the population danced, sang, and feasted at Pharaoh's expense, while within the temple Ramses, Kha, and a group of priests performed the ceremony inaugurating the new Apis. The culminating rite was the bull's sprint with the mummy of Osiris on its back—the reconstituted and resurrected body of the god who conquered death.

"How can anyone enjoy traveling?" grumbled Ahmeni. "And while I'm away, problems and emergencies are piling up on my desk!"

"For you to come here," observed Ramses, "you must have some important reason."

"Next you'll accuse me of spoiling the celebration."

"Have I ever found serious fault with you?"

The king's sandal-bearer lowered his head, muttering.

"Emperor Hattusili wasted no time replying," he revealed. "It's easy to see, reading between the lines, that he's angry. He disapproves of your attitude toward his daughter; the threats are barely veiled."

Ramses kept silent for quite some time.

"Since my arguments didn't convince him, we'll use a different strategy. Take a new papyrus, Ahmeni, and your best brush. My proposals will no doubt surprise my brother Hattusili."

FORTY-NINE

The negotiations are finished," Tanit told Uri-Teshoop. "The trader Narish has returned to Tyre, where he'll welcome Ramses with the mayor and a delegation of notables."

The Hittite gripped the handle of his ever-present iron dagger.

"Couldn't you get any more confidential information?"

"The itinerary isn't secret, and the monarch will be accompanied by his son Merenptah, the commander-in-chief of the Egyptian army, at the head of two elite regiments. Any attack against them would be doomed to failure."

Uri-Teshoop fumed; Malfi did not yet have enough men to wage a full-scale battle.

"Still, it doesn't add up," Tanit continued. "The senior administrators at the Double White House have made no special demands, as if the Pharaoh weren't even going to deal with economic problems. And there are disputed issues of the sort that Egypt doesn't usually ignore."

"What conclusion do you draw from that?"

"Ramses is concealing his true objective."

Uri-Teshoop was perplexed.

"You're probably right. We'd better find out what's really behind his journey."

"How can I do that?"

"Go to the palace, get the courtiers to talk, steal documents, whatever . . . You'll find a way, Tanit."

"But darling . . ."

"No excuses. I have to know."

Broad and safe, the track followed the foot of Mount Carmel and sloped gently down toward the sea. The sea . . . a strange sight for many an Egyptian soldier, an incredible limitless plain of water. The veterans warned the younger men: while wading in the foamy waves was not at all dangerous, if they swam out any distance an evil spirit might drag them to the bottom.

Ramses marched at the head of his army, just behind Merenptah and the scouts. All during the journey, the king's younger son had kept up the strictest security measures, yet the king did not seem worried in the least.

"If you take the throne," he told Merenptah, "don't neglect to make regular tours of our protectorates. If your brother Kha becomes king, remind him to do it. When Pharaoh's visits are too few and far between, the clouds of revolt can gather. His presence brings back the sun."

Despite the veteran soldiers' reassurances, the young

recruits were uneasy. The violent surf crashing against the rocky heights made them miss the banks of the Nile.

The countryside looked less forbidding: cultivated fields, orchards, and olive groves showed that this was a rich agricultural region. But the old city of Tyre faced seaward; a bay formed a kind of unbreachable moat, protection against attack by an enemy fleet.

New Tyre had been built on three small islands separated by shallow canals, along which lay the dry docks.

From atop their watchtowers, the Tyrians observed Pharaoh and his soldiers. Led by Narish, a delegation came out to meet the Lord of Egypt, greeting him warmly. Narish then enthusiastically guided Ramses through the streets of his home city. Merenptah kept his eyes riveted to the rooftops, a constant source of potential peril.

Tyre was a center of commerce. Glassware, gold and silver vases, purple cloth, and a variety of other merchandise passed through the port. The closely packed houses stood four or five stories tall.

The mayor, an old friend of Narish's, had offered Ramses his luxurious villa with a breathtaking view of the sea. The roof garden was a marvel, and the proud homeowner had even redecorated in the Egyptian style to help the Pharaoh feel at home.

"I hope you'll be satisfied, Your Majesty," declared Narish. "Your visit is a very great honor. This evening you'll preside at a banquet that will go down in our city's history. May we hope that closer trade relations with Egypt will develop?"

"I'm not against it, but on one condition . . ."

"Lowering our profits . . . I thought as much. It could be negotiated, provided we make it up in higher volume."

"That's not the condition I had in mind."

Despite the mild temperature, the merchant felt his blood run cold. In the wake of the peace agreement, Egypt had ceded the region to Hittite control, but in reality Phoenicia enjoyed considerable independence. Ramses must have grown power-hungry, seeking to tighten his hold on the area at the risk of violating the treaty and provoking a conflict.

"What are your demands, Your Majesty?"

"Let's go down to the port. Merenptah will come with us."

On the king's orders, his younger son brought only a limited retinue.

At the western end of the port were a hundred-odd men of varying ages and backgrounds, all naked and in chains. Some struggled to retain a shred of dignity; others stared blankly.

Curly-haired Tyrians were bargaining for the men, singly or in lots. They hoped to make a sizable profit on the sale of healthy slaves. The trading was active.

"Set these men free," demanded Ramses.

Narish was amused. "They're extremely valuable . . . Allow the city of Tyre to make you a present of them, Your Majesty."

"This is the real reason for my journey. No citizen wishing to trade with Egypt should deal in slaves."

Shocked, the Phoenician summoned all his self-control to stifle a vigorous protest.

"Your Majesty . . . slavery is a fact of life, and merchant peoples have always engaged in this trade!"

"There is no slavery in Egypt," said Ramses. "The gods forbid it. No individual has the right to treat another as an object without a soul or as merchandise."

The Phoenician had never heard such foolishness. From

anyone but the Pharaoh of Egypt, he would have thought such talk completely mad.

"But don't you take prisoners of war as slaves, Your Majesty?"

"According to the seriousness of their offenses, they're sentenced to varying periods of forced labor. Once they earn their freedom, they may do as they please. Most of them stay in Egypt, and many of them start families."

"Then you also depend on slave labor!"

"The law of Ma'at requires a contract between the party assigning work and the party executing it. Otherwise, there is no joy in the most sublime work nor the humblest task. And this contract is based on mutual agreement, on giving one's word. Do you think that our pyramids and temples could have been built by gangs of slaves?"

"Your Majesty, old habits are hard to change . . ."

"I'm not naive. I know that most countries will continue to practice slavery. But now you know what my demands are."

"Egypt may lose some important markets."

"What's essential is that Egypt preserve her soul. Pharaoh is not a merchant prince, but Ma'at's earthly representative and the servant of his people."

Ramses' words made a deep impression on Merenptah. For him, the journey to Tyre was a landmark.

Uri-Teshoop was so disturbed that to calm his nerves he felled a centenarian sycamore that shaded the duck pond, as Tanit's gardener cowered in the toolshed.

"Here you are at last!" exclaimed the Hittite when his wife came through the gate.

Tanit gazed on the destruction.

"Did you do this?" she asked sadly.

"This is my house and I'll do as I like with it! What did you find out at the palace?"

"Let me sit down, I'm tired," she said.

The little tabby cat jumped in its mistress's lap. As she listlessly stroked its head, it began to purr.

"Tell me, Tanit!"

"You're going to be disappointed. The real point of Ramses' trip was to halt the growth of the slave trade in Tyre and the surrounding region."

Uri-Teshoop slapped Tanit hard across the face.

"What kind of fool do you take me for!"

Trying to defend its mistress, the little cat scratched the Hittite. He grabbed it by the scruff of the neck and slit its throat with his iron dagger.

Blood-spattered, horrified, Tanit ran to her room.

FIFTY

Ahmeni was relieved; Serramanna brooded.

"With Ramses back from Phoenicia safe and sound, I can breathe easier," admitted the king's private secretary. "Why are you so glum, Serramanna?"

"Because Narish turned out to be a dead end."

"What were you hoping for?"

"To find proof that he had suspicious dealings with Dame Tanit. I could have threatened her with charges if she didn't tell me the truth about Uri-Teshoop."

"You're obsessed with that Hittite! Don't let it warp your mind."

"Are you forgetting that he murdered Ahsha?"

"We have no proof."

"Too true, Ahmeni."

The Sard could feel himself aging. Serramanna, stymied by the law! He might as well resign himself to admitting failure: Uri-Teshoop had been shrewd enough to get around the Egyptian police.

"I'm going home."

"To anyone special?"

"No, Ahmeni. I'm tired and I'm going to sleep."

"A lady is waiting for you," Serramanna's steward announced.

"I didn't send for a girl!"

"This one's no girl. A lady, I told you. I asked her to wait in the front room."

Intrigued, Serramanna hurried to meet his guest.

"Dame Tanit!"

The comely Phoenician rose and rushed into the giant's arms. Her hair was undone and bruises showed on her cheeks.

"Protect me, I beg of you!"

"I'd be glad to, but from what . . . or whom?"

"From the monster who's made me his slave!"

Serramanna was careful not to gloat. "If you want me to act in my official capacity, Dame Tanit, you'll have to press charges."

"Uri-Teshoop killed my cat, he chopped down my beautiful sycamore, and he beats me all the time now."

"Those are misdemeanors. He could get a fine, even forced labor. But that wouldn't put him out of commission."

"Will your men protect me?"

"My mercenaries are part of the king's royal bodyguard and can't intervene in private matters . . . unless they become affairs of state."

Drying her tears, Tanit pulled back and looked the hulking Sard straight in the eye.

"Uri-Teshoop wants to assassinate Ramses. He's in league with the Libyan Malfi; they formed their alliance under my roof. Uri-Teshoop brags about killing Ahsha with an iron dagger that never leaves his side. He plans to use it to kill the king. Would you call that an affair of state?"

A hundred men fanned out around Dame Tanit's villa. Archers climbed trees overlooking her garden; others stood by on neighboring rooftops.

Was Uri-Teshoop alone or with his Libyans? Would he take the household servants hostage if he noticed the stakeout? Serramanna had demanded total silence in the approach, knowing that the slightest incident would alert the Hittite.

And, inevitably, there was one.

Scaling the villa's outer wall, a mercenary lost his footing and fell into the shrubbery.

A barn owl hooted. Serramanna's men froze. After a few minutes of stillness, the Sard gave the order to advance.

It was too late for Uri-Teshoop to run, but he wouldn't surrender without a fight. Serramanna hoped to take him alive and bring him to justice before the vizier.

A glint of light came from Tanit's bedchamber.

Serramanna and a dozen mercenaries flung themselves onto the dew-soaked ground, crawled to the paving that surrounded the villa, and rushed inside.

The servant girl cried out in fright and dropped her oil lamp. It shattered on the floor. For a few seconds, confusion reigned; the mercenaries fought with the shadows and hacked at furniture with their swords.

"Calm down!" shouted Serramanna. "Give us some light!"

Other lamps were lit. Trembling, the servant girl was pinned between two soldiers pointing their swords at her.

"Where is Uri-Teshoop?" inquired Serramanna.

"When he realized the mistress had left him, he jumped on the back of his best horse and galloped off."

In frustration, the Sard slammed his fist into a Cretan jar. The Hittite's warrior instincts had taken over. Sensing danger, he had taken flight.

For Serramanna, being admitted into Ramses' stark office was the equivalent of entering the country's most secret inner sanctum.

Also present were Ahmeni and Merenptah.

"Dame Tanit has returned to Phoenicia after giving the vizier a deposition," Serramanna told them. "Several witnesses place Uri-Teshoop on the way to Libya. He's gone to join up with Malfi."

"That's guesswork," judged Ahmeni.

"No, it's for certain. Uri-Teshoop has nowhere else to go, and he won't give up the fight against Egypt."

"Unfortunately," reported Merenptah, "we haven't been able to locate the Libyans' camp. Malfi keeps moving around in the desert. All things considered, that may be a good sign: it proves that Malfi hasn't been able to form a real fighting force."

"We have to catch up with them," ordered Ramses. "An alliance between two evil and violent leaders constitutes a danger we can't ignore."

Serramanna drew himself up to his full height.

"Your Majesty, I have a request to make of you."

"Go ahead."

"I'm convinced that we haven't seen the last of this Hittite monster. I beg the privilege of fighting Uri-Teshoop and killing him by my own hand."

"Granted."

"Thank you, Your Majesty. No matter what the future holds, you've made my life a good one."

The Sard withdrew.

"Is something bothering you?" Ramses asked his son.

"It's Moses and the Hebrews. They're finally closing in on Canaan, which they consider their Promised Land."

"How happy Moses must be . . ."

"Yes, but the local tribesmen aren't. They fear their aggressive visitors. That's why I'd like to ask you once more for permission to take my troops and nip the problem in the bud."

"Moses will go as far as he must to create a country in which his faithful can live as they please. That's his right, my son, and we will not interfere. One day we'll open talks with his new nation; perhaps they'll even become our ally."

"What if they become our enemy instead?"

"Moses holds no grudge against his native land. You ought to be worrying about the Libyans, Merenptah, not the Hebrews."

The general let the subject drop. Although unconvinced by his father's arguments, he was an obedient son.

"We've had news from your brother Hattusili," revealed Ahmeni.

"Good or bad?"

"The emperor is thinking."

Even when the sun beamed, Hattusili felt cold. Within the thick stone walls of his citadel, he could never seem to get warm. With his back to the blaze crackling in the huge fireplace, he reread the Pharaoh of Egypt's proposals to his wife, Puduhepa.

"Ramses has incredible nerve! I send him a letter of reprimand, and he answers me with insults. He wants me to send him another princess to marry. What's more, he's asking me to travel to Egypt!"

"A wonderful idea," the empress told him. "Your official visit would be conclusive proof that the peace agreement can never be broken."

"You can't be serious. Why would I, the Emperor of Hatti, want to appear as Pharaoh's vassal?"

"No one is asking you to humble yourself. I'm sure we'd

be welcomed with all the honor due our rank. I've already written a letter of acceptance; you need only set your seal to it."

"I need time to think. There ought to be discussion first."

"It's too late for talks. Let's prepare to leave for Egypt."

"Since when do you make the diplomatic decisions?"

"My sister Nefertari and I were the ones who forged the peace agreement in the first place. The least you can do as emperor is make it last."

Puduhepa thought warmly of Ahsha, the most attractive man she had ever known. Ahsha, Ramses' boyhood friend, who had gone to his heavenly reward. For him, this day would be a joyful one.

FIFTY-ONE

When Mathor learned the news that had Egypt buzzing, namely the announcement of her parents' state visit, she thought it meant her return to favor. To be sure, she lived as a queen at the harem of Merur, enjoying the countless pleasures of her rank. Yet hers was merely a diplomatic marriage, and she wielded no true power whatsoever.

The Hittite princess wrote a long letter to Ahmeni, the king's private secretary. In the strongest terms, she demanded to occupy the role of Great Royal Wife in welcoming the Emperor and Empress of Hatti. She called for an escort to return her to the palace at Pi-Ramses.

The reply, signed by Ramses, was a categorical: Mathor would not attend the ceremonies; she was to remain at Merur.

Once her anger cooled, the Hittite reflected. What better way to thwart Ramses than preventing Hattusili's arrival? Energized by her plan, she made sure she ran into a priest of the crocodile god, a priest with a reputation for competence.

"In Hatti," she told him, "our priests often read omens to predict the future. They study the entrails of animals."

"You don't find that somewhat distasteful?"

"What methods do you use instead?"

"Only Pharaoh can see into the future."

"But surely you priests have your secrets!"

"There's a body of state magicians, Your Majesty, but they undergo special training."

"Don't you consult the gods?"

"In certain circumstances, the high priest of Amon asks questions of the god of creation, with Pharaoh's permission, and Amon replies through his oracle."

"And everyone follows his recommendations, I presume."

"No one would dare defy the will of Amon."

Sensing the priest's reluctance, Mathor dropped the subject.

Yet that very day, after ordering her household not to say she was gone, the queen left for Thebes.

Death had finally called for old Nebu, the high priest of Amon, at his little house by the sacred lake at Karnak. He died content in the knowledge that he had served the hidden god well and done the will of Pharaoh Ramses, the creator's earthly representative.

Bakhen, the Second Prophet of Amon, had immediately informed the king. And Ramses came to pay his respects, for men of integrity, men like Nebu, were what enabled the Egyptian tradition to endure in the face of the forces of evil.

The silence of mourning filled the vast temple of Karnak. After celebrating the rites of dawn, Ramses met Bakhen at the northwest corner of the sacred lake, near the giant scarab that symbolized the sun's rebirth after its nightly battle with the darkness.

"The time has come, Bakhen. Ever since we clashed as young men, you've been on my side. If the temples of Thebes are splendid, it's partly due to your efforts. You're a capable and honest leader. Yes, the time has come to appoint you as high priest of Karnak and First Prophet of Amon."

The priest's low voice rumbled with emotion.

"Your Majesty, I'm not so sure. Nebu, you know . . ."

"Nebu proposed you as his successor long ago, and he was a good judge of men. I entrust you with the staff and the golden ring that signify your new position. You'll govern this holy city and make sure it fulfills its sacred function."

Bakhen was already taking himself in hand. Ramses knew he would set straight to work in his new capacity without a thought for the prestige attached to it.

"My heart cannot remain silent, Your Majesty. Here in the south, your decision has caused a stir."

"Are you referring to the state visit from the Emperor and Empress of Hatti?"

"I am."

"It's caused a stir in the north as well. But the visit will take place, because it will set the seal on our peace agreement."

"Many religious leaders have asked to consult the oracle. If the god Amon gives you his consent, the protests will die down."

"Prepare the ceremony, Bakhen."

An administrator at Merur had sent Mathor to a valuable contact, a rich Syrian merchant who knew everything that went on in Thebes. He lived on a sumptuous estate on the East Bank, not far from the temple of Karnak, and received the queen in a hall with two graceful iris and cornflower columns.

"What an honor, Your Majesty, for a simple merchant!"

"This conversation never took place and we never met. Is that quite clear?"

The Hittite proffered a golden necklace; the Syrian smiled and bowed.

"If you give me the help I need," she continued, "I'll be very generous."

"What do you want?"

"I'm interested in the oracle's reading."

"The rumor has been confirmed: Ramses does plan to consult with Amon."

"What will he ask the oracle?"

"Whether the god approves of your parents' visit to Egypt."

Mathor was in luck. Fate had done most of the work for her; she only need finish it.

"What if Amon says no?"

"Ramses will be forced to capitulate. And I hardly dare imagine the Emperor of Hatti's reaction! Still, Pharaoh is a demigod himself . . . The oracle would never turn him down."

"I want the omen to be negative."

"What?"

"Let me repeat: help me and you'll be very rich. How does the god give his answer?"

"A select group of priests holds the bark of Amon while the First Prophet consults the god. If the boat moves forward, the answer is yes. Backwards means no."

"Bribe the priests, then. Amon has to contradict Ramses."

"It's impossible."

"Find out which priests won't take a bribe and use potions to make them sick. Then replace them with your own men. If you make it work, I'll shower you with gold."

"It's risky . . ."

"You no longer have any choice, merchant. You're already in league with me. Don't try to back out and don't dare cross me, or I'll show no mercy."

Alone with the bulging sacks of gold nuggets and gemstones that the Hittite had left as her down payment, the Syrian merchant pondered his situation. Some claimed that Mathor would never regain the king's trust, but others argued she'd reign again. And some of the Karnak clergy, he'd heard, resented Bakhen's rise through the hierarchy.

He'd never be able to buy off all the priests in charge of the sacred bark, but if he could just get the strongest ones, the god would appear to waver, then clearly show his disapproval.

It *could* be done . . . And he could be a very wealthy man.

Thebes was in an uproar.

In both the town and surrounding countryside, people knew that the "great feast of the divine audience" was about to begin, once again demonstrating the communion between Amon and Ramses.

Every important person from throughout the south was crammed into the great court of the temple where the ritual was to take place. The mayor, provincial officials, and great landowners refused to miss this exciting event.

When the bark of Amon emerged into the daylight, they held their collective breath. In the center of the gilded wooden boat was the tabernacle containing the sacred image, concealed from human eyes. Yet it was this living effigy that would decide for Pharaoh.

The priestly bearers advanced slowly across the silver flooring. The new high priest of Amon, Bakhen, noticed several new faces; he remembered hearing about stomach problems that had forced several initiates to drop out of the ceremony.

The bark came to a halt in front of the Pharaoh. Bakhen spoke.

"I, the servant of the god Amon, ask in the name of Ramses, Son of Light, whether Pharaoh may rightfully bring the Emperor and Empress of Hatti to Egypt."

Even the swallows had stopped winging through the blue sky. As soon as the god replied in the affirmative, the cheering for Ramses could burst forth.

The Syrian merchant's strong-shouldered recruits looked at each other and strained to move the bark backward.

It wouldn't move.

Their fellow priests must simply be pushing in the opposite direction. They tried even harder, but a strange force propelled them forward. Dazzled by the light streaming from the tabernacle, they yielded.

The god Amon had given his approval to his son Ramses. The jubilation could begin.

FIFTY-TWO

Here he was.

Slightly stooped, his hair graying but eyes still sharp, he could pass for a rather ordinary man, not worth a second look. Here he was, Hattusili, the Emperor of Hatti, wrapped in a thick woolen cloak to counteract the cold he felt no matter what the season.

Here he was, the chief of a warlike and conquering nation, the supreme commander of the Hittite troops at Kadesh, but also the co-author of the peace treaty. Here was the uncontested master of a rugged country where he had crushed all opposition.

And Hattusili had just set foot on Egyptian soil, followed by two women—his wife, Puduhepa, and a frightened-looking young princess.

"It's impossible," murmured the Emperor of Hatti. "Completely impossible. No, this can't be Egypt."

Yet it was no dream. It was really Ramses the Great advancing toward his former rival, to embrace him.

"How is my brother Hattusili?"

"Getting old, my brother Ramses."

Denounced by Tanit, Uri-Teshoop had fled the country, removing any potential obstacle to Hattusili's state visit. The fallen prince was now a hunted criminal and the sworn enemy of both Egypt and Hatti.

"Nefertari would have enjoyed this extraordinary occasion," said Ramses to Puduhepa, superb in her long red gown and adorned with Egyptian jewelry, a gift from Pharaoh.

"All during our journey, I couldn't stop thinking of her," confessed the empress. "No matter how long you reign, she shall always remain your true queen."

Puduhepa's remarks smoothed over any diplomatic difficulties. In the brilliant summer sunshine, the sparkling Turquoise City thronged with thousands of dignitaries from every corner of Egypt. They had come to welcome the royal guests from Hatti and participate in the many ceremonies planned in their honor.

The capital's beauty and wealth dazzled the imperial couple. Aware that the god Amon had given Ramses his approval, the population greeted the illustrious visitors enthusiastically. Beside the Pharaoh in his chariot pulled by two plumed horses, Hattusili experienced surprise after surprise.

"Doesn't my brother have any sort of security?"

"My royal bodyguard provides protection," replied Ramses.

"But all these people, so close to us . . . it hardly seems safe."

"Observe how my people look at me, Hattusili. Do you see any hatred or aggression? Today they're thanking us for giving them peace, and we're communing with them in joy."

"A population that's not governed by terror . . . how very strange! And how did Ramses manage to raise an army able to resist the Hittite forces?"

"All Egyptians love their country as the gods do."

"It was you, Ramses, who robbed me of the ultimate victory—you and you alone. But suddenly I don't mind anymore."

The Emperor of Hatti took off his woolen cloak. He no longer felt cold.

"I like this climate," he said. "It would be nice to live here."

The first reception, held at the Pi-Ramses palace, was grandiose. There were so many delicious dishes that Hattusili and Puduhepa could barely dip into them, sipping on vintage wine. Gorgeous bare-breasted singers charmed their ears and eyes, and the empress took note of the latest fashions worn by noble ladies.

"I'd like to drink a toast to Ahsha," suggested Puduhepa. "He gave his life for peace, for the happiness that both our peoples now enjoy."

The emperor agreed, but he looked discontented. "I see our daughter isn't here," he said.

"I won't rescind my decision," declared Ramses. "Although Mathor committed some serious wrongs, she will remain the symbol of peace. As such, she'll be given all the honor due her. Need I go into the details?"

"No, my brother. Some things it's better not to know."

Ramses thus avoided any mention of the Syrian merchant's arrest and his attempt to reduce his sentence by making accusations against the queen.

"Would Pharaoh like to speak with his future bride?"

"That won't be necessary, Hattusili. This second diplomatic marriage will be celebrated properly and in public, and our two nations will be gratified. But there will be no personal involvement."

"Nefertari is truly unforgettable . . . That's as it should be. I doubt that the princess I brought you, pretty but weakminded, would interest Ramses the Great. She'll discover all that your country has to offer and be happy here. As for Mathor, who never enjoyed life in Hatti, she'll mellow in Egypt."

Hattusili had just sealed the destiny of the two Hittite princesses. In this fortieth year of Ramses' reign, there was no further basis for dispute between Hatti and Egypt—which was why Empress Puduhepa's dark eyes were shining with genuine joy.

The city's pylons, obelisks, great forecourts, colonnades, scenes of offerings, and silver flooring all fascinated Hattusili, who was also interested in the House of Life, the library, storerooms, stables, kitchens, and offices where scribes labored. The Emperor of Hatti emerged most impressed from his meetings with the vizier and the cabinet; the architecture of Egyptian society was as grandiose as the country's religious monuments.

Ramses showed Hattusili how to burn incense, its fragrance attracting the gods to the dwellings that men had made for them. The empress was included in the ritual appeasing dangerous forces, which Kha conducted with his habitual rigor. Then there was the tour of Pi-Ramses' temples, notably the shrines dedicated to foreign deities. And then the emperor thoroughly enjoyed a moment of rest in the palace gardens.

"It would have been unfortunate for the Hittite army to destroy such a lovely city," he said to Ramses. "The empress is delighted with your capital. Since we're at peace, would my brother permit me to request a favor?"

Hattusili's relative passivity was beginning to intrigue Ramses. Struggling not to fall under Egypt's spell, his strategic mind was reasserting itself.

"The empress and I have seen marvels, yet I know there's another side to your city as well. Since we've agreed to assist each other in case of outside attack, I'd like to verify the state of the Egyptian army. Will Pharaoh grant me permission to visit the capital's main military base?"

If Ramses pleaded national security or steered the emperor toward one of the smaller bases, Hattusili would be forewarned. This was the moment of truth, the reason he'd agreed to make the journey.

"Merenptah, my younger son, is head of the Egyptian army. He'll be glad to take the Emperor of Hatti on a tour of his headquarters."

At the end of the banquet in Empress Puduhepa's honor, Hattusili and Ramses went for a stroll by a lotus pond covered with blue and white blossoms.

"I've discovered a feeling I never knew until now," admitted Hattusili. "I mean trust. Only Egypt could make a man your size, my brother Ramses. Forging an authentic friendship between two rulers prepared to destroy each other is something of a miracle. But you and I are growing older, and we should be thinking of our successors . . . Whom have you chosen, among your innumerable royal sons?"

"My oldest son, Kha, is a scholar, a deep thinker, who can moderate any discussion and convince without ever arguing. He'll be able to run the kingdom smoothly and weigh his decisions carefully. Merenptah has courage. He knows how to command and organize; he's won the military's admiration and the administration's respect. Either one of them would make a good king."

"In other words, you still aren't sure. Well, fate will send you a sign. With sons like yours, I'm not concerned about the future of Egypt. They'll both know how to carry on your work."

"And what about your succession?"

"The prospects are rather dim. Hatti is in decline, as if peace had unmanned us. But I have no regrets; the alternative was even worse. At least we'll have had a breathing space, and I'll have given my people a quality of life they never knew before. Unfortunately, I'm afraid they won't make good use of it, and our country will perish. Oh . . . I have one more favor to ask of you. I don't walk about so freely at home, and my feet have been killing me. I've heard that the chief physician of the realm is extremely competent and also a highly attractive woman."

Neferet left the banquet room where she was conversing with Puduhepa and came to care for the imperial toes.

"A condition I've seen before; I can treat this for you,"

she said after examining him. "The first step is applying a pomade of red ocher, honey, and hemp. Tomorrow morning I'll use another preparation—acacia and jujube leaves, malachite powder, and mussels, ground into a powder. This second salve will feel pleasantly cool, but you'll have to walk with your ankles bandaged."

"If I offered you a fortune, Neferet, would you come back to Hatti with me and be my personal physician?"

"You know I couldn't, Your Highness."

"I can never win against Egypt," said Hattusili with the hint of a smile.

FIFTY-THREE

Long Legs whistled a tune to the glory of Ramses as he trudged along with his donkey hauling pottery toward the northwestern edge of the Delta. Not far from the Mediterranean coast, the traveling merchant found the winding path that led to a small fishing village where he was sure to sell off his inventory.

Long Legs was proud of his nickname, bestowed by the girls who watched him and his friends run their footraces on the sandy beaches. He'd been undefeated for over two years. More and more girls came to admire the naked young runners, lingering to congratulate the champion. No wonder they called him the fastest man in the western Delta!

But there were drawbacks, too. Girlfriends wanted presents, and Long Legs had to work hard to uphold his status.

Cranes flew overhead as a strong wind buffeted low clouds. Observing the sun's position, Long Legs realized he wouldn't make it to the village before dark. He'd be better off spending the night in some reed hut along the way. Once night fell, dangerous creatures emerged from their lairs to attack the unwary.

Long Legs unloaded his donkey, fed it, then started a fire with flints and a fire stick. He ate two grilled fish and drank cool water from a jug. Then he stretched out on his mat and slept.

As he dreamed of his next footrace and the exciting aftermath, a familiar sound woke him. The donkey was pawing the ground with his front shoe. Between him and his master, it was an unmistakable danger signal.

Long Legs stood up, extinguished the fire, and crouched behind a thorn bush. Wise move, since thirty armed men wearing helmets and breastplates soon emerged from the shadows. The moon was full, giving him a good look at the man in charge. His head was bare, his hair was long, and his chest was covered with fleecy red hair.

"There was a spy, but he got away!" exclaimed Uri-Teshoop, sinking his lance into the reed mat.

"I don't think so," objected a Libyan. "Look at this pottery and the donkey here. It was only a traveling merchant who stopped to rest."

"All the villages west of here are under our control. We have to find this spy and get rid of him. Spread out, men."

Four years had passed since Emperor Hattusili and Empress Puduhepa had paid their visit to Egypt. The ties between Egypt and Hatti were stronger than ever; the specter of war had vanished. A steady flow of Hittite visitors arrived to admire the scenery and cities in the Delta.

Ramses' two Hittite princesses got along beautifully. Mathor's pampered existence had gradually quelled her ambitions; her younger counterpart was enchanted with life in Egypt. Together, and without regret, they concluded that Ramses the Great, at sixty-six years of age, had become a living legend, beyond their reach. And the Pharaoh, sensing their chastened attitude, allowed the two queens to participate in certain official ceremonies.

In Year Forty-three of his reign, at Kha's urging, Ramses had celebrated his fifth sed-feast, surrounded by the community of gods and goddesses. Their statues, imbued with their spiritual essence, or *ka,* were once again assembled in the capital. Henceforth, the Pharaoh must have ever more frequent recourse to this ritual rejuvenation as age bore down on him.

Ramses also had to consult regularly with Neferet, his chief physician. Ignoring her illustrious patient's occasional grumbling about old age, she cared for his teeth and kept his arthritis from progressing. Thanks to her treatments, the monarch's vitality remained intact, and he worked at an unrelenting pace.

After waking the divine power within the sanctuary and celebrating the rites of dawn, Ramses met with the vizier, Ahmeni, and Merenptah, whom he trusted to work out the details of his directives. In the afternoon he studied the grand state rituals with Kha, working toward their reformulation.

The king was slowly detaching himself from running the country, having placed it in excellent hands. He often went to Thebes to see his daughter, Meritamon, and meditate at his Eternal Temple.

When Ramses returned from Karnak, where High Priest Bakhen was performing to the satisfaction of all, a worried-looking Merenptah greeted him at the pier.

"A troubling report, Your Majesty."

The commanding general of the Egyptian army personally took the reins of the royal chariot, steering it toward the palace.

"If the facts are confirmed, Your Majesty, I'll feel partially at fault."

"Explain yourself, Merenptah."

"The oasis of Siwa, near the Libyan border, has supposedly been attacked by a band of Malfi's raiders."

"How old is this information?"

"I've just had the report, but the incident dates back ten days or so."

"And you don't think it's reliable?"

"Well, the officer assigned to the oasis isn't identified correctly, but that could be due to confusion and haste. If the oasis really has been attacked, we'll have to take action. And if Malfi is really behind it, we'll have to nip his rebellion in the bud."

"Why do you think you're at fault, Merenptah?"

"Because I haven't been vigilant enough, Your Majesty. The peace with Hatti has made me forget that war could break out in the west. And with Uri-Teshoop still at large, I worry. Will you let me go to Siwa and wipe out the insurgents?"

"For all your thirty-eight years, Merenptah, you still have the dash of a young officer! Send one of your top men on this mission. I want you to stay here and put our forces on a state of alert."

"I swear that they were Libyan bandits!" Long Legs repeated to the drowsy border guard.

"You're raving, boy. No Libyans around here, I tell you."

"I ran until I dropped; they were trying to kill me! Good thing I'm a champion, or they would have caught up. Helmets, breastplates, spears, lances . . . a regular army!"

The border guard yawned a few more times, then glared at the young man.

"Too much strong beer can make you see things. You ought to stop drinking."

"The moon was full," Long Legs persisted, "so I saw their leader before I ran. A great big guy with red hair all over his chest."

The guard's ears finally perked up. A sketch of Uri-Teshoop had been circulated to army, police, and customs outposts, promising a fat reward for the Hittite's arrest.

The border guard waved the sketch in front of Long Legs.

"Is this him?"

"Yes, that's the man I saw!"

The military had studded the band of desert along the western edge of the Delta with small forts, and settlements grew up around them. They lay a day apart by chariot, two days at a fast march, and the garrisons' standing order was to alert the generals in Pi-Ramses and Memphis to the slightest suspicious movement across the Libyan border. The high command made sure that this region was one they kept a close eye on.

When the border region's military governor received an unsettling report based on a traveling merchant's testimony, he took care not to pass it on to his superiors, for fear they'd laugh at him. The possibility of capturing Uri-Teshoop nevertheless prompted him to send a patrol to the area where the Hittite had supposedly been sighted.

That was why Nakti and his men found themselves on a forced march into an inhospitable, mosquito-infested region, with a single idea in mind: getting this unwelcome assignment over with as quickly as possible.

Nakti cursed every step of the way. When would he finally be posted to Pi-Ramses, to a comfortable barracks, instead of pursuing phantom enemies?

"Fort sighted ahead, sir."

The frontier guards may take us for imbeciles, thought Nakti, but at least they'll offer us food and drink, and we can spend the night.

"Watch out, sir!"

A soldier dragged Nakti backward. In his path lay an enormous black scorpion, positioned to attack. One more distracted step and he would have been bitten.

"Kill it," the officer ordered his rescuer.

The soldier had no time to draw his bow. Arrows flew from the fort's battlements. With the precision of trained archers, the Libyans under Uri-Teshoop's command mowed down the Egyptian patrol.

With his iron dagger, the Hittite prince cut each of the wounded men's throats.

FIFTY-FOUR

As he did each morning, the military governor of the Libyan frontier zone went to his office to consult the daily dispatches from his outposts. Ordinarily, it was a simple task, for all the wooden tablets bore the same message: "Nothing to report."

That morning, however, no reports had been delivered.

He wouldn't have far to look for the guilty party. The soldier in charge of the mail must have overslept. Furious, the governor vowed he'd demote the laggard to laundry detail.

In the fortress courtyard, one man listlessly pushed a broom. Two young foot soldiers were drilling with short swords. The governor walked briskly to where the couriers and scouts were quartered.

No soldiers lay on the reed mats.

The governor stood there, puzzled. No reports, no couriers . . . what could explain it?

He was still gaping at the empty mats when the fortress door was rammed open by a band of wild-eyed Libyans with plumes in their hair.

They hacked the sweeper and the two foot soldiers with their hatchets before bashing open the petrified governor's skull. He hadn't even tried to run. Uri-Teshoop spit on his corpse.

"The oasis at Siwa hasn't been attacked," an officer reported to Merenptah. "We were fed some false information."

"No victims?"

"No victims, no uprising. I traveled all the way there for nothing."

Merenptah sat alone, musing. If this was a diversion tactic, where was the real trouble spot? Only Ramses could gauge the extent of the danger.

Just as the prince was climbing back into his chariot, his aide-de-camp came running.

"General, a message from a garrison close to the Libyan border . . . a mass attack against our fortresses there! Most of them have already fallen and the governor's been killed, the report says!"

Merenptah had never driven his horses so hard. Jumping from his chariot, the king's younger son bolted up the stairs to the palace. With Serramanna's assistance, he broke into the audience Pharaoh had granted to select provincial leaders.

Merenptah's flustered face told Ramses at once that something serious had happened. The king adjourned the audience, promising another meeting in the near future.

"Your Majesty," declared the commanding general, "the Libyans have probably invaded the northwestern Delta. I can't tell how bad it is yet."

"Uri-Teshoop and Malfi!" exclaimed Serramanna.

"Yes, there is mention of the Hittite in the sketchy report I received. And Malfi has obviously managed to unite the warring Libyan tribes. Our reaction should be swift and merciless . . . unless this is another false lead, like Siwa."

"If it is a ruse and Malfi drew the greater part of our fighting force to the Delta, he could attack down by Thebes and meet no resistance. He'd put Amon's holy city to fire and the sword."

Weighing his decision, Ramses held the future of Egypt in his hands.

"Your Majesty," Serramanna said timidly, "you promised . . ."

"I haven't forgotten. You'll come with me this time, Serramanna."

Cruel black eyes burned in Malfi's square-jawed face. His men considered him the incarnation of a desert demon, with eyes in the back of his head and fingers that cut his opponents to shreds. He had brought nearly every tribe in Libya under his command, patiently fanning the flames of their long-standing hatred of Egypt. The Egyptians had grown far too used to peace, and now the Libyans would ride roughshod over them. What was more, they had the bold and experienced Uri-Teshoop on their side.

"Less than two hours' march in that direction," said the Hittite, gesturing, "are the first Delta settlements. We'll take them to begin with. Then we'll destroy Pi-Ramses, with its defenses reduced to the minimum. You'll be proclaimed Pharaoh, Malfi, and what's left of the Egyptian army will be placed under your control."

"Are you sure it will work, Uri-Teshoop?"

"Yes, because I know how Ramses thinks. The Siwa diversion has him upset and convinced that we're attacking on several fronts. His priority will be to protect Thebes and his temples; that's why he'll send two regiments south, probably under Merenptah's command. A third regiment is probably guarding Memphis. And since he's vain enough to believe he's invincible, the great man himself will head the force sent to wipe us out. We'll only be facing a few thousand men, Malfi. We can easily take care of them. I ask only one favor of you: let me kill Ramses myself with my iron dagger."

The Libyan nodded his agreement. He would have liked more time to get his troops in fighting shape, but their run-in with the traveling merchant had forced him to go on the offensive.

A single regiment would not daunt Malfi. The Libyans were fighters, their spirit increased tenfold by the drug he'd dispensed before the battle. They had every advantage over the unsuspecting Egyptians.

He'd given only one order: show no mercy.

"Here they come," announced Uri-Teshoop.

Malfi's eyes gleamed with eagerness. His country had been downtrodden too long. Now he would pay Egypt back, razing rich villages and burning cropland. Any survivors would be his slaves.

"Ramses is marching at the head of his troops," the Hittite reported excitedly.

"Who's that at his right?" asked Malfi.

"His youngest son, Merenptah."

"Didn't you tell me that he'd be diverted to Thebes?"

"We'll kill both father and son."

"Who's that to the king's left?"

"Serramanna, the head of his royal bodyguard . . . I can't believe our luck, Malfi! I'll skin the bastard alive."

Foot soldiers, archers, and chariots spread out along the horizon, in perfect order.

"There's not just one regiment," Malfi assessed.

The Libyan and the Hittite had to yield to the evidence: Ramses had risked confronting them with all four regiments, named for the gods Amon, Ra, Ptah, and Set. The entire Egyptian fighting force was ready to strike the enemy.

Malfi clenched his fists.

"You claimed you know Ramses well, Uri-Teshoop!"

"His strategy doesn't make sense . . . How can he risk bringing out his whole army?"

The Libyan looked around and saw that Nubian archers, commanded by Viceroy Setau, were blocking any retreat.

"One Libyan equals at least four Egyptians," Malfi shouted to his men. "Charge!"

As Ramses stood still as a statue in his chariot, the Libyans surged toward the Egyptian front lines. The Egyptian foot soldiers knelt to give the archers a better aim; their volley decimated the enemy ranks.

The Libyan archers returned the fire, but less accurately. The second wave straggled forward and was met by the Set regiment's infantry. Then the chariots counterattacked; on Merenptah's order, they pounded through the rebel troops, which despite Malfi's curses were beginning to disband.

The fleeing Libyans ran into Setau and his Nubians, with their devastating arrows and lances. From that moment on, the outcome of the battle was no longer in doubt. Most of the outnumbered Libyans laid down their arms.

In a frenzy, Malfi gathered his few remaining partisans around him. Uri-Teshoop had disappeared, the coward. Malfi didn't even care. All he wanted now was to kill as many Egyptians as he could lay his hands on. His first victim would be Merenptah, there within throwing distance.

In the confusion, the two men's eyes met. Ramses' youngest son could feel the Libyan's hatred.

In the same instant, their two spears flew through the air.

Malfi's grazed Merenptah's shoulder. The prince's spear ripped into the Libyan's forehead.

Malfi stood upright a few seconds longer, then swayed and fell.

Serramanna was having a wonderful time. Wielding his heavy double-edged sword with remarkable dexterity, he'd lost count of all the Libyans he'd hacked to bits. Malfi's death had discouraged the few rebel troops remaining, so now the hulking Sard could rest for a moment.

He turned to check on Ramses, and what he saw terrified him.

Wearing a helmet and protected by a breastplate that covered the reddish fleece on his chest, Uri-Teshoop had slipped through the Egyptian ranks and was approaching the royal chariot from behind.

The Hittite was going to assassinate Ramses.

A mad dash, knocking several royal sons out of his way, brought Serramanna between the chariot and Uri-Teshoop, but not soon enough to stop the Hittite from striking a mighty blow. The iron dagger went deep into Serramanna's chest.

Mortally wounded, the Sard had just enough strength left to grab his sworn enemy by the throat, squeezing it with his enormous hands.

"You didn't make it, Uri-Teshoop. You lose!"

The Sard loosened his grip only when the fallen prince had stopped breathing. Then, like a wild beast sensing its end drawing near, he lay down on his side.

Ramses cradled the head of the man who had just saved his life.

"You've won a great victory, Your Majesty . . . and thanks to you, what a wonderful life I've had . . ."

Proud of his final exploit, the Sard breathed his last in Ramses' arms.

FIFTY-FIVE

Mammoth vases and ewers in heavy gold-trimmed silver.
Gold and silver offertory tables of more than three hundredweight.
A gold-plated boat of Lebanese pine nearly two hundred paces long.
Sheets of gold to grace tall columns.
Close to a ton of lapis lazuli, two tons of turquoise.

This was only part of the treasure that Ramses presented to the temples of Thebes and Pi-Ramses to thank the divinities for granting him victory over the Libyans and saving Egypt from invasion.

And this forty-fifth year of his reign had seen the birth of a new temple dedicated to Ptah, Gerf Hussein in Nubia, where Setau had transformed a traditional sacred grotto into a shrine. The king had come to dedicate this miniature version of Abu Simbel, likewise carved out of a sandstone cliff. Here, as at many other sites, colossal statues of the monarch in the form of Osiris had been erected.

When the festivities were over, Ramses and Setau watched the sun set on the Nile.

"Have you caught building fever, Setau?"

"Nubia inspires me, Your Majesty. It blazes with heat that has to be channeled into stones and temples. They'll be the voice of posterity for you, won't they? Besides, soon enough we'll rest for all eternity. The point of our brief existence is to work; only what we accomplish will live on."

"Are you encountering any difficulty with your additional duties?"

"Nothing serious. During your reign, Ramses, you've put an end to war. Peace with Hatti, peace in Nubia, peace imposed on Libya . . . a creation as beautiful as a grandiose building, and it will prove your greatest memorial. Wherever he is, Ahsha must be happy!"

"I often think of Serramanna's sacrifice. He gave his life to save me."

"Anyone close to you would have done the same, Your Majesty. How could it be otherwise, when you're our spokesman in the great beyond?"

Planted early in Ramses' reign, the sycamore in the palace gardens at Thebes now provided welcome shade as Ramses sat listening to his daughter play the lute, accompanied by birdsong.

As they did each day in all of Egypt's temples, the priests had purified themselves with water from the sacred lakes and performed their rites in the name of Pharaoh. As usual, food had been brought to small temples as well as great ones, to be offered to the gods, then redistributed to Pharaoh's human flock. As usual, divine power had been awakened and Ma'at had reminded the king: *"You live through me, the scent of my dew revives you, your eyes are Ma'at."*

The daughter of Ramses and Nefertari set her lute at the foot of the sycamore.

"You're the Queen of Egypt, Meritamon."

"When you speak to me that way, Your Majesty, I sense a threat to my quiet life."

"Old age is catching up with me, Meritamon. Bakhen has his hands full taking care of Karnak; I'm asking you, my daughter, to become the guardian of my Eternal Temple. Its magic helped your mother and me to overcome adversity. Make sure that the rites and festivals are celebrated in proper order, so that the Ramesseum continues to pulse with energy."

Meritamon kissed the king's hand.

"Father . . . you know very well that you'll never leave us."

"Luckily, no man is exempt from death."

"Haven't the pharaohs triumphed over death? It's dealt you some rude blows, but you've resisted it; I even believe you've tamed it."

"Death will have the last word, Meritamon."

"No, Your Majesty. Death has missed its chance. Today your name is present on all the monuments of Egypt and your renown has spread well beyond our borders. Ramses can never die."

The Libyan revolt had been crushed, and peace reigned. Ramses' prestige never stopped growing. Yet problem cases continued to pile up on Ahmeni's desk, and he became grumpier by the day. Neither of Ramses' two sons, General Merenptah or High Priest Kha, would be any more likely than he to solve this latest conundrum. The vizier had already given up. To whom could he turn now, if not to Ramses?

"I'm not saying that Your Majesty is wrong to tour the country," declared Ahmeni, "but when you're away from the capital, problems tend to accumulate."

"Is our prosperity in peril?"

"I can't help thinking how the most minuscule flaw can topple a monumental structure. I don't work on a grand scale, but on everyday issues."

"Is this speech going to last much longer?"

"I've received a complaint from the mayor of Sumenu in upper Egypt. The sacred well that supplies the town has gone dry, and the local clergy have been unable to deal with the crisis."

"Have you sent help?"

"Are you accusing me of negligence? A slew of experts couldn't get it to work again. And now I have an unworkable well and an anxious population on my hands."

Several housewives had gathered on the banks of one of the canals that irrigated Sumenu's fields. In the middle of the afternoon they came to do their dishes, keeping their distance from where the washermen worked. They chatted, exchanging confidences, gossiping, and criticizing their neighbors. The sauciest tongue in town belonged to Morena, the pretty wife of a carpenter.

"If the well is dry," she said, "we ought to leave town."

"Impossible!" protested a servant girl. "My family has lived here for generations, and I don't want to raise my children anywhere else."

"How will you do it without well water?"

"The priests will fix it."

"They haven't so far. Not even the state magicians they called in could help."

Blind and limping, an old man approached the group of women.

"I'm thirsty. Please, ladies, give me something to drink?"

"Move along, you old coot," Morena said haughtily. "If you worked for a living, you'll find some water."

"I'm down on my luck, I've been sick, and—"

"A likely story! Move along, I say, or we'll stone you!"

The blind man shuffled away; the women resumed their conversation.

"What about me? Would you give me water?"

The women looked back and were silenced. The question came from a powerful-looking elderly gentleman. From his bearing, it was easy to tell that he was important.

"My Lord," said Morena, "we'd be glad to oblige."

"Then why did you refuse this poor blind man?"

"Because he's a good-for-nothing, always bothering us!"

"Remember the law of Ma'at: *'Have pity on the blind man, mock not the dwarf, do no harm to the lame, for we are all in God's hands. Care for everyone you meet.'*"

The flustered housewives looked at the ground, but Morena spoke up.

"Who are you to be talking to us this way?"

"The Pharaoh of Egypt."

Petrified, Morena hid behind her friends' skirts.

"A curse has fallen on Sumenu's main well because of your shameful attitude toward the less fortunate. That's the conclusion I've reached after several days of observation."

Morena prostrated herself before Ramses.

"Will changing our attitude be enough to save the well?"

"You've angered the god that inhabits it; I must appease him."

When the monumental statue of the god Sobek, a crocodile-headed figure seated on a throne, emerged from the sculpture studio at the House of Life in Sumenu, the townsfolk crowded to watch its passing. A team of stoneworkers slid it down a path of logs set on the dampened ground, slowly reaching the main well where Ramses awaited, reciting the litanies that asked Sobek to draw water from the *Noun*, the primordial ocean surrounding the earth, crucial to human survival.

Then the king ordered the craftsmen to lower the god to the bottom of the well, where he would do his life-giving work.

By the next morning, the Sumenu well was again dispensing its precious liquid. The citizens organized a banquet, where the blind beggar and the carpenter's pretty wife sat side by side.

FIFTY-SIX

Hefat had done very well in life. The son of an Egyptian father and a Phoenician mother, he was a gifted student, dazzling the royal academy's demanding mathematics professors. He had weighed his job offers carefully before joining the Hydrology Department, which regulated the Nile, predicting flood levels and controlling the flow of irrigation canals.

Over the years, Hefat had developed close relationships with the vizier, the cabinet members, and the provincial governors. His ability to flatter his superiors had helped him rise through the ranks. It also compensated for the fact that he had been an early admirer of Shaanar, the Pharaoh's older brother—Shaanar, a traitor to his country, but a masterful and fascinating politician.

Luckily, Hefat had never publicly supported Shaanar before the prince met his tragic end.

Now in his prime at fifty, married and the father of two, Hefat appeared to be at the height of his career, maintaining tight control over the inner workings of his department. Who could have guessed that he was the last important member of a network that Shaanar had created to pave his way to the throne?

Hefat's past alliance remained a distant memory until he

encountered the Phoenician merchant Narish. Assessing the foreigner's considerable wealth, Hefat came to realize that a man of his own intelligence, in his privileged position, might also become quite rich.

Dining with the Phoenician had opened Hefat's eyes. Ramses was heading into his seventies; he would soon leave the government in the hands of conventional men, incapable of bold initiatives. His eldest son, Kha, was a mystic, removed from the daily business of the administration. Merenptah obeyed his father blindly and would be at a loss once Ramses was gone. Ahmeni, an aging scribe, would certainly be shunted aside.

Upon careful reflection, the country's power structure was far shakier than it appeared. Despite increasingly frequent recourse to magical sed-feasts and the care of his chief physician, Neferet, Ramses was declining.

Perhaps the time had come at last to strike a decisive blow and make Shaanar's vision a reality.

Merenptah was showing the ambassador from Hatti into the great audience chamber at the Pi-Ramses palace. Usually the diplomat came with an entourage, bearing gifts; this time he was alone. He bowed at the sight of Ramses.

"Your Majesty, I bring sad news. Your brother the Emperor of Hatti has passed away."

From the battle of Kadesh to Hattusili's arrival in Egypt, a variety of scenes flashed through the Pharaoh's mind. The man had been a redoubtable adversary before his gradual conversion into a loyal ally. Together, he and Ramses had built a better world.

"Has his successor been designated?"

"Yes, Your Majesty."

"Will he honor the peace treaty?"

Merenptah swallowed hard.

"Our late emperor's decisions extend to his successors," replied the ambassador. "Not a single clause of the treaty will be called into question."

"Please extend my condolences and kind remembrance to Empress Puduhepa."

"Alas, Your Majesty, the empress was also ill, and her husband's death hastened her demise."

"Then assure the new Emperor of Hatti of my friendship and goodwill. He can rely on Egypt."

As soon as the ambassador left, Ramses spoke to his son.

"Contact our informers immediately and have them prepare a detailed report on the situation in Hatti. Tell them we need it right away."

Hefat entertained the Phoenician Narish at his plush Pi-Ramses villa. He introduced his wife and two children, with comments about their excellent education and the fine future in store for them. After a pleasant luncheon, during which a great deal of small talk was exchanged, the chief of the Hydrology Department and the foreign trader drifted off to a wooden gazebo with finely detailed columns.

"Your invitation is an honor," said Narish. "Forgive me for being blunt, but why did you ask me here? I'm a businessman, you're an engineer . . . we have nothing in common, as far as I can see."

"I've heard that you disagree with Ramses' trade policies."

"His ridiculous views on slavery have hurt us, certainly; but Egypt will come to realize how isolated his position leaves her and just how untenable it is."

"That could take years . . . and you and I would like to grow richer here and now."

The Phoenician was intrigued.

"I don't see where you're leading, Hefat."

"Today, Ramses is the unquestioned ruler. That wasn't always the case. His absolute power conceals a serious weakness: his age. Not to mention that his two potential successors, Kha and Merenptah, are equally inept."

"I don't deal in politics, especially not Egypt's."

"But you believe that profit is all-powerful, don't you?"

"It's the future of humanity, I agree."

"Let's make the future happen! We may be coming from different directions, but you and I both want to challenge Ramses. He's no longer an effective leader. But that isn't crucial; the important point is that we can profit financially from the decline of centralized power."

"What kind of deal are you talking about?"

"At the very least, tripling Phoenicia's wealth—and that's a conservative estimate. Needless to say, the man responsible for this happy state of affairs will be a hero. That man is you, Narish."

"And you, Hefat?"

"At the outset, I'd prefer to be a silent partner."

"What's your plan?"

"Before I unveil it, I need to be sure of your silence."

The trader smiled. "My dear Hefat, a man's word is law only here in Egypt. If you want to do business abroad, you'll have to leave your old-fashioned notions behind."

The chief hydrologist was reluctant to commit himself. If the Phoenician betrayed him, he'd end his days in prison.

"All right, Narish. I'll explain everything."

As Hefat outlined his idea, the Phoenician wondered how one of Pharaoh's subjects could have come up with such a bold scheme. But he, Narish, would be running no risk at all, and the Egyptian was right: if it worked, they could both make a fortune, and Ramses' reign would collapse.

Merenptah could not get the Libyan incident out of his mind. He was commander-in-chief, in charge of national security, yet he'd been unable to anticipate Malfi's moves. Without Ramses' clairvoyance and prompt action, the Libyans would have invaded the Delta, sacked the capital, and killed thousands of Egyptians.

Learning from the experience, Merenptah had personally inspected the forts along the Libyan border, instituting changes in patrol procedures, tightening discipline, and stressing what a vital service the soldiers assigned there were performing for their country.

Merenptah did not believe that the Libyan threat was gone for good. Malfi was dead, but other chieftains just as vengeful and bitter would take his place, preaching all-out war against Egypt. He therefore sought to reinforce protection of the Delta's northwestern flank, with Ramses' full agreement.

But how would the situation in Hatti evolve? The passing of Hattusili, an intelligent and realistic ruler, might well mark the start of an internal crisis that the ambassador was trying to play down. The Hittites were generally quick to use poison or daggers in their quest for the throne. And the old emperor had perhaps been mistaken in the belief that he had eliminated all opposition to his regime.

Impatient for reliable news from Hatti, Merenptah kept his regiments on high alert.

Though he didn't turn up his nose at fish, the dog Watcher had a marked preference for red meat. Sharp-eyed as the previous members of his dynasty, Ramses' companion enjoyed his mealtimes with his master. Food never tasted as good without conversation.

The king and Watcher were finishing their private luncheon when Merenptah arrived at the palace.

"Your Majesty, I've read all the reports from our observers and had a long talk with the head of our bureau in Hattusa."

Ramses poured some wine into a silver cup and held it out to his son.

"Don't keep anything from me, Merenptah. I want to know the exact truth."

"The ambassador from Hatti wasn't lying. Hattusili's successor is resolutely determined to uphold the peace treaty and maintain excellent relations with Egypt."

FIFTY-SEVEN

The Nile's flooding . . . a miracle renewed each year, a gift from the gods that unleashed the people's fervor and their gratitude toward the Pharaoh, who alone could make the river waters rise to make the earth fruitful.

And this year's inundation was remarkable: thirty-five feet! Since the beginning of Ramses' reign, the life-giving waters, springing from the depths of the celestial ocean, had never been wanting.

Now that peace with Hatti had been reconfirmed, the summer would brim with festivities and trips from town to town in boats refurbished during the winter months. Like all of his compatriots, Chief Hydrologist Hefat admired the grandiose sight of the Nile transformed into a lake with villages perched on hilltop islands. His family had left for Thebes to spend a few weeks with his parents, giving him room to maneuver.

While the farmhands rested, the officials in charge of irrigation were working hard. But Hefat had another way of looking at the inundation. The reservoirs were filled to capacity, held in by earthen dikes to be broken as water supplies were needed, and the engineer congratulated himself on the brilliant idea that was about to make him a man even richer and more powerful than Ramses the Great.

The high government officials had requested an audience with Ramses to submit a proposal they considered reasonable. They had independently reached the same conclusion.

The monarch listened attentively. Without refusing categorically, he advised against the undertaking, though he hoped it would work. Interpreting Ramses' words as encouragement, the Treasury secretary decided to call on Ahmeni. His colleagues appreciated his courage. That very evening, the secretary called on the king's sandal-bearer, whose staff had already gone home.

Approaching seventy, Ahmeni still looked like the student who had pledged his loyalty to Ramses when the young prince did not seem destined to become Pharaoh. He was as pale, slight, and skinny as ever despite a voracious appetite; his back ached constantly, yet he had more stamina than any man twice his size. He was a tireless, precise, and meticulous worker, sleeping only a few hours a night and personally reviewing every file.

"Is something wrong?" he asked the Treasury man.

"Not exactly."

"Then what are you doing here? I'm busy."

"We met under the vizier's direction, and—"

"Who is 'we'?"

"Well, the director of the Double White House, and the agriculture secretary, and the—"

"I see. And what was the reason behind this meeting?"

"To tell the truth, there were two reasons."

"Let's try the first one."

"For your service to Egypt, your colleagues in the administration would like to give you a villa in the locality of your choice."

Ahmeni put down his brush.

"Interesting. And the second item?"

"You've worked hard, Ahmeni, much harder than you were ever asked to. It probably doesn't seem that way to you, you're so devoted. But hasn't the time come for you to retire? A quiet life in a comfortable house, where you can enjoy your fine reputation."

Ahmeni's silence seemed a good sign.

"I knew that you'd listen to reason," concluded the Treasury secretary, thrilled with the outcome of his initiative. "My colleagues will be happy to learn of your decision."

"I'm not so sure of that."

"Excuse me?"

"I'll never retire," Ahmeni said emphatically. "And no one, with the exception of Pharaoh, will ever make me leave this office. Until he demands my resignation, I'll continue working at my own pace and according to my methods. Is that quite clear?"

"We thought it would be in your interest . . ."

"Don't give it another thought."

Hefat and the Phoenician Narish met again at the Egyptian's house on a hot summer day. The trader enjoyed the cool, refreshing beer that was served to him.

"I don't want to brag," said Narish, "but I think I've done an excellent job so far. Phoenicia's merchants are ready to buy Egypt. But are you ready to sell it, Hefat?"

"I haven't changed my mind."

"When's the exact date?"

"I can't bend the laws of nature, but we haven't much longer to wait."

"Nothing stands in our way?"

The chief hydrologist reassured him. "No, thanks to my position in the government."

"Won't you need the seal of the high priest of Memphis?"

"Yes, but that's Kha, who's lost in his spiritual quest and his love of old monuments. He won't even notice what he's signing."

"There's one thing I wonder about," admitted the Phoenician. "Why do you hate your country so?"

"Thanks to our arrangement, Egypt will hardly suffer and will finally open up to the outside world. We'll be freed from old superstitions and outdated customs, as my mentor, Shaanar, would have wished. He wanted to topple Ramses; now I'll be the one to get rid of the tyrant. By now he thinks he's invincible. But where the Hittites, the Libyans, and black magic failed, I'll prevail."

"The answer is no," said Ahmeni to the head of the province of Two Falcons, a big fellow with a jutting chin.

"Why is that?"

"Because no one province will enjoy special privilege to the detriment of its neighbors."

"But the Interior Department encouraged me!"

"It could be, but no government department is allowed to make law. If I followed all of the cabinet's recommendations, Egypt would be ruined."

"Is your answer final?"

"The irrigation system won't be modified. The water in the reservoirs will be released at the usual date, and not before."

"In that case, I demand to see the king!"

"He'll see you, but don't waste his time."

Without Ahmeni's support, the governor knew he had no chance of winning Ramses' approval. He might as well return to his provincial capital.

Ahmeni was intrigued.

Either by courier or in direct conversation, six heads of major provinces had asked him to confirm a decision supposedly made by the Hydrology Department in Memphis: the advance release of water from the reservoirs, in the hope of creating new cropland.

A double mistake, according to Ahmeni. On the one hand, there was no immediate need to develop agriculture. Furthermore, irrigation should proceed in a gradual manner. Fortunately the engineers in charge had no idea that the majority of provincial governors, with exemplary discretion, were in the habit of consulting the king's private secretary whenever they sensed they were heading for dangerous ground.

If so many problems weren't already crowding his desk, Ahmeni would have liked to launch an investigation and find out who was behind these irregularities.

The scribe began studying a report on the planting of willow in middle Egypt. Unable to concentrate, he set the scroll aside. This latest incident was definitely too serious to escape his attention.

Ramses and Kha stepped through the monumental gate to the temple of Thoth in Hermopolis, crossed a sunlit forecourt, and were welcomed by the god's high priest at the doorway to the inner sanctuary. The king and his son admired the rooms where only Thoth's clergy set foot, serving the god of scribes and scholars. Then they prayed in the chapel.

"Here my quest ends," declared Kha.

"Then you've discovered the Book of Thoth?"

"For a long time I believed that it must be an ancient text, hidden away in the temple library. But I finally saw that each of the stones in our sanctuaries made up the letters in the book, written by the god of knowledge to give sense to our lives. Thoth transmitted his message in each sculpture, each hieroglyph. The task of making the connections falls to us, just as Isis had to reassemble the scattered pieces of Osiris's body. Our entire country, Father, is a temple in the image of the heavens, and it's Pharaoh's role to keep the book open, to let the heart's eyes decipher it."

The joy and pride that Ramses felt hearing these sage words were something that no poet, even Homer, could have found the words to describe.

FIFTY-EIGHT

Though simple, Hefat's idea would be devilishly effective. The chief hydrologist would release the excess water stored in the reservoirs and chalk the mistake up to Ramses' inner circle, beginning with Kha, who would have signed and sealed the document giving his consent as the nominal supervisor of the canals.

Reassured by the fake studies that Hefat had circulated, the provincial governors had taken the bait and were clamoring for extra water to develop cropland and enrich their regions. By the time it was clear that a terrible mistake had been made, it would be too late. There wouldn't be enough water left for irrigation during the regular growing season, and all hope of an adequate harvest would vanish.

And after Kha, the blame would fall on Ramses.

That's where Narish and the Phoenician traders would come in, offering to sell the food Egypt needed, but at an exorbitant price. The Treasury would be forced to accept their conditions, and the old Pharaoh would be swept away on a wave of indignation. Hefat, meanwhile, would get an enormous kickback. If circumstances were favorable, he'd step in and replace the vizier; if not, he'd leave for Phoenicia a wealthy man.

One final formality—getting Kha's seal—and the plan could be set in motion. Hefat wouldn't even need to meet with the high priest; the prince would delegate the task to his secretary.

Kha's assistant greeted the hydrologist warmly. "You're in luck, the high priest is in. He'll be glad to see you."

"That won't be necessary," protested Hefat. "I only need a signature. I don't want to take his valuable time."

"Please come this way."

Jittery by now, the engineer stepped into a library where Kha, dressed in a tunic that looked like it was made of panther skin, was studying papyrus scrolls.

"I'm happy to meet you, Hefat."

"It's a great honor for me, Your Highness, but I didn't mean to interrupt your research."

"What can I do for you?"

"A simple administrative matter . . ."

"Show me the document."

Kha's voice was low, his tone commanding; the high priest was nothing like the dreamer Hefat had imagined.

"This is an unusual proposal. It demands close examination," Kha said at length.

The chief hydrologist's blood ran cold.

"No, Your Highness, it's a simple proposal for facilitating irrigation, nothing more."

"You're too modest! Since I'm unable to judge this document on its merits, I'll submit it to someone more qualified."

Ah, some other expert, thought Hefat, reassured. He'd have no trouble pushing the proposal through.

"Here's the man for the job," announced Kha.

Dressed in a fine linen robe with broad sleeves, Ramses wore his two famous gold bracelets inlaid with lapis lazuli ducks.

Pharaoh's eyes bore into Hefat's soul, forcing him to back away and bump into shelves piled high with papyrus scrolls.

"You've made a serious mistake," declared Ramses, "thinking that your technical knowledge would be enough to help you ruin your country. Don't you know that greed is an incurable disease that can make you blind and deaf? You might want to revise your opinion of how incompetent my government is."

"Your Majesty, I beg you—"

"Don't bother pleading, Hefat. Your word is worth nothing now. In your behavior I see the mark of Shaanar, the spinelessness that leads a man to destroy himself by betraying Ma'at. Your future is in the hands of the judges now."

It was Ahmeni's timely investigation that had spared the country from a very real danger. The king would have liked to reward his old friend, but such talk only annoyed the aging scribe. A meaningful glance had been enough, and Ahmeni had gone straight back to work.

And the seasons and days rolled by, simple and happy, until the spring of the fifty-fourth year of the reign of Ramses the Great, when the king consulted his chief physician, Neferet, then ignored her advice. Rejuvenated by his ninth sed-feast, the aged ruler felt the need to tour the Egyptian countryside.

The month of May saw the return of the hotter weather that soothed the king's arthritis.

It was harvest time. Laborers moved through the fields with wooden-handled scythes, cutting the ripe grain high on the stalks. Then the wheat was bundled in sheaves and laden on stalwart donkeys who carried it to the threshers. Building haystacks took skill; the truncated pyramids had to stand for the better part of a year. Two long sticks reinforced the structure.

As soon as the Pharaoh entered a village, the local dignitaries presented him with offerings of wheat stalks and flowers. Then the monarch would hold court in a gazebo and hear grievances. The scribes took notes and submitted them to Ahmeni, who demanded to read every report written on the trip.

The king noted that on the whole agriculture was doing well and that there were no ills without remedies, although perfection was unattainable. The grievances were not particularly vehement, with the exception of a bitter farmer from Beni-Hassan.

"I spend my days taking care of the crops," he complained, "and my nights fixing tools. My livestock is always getting loose, and I have to round up the animals. And now I have the tax inspector after me, trying to rob me! With his army of vultures he treats me like a thief, hits me when I say I can't pay, and locks up my wife and children! How could I be happy?"

Everyone was afraid of how Ramses might react, but he remained impassive.

"Do you have any other criticism to offer?"

The farmer was astonished. "No, Your Majesty, no . . ."

"One of your relatives is a scribe, isn't he?"

The man's face colored. "Yes, but . . ."

"He taught you a classic text studied in every school, exalting the life of a scribe and denigrating every other profession. You recited it quite well, but do you really suffer from all the ills you've just described to me?"

"Well, my cattle do get loose . . . It causes a lot of trouble."

"If you can't settle your own disputes with your neighbors, call in your village judge. And never suffer injustice, no matter how slight. That's how you can help Pharaoh rule the country."

Ramses inspected several storage facilities and ordered the grain measurers to handle the bushels with care. Then he opened the harvest festival at Karnak, placing the first wheat into one of the granaries on Amon's great domain. The priests and dignitaries noted that despite his age the Lord of the Two Lands still had a steady hand and a strong arm.

Bakhen, the First Prophet of Amon, accompanied his illustrious guest down a road where luxuriant fields surrounded a temple, leading to a landing stage. Fatigued, Ramses had agreed to travel by sedan chair.

Bakhen was the first to spot the shirker dozing beneath a willow tree. He hoped that the king wouldn't notice, but Ramses' eyes were still sharp.

"The man will be punished," promised the high priest.

"Just this once, go easy on him. Wasn't I the one who put willows all over Egypt?"

"He'll never know how much he owes you, Majesty."

"I've sometimes been tempted to do the same—doze off beneath a tree and forget my responsibilities."

Not far from the landing, Ramses ordered the bearers to set him down.

"Your Majesty," Bakhen said anxiously, "why walk?"

"Look at that little chapel over there . . . it's in ruins."

A small shrine to the harvest goddess (in the form of a female cobra) had suffered from time and neglect; weeds grew between the crumbling stones.

"This is a real crime," said Ramses. "Restore this temple, Bakhen. Make it bigger and install a stone door. Have your Karnak sculptors make a statue of the goddess to stand inside it. The gods made Egypt what it is; we mustn't neglect them, even in their humblest manifestations."

In tribute to the goddess, the Lord of the Two Lands and the high priest of Amon laid wildflowers at the foot of the little shrine. High above them, a falcon soared in circles.

FIFTY-NINE

On his way back to the capital, Ramses stopped in Memphis to talk with his son Kha, who had just completed restoration work on the Old Kingdom monuments and improvements to the Apis bulls' underground sanctuary.

Waiting for him on the dock he found his chief physician, Neferet, lovely and elegant as ever.

"How are you feeling, Majesty?"

"A little tired, and my back hurts, but I'm holding up. What's wrong, Neferet?"

"Kha is very ill."

"You don't mean . . ."

"A disease I'm familiar with, but one I can't cure. Your son's heart is worn out. My medicines can't help him anymore."

"Where is he?"

"In the library at the temple of Ptah, with the texts he's studied so carefully."

The king immediately went to be with Kha.

Approaching sixty, the high priest's harsh and angular face had become serene. His dark blue eyes shone with the inner peace of one who had prepared all his life to encounter the great beyond. No fear marred his features.

"Your Majesty! I was hoping so much that I'd see you before I leave . . ."

Pharaoh took his son's hand.

"May Pharaoh permit his humble servant to repose in his shadow, for there is no greater happiness . . . Let me go to the Land of the West and remain close to you. I've tried to respect Ma'at always, I've executed your orders, fulfilling the missions you've given me . . ."

Kha's grave voice trailed off gently. Ramses kept it inside him like an inalterable treasure.

Kha was buried in the underground shrine to the Apis bulls, near the beloved creatures whose animal form hid the expression of divine power. Ramses had placed a golden mask on his mummy and had personally chosen the treasure that would accompany him—furniture, vases, and jewelry, masterpieces created by the temple of Ptah's craftsmen to last him through all eternity.

The old king had led the funeral services with surprising vigor, mastering his emotion during the ceremony that opened his son's eyes and mouth in the next world.

Merenptah was constantly at his father's side, ready to help, though Ramses showed no sign of faltering. Yet Ahmeni sensed that his boyhood friend was drawing on his deepest reserves to rise to the occasion and retain an exemplary dignity in the face of this latest tragedy.

The cover was placed on Kha's sarcophagus. The tomb was sealed.

And once he was out of sight of his courtiers, Ramses wept.

It was one of those warm, sunny mornings that Ramses loved. He'd let the high priest stand in for him at the rites of day and would see the vizier only later in the morning. To try to forget his pain, the king would go on working as usual, although his energy was beginning to flag.

But when he tried to get up, his legs remained paralyzed. In his most imperious voice, he called his majordomo.

A few minutes later, Neferet was at the monarch's bedside.

"This time, Your Majesty, you're going to have to follow my orders."

"Don't ask too much of me, Neferet."

"In case you still doubted it, your youth is gone for good and you'll have to change your behavior."

"You're the most daunting adversary I've ever had to face."

"Not me, Your Majesty—old age."

"Give me your diagnosis, and don't try to hide anything from me."

"You'll walk again tomorrow, but only using a cane. You'll limp slightly due to the arthritis in your right hip. I'll do my best to relieve the pain, but rest is imperative, and you'll have to slow down. Don't be surprised if you sometimes feel stiff, as if you can no longer move. It will only be temporary, if you agree to several massages a day. Some nights you'll have trouble lying down; then liniments may give you some relief. Frequent Faiyum mud baths will complement your oral medications."

"Medicine every day? You must think I'm a helpless old man—"

"I've already told you, Your Majesty, that you're no longer young and you'll have to stop driving your chariot. But if you do as I say, you can avoid a rapid decline in the state of your health. Daily exercise, such as walking or swimming, will keep you mobile, as long as you don't overdo it. Your general condition is more than satisfactory for a man who's never rested in his life."

Neferet's smile comforted Ramses. No enemy had been able to vanquish him, except old age. He remembered how Nefertari's favorite author, the sage Ptah-hotep, had complained of it. But he had waited until the age of a hundred and ten to write his *Maxims*! Old age was a curse. The only bright spot was drawing nearer to the loved ones he longed to see again in the fertile fields of the afterlife, where there was no more fatigue.

"Your weakest point," added the chief physician, "is your teeth. But I'll watch them carefully to spare you any risk of infection."

Ramses gave in to Neferet's demands. Within a few weeks he had recovered much of his strength, but he had come to realize that his body, worn out by too many trials and struggles, was only a rusted tool, on the point of breaking.

Accepting that fact would be his final victory.

In the hushed darkness of the temple of Set, the terror of the cosmos, Ramses the Great made his ultimate decision.

Before making it official in the form of a legally binding decree, the Lord of the Two Lands convened the vizier, his cabinet, high-level administrators, and every dignitary in a position of responsibility, except for his son Merenptah, whom he sent on a mission to assess the Delta's economic viability.

The king conferred at length with the men and women who continued to build Egypt, day after day. Ahmeni was at his side, providing his ever-valuable notes.

"You haven't made many mistakes," said the king to his private secretary.

"Have you noticed even one, Your Majesty? If so, please point it out to me!"

"That's just my way of saying that I'm satisfied with you."

"That may be," grumbled Ahmeni. "But why did you send your commanding general on such an extensive mission?"

"Are you trying to make me believe that you haven't guessed why?"

Leaning on his cane, Ramses walked down a shady lane with Merenptah at his side.

"What did you learn in your travels, son?"

"The tax base in the part of the Delta you asked me to assess is 8,700 taxpayers. Each cattle rancher has 500 head, and I counted 13,080 goatherds, 22,430 poultry raisers, and 3,920 donkey drivers caring for several thousand livestock. The harvests have been excellent, and tax evaders few. As too often happens, the revenue service has been picky. I lectured them about leaving honest folk alone and going after cheaters."

"You understand the Delta now, son."

"This mission taught me a great deal. Talking with the farmers, I felt the country's heartbeat."

"Are you forgetting the priests, the scribes, the military?"

"I've already spent a great deal of time with such people. I needed direct contact with men and women of the soil."

"What do you think of this decree?"

Ramses handed Merenptah a scroll written in his own hand. His son read it aloud.

"*'I, Ramses, Pharaoh of Egypt, elevate the prince, Royal Scribe, Keeper of the Seal, and Commander-in-Chief Merenptah to the office of ruler of the Two Lands.'*"

Merenptah gazed at his father, leaning on his cane.

"Your Majesty . . ."

"I don't know how many more years fate will grant me, Merenptah, but the time has come for you to take the throne. I'm following in my father Seti's footsteps. I'm an old man; you're in your prime, and you've just cleared the final hurdle I set in front of you. You know how to govern, to manage, to fight. Take the future of Egypt in hand, my son."

SIXTY

Twelve years had passed, and Ramses, aged eighty-nine, had reigned over Egypt for sixty-seven years. In keeping with his decree, he had left it in Merenptah's care. But the king's youngest son frequently consulted his father, who remained Pharaoh in the eyes of his people.

The old ruler spent part of the year in Pi-Ramses and the other in Thebes, always in the company of his faithful Ahmeni. Despite his great age and multiple complaints, the king's private secretary continued to work according to his methods.

Summer was coming.

After listening to the tunes his daughter, Meritamon, had composed, Ramses went for his daily walk in the countryside around his Eternal Temple, where he had taken up residence. His cane was now his staunchest ally, for each step was becoming difficult.

During his fourteenth sed-feast, celebrated the previous year, Ramses had spent a whole night conversing with Setau and Lotus, who had made Nubia a rich and happy province. The robust snake charmer had also somehow grown old, and even lovely Lotus showed the effects of age. How many memories they'd shared, and what thrilling times they'd lived! None of them mentioned the future that they could no longer shape.

At the edge of the country road an old woman was baking bread in an oven. The tempting odor attracted the king.

"Would you give me a piece?"

The housewife's failing eyesight kept her from recognizing him.

"Ah, this is a thankless task."

"Let me give you something in return. Will this ring be enough?"

The old woman squinted at the golden ring, polishing it with the hem of her skirt.

"This would buy me a nice big house! Keep your ring. I'll just give you a taste of my bread. What kind of man are you, to possess such treasures?"

The crust was perfectly browned; when he broke it, it tasted of childhood, banishing the pains of old age for an instant.

"Take the ring," Ramses told the old woman. "I've never had such good bread."

Ramses enjoyed spending an hour or two with a potter. He liked watching his hands knead the clay into a jar that would hold water or solid food. It reminded him that the ram-headed god was constantly creating the world and humanity on his potter's wheel.

The king and the craftsman never exchanged a word. They listened to the music of the wheel. They silently experienced the mysterious transformation of shapeless material into a useful and pleasing object.

Summer was coming, and Ramses thought he might leave for the capital, where the heat would be less extreme. Ahmeni never left his airy office; when the king went to look for him, he was surprised not to find him at work.

For the first time in his long career, not only was Ramses' private secretary taking a break in the middle of the day, he was even sitting outside, exposing his pale skin to sunburn.

"Moses is dead," he said hoarsely.

"In the homeland he sought for so long?"

"Yes, Your Majesty. He found the place where his people will live in freedom. Our friend succeeded in his long quest. The fire in his soul turned into a land of milk and honey."

Moses . . . The man who had helped him build Pi-Ramses, the man whose faith had triumphed over endless years of wandering, the indomitable prophet. Moses, son of Egypt and Ramses' spiritual brother. Moses, whose dream had become reality.

The king and his secretary were packed to go. Before the morning was over, they would be sailing north.

"Come walk with me," the Pharaoh beckoned.

"Where do you want to go?"

"Isn't it a splendid day? I'd like to rest under the acacia tree by my Eternal Temple, the one I planted in the second year of my reign."

The old ruler's voice sent a chill down Ahmeni's spine.

"We're set to leave, Your Majesty."

"Come, Ahmeni."

The tall acacia near the Temple of Millions of Years gleamed in the sun, its leaves rustling lightly in the breeze. How many trees had Ramses planted—acacias and tamarisks, fig, persea, and pomegranate trees, willows and other tall creatures he so dearly loved?

Old Watcher, the last in a long line of faithful companions, had hoisted himself up to follow his master. Neither he nor Ramses was bothered by the noisy dance of the bees that tirelessly gathered nectar from the bursting acacia blossoms. Their subtle scent delighted both man and dog.

Ramses sat down with his back to the tree trunk. Watcher curled up at his feet.

"Do you remember, Ahmeni, what the goddess of the Western acacia says when she welcomes souls to the afterlife?"

" *'Take this cool water to soothe your heart, this water from the ritual font at the burial ground; receive this offering, so that your soul may reside in my shadow,'* " Ahmeni recited effortlessly.

"Our celestial mother is the one who gives us life," said Ramses. "She also places the spirit of the pharaohs in the starry fields of eternity."

"Perhaps you're thirsty, Majesty. I'll go get you—"

"Stay, Ahmeni. I'm tired, my friend, a deathly fatigue has come over me. Remember the old days, when we talked about true power? You thought only Pharaoh could wield it, and you were right. Only Pharaoh, as long as he follows the law of Ma'at, tirelessly fighting the forces of darkness. If that power wanes, the connection between heaven and earth is broken, and humanity is subjected to violence and injustice. The history of a pharaoh's reign should be the history of a feast, my father said. Both the great and the humble should receive their sustenance from Pharaoh, and both must have their just share. Today women come and go as they please, children laugh, old people rest in the shade of trees. Thanks to Seti, thanks to Nefertari, thanks to the friends and faithful souls who have worked for the increasing grandeur of our civilization, I've tried to make the country happy and act in rectitude. Now it's time for the gods to judge me."

"No, Majesty, don't go!"

Watcher sighed, a long sigh deep as the primordial ocean, peaceful as a sunset on the Nile. The last in a long, faithful line quietly expired at his master's feet.

Summer was coming, and Ramses the Great had just stepped into eternity, beneath the Western acacia.

Ahmeni did something he had never dared attempt in eighty years of unfailing friendship. He took the Pharaoh's hands in his and kissed them fervently.

Then Pharaoh's sandal-bearer and private secretary sat down in the classic cross-legged scribe's position. Taking a new brush, he drew hieroglyphs on an acacia tablet.

"I'll consecrate the rest of my life to writing your story," he promised. "In this world and the next, no one will forget the Son of Light."